# FISHERMEN'S COURT

ANDREW WOLFENDON

*Peace and Joy, Laura!*

Black Rose Writing | Texas

© 2019 by Andrew Wolfendon
All rights reserved. No part of this book may be reproduced, stored in a retrieval system or transmitted in any form or by any means without the prior written permission of the publishers, except by a reviewer who may quote brief passages in a review to be printed in a newspaper, magazine or journal.

The author grants the final approval for this literary material.

First printing

This is a work of fiction. Names, characters, businesses, places, events, and incidents are either the products of the author's imagination or used in a fictitious manner. Any resemblance to actual persons, living or dead, or actual events is purely coincidental.

ISBN: 978-1-68433-285-4
PUBLISHED BY BLACK ROSE WRITING
www.blackrosewriting.com

Printed in the United States of America
Suggested Retail Price (SRP) $21.95

*Fishermen's Court* is printed in Book Antiqua

*For Karen and Ken*

# Fishermen's Court

# Chapter 1

Ever see that old beer commercial: "Life doesn't get any better than this"?

That's what I'm afraid of.

· · · · ·

If I wasn't feeling bleak *before* entering Gauthier's Shop 'n Go, I am certainly getting the job done by the time I arrive at the Buddee's Hot Dog Flavored Potato Chips display and double back toward the Build-It-Ur-Self Nacho Station. Gauthier's is one of those discount food marts seemingly designed for one purpose only: to crush the human soul. There is not a single item on the shelves that a self-respecting, mentally healthy individual — not that I fit into either of those categories — would consume at gunpoint.

So why do I venture into Gauthier's two or three times a week, hoping to be dazzled by some sensational new dinner-for-one option? Answer that one, my friend, and I suspect you answer many other questions about me.

Cereal it is. I grab a box of off-brand Reese's Puffs, pay the sullen cashier with the nose pimple big enough to be mapped by Hubble, and make for the exit, flushing like a shoplifter.

Cold cereal, dinner of champions.

After scoring some off-season lager to pair with my naturally-and-artificially flavored corn balls, I cruise past the tire and exhaust shops of south Wentworth and park in front of my tired and exhausted old house. Well, my *parents'* tired and exhausted old house, actually; the place I grew up in. Legally it is mine now—I inherited it when Mom died last year and have been living alone there ever since—but it is still my parents' house in every way. I've done nothing to claim it as my own.

May I just say, nothing makes a thirty-eight-year-old feel more chipper about his life management skills than going to sleep every night in the same bedroom where he deflowered his first Victoria's Secret catalog.

I am, in case you haven't picked up on it, battling depression.

Well... *battling* is a strong word. The truth is, the fight went out of me ages ago. That's what most people who've never been depressed don't realize: the fight is the first thing to go.

I sit curbside in my vintage Hyundai, staring at the peach-colored, vinyl-sided bungalow and its twenty years of deferred maintenance; waiting, I guess, for it to transform into a sparkling seaside villa in France. When that doesn't happen, I step out of the car and let my feet start their programmed death-march toward the sagging front steps.

"Hey, asshole," says Clyde Gilchrist, my optimistically muscle-shirt-wearing neighbor, approaching me from his side of our scraggly dividing hedge. The man has a gift for crafting a conversation opener. "Can you do me a favor? Next time you decide to throw a bag of empties in my back yard, can you at least aim for the—?"

I cut him off with a flip of the hand. I've never, in fact, thrown *anything* into his yard—except disdain—but I'm not in the mood for Clyde Gilchrist this fine evening. I jam my key in the door and slip inside. The stale smell of last night's Kung Pao Shrimp assails my nostrils as—

A hard object—feels like a flesh-covered pipe—collides with my Adam's apple. My cereal box leaps from my hand as my bottled beer and car keys crash to the floor. My feet try valiantly to continue their forward march as my neck is jerked backwards with a sickening crack of cartilage.

The hard object, I realize, is a forearm. A muscled humanoid has me in a chokehold from behind. I can feel his biceps twitching and his hot breath in my hair.

My unseen assailant whips my body around in a smooth one-eighty and drags me backwards through the house, face up. I cannot breathe, and my eyes feel as if they're about to pop their sockets. My feet flail wildly, trying to gain purchase on the bare floor as my brain scrambles to make sense of the moment.

*What the hell is happening here? Why?*

I'm a second-rate computer game artist. I don't own anything worth stealing — a casual glance around the house would tell you that — and I've masterfully engineered my life so as to be of no real consequence to anyone. Ergo, I don't merit this kind of attention. Ergo, whoever this guy is, he has the wrong person. The wrong house. The wrong information.

Wrong, wrong, wrong. On every count.

I hope I can convince *him* of that. Whoever he is.

If only I could pull some air into my lungs.

As he jerks my body into the kitchen, I note, absurdly, that the ceiling is covered with black cobwebs. I haven't looked up in years, I realize.

The man's gym-forged arm forces me down into a kitchen chair, which has been set up in the middle of the floor, directly below the ceiling light, interrogation style. He releases the pressure on my neck just enough for me to gulp some air.

Standing in front of my parents' ancient Kenmore electric is a second man, smallish in stature, maybe five-seven or so. He's wearing a Star Wars storm trooper mask. The jaw section has been cut away to expose his real mouth. Perhaps so he can speak and be heard more clearly? I note a well-trimmed reddish beard rimming a set of small, even teeth.

The man wears latex surgical gloves and holds in his hands — almost comically, it seems at first — a branch cutting tool, the type landscapers use, with two long handles and a short, curved blade-apparatus.

The pipe-hard arm maintains its lock grip as Storm Trooper

addresses me in a soft, precise, and rather high-pitched voice that comes off as *almost* — but not quite — prissy. "This tool," he says, holding up the instrument for me to see, "is called a lopper. Did you know that? Most people don't. This particular model is a long-handled Corona High-Torque Bypass lopper. It can snip an inch-thick branch off a green tree as easily as slicing cake."

Storm Trooper lays the lopper on the kitchen table and picks up an iPad that's resting there. He holds the tablet device about a foot from my face, waits till my freaked-out eyes focus on it, and then taps it awake with a latex-covered finger.

On the viewing screen is a video, cued up and ready to roll. Its frozen image is that of a fifty-year-old man strapped into a metal garden chair, his arms and wrists duct-taped to the chair's tubular arms. Only the man's hands have been left free to move.

Storm Trooper taps the Play icon.

Trooper's own recorded voice issues from the iPad's speaker. He seems to be standing just off screen in the video. "I'll ask this question once and once only," Troop's high voice says to the taped-up man in the video. "Who knows about this besides the woman?"

Video-guy in the chair replies, "I haven't said a word to —"

Before he can finish his sentence, the open blades of the lopper lunge in from off screen like the jaws of a snapping turtle. They hook the man's left pinkie and ring finger into their curved bite and lop them off cleanly. A plastic bag is snapped around the man's hand to catch the blood. He lets out a keening *eeeee-eeeee-eeeee* of pure agony, as blood streams into the bag and sweat pours from his face. He shouts in the voice of a man whose balls are on fire, "Clarence Woodcock! Clarence Woodcock! Clarence Woodcock! Clarence Woodcock!"

My stomach clenches and I feel a violent urge to retch. Storm Trooper shuts off the video, puts down the iPad, and picks up the lopper once again.

"I hope that video was instructive," he says in his almost-but-not-quite-prissy manner. "The way we work is this: I give orders, you follow them without a moment's hesitation. Thus you avoid the lopper. Are we abundantly clear on that?"

I nod. Yes. Abundantly.

"My partner is going to release your neck now. You are to remain seated while he straps you into the chair. Clear?"

Again I nod. My list of alternatives does not stretch from sea to shining sea.

I feel Chokehold-man wordlessly pat me down and pull my cell phone from my pants pocket. He then wraps a band of rubbery, self-sticking fabric, eight inches wide or so, around my chest and upper arms several times, fastening me to the chair-back. He does the same to bind my ass and thighs to the seat.

The material feels elastic but tough, and I sense they've chosen it so as to avoid leaving binding-marks on my skin. They don't want me to look manhandled. I cling to this idea with a desperate thread of hope. Maybe the lopper is going to be used only for... emphasis.

Or as a last resort.

"Before we begin," Trooper says—begin *what?*—"let me explain something that I hope will put this situation in perspective and enlist your cooperation." Trooper Dan has my undiluted attention. "If you've seen many crime thrillers on TV, you may be thinking that because I am wearing this mask, I do not wish for you to see my face. Which, in turn, you might assume means that you have a chance of sauntering away from this encounter under your own power."

I do not want to hear whatever comes out of his mouth next.

"That, I'm afraid, is a faulty assumption. I wear the mask only out of an excess of caution. You *are* going to die today, Mr. Carroll. I get no joy out of telling you that, but I don't define the job parameters."

Adrenaline rips through every synapse of my nervous system. Not only does this guy know my name—my hopes of this being a case of mistaken identity have fizzled like spilt champagne—but also he intends to kill me. And apparently there isn't Thing One I can do about it. My heart and lungs pump in double-time. I stifle the urge to wriggle and scream.

"To employ a tired cliché," says the masked man with the lopper, "we can do this two ways..."

He pauses. At this moment I become aware of a detail I failed to take in before. The kitchen floor is covered with a sheet of clear plastic, *Dexter*-style. Not a hopeful sign for the protagonist, as a rule of thumb.

"Option A — cooperation — is better for all concerned, believe me when I say that, but we will revert to option B without qualm. Option B, needless to say, brings the lopper into play. A testicle sliced in half is a memorable experience, I'm told." His high, even voice has an almost hypnotic quality. "So... choose an option, Mr. Carroll."

Does he actually expect me to choose aloud? Apparently he does.

"Option A," I say flatly.

"The only choice, really," he says. "Still, it's surprising how often we have to go to option B. Let's begin."

He lays the lopper down again and reaches into a paper grocery bag on the table. His latex-gloved hands emerge holding three items: a plastic bottle of Svedka vodka — my brand, yippee — and two brown plastic prescription vials.

"This is a process I understand you're familiar with from past experience," he says. How could he possibly know I OD'd on vodka and pills half a year ago? "As you know, it's a no muss/no fuss procedure. Pleasant, almost. Though when you tried it last time, you didn't take enough of the pills to get the job done, did you? Today we're going to bypass the 'cry for help' stage and go straight for DOA."

He hands me one of the vials. "Your instructions are to take all the pills in both containers, wash them down with the vodka, and then continue drinking the vodka until you are rendered... non-functional. Then, bim bam bom, it's all over and we leave you to rest in peace."

I stare at the vial in my hand, knowing I have no choice but to obey the man, but trying to prolong the moment before my fate is sealed. In that brief moment, as I study the pill bottle, I become aware of another detail my conscious mind has failed to register till now: the soft *clack-clack* of my computer keyboard from the adjacent den — my "office." Chokehold guy hasn't left the kitchen, so that means there is a third member of this rogue Jehovah's Witness splinter cell.

What have I, Finnian Carroll, low-level computer artist and general life failure, done to merit a three-man criminal operation?

And what do they think they're going to find on my computer? The missing Snowden files? Yet, absurdly, a sense of violated privacy wells up within me.

"You're not going to find anything useful there," I shout toward the den.

"Oh, we know exactly what's on your computer, Mr. Carroll," says Troop. "Trust me. Come on, swallow the pills."

I turn the safety (ha) cap of vial number one and pour its contents into my palm. Cute little rounded rectangles with triple score-lines across them. Xanax. Close to a hundred twenty of them. My own prescription, as confirmed by the name "Finnian Carroll" on the label. I filled it just two days ago.

With my hand brimming with pills and about two seconds of grace time before the lopper is summoned into play, I review my survival options. One tactic might be to fling the pills, scatter them across two rooms. Buy myself some time to devise a better plan. Would that result in lopper discipline? Probably not. If these guys are going to all this effort to stage my death as a suicide, then the lopper is probably a bluff.

Probably.

Wasn't a bluff for the guy in the video, though.

"The pills, Mr. Carroll." Trooper-man eyes me through the mask, waits precisely two seconds, then turns and reaches for the lopper.

"I'm doing it!"

My hand, filled with pills, flies to my mouth. (Chokehold has left my forearms free to do the deed.) A few pills miss their target; most of them score a direct hit. Trooper hands me the bottle of vodka. "Drink."

I take an obedient swig, working the pills down my throat. I swig again. Storm Trooper takes the vodka from me and hands me the second vial of pills. These I recognize too. Diazepam—generic Valium. A script I filled but never used. I dump all of them into my hand. I believe there are ninety of the blue pills, a three-month supply. Ten-milligrammers. I cram about half of them into my mouth. Troop hands me the vodka to wash them down. I glug away.

I eat the other half of the pills and wash them down too.

Now it's just a matter of waiting for the results to come in. So to speak.

Well, this is what I wanted, right?

Fuck, what have I just done?

# Chapter 2

"Drink up, Mr. Carroll," says Storm Trooper, striding jauntily back into the room.

He has left me alone with Chokehold for a long while, to give the pills time to work their magic and so that he can confer around my computer with thug number three. In his absence, Choke has been dutifully nudging my arm every minute or two, and I've been taking measured sips of vodka, but now Trooper Dan seems eager to move my demise along at a brisker pace.

"Hurry, hurry, faster," he says, rapping the plastic Svedka bottle with his latexed knuckles. "We don't have all day. Things to do, Mr. Carroll, things to do."

Things to do.

For some reason, these three simple words snap me out of the fog of numbness I've drifted into. I will never, ever, ever have another *thing to do*, I realize. My thing-doing days are behind me. The comprehension that the world will really and truly go on without me blows through me like a polar wind.

Jesus, fuck, no! I will never eat another garlic, artichoke, and mushroom pizza from The Barnacle. I will never see another pretty woman in a summer dress. I will never dab paint on another canvas. I will never drink another pint of Arrogant Bastard Ale on the outdoor deck of Pete's Lagoon on Musqasset Island with my best friend Miles.

I will never again *set foot* on Musqasset Island, the only place on Earth where I was ever genuinely happyish. I will never again sit on the rocks at Mussel Cove with Jeannie, watching the seals bob in the waves, laughing so hard I feel sick.

I will never again make love to Jeannie. (Full disclosure, that customer left the barber shop years ago.)

My thoughts cluster surprisingly around Jeannie, whom I haven't seen in four years. Why did I let her go so easily? Why didn't I fight harder? What trivial principle had I been trying to prove? My soul for a do-over! Until this moment, I didn't even realize I wanted one.

I think, too, of all the things I have *never* experienced—thanks to pissed-away years of playing the tortured artist—and now never will. I will never have a child, never visit the Scottish Highlands, never master "Richland Woman Blues" on the guitar, never have my own gallery showing.

A hot blade of longing stabs my heart. Longing for the life I once held in my hands and failed to embrace, longing for the life I will never have.

Suddenly all my "struggles" of the past year—the half-assed suicide attempt, the endless search for "the right therapist," the maudlin boozing—unmask themselves as nothing more than drama. Posturing. I realize I haven't *really* been struggling with depression. (I've seen what a monster real depression can be.) No, what I've been struggling with is disillusionment. Clinical disappointment.

What a child, what an ungrateful tool.

Troop taps the vodka bottle again. I drink.

In my mind I replay all the decisions and circumstances that brought me to this place, and see the truth of my recent life with the crystalline insight of the soon-to-be-dead.

About four years ago, I left my beloved Musqasset Island to move back home to miserable Wentworth, Massachusetts, from whence I hail. Ostensibly, I made the move to care for my mother who had stage IV bladder cancer, but really I was just escaping a situation on the island that was too taxing for my poor, pain-averse psyche to handle. The six months Mom was given to live turned into three years, which I "endured" with outward valor, secretly grateful for the excuse it gave me not to make any affirmative choices in my own life.

Then Mom died, about a year ago, and I slipped into a serious downward spiral. Not because I was traumatized by her death, but because, upon being stripped of my "noble caregiver" role, I was suddenly faced with the void of a life utterly bereft of purpose. Storm Trooper dismissed my previous suicide attempt as a cry for help. I hate to admit it, but he's right. And not just about the overdose itself, about all of it. All my drama and self-flagellating. It was all a cry for attention, for pity. But from whom?

God? Tell me *that's* not the game I've been playing.

A powerful realization comes bubbling up from the depths of my awareness like a beach ball that's been stuffed under murky water:

I do not want to die.

Do not. Do not. Do not. Do not. Do not.

I want to live. I desperately, passionately, wholeheartedly want to live. No more fucking around. I have been cured of "suicidal ideation" for life. I want another crack at this thing.

True, I have a belly full of pills and am strapped to a chair under the glaring eye of a psycho killer, but a strong instinct rises up within me: my time's not up yet. Can't be. No. No.

But what are my options here? Seriously.

Try to talk my way out of it? Beg for sympathy? Not a chance. Bargain?

"What do you guys want?" I venture, my words slurring a tad. "What can I give you?"

Trooper Dan, his eyes obscured by the shaded plastic of the mask's eyeholes, leans over me and whispers, "What we want, Mr. Carroll, is for you to die so that we can get to Applebee's before happy hour ends. Sláinte!"

He waits till I take an obedient swig of vodka and then backs away.

I hear the clacking of the keyboard in the den again. "Whatever you're looking for on my computer, I'll tell you where to find it. Then you can let me call 911 and be on your way. I haven't seen any of your faces."

Trooper Dan doesn't even dignify that one with a response. So much for bargaining.

My lower legs are free, and so are my forearms. What if I Jackie Chan them? Spring to my feet and whip the chair legs around in a mad frenzy. Knock them both down. Then use my free hands to finish them off.

Sure.

What other options do I have? Only one, really. Make them think I'm already dead. Well, not dead. Faking dead is impossible when you're under the microscope, as I am. But maybe I *can* fake unconscious-to-the-point-of-no-return.

If I can convince them I'm down for the count before I actually am, maybe they'll leave while I'm still alive and I can call 911. It's not much, but it's all I got.

"Drink," says Storm Trooper.

I take another swig of booze and begin to map out my new strategy.

If I am going to sell the ultimate possum ploy—and survive it—I need to keep a mental edge. Not easy to do when you've just swallowed two hundred benzos in a lethal combo and you're drinking straight vodka by the mouthful. My challenge will be to outrace the real effects of the drugs with my faked performance. Can o' corn. Heh.

How much time do I have? I still seem to be sharp enough at the moment, but it's hard to judge. I try reciting the alphabet backwards. In my mind I say, Z... W... X... Y... A screw-up right out of the starting gate, not good. Z... Y... X... W... um... V... um... No clue what comes next.

Crap, I'm already mentally compromised.

I figure I probably have fifteen minutes, tops, before I become so foggy I sink into the chemical stupor that will end my life.

That means I have, at most, *ten* minutes to convince my captors I have slipped into terminal unconsciousness. I've got to get this show on the road. No sooner does this thought occur than I feel the tug of gravity yanking at my chin. Real sleep is hooking its nails in me. I need a strategy, fast. Something unexpected.

Instinct takes over. When Storm Trooper steps toward me to tap the vodka bottle again, I burst into a fit of laughter. It's so sudden and authentic, it takes *me* by surprise almost as much as it does Troop. I bray laughter till I'm gasping for air.

"I'll bite. What's so funny, Mr. Carroll?"

"You! With your little mask and your lopper. Taking yourself so seriously." I know I'm skating on thin ice to mock this guy, but I want him to think I'm losing it, throwing caution to the wind. "And the funny part is..." I break into whoops of laughter again. "The funny part is... We're on the same side! We both want the same thing. We both want this loser dead. I've been trying to get this job done for a year, but I always chicken out. All I needed was a little push. I didn't expect it to come from a Jedi stormtrooper, but fuck it, I'll take it."

With a big, forced smile on my face, I steer the bottle toward my mouth and begin swigging hungrily from it, staring defiantly at Troop. I want him to think I have not only *surrendered* to my fate but am welcoming it with open arms—that I just want to end things fast and go out drunk. Speed-drinking, I hope, will provide a credible reason for my passing out faster than expected. Of course, by doing this, I run the risk of *actually* passing out—or succumbing to alcohol poisoning. But I'm not in an ideal-world scenario here.

I drink manically for a solid minute or two, watching the bottle's contents go down by an inch and a half. I'm well past sloshed by now, but my "second awareness"—something I learned to harness years ago during my meditating period—has kicked in. A deeper part of me remains detached and watchful. I need to ride with that part. Zen my way through the chemical haze.

A burp escapes my belly. With a mock-serious face, I pronounce, "Hints of sweetness with a pleasingly yeasty body and a peppery finish." I dissolve into fits of giggles again.

Storm Trooper's red-bearded mouth curls into a tiny smile below his mask. "Might as well go out laughing, eh, Mr. Carroll?"

"With a whimper, not a bang," I agree, toasting him with the bottle. "I mean with a bang, not a wimple. Ha, ha, wimple!"

I sit up rod-straight as if I've suddenly remembered something urgent. I make a horrified face and let the bottle slip from my hand. Trooper Dan catches it. I look at him as if seeing him for the first time and say with deadening mouth muscles, "I guh go. I guh go."

I pretend to try to rise, to make my exit. As I do, I feel a strong pull from below, as if my arms are being dragged down by a puppeteer hiding beneath the floor. The drugs in my system are making another play for me even as I'm trying to fake the same effect.

I take a panicked look all around me, breathing hard, pretending I have no idea where I am. As if trying to make a frantic burst for the door, I push off with my right leg, causing the chair to topple to the left.

My head strikes the plastic-sheeted floor and bounces hard, once. My eyes roll up in their sockets, and my eyelids shut.

I am officially down for the count. Win or lose.

Silence reigns as my captors and I remain motionless.

I can hear their breathing. Studying me for signs of consciousness.

I am turnip, watch me vedge.

Time flattens into eternity. Not a word from my captors. Not a twitch from me.

At some point, one of the men crouches and flicks my cheek. I don't react.

More wordless breathing.

A hand shakes me by the shoulder. I let my body wobble liquidly. I allow my breath to become shallow, labored, ragged.

I don't know how long I lie there like that. Clock-time no longer exists.

At one point, my brain literally blinks out, like a faulty light bulb, then blinks back on again. Shit. I am minutes away from real and permanent turnip-hood.

I feel the warm breath of one of the men as he moves his face within inches of mine. What is he going to do, kiss me? ...Is he?

"That was an inspiring performance, Mr. Carroll," Troop whispers in my ear. My heart flips like a dying fish. "But you don't fool me. I know you're fully conscious. And so here is what's going to happen. I'm going to position the lopper blades on your nose."

I feel the brush of sharpened metal on either side of my nose. My Zen state retreats. I must use all my willpower not to flinch.

"When I count to three, you will open your eyes. If you fail to do so, I will lop the nose off your face. One..."

Troop is only testing me. Has to be. I'm betting my nose on it.

"Two... Three..."

Troop pauses for a moment and does nothing.

*I do nothing.*

The lopper blades tighten ever so slowly against my nose. I do not throw my eyes open and beg for mercy. I, rutabaga.

The blades halt without breaking the skin. They stay poised in that position, pinching my nose flesh, for what seems like a month. Then Storm Trooper opens the blades, withdraws the lopper, and stands up, his knee cartilage crackling again.

"He's gone," he says to his partner. "If not, he would have cracked."

My heart leaps with crazy hope.

Chokehold whips the plastic sheet out from under me like a magician doing the tablecloth trick. He starts cutting my chest strap with a knife. Yes! They're getting ready to leave. And if this is to look like a suicide, they can't leave plastic sheeting on the floor and me strapped to a chair. Choke lifts my body and cradles it a foot or so above the floor as he finishes cutting the binding fabric. Then he releases me and lets me drop, tossing the chair aside.

Whap! I hit the floor like a bag of grapefruit. My cheekbone sings out in pain, but I think I have remained limp. I don't think I have tensed or winced.

"All set here," Choke reports to Troop. His first spoken words. What's that accent? No "r" at the end of "here." Boston? Brooklyn? I would need to hear more.

"Good," says Trooper Dan in his high, almost-prissy voice. Then he utters the words that crush my hope like a sat-on birthday cake. "We'll give it another ten minutes to be sure he doesn't puke or pull any surprises, then we'll be on our way."

*Ten minutes?* No way can I hold onto consciousness that long. As if to confirm my fears, I feel a wave of heaviness spread through my body from the base of my spine outward. My brain blinks off again.

The opening bars of Schubert's "Ave Maria" ring out in an angelic female soprano. For an absurd moment I think I've died and gone to Catholic-school heaven. Then I realize it's a ring tone. Storm Trooper steps out of the room to take the call in private.

Twenty seconds later he returns. "Time to go," he says to his partners. "Let's do a quick clean-up, grab our stuff, then we're out of here. Bim bam bom."

I hear Chokehold bunch up the plastic sheeting. Three sets of footsteps begin clomping through the house, one heavy, one light, one medium. The three bears. I hear someone fill a bucket in the laundry room and begin cleaning up the spilled beer and broken glass in the entry hall with a broom and mop.

*Faster*, I silently urge the men as my brain fights to avoid blinking out once again. The next time it blinks may be the last. My chances of being able to walk out of here on my own two feet are dimming by the minute.

The downstairs toilet flushes. I hear other cleaning-up noises and the sound of the mop being rinsed and returned to its place.

*For fuck's sake, get a move on.*

I feel a sharp pain in my gut. Hmm, has a foot just kicked my stomach? Yes! Chokehold checking on me one last time. The only reason I didn't react is that my brain had zonked out again. It is the kick that revives me and, in a brilliant twist of irony, probably saves my life.

Several quiet seconds pass. What now? I hear Troop say, "Finis. Let him die in peace." He drops the quarter-full plastic vodka bottle on the floor near me. And with that, the three home invaders exit by the back door.

A finger of the spilled liquid coldly touches my arm.

I force myself to wait till I hear the distant sounds of car doors closing and a vehicle driving away before opening my eyes.

I try to sit up and find my body now weighs a pleasant five hundred pounds. After three failed attempts, I manage to heft myself to a sitting position. I wait for my mental fog to ebb a bit, then grab the edge of the table, pulling myself to a stand. I notice the empty pill vials. Somehow I summon the presence of mind to stick them in my pocket so the ER staff — if I can make it to the hospital — will know what I OD'd on.

The mad puppeteer beneath the floor is pulling my limbs down with all his might.

I start toward the wall phone, then remember I stopped paying for the landline after Mom died. I need to use my cell. But where is it?

Chokehold took it from me. I'll need to get to a neighbor's phone.

I lumber toward the front of the house, feeling as if I have twenty-pound weights strapped to my ankles. To get to the door I must pass through the den/office, which now seems the length of a football field. As I plod across the old wooden floor, my heavy footfalls jiggle the mouse on my computer desk, causing the screen to awaken.

A Microsoft Word document pops open. This grabs my attention, even through the mental fog. I haven't used Word in over a week.

I stare fuzzily at the screen. I need to be on my way, but I also want to know what these guys were looking for on my computer. And what they found. Stepping closer to the desk, I try to read the title of the document, but the letters are swimming around and doubling up in my vision. They've become animated, abstract symbols. Cuneiform in motion.

With all the concentration I can muster, I force my vision to lock in on the document's heading, which is in bold fourteen-point font. It reads, "Finnian Carroll's Absolutely Final (This Time I Mean It) and Incontestable Suicide Note and Last Confession."

What? Sounds like something I would write, but...

But I *didn't* write it. Of that I am certain, even in my massively compromised state.

Damn. Those guys weren't trying to take something *from* my computer, they were planting something *on* it.

I try to read the body of the note, which is in smaller font, but I can't get my eyes to work in synch. The letters are dancing apart and bunching together like ants at a barn dance. I can only make out isolated phrases. Still, the few chunks of text I *am* picking up, in those floating bits and pieces, are suggesting something horrifying and impossible.

A wave of nausea overtakes me. My knees buckle and I fall to the floor.

The feel of the hard floor is bliss. I want very badly to sleep—for a long, long time. I come perilously close to giving up the fight right then and there, but I manage to tap into some unsuspected reserve of mental toughness and force myself to my feet again. I try to read the words on the computer screen again, but something inside me screams, "No time! Get moving! Now!"

I obey. I stagger heavily to the front door, then out onto the porch. I plunge down the front steps, across the sidewalk and into the street. No neighbors anywhere in sight. I turn and see a yellow step van with a cartoon face painted on it bearing down on me from the upper end of Bell Street. I drop to my knees and use the last ounce of my strength to throw my arms up.

And that's the last thing I remember.

# Chapter 3

"This release-form states that you are leaving the hospital against the advice of the treatment team," says the social worker in a voice so slow she must be going for comedy.

"Understood," I reply, my knee dancing a feverish jig. I'm sitting in the day room of Saint Dymphna's, the psych ward of Calvary Mercy Hospital, signing my discharge papers.

"Before you sign the release, Mr. Carroll," labors the social worker, "I'd like you to read this document and initial that you understand it."

She hands me an information page detailing the perils of the particular combo of benzodiazepines and alcohol I ingested (I vaguely remember hearing the ER doctor refer to it as "the full Whitney Houston"). The paper lists two dozen possible symptoms, side effects, and disastrous consequences, including:

- Confusion
- Slurred speech
- Disorientation
- Stumbling
- Dizziness
- Loss of consciousness
- Brain damage
- Muscle weakness
- Difficulty breathing
- Hallucinations

...and of course, that grande dame of all side effects:
- Death

I speed-scan the rest of the document. Fine. I need no convincing that the chemical cocktail I ingested is a bad idea. After getting my stomach pumped in the ER, receiving activated charcoal treatment, and undergoing sixteen hours of vital-sign management under glaring fluorescent lights, I'm all set on that.

Following my medical treatment, I was shipped, FedEx Express, to the psych ward upstairs. Having stayed there once before, I knew the ropes a bit. Rope number one: when you come in on a "voluntary," you cannot be held for more than seventy-two hours without a commitment. Technically, my admission was voluntary, so one of the first things I did, after sleeping for almost twenty-four hours straight, was sign a so-called "three-day note."

And now I fully intend to honor it. I don't need suicide counseling and I don't need protection. From myself, anyhow. What I need is to go home, stat, square things with my job, and try to figure out what the hell happened at my house last Friday.

During my four-day stay at happy valley, I said as little to the counseling staff as I could get away with. I didn't tell anyone about my encounter with deranged masked assailants or the fact that my suicide attempt had not exactly been voluntary.

Why not?

Because if the staff thought I was having paranoid delusions, they might have extended my stay. And if they thought I was telling the truth, they would have brought the police in. I don't want anyone going through my house — or my computer. Not till *I've* had a chance to do so.

I sign the warning/information page and the release form.

"This is your discharge summary and treatment plan," the social worker's voice slogs on through snow and rain and gloom of night. "Counseling sessions twice a week are recommended. This page has your prescriptions." No, thanks. "And here are your personal items."

She hands me a large reusable manila envelope containing my wallet and my belt.

"Mr. Carroll... May I call you Finnian?" *Not a lecture, please. I didn't pack a lunch.* "This is your second stay with us. When patients come back a third time, the staff starts to refer to them as 'regulars.' Don't become a regular."

"I won't," I say. I mean it too.

The truth is, despite the circumstances, I feel more alive than I have in years.

• • • • •

I've only been away for five days, but as I step out of the cab, my parents' place looks a bit alien to me — shrunken, dark, angular. I try the front door. Unlocked. Handy, since I don't have my keys; they were inside the house last I saw them. I step into the entry hall, flinching involuntarily. No attacker grabs me by the throat. Still, the silence feels fraught.

"Hello?" I shout. Hidden assailants, as we all know, are rendered defenseless by the shouted hello. Needless to say, no one responds.

I do a quick walk-through of both floors to see what sort of tracks my "visitors" left behind. Did they sack the place? Take anything? I make a pass through my upstairs bedroom, which I am still treating as temporary quarters four years after moving in. It's clean. Which is to say filthy, but in the customary way.

I check my mom's room, which, since her death, I've been using mostly as storage space for crap I don't want to deal with. Nothing's been moved.

It isn't till I step into the kitchen, downstairs, that a chill creeps across my skin. All the kitchen chairs are arrayed neatly around the table — not how I left them — and there is no trace of the vodka bottle. No spilled booze on the floor, no stray pills. It is as if nothing untoward has taken place here.

Which can mean only one thing. Trooper Dan and his buddies returned to the scene of the crime. Finding no body, they cleaned up the "suicide" traces. Why, I don't know. But one thing's for sure: the bad guys know I'm still on the sunny side of the grass.

Therefore, I am unsafe in this house.

I find my keys splayed on the kitchen counter where I always leave them, along with my cell phone. The phone is a surprise. I figured, for some reason, my assailants would have kept it or destroyed it. Why? Suddenly I'm Jason Bourne?

I turn the phone on. No recent activity except a few missed calls and a text from work. I'll give my boss a call in a minute.

My computer. I've been saving that for last.

I step tentatively into the den where my workstation is set up and roll the mouse to awaken my Mac. Only my desktop wallpaper (a painting I did of Fish Pier on Musqasset Island) appears on the screen. No suicide note. *Where the hell did it go?*

My captors must have deleted the note when they returned to the scene. I sit in my eighty-dollar HomeGoods office chair and open Microsoft Word. Moving the cursor to the File menu, I select Open Recent. A blank list pops up. Someone has cleared the Recent files list. Not I. I click the Trash icon to see if the deleted document is there. The Trash has been emptied. Again, not by me.

What other ways are there to find a recently created and deleted document? I do a Spotlight search. Nothing. I go into Finder, click All My Files, and arrange them in order of date. Nothing on the date of my assault. I check the folder where AutoRecovery files go. No joy. Maybe my booze-and-drug-addled mind dreamt the note up.

My anxiety is mounting. If Trooper and company came back here at some point—and obviously they did—then they're no doubt aware I was hospitalized and probably also know I've been discharged. They might be planning to swing by for a visit at any moment.

They might be here right now. It's not out of the question.

I listen again. Nothing.

I need to vanish, pronto. But go where and do what?

Wait. Better TCB first. Call work. Check my emails. But hurry.

I work for a computer game company in Cambridge, creating artwork for animated adventure games for the iPad. It's an okay gig, though miles from my former dream of becoming a museum-level oil painter. Being a puzzle-minded guy, I pitch in on the game designs too.

I'm a 1099er, not a salaried staffer. The pay is tragic, but the freedom agrees with me. I show up at the office once or twice a week for design meetings. The rest of the time, I patch in from home.

I call Rajam, my boss, and tell her I've been dealing with a medical emergency but I'll make up the work later. She says fine and she hopes I'm blah-dee-blah.

I consider calling the police, but what would I tell them? My visitors left no traces, and I can't identify any of them except to say that one of them had a reddish beard and small, even teeth. But of course, the larger issue is that until I know what happened to that "suicide note" I saw — and until I read its full contents — I don't feel too jazzed about bringing in the cops.

I check my emails. There are several from the programming and design teams at work regarding concept art for a new game called "Monty Zuma's Revenge" (don't ask). They can wait. I also find a note from my sister Angela, saying she's worried about me. The hospital must have called her. I gave her name as next of kin.

Angie lives in Wentworth too. She helped me with the Mom duties whenever she, Ange, was sober. Unfortunately, that wasn't all too frequently, and she and I haven't talked a lot since Mom went to her big Parish Bingo Night in the sky. Complicating matters is the fact that Mom bequeathed the house to me, not Angie, which is a touchy spot between us. I briefly consider asking Ange if I can stay at her apartment for a couple of days, but I don't want to put her in danger, and I *really* don't want to deal with her drinking.

I need to find that deleted suicide note before I leave. Supposedly it's hard to fully delete a file from a computer; it can almost always be recovered. But I have no idea how. For a guy who works in a technical field, I am astoundingly low-tech.

A muffled thump issues from somewhere toward the back of the house. I freeze. Small mammal or assassin? I don't *think* Trooper Dan and company are hiding in the house right now, but still, my urgency to vacate the premises shoots into the red zone.

Screw it, I'll look for the Word file later.

I run upstairs to my bedroom, dig out a mid-sized backpack, and throw in a few haphazard changes of clothes, some toiletries, a few books, and a phone-charger cord. Grabbing my all-weather jacket, I make a quick trip out to the car, then head back inside to fetch my iMac.

As I'm reentering the house, though, a powerful intuition tells me to turn around and get the hell out of there as fast as I can. I heed it, leaving the computer behind.

# Chapter 4

I pace the floor of my sad single standard at the Oak Crest Motel (nary an oak to be glimpsed), trying to ignore the thick smell of bleach—I hope it's bleach—in the air. I chose this place because of its off-the-beaten-path location and its rear parking lot. I don't want my car to be seen from the road.

I haven't come up with a plan beyond "house bad, motel good." The anxiety in my chest feels like a physical mass. I long to talk to someone I trust but realize, tragically, I have no one to call. Angie, whom I love dearly, is probably hammered to the nines by this hour and, alas, is also physically incapable of listening. I don't want to argue about the house either.

There was a time I would have called my friend Miles in a situation like this. He's a pretty good listener, or at least pretends to be. But we had a "cooling off," shall we say, when I left the island, and he and I have some ground to cover first.

Besides, if that note said what I thought it said, my relationship with Miles has just taken on a troublesome new twist. I still have a few other friends on Musqasset, but we don't really have "chat on the phone" relationships, and besides, I'd rather they thought I was painting in a loft in Bruges.

That damnable suicide note is eating at my mind. There should be some trace of it that can be reconstructed. I regret having left my iMac behind. I wish I could tool with it right now. With darkness approaching, though, I don't feel safe going home to get it.

If only I had some way to tap into my computer remotely. I know this is possible theoretically, but I have no idea how. I rack my brain to come up with a solution, but low blood sugar has turned my skull into an ever-tightening vise. I've got to put something in the ol' Twinkie-hole.

• • • • •

I'm sitting at the bar at J.B.'s Pub, a rural roadhouse with poor self-esteem and a truly frightening jukebox lineup, scarfing down a Cowboy Burger and watching a cornball old movie starring George Segal and a fresh-out-of-acting-school Denzel Washington. Segal discovers he has a black son he didn't know about, hilarity ensues. The movie is called *Carbon Copy*. Each time the title comes up I feel a tickle in my gut, but I can't nail down why.

Then, mid-burger-bite, it hits me. There's an online service called CarbonCopy — it provides remote backup of personal computer files. I have it on my iMac; its icon sits there between Dropbox and Plaxo in the upper right corner of my screen.

My skin prickles with excitement. CarbonCopy makes daily backups of your files and archives them! That means even if my home invaders eliminated all traces of the suicide note from my computer when they came back to my house, there's a chance a copy exists on my backup. And I can access my backup from any computer.

My burger instantly loses all its scant appeal. I need to get into my CarbonCopy account. That means I need to get my hands on a computer. My phone won't do. Technically, it's an Internet portal, yes, but it's a Barney Rubble iPhone with a tiny, banged-up screen. I need to get my hands on a real computer. Where can I find one at seven forty-five on a Wednesday evening?

Wentworth Public Library has a slew of them, as I recall. What time does it close? Going online with my phone, I learn the library closes at eight tonight. Not helpful. Where else can I access a public computer? Do Internet cafés still exist? I google "cyber café" and find there is, indeed, a brew-house in nearby Haverhill that rents computer time. It is open till eleven and only about nine miles away.

I inhale a few more bites of my Cowboy Burger, slap a twenty on the bar, and head out the door to saddle up my trusty Hyundai. Yee-ha.

•     •     •     •     •

Brew Moon is a wannabe-hipster joint that suffers from a pronounced dearth of hipsters. Other than the requisitely goateed and eyebrow-impaled barista, who crafts my iced Vietnamese Cà Phê Dá with studied indifference—ten bucks says his name is Bennett or Django—the rest of the tiny night-crowd is woefully unhip and borderline desperate-looking. All but one of the computer stations are available. I pay for my Cà Phê Dá, which comes with a free hour of computer time, and settle into a Mac station in the darkest corner of the room.

I google CarbonCopy and go directly to its website. I am quickly able to access my account and view the mirror image of my home hard drive. After a bit of clicking around, I learn that CarbonCopy lets you restore any folder to an earlier version by date.

I go to all the obvious folders where a Word file might have been saved, and restore them to their state of five days earlier. Nothing.

Then I remember good old AutoRecovery. Even if the bad guys didn't save a named copy of the document anywhere on my hard drive, Word might still have auto-saved a copy. I checked the AutoRecovery folder at home, but I want to see what that folder looked like five days ago.

I do the restoration process and—I can't believe my eyes—something pops up. At the top of the AutoRecovery file list is a Word file created on August 23, the date of my home invasion. The file has a generic, auto-generated filename. I double-click on it and hold my breath as the pre-Obama-era computer churns away, trying to open the file.

Holy crap. There it is: a document with the heading, "Finnian Carroll's Absolutely Final (This Time I Mean It) and Incontestable

Suicide Note and Last Confession." With my brain now free of toxic chemicals, I can read the text quite easily. I wish I couldn't.

*Friends, Romans, Countrymen,*

*I, Finnian Carroll, have opted to "put in for early reincarnation," i.e., terminate this failed attempt at an earthly existence. I do this because I can no longer come up with a defensible reason to crawl out of bed each morning. Thus have I swallowed a large quantity of the very pills intended to keep me alive, along with enough vodka to kill a Russian game programmer (or at least get him mildly buzzed). I apologize to whoever discovers the "results" of my actions – hope it wasn't too grisly a scene (unless it was you, Clyde Gilchrist, then I hope it was straight out of* Battle Royale*).*

*They say confession is good for the soul. I hope that's true, because my soul is going to need all the help it can get.*

Suddenly the tone takes a less smarmy turn.

*Eighteen years ago, on May 12, 1999, the night of my college graduation, I made a lethal mistake, which I failed to atone for.*

I pull in a breath, stand up, and walk away from the computer, blowing air from my cheeks. I'm starting to hyperventilate. I need to calm down. I don't want to call attention to myself. I take a slow breath from my diaphragm, then sit back down and continue reading...

*That night, I went to a graduation party at a professor's farmhouse in Bridgefield, Mass. There was a lot of drinking. Late in the evening, a close friend and I went outside to share a goodbye toast in private.*

*Somehow we'd gotten our hands on an expensive bottle of Glenmalloch single malt scotch. We passed it back and forth, sitting by a stream behind the house, talking and reminiscing. I had never drunk scotch before and had little experience with hard liquor in general. I did not realize how drunk I was getting (not an excuse, just an explanation).*

*I left the patry* – my eyes note the misspelling – *alone. Foolishly and regrettably, I got behind the wheel of my car, taking the scotch bottle with me.*

*As I was driving home — on the "back roads" — I dozed off at the wheel and almost struck the stone wall that borders the Dempsey Bridge. I jammed on the brakes, making a loud squeal, and went into a panic. What if the noise attracted attention? I'd had way too much to drink and was carrying an open container of alcohol. I had to get rid of the bottle.*

*What I did next was an honest mistake, but the costliest one of my life. I threw the half-full bottle over the bridge. I won't describe the consequences of my action here, but for those interested in knowing...*

Here the note provides a link, presumably to a news article (I see the name *bostonglobe* embedded in the long URL).

*Where I erred, morally speaking, was not so much in making the initial mistake but in failing to own it once I realized what I'd done.*

*I have regretted my actions every day since, and it's not an overstatement to say they have ruined my life. I deeply apologize to all those whose lives I have affected. Thanks for reading this.*

*Until next life,*
*Finnian Carroll*

I feel like I have a blowgun dart in my neck. This note is a flat-out impossibility. Shock waves bombard me and I can't make sense of my world. I wobble to my feet. If I don't get some air, I'm going to pass out, right on the floor of Brew Moon.

# Chapter 5

I hang an "In Use" tag on the monitor and tell Barista General Django I'll be back. I punch the door open and stumble out into the chill night air.

I need to walk, process what I've just seen. My legs are on autopilot. I jam my hands into my pockets and head straight up Washington Street, past the sleepy pubs and closed thrift shops. Without consciously intending it, I'm walking straight toward the bridge over the Merrimac River.

There are so many disturbing elements to the note, I have trouble putting them in order of enormity. Questions tumble in my head like clothes in a dryer. Which one holds the key to the others? Which do I need to answer first? Logic can't gain traction in my brain.

Okay: first and foremost, there are elements in the note *no one could possibly know about*. No one on the entire planet but me. No one. Then there are other details only Miles and I would know. At the same time, there are crucial facts that are flat-out wrong or omitted. Why? How? Either someone is lying or doesn't know the whole story.

Who could be behind this? Who could possibly have learned these private and unknowable truths? And whoever it is, why are they making a move now, after eighteen silent years? And, oh yes — don't want to forget this trifling little detail — why does someone want me dead because of it?

Of course, the biggest question of all — and the one I know I must answer before this evening is over — is *What actually, factually happened after the bottle was thrown that night?* My entire adult life has been an exercise in stuffing that jack into its box. But tonight, when I get back to that computer at Brew Moon, the jack will be sprung, baring its grinning teeth. I will learn the facts. At long last. I am both terrified and relieved.

I arrive at the Comeau Bridge and look down at the rushing black Merrimac far below. I reflect that if a certain glass bottle had landed in these waters all those years ago, as intended, the worst crime to have been committed would be littering.

The flowing water has a hypnotic effect. I allow myself to be carried back to a night I spend as little time thinking about as possible.

• • • • •

*May 12, 1999. Miles and I did indeed go to a party, at a farmhouse in the rural section of Bridgefield, where a sociology professor we knew co-ran a small organic farm.*

*The Godwin College graduation had taken place that afternoon, and I was now a certified Bachelor of Arts. Stand back, world. Godwin, a small private college in blue-blooded Bridgefield, Massachusetts, catered largely to upmarket students who didn't make the Ivy League cut but still wanted to go to a college that looked the part. About two-thirds of its students were out-of-towners who lived in the dorms or in nearby college apartments. A third were local commuters. Townies. Like me. I lived in Wentworth, the neighboring blue-collar city, with my parents, and never could have afforded Godwin if not for a full scholarship.*

*I drove Miles and his live-in girlfriend Beth to the party that night. They were planning to return the next day to Miles' home state of Connecticut, there to take up their rightful places in the world of privilege-by-birthright that I knew only from behind a glass wall. This was to be our last night together as college friends.*

*Jeannie, my unofficial girlfriend, came to the party too but tellingly did not come with me. We were already starting to do the emotional mitosis necessitated by the fact that she had taken a job in Quebec and I was planning to go to grad school at RISD. Jeannie and I were planning to have our grand goodbye the following weekend.*

*The beer was flowing freely, but I was trying to be cautious. I knew I would be driving later, and I suspected the local constabulary would be out in force on this celebratory night.*

*May 12th was a gorgeous spring evening, strident with frog song, that seemed to stretch on forever. There was a pass-the-guitar session around a fire pit, and I yowled out a couple of Cohen tunes. There were sloppy toasts and long goodbye hugs and tearful reminiscences.*

*Toward the waning part of the evening, I managed to get Miles alone for a private goodbye. Miles Sutcliffe was my best friend. We came from different worlds, but we had bonded at a level I'm not sure I understand even today. I was working-class all the way, deeply self-conscious and insecure. Miles was cool and self-assured, from old Connecticut money (though I think the bulk of the family money had taken its show on the road a generation or two earlier, leaving mostly old Connecticut* attitude*).*

*Our friendship grew from the fact that we both loved to talk endlessly about topics no one else was remotely interested in – Castaneda, game theory, obscure Monty Python sketches. We tended to drive other people away with the fervor and exclusivity of our conversations. I guess it was natural that we became friends.*

*Miles was a handsome son of a bitch, with a smile that made estrogen boil. For the first three years of college, he had an endless, overlapping stream of good-looking, brainy, and cool girlfriends. In fact, I can't remember a single girl (except Jeannie) who ever spurned his advances. It wasn't till senior year that he became exclusive with Beth, who, oddly enough, was the "plainest"-looking girl he'd ever dated, as well as one of the least philosophical and imaginative. Well, maybe not so odd when you realized how much her dad was worth.*

*The dudes loved Miles too. Yep, all the preppy boys and girls genuflected at the altar of Miles Sutcliffe. And because I was his friend, and a reasonably funny guy, I got to nibble at some of his social crumbs. But when push came to shove, I think most of his friends regarded me as little more than smart-assed white trash. I was fun to have around in a group setting – a capuchin monkey in a bellhop cap – but wasn't really invite-on-the-ski-trip material.*

*Here's the thing about that fucking bottle of scotch: I bought it for Miles* as a gift, and I didn't take it home with me. ...And I was not the one who tossed it.

About ten-thirty or eleven o'clock that evening, I went looking for Miles and found him embroiled in a flirt session disguised as a political debate with a pair of comely female underclassmen.

"Sutcliffe," I said, holding up two heavy-bottomed whiskey glasses I'd appropriated from the house. "Come with me, I want to give you something."

"A kiss? You can do that here," he said. "Everybody knows." The gals laughed. It was an open joke that certain members of the male student body thought Miles and I were gay because of our constant and enthusiastic companionship.

I wiggled the whiskey glasses like fishing lures and started down the path to the stream that ran behind the farmhouse. Miles followed, grabbing one of the Coleman lanterns stationed around the yard. When we got to the banks of the brook, which was bursting with early spring growth, I surprised him with the bottle I'd hidden there. It was the Glenmalloch, his dad's favorite single-malt. This was the sixteen-year stuff, and it came in a special, limited edition, decanter bottle, rectangular-shaped and made of heavy glass. It had set me back eighty-something bucks. I was proud of it.

"I want to have a private toast with you," I said, "and I want to do it with a man's drink, not something from a red Solo cup."

I handed Miles the bottle. He responded with an overly hard hug that I took as evidence he was already pretty well lubricated. He uncorked the bottle expertly and poured us each a finger. We clinked our glasses and drank. To my uncultured tongue, the stuff tasted like Listerine. But Miles, as in so many other things, was light years ahead of me, taste-wise. He rolled the nectar around on his tongue, savoring the texture and flavor. "That's whiskey as God intended it," he proclaimed. "Blended scotch ought to be used for soaking machine parts." A ridiculously pompous statement for a twenty-one-year-old but the kind of thing Miles could get away with.

I was soon to learn that Miles, who was always judicious in his consumption of beer and wine, was powerless under the spell of single malt. Over the next hour, as we swapped memories and promises by lantern light, he bogarted the bottle and swigged from it like it was a hiker's canteen. His speech got progressively sloppier as his tongue got progressively looser.

*Miles was typically a guarded guy beneath his cool exterior. I think he always felt he was carrying the weight of his family name and had to keep himself on a tight leash. He liked to have fun but not too much of it. He talked like an anarchist but was careful never to do anything that could get him into real trouble.*

*Not tonight, though. Tonight he was throwing off the moorings. Sharing his family scandals with me, offering scathing analyses of all our friends. "What's the over-under on when Timmons gives up the hetero act and starts begging for cock? I give him three months in Manhattan, tops." Whoa. My window of opportunity for getting Miles home conscious was slipping shut.*

*"Wait here, brother. I'm gonna go find Beth."*

*I took a walk around the property, looking for Beth amongst the lingering partygoers, but she was nowhere to be found. I didn't want to leave without her. Someone finally told me, "She left with Fitzy and Deb, like an hour ago." Beth often became impatient with Miles and me as a duo, so it didn't surprise me that she'd found her own way home.*

*I packed Miles into the car. I was pretty clearheaded for driving, but still, I did have more than trace quantities of alcohol in my system, so I stuck to the back roads on my way to Miles' apartment. Miles clung to the Glenmalloch and continued to hit it like it was Dr. Pepper.*

*We hadn't driven more than a mile or two when he let out a wounded-animal wail and buried his face in his hands.*

*I found a place to pull over, a picnic area at the edge of the state park. There, Miles proceeded to have what I can only call a breakdown. Jettisoning his usual self-control, he threw himself on the ground and proceeded to blurt out all the fears and doubts he'd been stuffing inside for years. Fears about his future. Fears about the expectations that had been hung on him by his family and himself. Fears about his upcoming marriage to Beth. "I want what you have with Jeannie. I want to be an artist and a gypsy like you. You're so fucking lucky. You can live the life you choose. Love whoever you want."*

*I think I offered him some thin counsel, but he was too drunk to hear it. Just as well. He finally staggered to his feet, wrung out, and stumbled back to the car.*

*After driving another mile or so, I spotted a police car parked in the shadows on a wooded section of Carlisle Road. Watching for speeders and drunks. My heart started to rev.*

*"Shit," I said to Miles, "The bottle." Massachusetts law forbade "open containers" of alcohol in moving vehicles.*

*As I drove out of the woods onto an open stretch of road, I kept my eyes glued to the rear-view mirror, certain the cop would be tailing us any minute. I didn't notice we were going over a bridge, but Miles evidently did.*

*Before my brain could register what he was doing, he rolled his window down. I heard him slur the words, "My apology to the river gods," then his window went back up. My eyes were still riveted to the rear-view mirror, watching for the cop.*

*Moments later, we were passing an old carved-wood sign with a crucifix on it when I heard — or thought I heard — a faint series of sounds that didn't make immediate sense to me.*

*"Did you hear that?" I asked Miles.*

*"Hear what?" he said, his head wobbling precariously.*

*I glanced at Miles' lap and noticed it was empty.*

*"What did you do with the bottle?" I asked him.*

*"Tossed it in the Merrimac," he said. "Ba-bye."*

*It was then I noticed headlights following us at a distance.*

*"Fuck, Miles, that's the cop behind us. What if he saw you throw it?" I didn't think the cop could have seen anything; he wasn't behind us at the time, but still...*

*"Jeez, I was jus' try'na help."*

*"Shit, man, we're screwed."*

*I drove a little farther, hewing to the speed limit, and the headlights continued to follow us. And then the dreaded thing happened. Blue lights. My heart hammering, I started looking for a place to pull over. That was when I noticed another bridge up ahead of us on Carlisle Road.*

*My body must have put two and two together before my conscious mind did, because a wave of nausea rose up from my gut. "Oh no, Miles," I said. "This is the bridge over the Merrimac! This is the bridge over the Merrimac!"*

*I parked the car as the full weight of the realization sunk in.*

*If this was the bridge over the Merrimac, that meant only one thing: the previous bridge had been the bridge over route 495.*

*Oh God. Oh shit. The sounds I'd heard — or thought I'd heard — when we were passing the crucifix now made damning sense. They were the distant sounds of squealing brakes, shattering glass, and smashing metal.*

*The blue lights loomed larger in my mirror. Life as I knew it was about to end.*

*But instead of pulling to a stop behind me, the police car turned on its siren, did a quick three-point turn, and sped off in the direction from which it had come.*

*I should have been massively relieved that the cop was rushing off to deal with an emergency but was only more deeply sickened by the implications. "Miles," I said, gathering my strength to tell him what I now knew. "You didn't throw the bottle into the river, you threw it onto the highway."*

*But as I turned to look at Miles, he was passed out, stone cold.*

# Chapter 6

I stare, spellbound, at the rushing black water below. There's no question what my next move must be, though I long for an excuse to stall.

I drag myself back to Brew Moon, giving Django the Brave a little nod as I enter. He fails to acknowledge my existence with even the tiniest of facial tics.

Jumping back onto the rented computer, I pull up the file—my "suicide" note—and stare at that hypertext link on it, ripe with odious promise. I click on the link before I can change my mind. The elderly iMac starts to churn.

Moments later, a Boston Globe news article from 1999 is sitting on my rented screen: "Police Investigate Fatal Three-Car Collision in Bridgefield."

Ah, shit. Ah, no.

No, no, no.

I take a shaky breath and start in on the news story. I want to throw up. I want to run away. I want to drink something infinitely stronger than a Cà Phê Dá.

I can't believe what I'm reading, yet the words strike home with the fatedness of cancer after a thirty-year smoking binge.

*A fatal car accident occurred at 1:21 a.m. Sunday on Route 495 near the Carlisle Road exit in Bridgefield, say police. According to an eyewitness who was peripherally involved in the accident, a 1987 Chevrolet El Camino driven by Edgar Goslin of Wentworth lost control "for no apparent reason" and veered into the passing lane where it collided with a 1998 Ford Aerostar occupied by Paul and Laurice Abelsen and* — please no — *their two-year-old daughter. The Abelsens' vehicle veered off the highway, rolled over and struck a tree, where Goslin's car struck it a second time, crushing both the roof of the Abelsen's vehicle and the front end of Goslin's car. All three of the Abelsens were pronounced dead on arrival at Wentworth General Hospital. Goslin is listed in critical condition with multiple undisclosed injuries.*

*A third vehicle, driven by the eyewitness, Jeremy Halsey of Methuen, reportedly collided with debris from the other two vehicles and was damaged slightly. Halsey was uninjured. Police have not ruled out alcohol as a factor and are continuing to investigate.*

I read the words again.

Then again. And again.

Fuck.

Sweet holy fuck.

I think back to that night long ago. I remember my decision, after the cop sped off, to drive away and let Miles remain unconscious. I remember convincing myself I probably hadn't actually heard any crashing noises at all. And if I had, the accident probably wasn't as bad as it sounded. And if it *was* bad as it sounded, Miles' tossed bottle probably had nothing to do with it. And even if the worst possibility was true, that Miles had inadvertently caused a serious accident, what good could possibly come of getting him in trouble? It was his graduation night. He was about to embark on an exciting new life. Why kneecap his destiny? Whom would it help, really, to assign blame? The cops had the situation handled.

And anyway, I probably didn't hear anything. Right?

So probably nothing happened. Right?

The day after the "incident," though, I shocked my parents by announcing I had changed my mind about going to grad school in Providence. I wanted to take a year off to think about it, I said. I had decided, instead, to accept an invitation from a couple of college classmates to drive to California with them and hang loose for a while. Seek my fortune — by way of minimum wage — in the Land of Milk and Honey.

My folks tried to reason with me, but my mind was made up.

I remember keeping myself busy all day on May 13, 1999, packing duffel bags, closing my bank account, returning library books, selling my old Chevy at a used car lot, and saying goodbye to Jeannie a few days earlier than planned. I studiously avoided looking at newspapers and televisions—if nothing was confirmed, then as far as I knew, no accident had happened. And, then, on the morning of May 14, I jumped into a thirteen-year-old Aries K-car with two stoners from Godwin I didn't even like very much and headed for the Golden West.

I didn't return to Massachusetts for over five years. Now I ask you, is that the behavior of someone with a clear conscience and a bright future ahead of him?

My attention snaps back to my Brew Moon environs. I study the suicide note on the computer screen again, mystified by both its accuracies and its inaccuracies, and dumbfounded as to its purpose. Who wrote it and why *now*?

I need to keep a copy of it. I ask the barista if he sells flash drives. He micro-shakes his head no—man, does this dude need a hug—so I log into my Gmail account, copy the text of the note into an email, and send it to myself.

I do the same with the Globe article.

• • • • •

Twenty minutes later, I'm lying on my bed at the Oak Crest Motel, drinking a beer, staring at the cracked ceiling, and listening to the rattle and hum of the barely functional air conditioner. My mind wants to spin out of control. I don't have the slightest idea how to process the events of the past few days, and I don't have a clue about what I'm going to do when I get up in the morning. Or any morning thereafter, for that matter.

It's ten-thirty at night, and I know what I *want* to do: call Miles. I have an almost physical urge to get him on the phone, hear his voice, share the burden of what I've just learned. But the hour is late. And besides, what would I say to him? What *should* I say? I can't just dump those ancient deaths on him now.

Do I even have a *right* to dump them on him? After all these years? To throw such a crowbar into the machinery of his carefully executed life? The man is a state senator, for God's sake, and a partner in one of New England's finest law firms. What possible good could come of sharing this information? It would either ruin his career or destroy his peace of mind. Or both.

No. My time to speak was eighteen years ago, when I heard—or did I?—that distant sound of smashing glass and metal. Not now.

On the other hand, do I have any right *not* to tell him? Who appointed me Truth Fairy? Does he not have a fundamental right to know something of such vital import to his life?

That is the question.

I turn on my phone, play a little gem-matching game called *Cascade* for a while, trying to numb my brain. It doesn't work. I look at the time again. Ten forty-three.

Screw it. I lose the battle of will. I won't *call* Miles, but I'll text him, see if he's still up. *Long time, brother,* I type. *Sorry for the radio silence. Hope all's well. Didn't want to call this late and piss Beth off, but if you're awake, so am I.*

Less than a minute after I hit Send, my phone rings. Miles. The instant I slide the answer button, I hear a flat voice: "So you didn't die in a freak circus accident."

"Is there any other kind of circus accident?" I reply, then retreat to the safety of the goofy Maine Yankee accent with which Miles and I have amused each other since college. "Anyway, I heah these new smaahtie-phones work both ways: sendin' *and* receivin'."

"Ay-yup," says Miles, playing along, "that's what Maahge down't the Radio Shack tells me." He drops the shtick. "Man, it's fucking great to hear your voice."

"Yours too."

There's a pause. We both know there are fissures to be mended, and we are both weighing whether now is the time to mend them. By silent accord, we agree to save the harder conversation for later. We are both happy to be reconnecting. That's enough for now.

We spend the next few minutes playing catch-up. What am I up to these days? (I spin the living shit out of that one.) How's Miles' four-star career going? How are Beth and the kids? When the grace period for bullshit expires, Miles says, "But I'm guessing you didn't call after all this time just to find out if Kelsey made the freshmen soccer team."

He's right. But of course, I can't tell him what really prompted my call. Not by phone. No, if that conversation is ever going to take place—and that's a very large *if*—it will need to be face-to-face.

I suddenly realize there's a deeper, truer reason I've called him. It's simply because I miss my friend and I need to hear his voice right now.

"I'm scared to death, Miles," I say. I proceed to blurt out the whole story of the home invasion, the attempted forced suicide, and the later clean-up of the evidence. It just comes spilling out of my mouth unfiltered. The only part I omit is the suicide note, because that would lead us into complicated turf. It takes me fifteen minutes to get through the story. The whole time, Miles doesn't say a word, but I can feel his listening presence like a silent beacon.

When I'm done, he asks me to hang on. He puts me on hold for a couple of minutes, then comes back on the line and pronounces, "Here's what you are going to do. You are going to get some sleep. Mainline some Nyquil if you need to. Then you will get up early in the morning and drive directly to New Harbor, where you will get on the ten a.m. ferry to Musqasset." Yes, Miles owns a summer home on my beloved Musqasset Island—a place he didn't even know existed until I browbeat him into visiting me there—and I am living in my parents' house in Wentworth. How that blasphemous twist of fate came about is a subject for later discussion.

"Beth and I and the kids are out on the island for the Labor Day weekend," he says. "You are going to stay with us. You will be safe here, and you and I will figure out exactly what the hell is happening and what to do next."

"I'm sure Beth would love that," I say.

"I already talked to her, and she thinks it's a great idea. She'll be thrilled to see you, I promise. Listen to me, Finn: it's important you get on the morning ferry."

"Why?"

"You *do* watch the news, don't you?" Actually, I've been a smidge preoccupied. "That tropical storm off the coast? The waters are supposed to get really nasty, and the morning ferry may be the last one leaving the mainland for a couple of days. Tell me you understand, and you're going to do what I say." Why is he talking to me like I'm seven?

"I don't know, Miles. You know I haven't been back to the island since Jeannie and I..." No need to finish my sentence. "I'd have to think about it."

"Okay, then, think. I'll give you ten minutes. Then I'm calling back, and I want to hear your decision, and I want it to be yes."

He hangs up.

Go to Musqasset Island? Me? Tomorrow?

I haven't been back there since I left four years ago. Jeannie and I had just broken up for the second and final time. There were changes taking place on the island—Miles was in the thick of them—and the place just didn't feel right to me anymore. My mom's health problems gave me a handy excuse to return to Wentworth. So I just quietly packed my bags one morning, stepped aboard the ferry, and closed the door on the "Island Artist" chapter of my life.

But since that time, not a day has passed that I haven't thought about Musqasset. As I close my eyes right now, I can hear the screeching of the gulls and the rumble of the lobster boats. I can see the seals basking like drunken cruise-ship passengers on Table Rock. I can feel the welcoming warmth of Pete's Lagoon, The Mermaid Café, Mary's Lunch.

And the light. Oh God, the light. There is a reason Musqasset attracts painters from all over the world. Everywhere you focus your eyes, from the tightest close-up to the grandest panorama, you see an oil painting—a tiny purple flower peeking out of a crack in a rock, a pile of lobster traps in the tall grass, the lighthouse silhouetted against a translucent sea. It's an artist's wet dream.

Leaving was agony. But the wounds have healed, the breaks have mended. And I know I can't go back.

Maybe for a few days, though.

Arrive unannounced, stay at Miles' place, fly below the radar.

The idea actually makes logical sense, under the present circumstances. For one thing, I'm clearly not safe here in Wentworth. For another, I have no freaking clue what my next move is. It would do me enormous good to spend some time in a safe place with old friends. Take a step back from my predicament, figure out what the hell is going on. Think and strategize a bit.

Then, of course, there's the fact that I may need to have a very serious conversation with Miles.

The idea of going to the island starts to acquire momentum in my mind. If I slipped out of here in the pre-dawn hours, I could make it to New Harbor by eight or eight-thirty. Be out on Musqasset before noon. The brewing ocean storm actually gives me added incentive. By the time my assailants could possibly pick up on my trail, they won't be *able* to follow me, at least for a couple of days. The ferry will be down. I'll be safely unreachable, several leagues out to sea.

The logic seems ironclad.

But ultimately it's not logic that moves my decision needle. It's the fact that I *feel* safe on Musqasset. Safer than anywhere else I know. It is still home to me. Deep down, I've been longing for an excuse to return there for years. If only for a visit.

Miles calls back.

"I'll see you in the morning," I tell him.

• • • • •

I lie back on the lumpy motel-room mattress and let my mind wander to the suicide note again. Of all the many disturbing, unanswered questions it raises, I know the one that will gnaw at my sleep most of all is this:

Why and how does the note sound exactly like something I would write—from its feeble attempts at gallows humor, to its linguistic style, to its specificity of details (like the Clyde Gilchrist reference), to its misspelling of the word "party" as "patry," a habitual typo of mine?

How could any other person have captured *me* so perfectly?

I'm scared about the places this question is taking my mind. And I wonder if there's a deeper reason I don't want to get the police involved in this. Or talk to Miles about it.

# Chapter 7

I'm up and dressed by four forty-five. I wouldn't have been able to sleep even if the mattress *weren't* stuffed with dead squirrels, so I figure the earlier I hit the highway, the better. As I throw my few belongings into my backpack and do a final room check, I can't tell if I'm excited or terrified. Maybe there's no difference. But one thing is certain: I feel more alive than I have in years. Being almost murdered has done wonders for my state of mind. Can't say I recommend it for everyone, but still...

As I slip out into the pre-dawn darkness of the Oak Crest's unlit parking lot, a brisk morning breeze greets me. Must be the western edge of that ocean storm. It smells of the sea, even this far inland. It smells of adventure too, if I'm being honest.

I consider driving back to the house and grabbing my iMac, but I'm worried the house is being staked out. Better not. I just jump into my car and head north.

Route 95 is practically deserted at this hour; most of the trip I see no one behind me for more than half a mile. Still, I take couple of detours onto the surface roads just to be sure I don't have a tail on me. And to gas and coffee up.

No cars come anywhere near me, except to pass. I'm confident I'm alone on the road.

I find a supermarket in Damariscotta that's open early and buy some freshly baked crusty bread, a couple of bottles of decent wine, one red and one white, and the makings of a pasta puttanesca and a Caesar salad. I don't want to show up empty-handed at Miles', and I know grocery options are extremely limited on the island.

I arrive in New Harbor at seven fifty, plenty early for the ten o'clock ferry. I park in the grassy field designated for long-term parking, open the car door, and pull the swirling ocean air into my lungs. Damn, that smell stirs my blood. I think on a deep cellular level I can still remember my ancestral sea-dwelling days. I probably had a nice paddlefish family that loved me.

Trombly's Boat Tours and Ferry provides ferry service to "The Three Ms"—Monhegan, Matinicus, and Musqasset islands, the three remotest inhabited islands off the coast of Maine. Musqasset, roughly equidistant from the other two and a bit farther east—thirteen miles from the mainland—is primarily a "walking" island. Some of the residents and businesspeople own vehicles, but visitors can't bring cars over; the ferry is for pedestrians only.

As I approach the office of Trombly's, I see wild whitecaps streaking the Gulf of Maine and billowing masses of gray crowding the eastern sky. I hope the morning ferry run is still on. If so, it's going to be a two-Dramaminer. I'm glad I wore a weatherproof jacket.

I step inside the ferry office to an atmosphere of controlled frenzy. An early crowd of gabbing, raingear-clad passengers has already formed. Phones are ringing, keyboards are clacking, and outside the back door, deckhands are toting boxes of groceries and plastic tubs wrapped in bungee cords. On a big TV screen tuned to a local weather station, the announcer talks about twenty-to-twenty-five-foot waves and winds off the coast gusting to forty-five knots, getting worse over the next thirty-six hours.

I suddenly realize, dumbass that I am, I should have called ahead to buy my ticket. Mainland living has made me soft in the head.

I recognize the woman at the ticket counter from my past years of ferry usage, but she looks too harried for *hey-how-are-you*s. I ask the question she must have heard fifty times this morning, "Is the ten o'clock going to run?"

She fires off her answer by rote, "Captain hasn't made the final call yet. It ain't the ride out he's worried about, it's the ride back. He'll let everyone know in ten or fifteen. Stay tuned."

"Can I buy a ticket anyway?"

"Sold out, my friend."

Damn. Fuck. My incompetence knows no bounds.

"I can put you on the wait list. Dozen people ahead of you, though." Folks are scrambling to get out to the island before the storm shuts everything down. Of course.

"Hold on—your name's Carroll, right?" she says. "Finnian?" Nice to be remembered. "Didn't you buy a ticket online?"

"I wish."

"Looks like someone bought one for ya." Miles. Bless his anal-retentive soul. I gratefully take my ticket and buy a travel pack of Dramamine. I swallow two immediately.

Backpack and shopping bag in hand, I wander out onto the dock to await the captain's verdict. The air feels more like late October than early September. I zip my windbreaker/rain jacket up to my neck.

Standing on the dock is like slipping into a pair of well-worn sandals. I used to set up my easel here a few times a week. Did quick acrylic miniatures for twenty-five bucks a pop. Tourist fodder. Yup, I was *that* guy. Some of my fellow artists on the island used to make fun of me for it, but the gig could be surprisingly lucrative. On a summer weekend morning, you could catch the overlapping crowds going out to all three of the Three Ms. Passengers just sitting around waiting, their pockets stuffed with vacation spending cash.

I notice a couple of geezers—island guys—standing near me. They're bemoaning the impending loss of business over Labor Day weekend due to the storm. Sometimes when I'm romanticizing life on Musqasset I forget how brutal it can be for the shop- and B&B-owners. A few bad holiday weekends can sink a season. A whole business.

The outdoor loudspeaker crackles at last, and the ticket woman's voice bullhorns, "Attention, please. The ten o'clock ferry *will* be running this morning. Boarding starts in forty minutes." Immediately a line starts to form at the roped-off gangway. What's the rush, folks? We're all going to be in the same boat. Literally.

• • • • •

As I board the *Knot for Sail*—yes, tragically, that is the ferryboat's name—I feel a thrill of excitement about seeing Musqasset again, even under less-than-optimal circumstances.

"Hey, Mr. Carroll," shouts a smiling deckhand, about seventeen or eighteen, hurrying by with a rope and bucket in his hands. He looks familiar, but I can't quite place him. "Preston Davis," he says, seeing my confusion.

"Of course! Preston! Holy shit, look at you. I'll catch up with you when you're not busy." I gave Preston painting lessons when he was still a pudgy kid. Now he's grown into a handsome young man with scruffy whiskers. Better brace myself for more changes.

The ferry has an upper and a lower deck. The lower deck offers both indoor and outdoor seating, but I decide to seek a spot on the open upper level. It'll be less crowded up there, with the weather as it is, and I want to be alone. I climb the steps, hearing the familiar clang of my shoes on the metal grating. I find an open deck table in the rear corner and claim it with my shopping bag and backpack.

The boat is already dipping like a tilt-a-whirl car, though we haven't left dock yet, and the wind is whipping my hair, but I feel incongruously calm and even-keeled. The sludge of depression that has been gumming up my life of late seems completely absent. I find I can move and breathe with unaccustomed ease.

I'm glad I made this decision to get away. I do feel a bit awkward about descending on Miles' family—especially Beth, whom I've always suspected enjoys my company about as much as she enjoys a nice root canal—but I intend to stay out of everyone's way. Their house is huge and if I can't find a quiet corner to read in, I'll hike the trails (weather permitting) or slip off to the village or out to Studio Row. There are a few people I wouldn't mind saying hi to.

Which brings me to a topic I've been strategically avoiding. Jeannie. She still lives on the island. It was "her" place before I moved there, and it seemed only right that it should revert to her after we broke up.

That was one of the reasons I left. It's a small community, Musqasset is. Fewer than a hundred people live there year-round. Socially, things can get a bit "close."

I've heard she had a child with my replacement dude. I don't know if he's still on the scene—my replacement—and frankly I don't much care to find out. Do I want to see Jeannie? Well, she's only the most beautiful woman I've ever laid eyes on. I'm not even joking. So on a selfish, testosterone-driven level, of course I want to see her. Do I think it's a good idea? Not even close. I'm sure we're both over the breakup and would behave politely toward each other. But I'm certainly not her favorite human on Earth, and I don't want to rock the boat of her new life (or, if I'm being brutally honest, to find out I am impotent to do any rocking).

Besides, I've got enough things to worry about as is. Why pile on?

The captain's voice comes over the P.A. "Okay, folks, we're going to be shoving off. Waters are pretty choppy, as you've probably noticed. We'll do our best not to t-bone the big rollers, but still, it might not be pretty." He proceeds to give half-joking instructions on what to do if you need to barf, which, of course, instantly makes me want to barf.

I look over the railing and see Preston Davis pulling up the rubber dock fenders and untying the moorings. My mind pulls a U-turn and I decide this is the worst idea I've ever had (no minor achievement, given my track record). I seriously consider bailing—grabbing my stuff, running downstairs, and heading for gangway, which will be closed off any second now.

But as I watch the deckhands detach the gangplank from the boat, I remain glued to my seat. My ass, not for the first time in my life, has made my decision for me.

The captain blasts the horn. The folks on the dock wave goodbye.

We're off. Like dirty skivvies, as my dad used to say.

· · · · ·

I try to read a book, but the motion of the boat, combined with my inner turbulence, makes concentration impossible. After reading the same paragraph eight times, I give up. A coffee would perhaps be therapeutic.

Leaving my bags to mark my spot at the table, I head for the downstairs snack bar. The cabin is jammed with gabbing passengers, some drinking coffee, some hoisting ten-a.m. Pabsts and Sutter Home singles, yo ho ho. The choppy waters have everyone laughing a bit harder than strictly necessary and struggling to find their sea legs. I move to the end of the customer waiting line and take my place. I suddenly realize how zonked I am from lack of sleep. I plant my feet wide apart for balance and let my eyelids drift shut. The chattering voices meld together in my mind and become the echoey "rhubarb" of a movie mob. The sound has a soporific effect, and I find I'm getting drowsy on my feet.

I think I actually do doze off for a second or two, in spite of the boat's rocking.

Something snaps me to attention—three syllables, leaping out of the random noise of the crowd behind me: "Bim bam bom."

Nope. Didn't hear that. Not possible.

My impulse is to whip my head around and try to pinpoint where the voice came from, but I force myself to keep my gaze trained on the Harpoon Ale sign on the wall. My legs feel numb as I shuffle forward with the wobbly-legged snack line.

Did I really hear what I think I just heard?

Once again, my brain spins wildly as it tries to make sense of the incomprehensible. No way Trooper Dan could be on this boat. I left Wentworth in the dead of night, from an obscure fleabag motel where I paid with cash, and there were no cars anywhere near me on the road.

And yet, "bim bam bom." Who says that? And did I even hear it? The voice I *think* I heard was definitely in the same upper range as Trooper Dan's. But I might have drifted into a REM state for a moment there and dreamt it. Or maybe my stressed-out brain distorted some similar-sounding syllables. I try to think of phrases in English that are phonetically similar to "bim bam bom." I come up with precisely jack.

Still, Trooper Dan can't be on this boat—*can't* be.

But what if he is?

Then two things are true. One, he's watching me like a cat. Two, he's not wearing his Storm Trooper mask. I have no idea what he actually looks like, except he has a short reddish beard and small, even teeth. Nor do I know what his cohorts look like or whether they are traveling with him today.

I don't want to look as if I've become suspicious, so I force myself to stay in line and buy the coffee I no longer want. When I get the lidded Styrofoam cup in hand, I stroll back through the crowd, exchanging friendly glances with the faces I encounter. I pass a trio of middle-aged women, the two island geezers from the dock, a couple of teenaged boys...

I wander out onto the exterior deck and stroll around the whole perimeter of the boat, nodding greetings at my fellow passengers. I encounter only one reddish beard, but it's longish and attached to the face of a tall, gaunt guy with Coke-bottle glasses. Anyway, Trooper Dan might have shaved his beard by now, or dyed it. So the beard isn't much to go on.

I go back upstairs and repeat the same procedure, walking around the whole upper-deck perimeter wearing my rendition of a friendly expression. I spot only one *possible* Troop candidate leaning on the rail, smoking an e-cigarette, looking out at the water—a guy about five-seven or so, trim of build—but his lips seem a bit too dark, his beard too wispy and light in color. I think I'll know my guy when I see him, and no bells are ringing. Not loudly anyway.

I return to my spot at the rear table, yawn and stretch and look around inconspicuously. Only two new parties have moved into the table area since I left. One is a couple in their sixties with puffy pale-blue winter jackets and lots of camera equipment, the other is what appears to be a family of three: a husband and wife in their upper forties and an adult daughter in her twenties. They look vigorously "down east"-y in their fisherman's hats and L.L.Bean rainwear.

I ask myself, being strictly logical and unemotional, which scenario is more likely: that a stranger uttered the phrase "bim bam bom" or that Trooper Dan is actually on the boat? I must give high odds to the former, though I'm not too bullish on the wager.

I try to banish fear from my mind and go back to my book. But as the boat churns its way over the endless hills of water, I begin to feel that every person who glances in my direction wants to murder me. Maybe that's because we're all feeling pretty seasick by now. The ceaseless rise and fall of the *Knot for Sail* has put a dark look in everyone's eyes.

The watched feeling grows stronger by the minute, though I have no concrete reason to give it credence. The only passengers facing my way are the old photographer couple and the L.L.Bean family. The latter are in their own world. Daughter is asleep with her head on Dad's shoulder. Dad is willing himself to sleep with a crunched frown on his face. Mom, an intriguing shade of green not theoretically attainable by mammals, is trying to read her Kindle.

Several other passengers have begun milling about, though. I notice e-cigarette guy turn and look in my direction a couple of times. Am I imagining things or does he also shoot a meaningful glance at another guy sitting on the opposite side of the deck—a bigger guy wearing a slate-grey slicker with a hood?

If Trooper Dan *is* on board, I must find a way to force his hand and make him reveal himself. The prospect of being stuck on a small island with a psycho like him—with no means of escape for several possible days—is unthinkable.

So how can I flush him out? I ask myself what I would do if I were a character in one of the adventure games I work on for a living. This is a mental trick I sometimes use for problem-solving. Thinking like a game character, I come up with an idea. A ridiculous one, admittedly, but maybe worth a shot.

I pick up my cell phone and locate VoxFox, a digital recorder app I use for work meetings. I open it and hit Record. Then, inviting attention, I go digging loudly in my grocery bag as if hunting for a snack. I secretively slide the phone into the white paper bag containing the crusty bread and then bunch the bread bag closed.

Next, I take my idea notebook out of my backpack and begin looking around conspicuously. I try to convey the impression that I'm getting *juuuust* a tad suspicious about being followed, without overdoing the act. I start writing some notes, as if I'm recording my suspicions. As I do this, I make eye contact with every male who looks my way, as if to say, *I see you*. I'm actually writing random observations, but I hope to pique the curiosity of Trooper Dan, if he's here. I carry on with this for a while, then pretend I'm feeling sick. I stand up, holding my belly. I "surreptitiously" hide the notebook in the shopping bag, atop the crusty bread, and cover it with groceries. Then I lay my rain jacket over the bag and head for the stairs.

Here's my thinking: if I'm being watched, my watcher is going to want to know what the hell I've been writing—i.e., am I on to him? By my going to the bathroom for a sick visit, I am offering him a grand opportunity to check out my notes. There's a long waiting line for the bathroom right now, so he can safely assume I'll be gone for a while.

And if he goes through my bag, aha, my phone will record him. I'll hear the recorded jostling of the groceries and whatever other sounds he makes. This may not tell me *who* my stalker is, but it will at least confirm my suspicion that I'm being followed. And that's a start.

What if he—or *they*, as the case may be—finds my phone/recorder in the process? I really don't think they'll look in a bread bag for a phone, but even if they do, *they're* the ones with the problem. See, if they shut off my phone, or steal it, or tamper with it in any way, I'll still know they went through my stuff. Pretty clever, eh?

Okay, no, but got a better idea?

I wait in the long line for the unisex toilet. At one point I turn and see L.L.Bean daughter waiting behind me. She's cute, I realize—*really* cute—despite the current pallor of her skin. We exchange playful glances, but the tang of fresh bile in the air, our mutual nausea, and our age difference nix any actual flirting.

The guy in the slate-grey slicker—actually, I'd use *Davy's* grey if I were going to paint it; slate with a tinge of green—strides by after a while, casting a hooded glance in my direction. Checking to see if I'm still occupied? I finally make it into the bathroom—gad, what a horror show, we shall never speak of it—and then go hang out in the snack bar area for a while.

At last I go back upstairs and reclaim my spot at the rear corner table. I'm careful not to open my shopping bag for a while. When it feels natural to do so, I remove the rain jacket from the top of the bag, reach inside, and slip the phone out. Pretending to pull it from my pocket instead, I make a show of flipping through some menu screens and plugging in earphones. I lean back in my seat, tapping my hand in idle rhythm, as if listening to music.

What I'm really doing, of course, is listening to the audio recording I've just made.

For the first few minutes of the recorded session I get nothing but a hiss and a low rumble: the background noise of the ocean and the boat engine.

Then I hear something that puts me on high alert.

The bag is rustled and a voice says something that sounds like, "You stay on that side." It's a voice I believe I know, but I can't be sure. One thing is certain, though. If this guy is talking to someone, he's not traveling alone.

I hear about five seconds of rifling noises that drown out whatever the voice says next. Then the voice, just above a whisper, says, "Here it is." It's him. I'm certain of it. Trooper Fucking Dan. I feel a fresh surge of nausea. I stand up, turn around, and look out over the back deck-rail for fear my face will betray the horror I'm feeling.

"Doesn't seem to go in order," comes a second recorded voice, a deeper one with a heavy Boston—Brooklyn?—accent. Must be talking about my written notes.

"Here's some stuff, dated today," says the Trooper voice. There's a fifteen-second pause before he says in his high tone, "It's nothing. Just random bullshit. He's clueless."

I hear the bag being repacked. Then I hear cloth zippers being opened: my backpack, I assume. "Oh look," says Troop in an aww-isn't-that-cute voice, "he bought a round-trip ticket."

Recorded Chokehold laughs as if this is the funniest joke he's heard in quite some time, and then I hear the two men clomp away.

I shut off the recording. I don't want to turn around until I've regained my composure, so I remain standing at the back railing staring out at the water. As I watch the wake of the boat melding into the rolling waves, I feel as if I'm watching my entire past slip away behind me.

Only the present remains.

The terrible, poisoned present, in which I am royally screwed.

I do have one possible advantage, though. I know these jagholes are following me. But *they don't know that I know.*

# Chapter 8

The sight of Musqasset's domed silhouette on the horizon does not lift my spirits as it always has in the past. I feel like a baby mouse about to be set loose in a snake terrarium.

Several concerns vie for attention in my fear-hijacked brain. First and foremost, I need to make sure Miles does not meet me at the dock. I mustn't lead a psychopath posse to my friend's home. Staying at Miles' house is officially off the itinerary. I text him: *Miles, if you were planning to meet me at the ferry, don't. I'll explain later. Hate to sound cryptic, but DO NOT come to the ferry. IMPORTANT. Trust me.*

Miles texts back a minute later: *Roger that, but I WILL want an explanation ASAP.*

My second concern is that I must find a way to ditch my pursuers as soon as I set foot on the island. I must do this (a) without knowing who they are and (b) without betraying that I know I'm being watched.

Third—and this is the biggie—I've got to figure out a way to get back on this boat for its return trip. The ferry won't be staying on Musqasset overnight. It always docks on the mainland, so it *will* be going back today, regardless of weather, and I need to be on it.

As if reading my thoughts, the ferry captain comes on the P.A. "Ahhhhh, listen, folks we're going to be doing a quick turnaround. I doubt we have any day-trippers on board today, but if you or anyone you know has a ticket on the four o'clock back to New Harbor, tell 'em we'll be heading back early, as close to one-thirty as we can make it. It's twelve-thirty now."

Normally the ferry stays on the island for four-plus hours, giving the day-trippers time to poke around the shops and grab some lunch. Not today.

The stepped-up schedule means I have less than an hour to figure out how to get back on the ferry without being stopped or followed by Trooper Dan and company. Working in my favor is the fact that they don't know I'm on to them. The last thing they'll be expecting is for me to turn around and get right back on the ferry I just arrived on.

So goes my theory.

• • • • •

The crew has a tough time docking the *Knot for Sail* because of the rough waters, but they finally manage to get the gangplank in place. It's moving up and down like a bellows as the passengers disembark. I never got a chance to talk to Preston Davis, I realize. Oh well, now's hardly the time for grand reunions. He's busy assisting passengers anyway.

Anxious as I am to get off the boat, I stick to the rear of the exiting crowd. I want to be a watch*er*, not a watch*ee*, see if my pursuers reveal themselves in any way.

It's been storming on the island already, I see; everything's soaked, and some pretty hefty debris has been blown about. But the rain, if not the wind, has stopped for the time being.

Parked near the dock—here's a ritual that hasn't changed—are transport vehicles for all the major inns, waiting to pick up arriving guests and their baggage. The Sea Grass Inn and The Hotel Saint-Étienne, the two upscale hotels, deploy passenger vans with cargo racks on top. Harbor House and Musqasset House, the mid-priced places where you "rough it" by sharing communal bathrooms, send out pickup trucks for their guests. You just climb into the truck bed along with your bags. Guests renting private houses or staying at the smaller B&Bs can take Dorna Caskie's electric-cart shuttle or just walk to their destinations. It's not a big island.

Economic stratification, let me say briefly, is not a subtle thing on

Musqasset. Both of the upscale inns, along with some high-end B&Bs, are located on the western side of the island, called The Meadows. That's where the pricey private homes, higher-end art galleries, and a wannabe-gourmet bistro are also located.

Clustered around the middle of the southern bay, where the ferry docks, is "the village," a small collection of tourist shops and galleries, a few restaurants, a grocery/supply store, a donut shop/post office, three or four B&Bs, a tavern, and Musqasset House and Harbor House.

The eastern side of the bay, a section called Greyhook, belongs mainly to the working people—lobstermen, bartenders, tradespeople. Greyhook hosts a few small apartment buildings and rooming houses where the summer help—mostly young exchange workers from Eastern Europe these days—stay, in tiny quarters, two to a room. There's also a bar there that serves cheap(er) drinks for the lobstermen and blue-collar folks. You won't get killed for wandering into The Rusty Anchor unaccompanied by a local, but you might get seriously glared at.

The central and northern part of the island consists mostly of wilderness and hiking trails, along with a network of houses with attached art studios and galleries, called Studio Row, where many of the island's famous and semi-famous artists live and work. It's a major attraction for tourists with cash to burn.

My uninvited guests must have made lodging arrangements. I wonder which part of the island they're going to. Perhaps they'll wait to see where I go first. In that case, maybe I can force them to reveal themselves. After debarking, I hang around the dock for a while, waiting for all the foot traffic to disperse, deliberately stalling before choosing a vehicle and destination.

The van for the Sea Grass Inn takes off with its three guest-couples. A minute later the St. Étienne's van departs, carrying two couples and a dowager queen type who is grasping her hat as if she's already regretting coming to a place so barbaric as to have weather.

I notice e-cigarette guy standing with the bigger guy in the Davy's grey slicker, near The Dockside, a snack and souvenir shop. So these guys *do* know each other. Noted. I climb onto the back of Musqasset

House's truck to see what move they'll make.

Sure enough, a minute later, the two guys casually climb aboard the Musqasset House truck too. My heart starts to pound.

I wait till the driver yells, "Musqasset House," then I pretend to notice I'm on the wrong vehicle. I jump off and climb aboard the Harbor House truck, where the old photographer couple with the puffy blue jackets and four or five other guests sit nestled amongst the luggage.

I'm betting e-cigarette guy and Davy Grey will now switch trucks. They don't. The L.L.Bean family and a chunky guy in a Patriots sweatshirt come rushing out of The Dockside and are the last to board my truck before it starts off with a shout of "Harbor House."

Our truck follows the Musqasset House truck for a while. When we slow down to let some pedestrians in oversized rain gear cross the street, I grab my bags and jump off the truck.

I scoot down a narrow alley between Hook Me Up, a fishing gear shop, and I Scream, a goth-themed ice cream joint I'm shocked to see is still in business. The shops and houses lining the bay are built on pilings. Ducking beneath their floors, I make my way along the waterfront to a small overgrown yard a few buildings away. I crouch among the reeds and scrub bushes.

With little time to act before the ferry departs, I again try to think like a game designer. If I were designing a puzzle for an adventure game, what would be a good strategy for sneaking back onto the ferry?

A couple of water drops slap my face. Damn. Looks like the rain that's been on break has decided to clock in again.

But wait, maybe that's my answer. Rain. Maybe the way to get back on the ferry unnoticed is to hide in plain sight. Cover myself in some serious Maine raingear. I don't think anyone sells that kind of gear on the island, though, and I don't have time to shop around.

Where can I get my hands on some?

An idea strikes almost immediately. Billy Staves. He has one of the few permanent residences in the village proper. Billy's a lobsterman. He and I were Scrabble buddies back in the day. We'd meet for a beer and a match on the porch of Harbor House two or three times a week in the summer. He kicked my ass on a fairly aggressive schedule. He had a partner, Dennis, who sold lobster and crab rolls from a tiny sandwich shop attached to their house. Jeannie and I had them to dinner once or twice, and I always helped Billy put up his traps for winter.

It should be safe to walk a *short* distance on the main road—my followers can't be everywhere—so I scurry out to Island Avenue and make my way toward Billy's. After walking a hundred yards or so, I see a hand-painted sandwich board just past Black's Emporium, "Lobster Rolls. Crab Rolls. The Island's Best," with an arrow pointing to the right. Still there. Yay.

Dennis's sandwich counter is around the back side of the building, facing the bay, so I cut through the narrow alley between Black's Emporium and Billy's place, stash my bags in the open space beneath Black's, and approach the food counter from the ocean side. Damn. Normally there's a wide, rocky beach here. Waves are now covering most of it.

Dennis, a hefty, ruddy man with a curly, graying beard and suspenders, is sitting behind the counter reading The New York Times. Not a lot of customers on a day like this.

"Look what the catamaran dragged in," he says, in a not particularly jovial manner.

"How've you been, Dennis?"

"Can't complain since they closed the complaints department," he says, putting an audible period at the end.

Okay, I'm not in a mood for small talk, either, but I wonder why the cold reception. Dennis and I always got along well. Trying to elicit a little more chattiness from him, I say, "Hey, is it true what I heard about you and Billy?"

He dutifully holds up his hand to show a gold band around his thick ring finger. "Ayuh, the great state of Maine now recognizes us as a jointly taxable entity."

"Wow, that's amazing. Congratulations. Hey, I'm having sort of a storm-related emergency. Is Billy around?"

He shakes his head no and snorts. "Still out on the boat battening down the whatevers as much as possible. Obviously, he can't dock at Fish Pier anymore." Looking at me in a vaguely accusing way, he adds, "But I guess you know that."

I don't. I have no idea what's been happening with the Fish Pier situation since I vacated the island. It was getting ugly at the time I left, and I'm guessing it's gotten uglier.

"Ayuh," Dennis continues, "he has to anchor out in the bay now and row in."

I don't have time to wait for Billy's return. "I really need to get my hands on some rain gear, Dennis, just to borrow for a bit. Long story, but it's kind of urgent."

"He's got his good gear out on the boat with him today," Dennis says, "but..." He looks me up and down and sighs, decides it wouldn't be right to deny me basic courtesy. "I guess you can look through his old stuff if you want."

Dennis silently leads me through the house and points into a closet, where two or three retired rain outfits are folded up under a box of Christmas decorations. One of the suits, liberally patched with duct tape, is exactly what I'm looking for. Bright safety orange in color, it's a two-piece Acadia-style affair, with pants and a spacious hooded jacket. The hood has a visor on top and a high collar that covers the lower part of the face. Perfect for traveling incognito.

I thank Dennis and buy a crab roll from him, which he sells me only grudgingly, then I scurry around the corner of the building and duck under Black's to put on the rain suit and eat my sandwich. The food gives my blood sugar a needed kick. I recall that I still have my travel bags to deal with. They might give my identity away if I carry them openly. I head for Musqasset Mercantile, a grocery and supply store a little farther east on Island Ave.

The rain is picking up and whipping sideways in sheets, so I don't look out of place as I tramp down the main drag in my full-body raingear. No one's out on the streets anyway, though I do get one "Hey, Billy" from a t-shirt shop worker in her doorway. Guess she recognizes the duct-taped rain suit.

I enter the Mercantile, where the clerk behind the counter is Barbara

DeCamp. I once did a painting of her cat and helped her clean out her tool shed after her husband died. I don't identity myself as I buy a box of Glad Lawn & Leaf bags, and she doesn't greet me by name. Just rings me up and says, "Nice weather for lobstas." Good. The disguise is working.

I go back under Black's, fetch my shopping bag and backpack—the surf is getting wilder by the minute—and place them inside a black trash bag to conceal them. According to my phone's clock, I've still got twenty-five minutes till the ferry leaves. My plan is to be the last passenger to board, which means I've got a bit of time to kill.

A singularly bad idea begins to ooze from the three-pound chimpsteak in my skull: dare I try to get a glimpse of Jeannie? It would be a shame to come all this way and not even take a peek. And hey, she won't recognize me in this ridiculous getup.

Jeannie's house—*our* old house—is up near Studio Row. I don't have time to safely make it there and back on foot. But I wonder if she still tends bar at Pete's Lagoon. That was where I ran into her, about nine years back, for the first time since college, and where, upon seeing her face behind the bar, my life's path took a sharp left. She worked there the whole time I lived with her on the island, so maybe she still does. Maybe she's on duty now.

And what if she is? Do I really want to load up my brain's hard drive with fresh images of Jeannie to hijack my dreams and ruin my nights?

I pace back and forth between Billy's and Black's, trash bag over my shoulder like a demented Santa Claus, debating whether to try to see her. I actually say aloud to myself, "Don't be a fucking idiot. Don't be a fucking idiot."

As if such an existential choice were mine to make.

• • • • •

Pete's Lagoon perches on the bay on the eastern edge of the village, near the western side of Greyhook. It's a bustling bar and restaurant that attracts a mix of people from all over the island—tourists, artists, boat captains, shopkeepers, even some of the "landed gentry" from The Meadows. If there's a default gathering spot on Musqasset, it is Pete's. I was known to murder a six-string there of an odd Thursday evening and to muck in as a bartender occasionally.

No one's on the outdoor deck of Pete's today, naturally, and from what I can tell from a distance, the indoor crowd is pretty thin too. No chance of blending.

So what's the plan? Stand outside in the rain in my hooded gear, gawping in the window like a Hollywood axe murderer?

*Don't over-think it,* I tell myself. I step up to the front door and go inside. I stride through the place, looking purposeful but staying well hooded. I get another "Hi Billy," which I don't correct. I make a circuit of the whole bar, upper and lower level. I'm pleased to note a seascape of mine is still hanging over the fireplace. Jeannie's not behind the bar, though, unless she's had a sex change, put on eighty pounds, and become an African-American. Maybe she doesn't work here anymore. Maybe she doesn't even live here anymore.

As I'm looping back toward the exit, the Daily Specials board catches my eye: Jeannie's printing, in chalk, no doubt about it. Her words too. The Bos'n Burger, today's special, has the write-up: "We start with a dead boatswain, grind and grill him to perfection, then inexplicably add slaw and a store-bought bun. Fries mandatory."

Pete used to get furious when she did these goofy negative write-ups, but then they became a thing. People would come in just to read the Specials board. Looks like they still do.

Smiling to myself, I'm about to head out the door when I hear it. That laugh.

Oh, man.

I peer into the kitchen and there she is. Facing away, one-quarter view. Wild hair barely constrained by a clasp, swan neck, bone-thin wrists, dancing hands. She's towering over a couple of younger waitresses who look delightedly scandalized as she tells them a story. My feet are nailed to the floor.

I know I can't continue staring like this—Jeannie has an unerring stare-detector—but I can't pull my eyes away. Sure enough, she turns.

She looks right at my face, though I'm sure it's unidentifiable in the flaps and shadows of the rain suit's headgear. She lets her gaze linger for a couple of beats, then turns back to her coworkers.

I can't get out the door fast enough.

•   •   •   •   •

Five minutes till the ferry leaves. Time to make my move.

I march, businesslike, down Island Avenue in my Billy Staves costume and turn left toward the dock. I have my ticket in my hand and my hand in my pocket. I don't see anyone hanging around the rain-swept dock area, but that hardly means I'm in the clear.

My plan is to wait till the boat crew starts pulling up the gangplank and then dash on board at the last second, giving no one a chance to follow me.

I'm walking past the old bait shack across from The Dockside when a hand shoots out and grabs my arm.

# Chapter 9

I haven't been in a fistfight since high school, but instinct kicks in. I start punching at the shadowy figure grasping my left arm. He's a pretty husky guy, I can see, but I land a couple of jabs and hooks with my right hand.

"Whoa! Whoa! Easy there, pal!" he whisper-shouts.

It's dark in the windowless bait shack, but I can see there's a second man in here too. Both men are wearing hooded rain jackets. The larger of the two guys continues to grip my arm and block my fist as I flail at him with my free hand. I land a solid blow to his biceps, breaking his grasp. I wheel about and kick the door open, but before I can make my escape the other dude lunges and grabs me around the chest from behind.

It takes me several seconds to register his voice saying, "Finn! Finn! Calm down! Finnian! Whoa!"

He waits till I stop struggling, then spins me around by the shoulders to face him.

"Miles! What the hell!"

"Yeah, Finn, pretty much my words exactly."

"What are you doing here?" I ask.

"Um, let's see, I invited you out to the island, remember? You're going to be a guest at my house."

"I told you to stay away from the dock. I said I'd be in touch later."

"Yeah, well, I was already *at* the dock when you texted, so I decided to stick around. I didn't like the tone of that text. Not one bit."

"I told you I'd explain things *later*, Miles, and I will. But not right now. I've got to get back on that ferry. You have to trust me on that."

I pull away from Miles, but the bigger guy steps in front of the door.

"No one's going anywhere just yet, Mr. Carroll," he says in a polite don't-fuck-with-me voice.

"Finn, this is Jim," says Miles. "He's with the Maine state police."

"What?"

"Relax. He's not on duty. He's just a friend of mine who's on the island for the holiday weekend. After hearing that stuff you were telling me on the phone last night, then seeing that text, I was... I don't know, Finn. I felt I should give him a call."

Jim holds up a pair of binoculars. "We've been watching you since you got off the boat, Mr. Carroll," he declares, as if this fact alone should explain Miles' concerns.

I think about how bizarre my behavior must have appeared to these guys. Jumping off a moving vehicle, hiding in the reeds, talking to myself with a garbage bag over my shoulder, stalking Jeannie at the bar. Cripes.

I open my mouth to defend myself, but no words come.

"What we're going to do," says Miles in the capable, persuasive voice that must have won his law firm many a client, "is give you a few minutes to settle yourself down, and then Jim is going to drive us to my—"

"No, Miles, sorry. That's not what we're going to do. We can't go to your house because that will put you, Beth, and the kids in danger. Those guys who tried to kill me? They *followed me out to the island*, Miles, and they will find me at your house."

The two men stare at me like cigar store Indians.

"If you don't believe me..." I dig out my phone and fumble open the VoxFox app. In my agitated state, I can't remember how to play a recording. I can't even find a recording *to* play. Where the hell does the stupid program store its files? "I'll play it for you later."

I edge toward the door of the bait shack, explaining, "I wish we could have spent some together. I love you, man, and I'm grateful for the invite. But I *need* to get on that ferryboat now. I'll call you as soon as I get things sorted out."

I make a burst toward the door, but again Jim blocks my way. The two men move in on me gently but firmly, sandwiching me between their bodies and locking me in with their arms. No one says a word. It's an awkward tableau, to say the least.

I hear the blast of the ferry horn.

Fantastic.

The lid is on the snake terrarium.

• • • • •

"Beth, look who's here!" Miles calls out as I follow him into his kitchen. He's carrying my backpack and shopping bag.

Beth comes running in from another room with a squeal and a lit-up smile and practically leaps into my arms for a hug. "Finn! Oh my God! I can't believe you made it out here in this weather!" Her enthusiasm throws me. Maybe absence does make the heart grow fonder.

"Kelsey, Dylan, come say hi to uncle Finn!" she shouts.

I'm not really the kids' uncle, we just say that, but I am Kelsey's godfather. Kelsey comes prancing into the kitchen, smiling through her braces, a fourteen-year-old foal in short-shorts who's all leg and almost a foot taller than the last time I saw her. We do the lean-in hug. Dylan, who must be twelve now, backs out of a room down the hall, doing a robot shuffle and holding an Xbox controller. He robo-waves at me.

"Uncle Finn's had a long trip," announces Miles. "I'm going to show him his room, let him rest for a while, and we'll see him at dinner." Oh, okay, nice to have my schedule worked out.

It is emblematic of Miles' and my relationship that I have let him talk me into coming to his house after I'd resolved with all my heart not to. I am terrified that he and his family may be endangered by my presence, but Miles believes everything is fine and "We all just need to chill." And so I have allowed his version of reality, as usual, to trump mine.

He escorts me to a preposterously inviting guest bedroom in the back part of the house on the first floor, landward side. It has a hideaway TV, motorized curtains, and a full attached bathroom with heated floor and whirlpool bath. It looks like the demon spawn of Martha Stewart and the Anthropologie website. There are more pillows in here than have touched my head in a lifetime.

"Why don't you take a warm shower," says Miles, "then maybe nap for a few hours, or read a book, whatever will help you chill. Later on, we'll have a glass of wine with Beth before dinner and catch up. After dinner, you and I will find someplace where we can... talk."

Miles has a way of making suggestions that are actually edicts. "I *might* do that," I say, just to assert some autonomy—an old dance of ours—"or I might take a walk into the village or out to Seal Point to watch the storm."

"Why don't you just make yourself comfortable here?" he responds, upping the insistence factor *juuuust* a hair.

"Are there bars on the windows I should know about?"

"Yes," he fires back in a Peter Lorre voice, rubbing his hands together, "you are our very *special* guest, heh-heh-heh. All we ask is that you never look in the basement, heh-heh." He laughs and starts to head off but then stops and turns to me with an earnest expression. "Finn, I need to put this out there, so there's no... dishonesty between us. Your sister Angie called me five or six months ago, when you were in the hospital after that..." He doesn't have to say the words. "I didn't call you then because I wasn't sure if you'd want me to know. The point is, I'm aware you've had some... issues of late. And I just want to tell you, there's no judgment from me. You're safe and loved here and... that's all. We'll talk later."

He leaves, closing the door before I can reply. Another annoying Miles habit. I love the man, but sometimes I want to jump up and down on his face with hard shoes.

I flop onto the bed. It's stupidly comfortable, as I knew it would be. I'm sure the mattress cost more than my car. Damn. So Miles and Angie chatted after my first fling with pills and booze. That certainly puts a fresh spin on things.

The situation at hand suddenly becomes Poland-Spring-clear to me. Miles doesn't believe a bloody word I've told him. Not about the bad men in my home, not about being followed on the ferry, not about the danger I'm in here on Musqasset. He thinks I'm three scallops short of a fisherman's platter. He believes my recent brush with death was exactly what it appeared to be on the surface—another suicide attempt—and that I made up the bad-guy story, either because I'm embarrassed to admit the truth or because I'm flat-out bonkers.

I need to convince Miles I'm telling the truth. Because if he doesn't believe me about the danger I'm in, then I'm not the only one in danger here. And I can't stay in this house.

Luckily, I do have that digital recording from the boat.

Or do I? I check the app on my aging phone again, confident I simply overlooked the location of the recording in my earlier anxiety. But there's only one place the file could be stored: under "Recordings." And that whole screen is blank. How did I do it? How did I manage to delete the file? Why does technology hate me? God damn it! Alone, the recording didn't prove much, but in context it provided pretty good corroborating evidence.

• • • • •

Miles and Beth allow me to make dinner, so I assemble a pasta puttanesca and Caesar salad with the ingredients I brought along. Chopping and sautéing at a leisurely pace, I'm able to stay busy for a couple of hours and channel some of my nervous energy—while keeping a vigilant eye on the road and grounds through the kitchen's bow windows.

During dinner, I find it pretty easy to keep the conversational focus off myself. First, Beth talks about some New Age-y webinar she's involved with called *The Power of Words*, which sounds a bit cultish and full of daffy-sounding affirmations and wishful thinking to me, but which she seems to take very seriously, and then I manage to get Miles talking about himself, never a difficult task. As he tells me about his recent career exploits that led to his winning a seat in the Maine state senate, I begin to feel steadily queasier.

Why? Well, first a bit of background on Miles' career:

When Miles was fresh out of law school, Beth's dad, a big Maine real estate developer with his finger in many pies, pulled some strings to get Miles into the top-echelon law firm where Miles is now a partner. Miles chose to specialize in real estate and environmental law. Over the years, he did the legal work for several projects Beth's dad was involved in — a PGA golf course, a resort hotel, a riverfront shopping complex. Helped him get around some pesky environmental speed bumps. I've often chided Miles for being, not to put too fine a point on it, Beth's dad's bitch, and for betraying all the values he stood for in college.

But in the years since he last saw me, Miles explains over dinner, he has started working his way back onto the green side of the fence. A few years ago, over his partners' objections, he decided to represent the Penobscot Indians, on a pro bono basis, in a case involving a new power plant on the Penobscot River. The tribe claimed it owned the water rights. "Long story short, our litigators prevailed in court. The story got some positive press. Made the firm look like a company with a conscience."

"Since then, his partners have backed off, and he's taken the lead on a couple of other big pro bono cases," adds Beth. "He saved an area near the Appalachian Trail from development. He also got the laws changed around noise pollution in Maine's state parks."

"It's a win/win/win," as Miles describes it. "The firm gets some positive press, the environment gets some protection, and I get my face in the papers as a champion of the blah, blah." Meanwhile, Miles explains, he continues to work behind the scenes for his high-end developer clients. Got to pay the bills, after all.

The publicity he got from the pro bono wins was what allowed him to samba into the seat for Maine state Senate District 29, he says. And he now has his eyes on bigger prizes. He leans over the table, lowering his voice to conspiratorial level. "There's a situation shaping up, knock on wood, that could — *could* — land me in Washington before long."

"Holy crap," I say, duly awed. It makes sense, actually. With his Hollywood looks, graying temples, legal smarts, and easy charm, the possibilities are endless.

"Maybe we should wait till we know more about that before saying anything else," Beth chastises him with a smile.

The whole time Miles has been talking, Beth and Kelsey have been gazing at him with near worship in their eyes. (Dylan is absorbed by a complicated spaghetti-art project on his plate.) As for me, my belly has turned to lead, and not from the pasta. What's making me queasy? Well, I already knew Miles was enjoying a lucrative law career and making strides in the political arena, but hearing this latest development—and seeing Beth's and Kelsey's faces light up as he alludes to it—has brought my dilemma into bold relief.

What am I to do with the terrible facts I learned last night?

After we clear the dinner dishes, Beth pours Miles and me a brandy and says, "You two probably want some time alone." She adds in a teasing tone, "And you're probably going to go off on one of your wild conversational... *excursions*, which I don't understand *at all*, so I think I'll excuse myself for the evening. I've got some journaling to do for my course. But maybe we can all do something tomorrow." We say our goodnights, and Beth departs.

I had hoped Miles and I could go somewhere private, outside the house, to talk, but rain is whipping the windows like strands of wet seaweed. We're not going anywhere.

I'm hoping Trooper Dan has gone to ground for the night as well.

Miles suggests a move to the study—yes, he actually has a "study," which he refers to without any apparent irony. And so we stand up and do something I never thought I'd have the chance to say I did in my lifetime: repair to the study for a brandy.

# CHAPTER 10

Miles parks his brandy on the oak mini-bar and says, "I think I'm going to have something else instead." He stoops and reaches under the counter, and I know with alarming certainty what his hand will be holding when he rises.

He does not disappoint. Was there any doubt? The Glenmalloch.

Fate? Karma? Cosmic joke?

He sets the bottle down on the mini-bar, where it proclaims its presence like a telegram from beyond the grave.

"How 'bout you?" he asks.

"I think I'll stick with the brandy."

Gazing at the Glenmalloch bottle, my head begins to swim, and I feel as if I'm standing on the ledge of a skyscraper. But then I realize the bottle is offering me an opening, a chance to jump straight to a topic I thought I would have to weave my way toward ever so gingerly.

I grab the bottle and blow a laugh out my nose, pretending the distinctive black-and-gold label has just now jarred a memory loose. "Do you remember our college graduation night?"

"Oh God," says Miles, shaking his head. "*Parts* of it. Without a doubt *the* drunkest I have ever been in my life. An epic cringe-fest, from start to finish."

"Do you remember the Glenmalloch?"

"Duh. You gave me that beautiful bottle as a gift. It was even better than this twelve-year stuff. Sixteen-year, right? Came in a special bottle. It must have cost you a fortune. And I, like an ass, proceeded to swig it like it was PBR. Got completely toasted, for no apparent reason."

"I think you had stuff you wanted... *needed* to get off your chest. Do you remember how we got home that night?"

"I know we left without Beth. I caught endless shit for that. I have these strange memories of being out in the woods somewhere, thrashing on the ground. So drunk. I remember you standing there patiently, trying to get me back in the car. I woke up on my sofa the next afternoon with one shoe on and... a *hospital wristband*. What the hell was that all about?"

I have a question of my own to ask first. "Do you remember the cop? On Carlisle Road?"

"Oh God, I'm not sure. You and I got pulled over a *few* times in those days."

"Yes, we did." I pause meaningfully for a moment—he knows why—and then say, "But on *that* night, we saw a cop at a speed trap on Carlisle Road. Remember? We thought he was going to follow us, so we had to get rid of the bottle."

"No! No!" He groans theatrically. "Tell me we did not toss a bottle of sixteen-year-old Glenmalloch on the side of the road. Please tell me that, I'm begging you, Finn."

I shrug a *what-can-I-say*.

"No!" he groans again, grimacing. "I always hoped you kept that bottle and drank the rest of it yourself. Maybe had a nice goodbye toast with Jeannie. I certainly proved myself unworthy of it." He looks me in the eye and shakes his head in tragic disbelief.

Gazing into Miles' eyes, I am positive he's recalling that night for the first time in eighteen years. This reaffirms what I already knew: Miles has precisely *zero* memory of throwing that bottle and zero knowledge of what happened in the aftermath. I was sure about it already, but I still had to ask. Why my certainty? Because Miles passed out so badly that night, I had to take him to the ER, where he was treated for alcohol poisoning. So yeah, he was about as conscious as a bowling trophy by the time the cop's blue lights came on. And even if, by some form of alien telepathy, he managed to acquire trace memories of what went down on Carlisle Road that night, Miles is quite literally *the* last person on Earth who'd want to awaken that long-sleeping dog and start the police asking new questions about it. He has nothing to gain, everything to lose. He was *not* the source of the private knowledge in that suicide note.

So who was? And where does that leave me?

I now see, with clear eyes, my only viable path forward with Miles.

I plop myself into one of the study's brushed-leather armchairs, clap my hands to my thighs, and fix Miles with a gaze. "I need to be straight with you, bro."

"Okay," he says, intrigued by my sudden shift in tone. "Fire away." He sits in the armchair facing mine.

"I think you invited me out here under false pretenses."

He probes my eyes to see if I'm messing with him. "What do you mean?"

"I didn't know you had talked to Angie back in March."

"I'm sorry, Finn." He pauses. "But that changes things... how?"

"Oh, come on, Miles. It changes everything. For starters, you know that I swallowed some booze and pills and was hospitalized once before. I'm sure you also heard Angie's amateur diagnosis of my fragile mental state. But see, *I didn't know* you had that information when we spoke last night. So, crazy me, when I was telling you about that shitstorm in my parents' kitchen, I thought I was talking to a friend who was believing every word I—"

"Finn, I do believe—"

"Shh, Miles. ...A friend who was believing, *literally*, every word I was saying and wanted to help me because—"

"I do want to help you."

"I know, Miles, but you want to help me in the my-poor-friend's-out-of-his-fricking-gourd kind of way. And I thought you were offering to help me in the my-friend's-life-is-in-danger-and-together-we're-going-to-get-to-the-bottom-of-it kind of way."

"I want to help you in whatever way you need or want help," he says, reaching out to touch my hand.

"I appreciate that, Miles, but tell me honestly: when I was describing my run-in with those thugs, did you believe that really happened or did you think it was just another suicide attempt on my part?"

Imagine the face of a hooked trout. That's what I'm looking at now.

"What does... 'really' even mean?" he stammers. "What we *call* reality is just a series of neurological events. If *you* believe what happened was real, then it *was* real. To you."

"Let's skip the neuro-epistemology lesson tonight, Miles. Tonight I just want to know what game we're playing, you and I, as friends. I need you to tell me straight: do you believe me, *factually*, or not?"

"Finn..." The man is squirming as if an electric eel has crawled up his ass.

"It's okay, Miles, I already know the answer. I just need to hear the words from your own mouth."

"Okay—do I have doubts about you being pursued by psychopathic hit men who are trying to make you commit suicide for no apparent reason? Finn, I mean, Jesus. Step back and look at this objectively. Which makes more sense, that you've had a mental breakdown or that these 'events' are really happening? You just got out of a psych hospital *yesterday*, for crying out loud. I'm sorry, man. This is killing me to say..."

"It's okay, Miles. It's okay." It's time to let the trout off the hook. "For what it's worth, I think you may be right."

"What?" If he were a dog, he'd be cocking his head diagonally right now.

"I think your instincts were dead on," I tell him. "I think inviting me out to the island—getting me away from everything—was absolutely the right call. In just the few hours I've had to myself this afternoon, I've already started to have *my own* doubts about what happened. The shrink told me hallucinations and delusions are a common effect of the chemical cocktail I took. And I was already in an iffy mental state *before* the... incident. So I'm starting to think it's possible I concocted the whole thing in my mind, as a way of—"

"It's okay, Finn," says Miles. "No judgment here, just friendship."

"Here's what I propose: Let's stick to the 'treatment plan.' I'll stay here as we agreed, get as much R and R as I can. Probably spend a lot of time alone, if that's okay. In a couple of days, when this storm has blown over, so to speak, we'll... reassess."

Miles' relief is palpable. "I think that's a brilliant idea."

He stands and takes my brandy away, as if suddenly realizing that giving me booze might not have been the wisest thing to do. He offers to make me a cup of herbal tea and bring it to my room. I accept, agreeing an early bedtime for me is a capital idea, eh wot.

• • • • •

I sit in the guest bedroom, sipping my warm tea and watching the rain lash the window. I dread going out in the storm, which I'll need to do before long.

You see, that crap I told Miles about accepting my delusionality was grade-A cow shit. Over the course of the evening, I have come to see a couple of things clearly. One, Miles truly believes I've had a nervous breakdown. Period. Therefore, he is not going to take precautions against the danger I'm in. Therefore, he and his family remain in danger.

And two, the only way to make him believe me would be to tell him everything. Pull out all the stops. Show him the suicide note. Show him the Boston Globe article. And I can't do that. I can't derail this man's top-shelf life and career.

Not now. Probably not ever.

No, it seems I will have to bear that burden alone, and pay whatever price it demands of me. And that is probably as it should be. *My* guilt, after all, is far greater than Miles'. Isn't it? Miles has no idea what he did; *I'm* the one who made a conscious decision to keep a secret on that fateful night so long ago.

Best for Miles and his family if I remain a delusional nutjob in their eyes.

And so here is my plan. I will wait until the house has gone to sleep for an hour or so. Then I will borrow a flashlight, a gallon of water, an old blanket or sleeping bag, and a few CLIF Bars from the cupboard. I'll sneak out of the house, taking all my belongings with me, and find a hideaway on the island where I can hole up until the storm is over. I don't care if it's a tool shed or a moldy boathouse. (I've been living at my parents' house; I can survive anywhere.) I will stay hidden from all eyes and avoid all contact with Miles. Once the ferry is running, I will board it. And the moment it docks, I will seek police protection, even if that means telling them the tawdry tale of the scotch bottle and taking all the blame for it.

By the way, no, there is no full-time police department on Musqasset. We share one part-time peace officer with Monhegan, and he's stuck on the other island till the storm passes. We have no jail or protective custody facilities either.

• • • • •

My chin bobs off my chest and I pull in a ragged snore. I notice my tea has gone cold and rain is no longer pelting the window. I must have dozed off and drifted into a heavy slumber. The wind is still howling, but the windowpane is mostly dry.

Was it a sound that jarred me from sleep? I freeze and listen.

Seconds pass and I hear it again. A pebble tick on the window glass? Really?

No way. No one has seen me on the island, except Dennis. And he doesn't know where I'm staying.

That suggests only one possibility. My bowels tighten.

I wait again. Another tick.

I look out through the glass, but a rhododendron bush blocks most of the view, and the darkness beyond it is inky.

I throw on my rain jacket—I don't know where Beth and Miles put Billy's rain suit—and sock-foot my way through the sleeping house. I pull a butcher knife from a wooden rack in the kitchen and locate my shoes in the mudroom. Grabbing one of the flashlights hanging near the door, I step out into the gusting wind.

It's pitch dark outside, as it always is at night on Musqasset. The island does not have streetlights. In fact, it still shuts off its electric power at eleven o'clock at night. The only buildings that have power after eleven are those with gas or propane generators. And even they don't use outdoor lighting. No one does on Musqasset. Nighttime is nighttime here. Old school. If you go for a walk at night, you bring a flashlight.

I tiptoe toward the blackness of the back yard, not wanting to turn my flashlight on and reveal myself until I know what I'm up against. The idea that my Wentworth stalkers would *invite* me to my doom by pebbling my window like a high-school suitor seems absurd, and yet here I am, bait taken.

As I'm rounding the rear corner of the house, feeling my way along the rhododendron, a flashlight ignites ten feet away, bottom-lighting a face in a hooded jacket.

## CHAPTER 11

"So, Finnian Carroll," says the hooded figure, "you walk right into Pete's and you don't even say hello?"

Jeannie.

"How'd you know that was me?" I ask, sliding the butcher knife into my jacket pocket and turning on my flashlight.

"Come on, Finn, this is Musqasset," replies Jeannie.

She's right, of course. A secret on Musqasset Island has about the same odds of survival as dignity at a Renaissance fair. "You recognized the rain suit," I say. "And then you talked to Dennis or Billy."

"Give me a little credit. I knew it was you the second I laid eyes on you," she says. "Raincoat can't hide a vibe."

"How'd you know I'd be staying at Miles'?"

She doesn't even have to answer that one. Jeannie knows every blade of grass on the island, every piece of news that blows ashore here, every nuance of every island relationship. She absorbs it all by psychic osmosis and by working at Pete's. That's why I knew I couldn't stay on the island after we broke up; I would never be able to establish my own boundaries.

So did I really think I was going to visit Musqasset without Jeannie knowing about it? I guess I did, because I am thoroughly unprepared for this encounter. I have thought for years about what I would say to Jeannie if I ever saw her again, and now my skull is an empty jar.

She aims her flashlight at my face like an inquisitor's lamp and says, "What in the Jumping Jiminy Fuck are you *doing* here, Finn?"

Never one to beat around the bush, Ms. Jean Eileen Gallagher.

The wind howls, accentuating my silence. I can't very well blurt out the whole truth, so I just say, "Miles invited me out for the holiday weekend."

"You two are talking again?"

"We were never 'not talking'; we just hadn't spoken in a while."

"Wow, there's a Finnism, sure and true."

"Something came up yesterday. I called him, we talked, he invited me out to the island. It was all very spur-of-the-moment."

"So that's why I didn't even merit a heads-up?"

She shines the flashlight on my face again for a couple of seconds, then turns and aims it into the wind-whipped bushes. She strikes off down a trail that leads out of the yard. I guess I'm meant to follow her. You never know with Jeannie.

"I wasn't necessarily planning to see you," I say, hustling to keep up with her long-legged stride. "I wasn't sure you'd want to see me or what your situation was."

She marches ahead into the scrub-pine woods that surround the shore properties here in The Meadows. We walk in silence for almost a minute, and then she says, "My situation—the part that's any of your business—is: I'm still pissed at you. The way you left here sucked. No goodbye, no forwarding phone number. You even killed your Facebook page and email address. Not cool, Finn, not cool. There were things that needed saying."

"I could have handled things better."

She ignores me and continues through the blowing scrub, lighting the narrow trail ahead. I feel myself getting sucked into a familiar old dynamic. Jeannie would say or do something thoughtless or mean or downright wrong, and I would react badly to it. Then we'd get hung up on analyzing *my* shitty reaction, while avoiding discussing her original behavior.

In the case of our breakup, Jeannie pulled the big A. She had an affair. Now here we are, talking about what an asshole I was for leaving the way I did. Typical. Suddenly I am not feeling so wistful about the

Jeannie days.

We come to a fork in the trail and stop short. Do I hear the sound of footsteps following us, a few yards behind?

No, just a shore bird scurrying through the brush... I think.

"A lot of changes since you left," she says in a reproachful tone much like the one Dennis used on me. She shines her light down the right-hand path, the one that leads to Fish Pier. Or used to. "You need to see something."

We walk in silence among the gnarly pine shrubs for a minute or two, following our bobbing light-beams closer to the water. When we get to the shore of the inlet between The Meadows and the village, where Fish Pier stood last I knew, she stops and shines her light on a hanging wooden sign I've never seen before. Twisting in the wind, it reads *Marina and Yacht Club at The Meadows*.

"Has Miles given you the grand tour yet?"

I shrug no.

"Didn't think so. Brace yourself."

She sweeps her light-beam around the inlet, revealing a huge network of newly constructed private docks where the old fishermen's pier once stood. Yes, Fish Pier is *gone*. I pull in a breath. Pausing dramatically, she raises the light above the docks to reveal a massive cluster of dockside retail buildings. The complex looks so *wrong* here my visual cortex actually wants to reject the image. It includes a pretentious-looking restaurant with outdoor tables called Haar; two or three art galleries; a specialty wine, cheese, and pâté shop (North Atlantic Charcutiers); and, holy shit, a new upscale hotel by the name of — gag me with a marlin lure — Kaiyo. There's also a marine repair shop and a dockable gas station, complete with a preciously country-store-styled convenience shop where Fish Pier's ice-making machinery once stood.

Taken as a whole, the marina complex looks completely out of character and proportion for humble little Musqasset Island.

"What the fuck *is* this?" I ask, aghast.

"Don't look at me," she says. "Miles and his crowd *own* this end of the island now. They just dock their frickin' Catalinas and stroll right up to a restaurant or hotel, or take a golf cart to their million-dollar homes, without ever having to sully themselves amongst the commoners."

"God, this is not what this thing was supposed to be."

"No shit, Princess Buttercup." She shines her flashlight in my face again and clucks at my incredulity.

"Miles' original proposal—the one I supported—was nothing like this. You know that. It was a good idea. It would have *helped* the fishermen. It would have helped the *island*."

"Yeah, well, things went off the rails, as you well know."

"Yeah, but not to this extent. Jesus. How'd they push this monstrosity through?"

"The shit show just got worse and worse after you left."

After Miles bought his place here, he became a mover and shaker on Musqasset, much to my chagrin. He and some investment partners came up with a plan for a modest-sized yacht club and marina complex that was originally supposed to include rebuilding and maintaining the old Fish Pier in perpetuity, not hauling it away on a salvage barge.

Fish Pier, you must understand, was the heart of Musqasset's fishing and lobstering trade. The heart of Musqasset itself. Islanders and guests could fish off the end of it, and all the fishing boats used to dock and unload their catches there. The pier itself was public property, but for decades a guy named Bo Baines ran a private outfit at the base of it called the Seafood Exchange. He bought the fish and lobsters from the local fishermen at the end of each day, then took the whole haul to the mainland and sold it at a modest profit. It was a good arrangement for everyone. It meant the fisherman didn't have to lug their individual catches all the way to New Harbor or Port Clyde, so they were able to shave hours off their workday. Bo sold gas too, and supplied the boats with ice, and was known to fix a bent propeller shaft or two.

But for years Fish Pier had been falling into disrepair and no one could agree on who was supposed to pay for the renovation. That was where Miles' development plan came in. Yes, it included a new yacht club and marina, which rubbed a lot of island people the wrong way, but it also provided for a complete overhaul of Fish Pier and ongoing funds for its maintenance. Under the plan, the new developers would own the Seafood Exchange, and it would get a facelift, but Bo Baines would continue to run it. Though many locals griped about the change to the "character" of the island, to me it seemed like a win/win. Not only would Fish Pier get a badly needed rehabbing but the town would also get a huge tax windfall, which it could use to build a new schoolhouse, hire a full-time police officer, upgrade the electric grid, fix up some of the public buildings, and more.

"What happened?" I ask Jeannie.

"You saw the beginning of the end while you were still here. Once everyone in town got a giant stiffy for all that new tax and tourist money, the parade of amendments started. Let's add this, let's change that. Right after you left, Miles and his boys came back to the approvals board, claiming the slump in the local fishing industry had changed their 'projections for that part of the revenue stream,' and they might have to 'rethink the fishing component.'"

"I was still here when that happened."

"Oh, that's right. Well, then they brought in some new tourism 'trend charts' showing the island could support a bigger retail complex than they originally thought. They just wore the opposition down with dollars and promises.

"A lot of people see them as saviors, though," she goes on. "The new schoolhouse has already been built—'course there are only twelve kids in it—and Greyhook just got a quaint little park, courtesy of the new tax funds. The island's hiring a full-time cop next spring."

"But not everyone is thrilled, I'm guessing."

In response, she just shines her flashlight on her own unsmiling face.

She heads back up the trail that led us here. We walk without talking for a while, hearing only the changing sounds of the wind. And... wait, do I hear footsteps behind us again? I stop and say, "Shh. Did you hear that?"

Jeannie strides on. Eventually she turns onto an uphill trail leading to the north edge of the island. We hike for a bit longer, then ascend Lighthouse Hill to the top, passing the lighthouse on our right. Next, we work our way down the steep cliff-side trail that descends to Table Rock, lighting the slippery path with our flashlights.

Table Rock is a flat, wide, slightly raked, slate-rock structure on the water's edge, where The Shipwreck, an island landmark, resides.

"Lots of other changes happening," Jeannie says. "Brace yourself."

She stops in her tracks when we're still twenty yards or more above sea level and shines her light down in front of us. Massive waves from the storm are crashing on Table Rock, and something looks off to my eyes.

"The Shipwreck," I say. "It moved."

"It's mov*ing*," she says. "I think this storm is going to take it out to sea."

*What?* The thought chills me to the marrow. We sit and watch the giant waves crash in the light of our flashlight beams, mesmerized by the spectacle.

The Shipwreck has been a Musqasset icon for decades, as well as the subject of at least eighteen bajillion oil paintings, including a few of my own. The story is that in the late 1940s a mail boat named the *K.C. Mokler* ran aground here in a storm at sea, and its rusting metal hull has remained dry-docked on Table Rock ever since.

The Shipwreck holds a boatload of history for Jeannie and me. It was our designated place for bad behavior. During the day it belonged to the tourists, but at night it was ours. Whenever we felt like smoking a joint, or drinking some Chartreuse, or being sexually... *resourceful*, we'd end up at The Shipwreck. You could climb up on top of it or go inside the hull, depending on the weather — and your inclinations. The risk of getting caught, of course, always added an edge of danger to our activities. And in keeping with the theme of the landmark, we were usually pretty well wrecked whenever we found ourselves there.

"I quit drinking," says Jeannie, as if tapping into the stream of my thoughts.

"Wow, really?" I say. Sometimes my font of eloquence is positively bottomless.

"Over three and half years ago now," she says. She watches another wave crash on The Shipwreck, then adds, "Not that I owe you an explanation, but: I'm not the way I... *was* anymore, Finn. I just thought you should know that."

As a statement, it couldn't be vaguer, but we both know what she's referring to. I won't say Jeannie was promiscuous—that's not accurate—but she had issues with monogamy and was not willing to give up her sexual autonomy for anyone, including me. There were men who preceded me, and whom she quietly continued to see from time to time, even after she and I were an item. Her belief in her entitlement to these ongoing assignations was built on some obscure moral foundation I was never allowed to glimpse in full.

The men weren't island guys; she didn't want that kind of entanglement. Rather, they came by sea. One was a ship's captain, another owned a yacht so big it couldn't dock in the harbor. (I prayed that wasn't a metaphor.) She shielded these encounters from me, and I sensed that if I were ever to insist we confront them openly, I would lose her. So I didn't. But this "pattern" of hers—and my utter ineptitude at dealing with it—formed the fault line in our relationship that eventually led to the quake that undid us.

"You coming back here was a mistake," declares Jeannie.

I don't reply at first. Instead I watch the tide hammer Table Rock for a minute. As if to confirm Jeannie's earlier prediction, a monster wave crashes, spraying us from below. When it hauls itself back out to sea, I hear the deep cetacean groan of submerged metal dragging on rock. It's a sound that ices my skin. The *K.C. Mokler* inches closer to the Atlantic.

Still gawking at the historic drama unfolding below, I ask, "Why do you say that?"

I turn to look at Jean. She is gone.

# Chapter 12

As I'm passing the lighthouse on my way back to Miles', the wind carries a sound to my ear. A seashell crunching in the dirt. Jeannie? I turn my head and see nothing, but that's unsurprising given the darkness of this starless night. I don't want to spin around and shine my light on whoever it is, because if it's just a stranger out for a stroll, that would be a breach of island etiquette. And if it's someone trolling for trouble with me, I'm not eager to light that fuse.

I shut off my flashlight and step up my pace, hoping I can navigate the route back to Miles' house in the dark without breaking my fool neck.

I haven't gone twenty feet before my foot snags on a creeper and I go sprawling on the ground. So much for hope. I rise, listening intently. I hear only the whistling and howling of the wind, but my gut tells me I'm not alone out here.

I reach into the pocket of my jacket to see if I have my cell phone with me. Yes, it's there. I don't know whom I'd call for help or how they'd find me out here, but still, the phone feels comfortingly warm in my pocket.

I walk on, my eyes adjusting somewhat to the absence of flashlight, and come to a familiar fork in the path where the scrub pine starts to turn into real woods. The right path is a pretty direct route back to Miles' house, but by taking it I'll run the risk of leading my possible pursuer there. The left path is longer and twistier but will lead me into the village, the island's most "public" place.

I pause to make up my mind when a flood of light strikes me from behind.

Like an idiot, I turn.

About a hundred feet behind me, three bright circles of light throw their beams at my face. Flashlights. All three shut off at once. Island courtesy or am I being messed with?

Being a cup-half-empty kind of guy, I put my chips on the latter.

I scurry down the left path, the one that leads to the village, at the briskest pace I can manage without using my light. It's a well-worn path, so I'm able to walk it pretty fast. But with each step, my apprehension mounts.

I go a hundred feet. Two hundred. The wind whipping the trees is loud enough to mask the sound of any footsteps behind me, but I can *feel* a presence gaining on me. I remember I still have the knife in my pocket, though exactly what I'll do with it I have clue zero. I grope for its handle. Goosebumps tickle my back. Nervousness starts to give way to panic.

I spot a tiny, overgrown path snaking off to the left, through a stand of pine. If memory serves, it leads to an old abandoned property. I ditch the main path, hoping my detour isn't noted.

I can't see John T. Shit as I pick my way through the wet spruce pincushions pressing in on me from either side of the narrow footpath. I get a face-full of spider web at one point and step in something squishy and bitter-smelling. I'm trying to move as quietly as possible, but the path is riddled with sticks that snap and vine runners that snag my shoes. My jeans are getting soaked from water beading on the fat needles of the branches.

Up ahead, about twenty-five yards or so, I can dimly sense a clearing in the trees. I head toward it, letting the old scratch-mark of a path guide my feet.

I dare not turn on my light, but I can make out a couple of shapes in the dark clearing. One is a rectangular patch of inkier blackness on the ground, which I believe to be the foundation of an old cottage. How deep it is, I can't tell. The other appears to be a rotting, upside-down dory I recall from my old island excursions.

Instinct tells me to hide under the dory, though I'm not sure why. If someone follows me this far, they'll definitely look under it. But instinct wins. I lift the port side of the boat, allowing time for any resident fauna to disperse, then duck beneath its bowed gunwale. It stinks of wet, decaying wood and vegetation under here, but the hull is bowl-shaped and deep enough for me to sit up a bit. I resist the temptation to turn on the flashlight and see who my zoological co-tenants might be, and just sit in silence, letting my heart rate resettle.

Time dissolves. Sitting there in the almost perfect darkness, my senses — and perhaps my imagination too — shift into overdrive. I am almost certain I hear the approach of stealthy footfalls below the sound of the wind. Someone creeping into the clearing. *More than one someone.* I think I hear a "shh," though I can't swear it isn't a trick of the wind catching a pinecone scale or a curled leaf.

A small twig cracks.

Something flutters. A piece of fabric flapping in the wind?

A sixth sense — or maybe a fusion of my conventional five — tells me several human beings are standing stock still in a semi-circle around the perimeter of the flipped dory. Why aren't they moving? Speaking? Why aren't they looking under the boat? What game are they playing? Every nerve and muscle in my body is at DEFCON 1.

I suddenly become absurdly certain my cell phone is going to ring, but I don't want to make the move to shut it off, afraid the slightest rustle of Gore-Tex will give me away.

Minutes pass. I remain motionless.

I hear a light rapping on the hull. I almost scream, but then I realize it's just the rain starting up again. Within seconds, it starts to whoosh down harder.

I hear a faint "ssst," like a signal — but again, it could be an artifact of the wind. Then I hear — or *sense*, rather — the figures moving away. Or am I just imagining that? Did I imagine their presence in the first place?

I can't stand the tension, the uncertainty, any longer. In one swift, coordinated move, I turn the flashlight on, thrust the boat-edge upward, let out a lunatic yell, and charge out from beneath the dory.

Holding the knife by the handle, I slash at the air while shining the light around, screaming like a crazed baboon.

No one is here.

I sweep the light around the whole clearing. Vacant.

I stand in place, panting, for a solid minute or two.

I start back toward the main trail, about to write the whole thing off, when my face smacks into something wet and slimy suspended on a branch in the middle of the path. It falls to the ground with a flabby thud. When I see what it is, my head goes woozy.

A dead mackerel. A two-inch thorn has been jammed through one eye and out the other. It was placed there for me. A message. From Trooper Dan and friends.

How they found me so easily in the dark, I have no idea, but one thing is certain: they could have confronted me, or taken me, or done whatever, but chose not to. Why, I don't know. Maybe they're just toying with me, like a cat with a mouse, but I suspect the reasons run deeper. I'm freaking terrified.

I decide, screw it, to *run* to the village. Keeping my flashlight on, I book it back down the brambly path, turn left onto the main trail, and run, full speed, till I reach the short dirt road leading to the village. Then, what the hey, good children, I run some more.

Standing in the rain and wind and darkness in the center of the village, hauling air into my lungs, I feel both safer and more exposed. All the shops are closed, of course, and the lights are all off. I shine my flashlight back in the direction I came from and see no sign of pursuit from the woods.

I feel like I'm coming unspooled. Maybe there was no one following me. Maybe I imagined the whole thing. The presence I detected in the clearing? Raccoons stalking one another for a fish. Sure, why not? I scared them away and they ran up a tree, dropping their prize on the way up. The thorn through the mackerel's eye? Just an accident of the forest.

And yet the thought of going all the way back to Miles', collecting my belongings, and then prowling around the island some more, in the dark and the rain, looking for some possum-infested shed or rotted old boathouse to hide out in for the next day or two, feels like a terrifying prospect. I'm exhausted, nerve-fried, soaking wet, and freezing. Neither the island nor my own mind feels like a safe place to me right now.

What I really want to do is sneak back into Miles' house, go to sleep in that big, soft, stupidly comfy bed, and take a fresh look at everything in the morning.

Maybe that's what I'll do.

Yup, new plan.

# Chapter 13

I awaken at nine in the morning, hours past my usual wake-up time, and sit up on the edge of the bed. I feel oddly rested and recharged. My situation hasn't changed, but something has subtly shifted inside me. I suddenly feel as if I have access to inner resources that have been walled off for ages. Like I might even have some fight in me.

I replay last night in my mind. Despite the threat I'm dealing with, the foremost thing on my mind is Jeannie. I won't say it was "good" to see her—binary terms like good and bad don't apply where Jeannie is concerned—but it was illuminating. A truth I've been denying for years has become as plain as the taste of oyster cracker a la carte: I'm still in love with her. I was in love with her in college but too thick to know it. I fell in love with her again when I ran into her on Musqasset Island several years later, and I am in love with her now. I know, I know: love, in itself, doesn't change anything; that and a five-dollar bill will buy you a caramel macchiato. I'm sure Jeannie is not even "available." And even if she were, it's colossally unlikely that she would subject herself to another go-round with the likes of me.

Still, it's good to know my own truth, for better or worse, and to name it. Maybe *that's* what has shifted in me. Truth is power, maybe that's really so.

I think back on my experience in the woods. A night's sleep has not convinced me the threat was imaginary. Quite the contrary. I feel doubly certain there *were* men in that clearing. Trooper Dan was fucking with me. The dead fish was intended for me, and its meaning seems clear: *You're dead, but at the time and place of* our *choosing.*

Maybe, maybe not, assholes.

I open the window curtains, using the remote on the nightstand. Motorized curtains—Jesus, Miles. The rain has returned, I see. In spades. I switch on the bedroom TV and surf for a weather report. I find a live broadcast of a yellow-slickered imbecile with a mike standing on a sea wall as waves crash behind him. "The storm system is feeding off unusually warm waters in the Gulf Stream," he yells over the wind. "Its forward progress has been stalled by a high-pressure zone, and right now it's 'parked' over the ocean south of Nova Scotia and spinning like a top. That means we can expect high seas to continue for coastal Maine and the islands, perhaps through the holiday weekend, along with intermittent rain and—as you can see!—strong winds."

I'm not getting off this island till Sunday or Monday.

So be it. I refuse to spend that time feeling trapped and afraid. Fuck that. I intend to *do* something. *What*, I haven't the remotest idea, but something.

I look for my jeans and see them folded on the dresser, along with yesterday's shirt. Some early riser has thoughtfully washed and dried them for me. Shit. That means Miles and Beth know I was out last night. I suppose I'll have to explain that.

• • • • •

Dressed and as groomed as I get, I venture out of the guest room. As I wend my way to the kitchen, I can see Miles sitting at the table, talking to someone in a low voice. I pause before entering the room, trying to catch a glimpse of the other party.

Miles spots me before I can ID the visitor and shouts, "He's conscious!"

"Let's not say things we can't take back," I reply, stepping onto the imported, handmade tile of the kitchen.

"Finn, you remember Jim." Damn. The off-duty statie.

"Hey there," says Jim, standing for a handshake. "Don't punch me this time," he adds, doing a mock flinch. Ha, so funny. Jim is tall and broad, and I swear his head has a permanent groove around it from twenty years of wearing a state policeman's hat. "You've got a pretty fair right hook for an artist."

"Finn grew up in Wentworth, Mass," says Miles, as if that explains everything. Jim laughs heartily.

There's a bit too much forced bonhomie in the air. I wonder why. Then I notice the butcher knife sitting in the middle of the kitchen table. Crap, I forgot to return it to the rack last night. Miles or Beth must have found it in my room, along with my wet clothes. I nod at it pointedly and say, "I assume you're going to ask me about that. Mind if I grab a cup of coffee first?" Miles throws his palms open as if to say, *This isn't a locked ward.*

Armed with my small-batch-roasted, single-origin, fair-trade Guatemalan coffee, I join the men at the table, and we make a couple of fizzling attempts at small talk. The Sox, the storm. Then Miles gets down to business. "So... seems you were 'oot and aboot' last night."

"I didn't realize I was under house arrest," I say, leaning back and folding my arms. I'm in no mood to be treated like a mental patient this morning.

Miles snorts dismissively. "You're our guest. Obviously, you're free to come and go as you please," he says, "but I thought we had agreed on a basic script."

"Yeah, well, the writers and I got to chatting last night," I reply. No one laughs. I tell him about seeing Jeannie.

He winces as if a crab just pinched his scrotum. "Do you think that was wise?"

"It wasn't a date, Miles. I didn't plan it."

"Really? You just happened to run into her after going to bed in my house? I thought the whole idea was for you to relax and stay emotionally calm. I can't imagine seeing Jeannie was an emotionally calming experience."

"It wasn't. She took me to see the new Disney World over there at Fish Pier. Wow, Miles."

"That's a subject for another time, Finn. Right now, let's keep the focus on you."

"Haar? Kaiyo? North Atlantic Charcutiers? Really? No wonder you want to keep the focus on me."

"See? This is exactly my point. This is what Jeannie does. She stirs things up. She stirs *people* up. She's a one-woman wrecking crew..."

"*She's* a wrecking crew? Seriously, Miles?"

"...And I don't think seeing her is particularly wise, given your current—"

"Whoa there, gents," interrupts Jim. "I'm less concerned about who's dating who than I am about *this*." He picks up the butcher knife and twirls it weightily in his hands. "Can I ask why you felt the need to take a weapon with you last night, Mr. Carroll?"

I think I can pretty easily justify that decision, actually, given the circumstances, but I don't feel I owe Jim Hat-Head an explanation. "Can I ask why you're here, Jim? Not to be rude."

He ignores my question. "You see, Miles here was under the impression that you'd given up on this... *notion* that you were being chased across the Gulf by crazed psycho killers. But then you sneak out of the house late at night with a sharp knife in your hands, and we don't know what to think."

"It's not your job to think about it, Jim."

"Well, now, that might not necessarily be true. From a law enforcement perspective, the question arises as to whether a person might be a danger to himself and others. And with your recent— *extremely* recent—psychiatric history..."

"What's the bottom line here, guys?"

Working in tandem, the two of them trot out a proposal they obviously hatched before I awoke. They would like me to "see" a woman on the island they think can help me. A counselor. Wow, so Musqasset has its own shrink now; *that's* miles past overdue.

I stand up. I've had about enough of this. The only reason I copped an insanity plea last night was to placate Miles so I could sneak out of his house and vanish. Now I'll need to make my exit more obtrusively. Time is short and I have a rather serious problem to solve.

I go to the guest room, pack my clothes and belongings, and head back into the kitchen wearing my rain jacket and carrying my backpack.

"Thanks for the invite, Miles," I say. "But I can't stay here. I shouldn't have come in the first place." I make a move toward the door and feel Jim's strong fingers clamp my upper arm. "Jim, you have about two seconds to remove your hand."

"You want to think *very* carefully about your next words and actions, Mr. Carroll."

"Or what, Jim? You have no authority to hold me or stop me. I haven't been charged with a crime, and I'm not under psychiatric commitment."

"That could change."

"In the state of Maine, you need a blue paper"—an involuntary commitment—"to hold someone against their will," I tell him. "And I'm pretty sure it needs to be signed by a psychiatrist, not a licensed social worker who sells Herbalife on the side."

"In special circumstances, such as a storm like this, Mr. Carroll, if there's a clear and present risk, I can get a blue paper approved by phone on an emergency basis."

I suspect he's full of shit and tug my arm away from him to test that theory. He lets go. Theory supported. I push the door open, make my exit, and march up the walkway that leads away from Miles' house. I barely notice the rain stippling my face with hard pellets.

Miles charges out the door behind me.

"Finn!" he shouts. "Stop! God damn it, I am *ordering* you to stop."

Ordering me? That's a new one. I keep walking. Miles catches up but walks two paces behind me.

"Classic Finn. Charging off with your head up your ass instead of facing reality."

The wrong thing for Miles to say to me at this particular juncture. I wheel about and face him, my neck flushing with heat. "*Me* face reality? You don't know fuck-all, Miles! And you never have. You live in your little world of..." I stop myself there.

"Say it, Finn. Come on, get it off your chest."

I have something on my chest, all right, but it's not what he thinks.

"Come on, Finn. Clear the air. Say what's on your mind. Because it's been poisoning our friendship since freshman year of—"

"Friendship? Is that what you call this? 'Cause that's not what it feels like right now." I walk on, my feet slapping the mud.

Miles follows. "Finn, come on..."

"I need a *real* friend today, Miles, not a social worker, not a cop, not a—"

"Then convince me, god damn it!"

"Of what?"

"That you're not out of your god-damn mind!"

My gait falters for a hitch, but I don't stop. "I'm afraid I can't do that."

"Then let me get you some help and together we'll—"

"I can't do it because I would have to tell you things... I'm not able to say."

"What are you talking about?" He draws up abreast of me and clasps my jacket sleeve. "Finn. What the hell are you talking about?"

Before cooler heads can prevail, I blurt out, "I didn't tell you the whole story of what happened to me, because I didn't want to burden you with it. I was... protecting you. As usual." I reach the road and keep walking. Miles stays glued to me, awaiting more. "There's a reason those men came to my house," I say. I turn and notice Jim following us, several yards behind. I lower my volume. "And it has everything to do with you."

Jesus, what am I hearing from my own mouth? Only yesterday I swore I would never share my awful secret with Miles. But now it seems like the only path forward.

"Me?" says Miles. "You'd better explain yourself, Finn."

"I can't."

"You have to."

"I can't!"

But we both know there's no stopping this train now.

## CHAPTER 14

Miles and I sit side by side on a pew in the island's tiny nondenominational chapel. I didn't want to talk at his house, or in a public restaurant, or outside in the driving rain. There's no one else using the chapel on this rainy Friday morning, and the setting seems fitting for the confessional work at hand.

"Those guys at my house?" I say, hushing my voice for no good reason. "That really happened. Not just in my mind. I'm not crazy, Miles. Someone tried to kill me. When they left me for dead, *this* was showing on my computer." On my phone, I pull up the suicide note.

Miles reads the text, his face a stone sculpture.

"But *you* wrote this, right?" he asks.

"No. I know it sounds like my words, but no I didn't."

If Miles wants to challenge me on this point, he doesn't. "It says you were alone in the car that night."

"Right. Why would *I* write that? Or some of this other crap?"

"Okay, so what's this big incident that's being alluded to? What's all the drama and guilt about?"

"People died, that's what."

"Died? What do you mean?"

"That Glenmalloch bottle? We didn't toss it on the roadside, Miles."

I pause before delivering the *coup de grace*, knowing that what I tell him next can never be taken back. Doubt rears its head again. What right do I have to dump this stuff on him? To torpedo his career and his family? His actions that night were careless, not evil. He has no real moral stain. Not yet, anyway. Not till he knows.

I suddenly see another option, a way to tell him *almost* the entire truth by changing one little detail. In this way, all the major implications will remain the same, but Miles can be spared the actual guilty hand.

"We needed to get rid of the bottle," I say. "We were driving over route 495, but... you told me it was the Merrimac. You were drunk, you didn't know. I grabbed the bottle from your hand and threw it over the bridge without thinking. It was only when we got to the next bridge that I realized we'd made a mistake. I had thrown the bottle onto the highway, not in the river."

Miles tenses, waiting for more.

"I thought I heard crashing sounds from below," I continue, "but I wasn't sure. You had passed out by that point, and I couldn't wake you, so I couldn't talk to you about it. I didn't know what to do. So I just drove off, told myself it was nothing."

"And...?"

"It wasn't nothing." I show him the old Globe article from 1999 that I emailed myself. He reads it. His face visibly drains of blood, and his breath becomes shallow and audible.

"Jesus, Finn," he says, unconsciously pressing his palms together like praying hands. "How long have you known about these deaths?" Suddenly I'm not crazy anymore.

"Only since I clicked the link in that 'suicide' note. The day after graduation, I avoided reading the papers or watching the news. I left for California a day later."

"Jesus, Finn," he repeats. "Jesus." A sheen of perspiration has blossomed on his forehead.

"Now do you believe me? Now do you see why someone might be upset enough to want to hurt me? Now do you see why I can't be staying at your house?"

But Miles doesn't seem to hear me. He stands up and walks out of the church with his mouth hanging open and a benumbed look in his eyes. I start to follow him, but he warns me off with a sweep of his hand.

• • • • •

I've rented a room on the third floor of Harbor House—to distance myself from Miles' home and family. Ordinarily there would be no vacancies on Musqasset on a holiday weekend, but because of the storm there have been numerous cancellations. I asked JJ, the manager, for a quiet room away from other guests, and he was able to put me in 313, in the back corner of the third floor, with no one occupying the next two rooms.

I'm under no illusion that I'm safe here, though. If Trooper Dan and company were able to find me in the pitch dark last night, in a storm, in the middle of an island unfamiliar to them, then I assume, going out on a limb, they can find me in a public inn. But what can they do about it? That's what I'm pondering as I sit here on the edge of the bed, biting furiously at a hangnail. Would these guys really dare make a move on me here, in this old wooden inn where noise carries like electric current? Or in any public spot on the island?

Or will they need to isolate me somewhere, far from the madding crowd?

But they had their perfect opportunity last night in the woods, and they didn't act on it. Why? I haven't a clue. That's because I have no idea who these guys are or what their motivation is. So how can I gain better clarity? I decide to give mind-mapping a whirl. It's a visual brainstorming technique I sometimes use for developing creative ideas in games. I'm digging in my backpack for my notebook when there's a knock at the door.

Suicidally, I turn the knob and peek out.

It's Miles. He pushes the door open. Carrying a laptop computer, he strides purposefully into the room. "Let's assume everything you said is true," he announces without preamble. "Who could possibly know about that night, and why would they care?"

I have no idea what has caused this sudden shift of attitude, but Miles plunks his laptop down on the room's small desk, tosses his rain jacket onto the bed, and rolls up his sleeves as if he's ready to work. "Let's start by going over what we know for sure," he says. "See where that leads us." His energy is all business.

Fine, I'm game.

We convert my room into a makeshift "war room," using the desk as a table and snagging an extra chair from down the hall. We both agree that my only real hope of thwarting my purported stalkers is to figure out who they are and what they want. We know the odds of our being able to solve this puzzle from the remote location of Musqasset Island, in a storm, on a holiday weekend, with two rank amateurs at the helm, are slim, to put it wildly optimistically. But slim beats nonexistent.

Miles tells me he has already put out feelers to all the inns, asking if any suspicious-looking men traveling in twos or threes have checked into their establishments, but that has yielded no results. No shocker there. The bad guys, after all, are probably not wearing bandit masks and carrying violin cases. Besides, we have absolutely no authority to question anyone, even if we suspect them. And the "facts" we possess, at least at this point, are far too sketchy to bring Jim into the picture. So for now it's Miles and me against the world.

"Before we go any further with this," says Miles, booting up his computer, "I want to state something 'for the record.'" Oh joy. "I'm choosing to believe you, and I want to help you, but... here's my dilemma. Now that I know what happened that night, I can't unknow it. And the more information we unearth, the harder it's going to be to pretend I can. What I'm trying to say is: in my position, I can't be guilty of covering up... misdeeds."

"Don't worry about me, Miles. I'm prepared to step forward and accept complete responsibility for my actions at the appropriate time." It's true. I am.

"Are you sure?"

I nod. He nods. We lock eyes across the table for several long seconds.

"Then let's do this."

I go to turn on my phone recorder to capture our conversation—a habit of mine from work meetings—but before I touch the phone, it "wakes up" as if a text or call has come in. Nothing shows up on the screen, though. Whatever message was snaking through the ether, trying to find me, has been lost in the storm. I tap "record" on the

VoxFox app.

"The most fundamental question we need to ask," says Miles, "is who besides you and me could possibly know about your connection to that accident? No one else was there." He leans back, flaring his palms out. "Possibility number one: you or I told someone. Since I had nothing to tell until now, that kind of eliminates me." Miles drills his eyes into mine, doing his lawyer thing. "Over the course of the last eighteen years, have you told *anyone* what happened in that car? Anyone at all?"

Easy answer: "No."

"Are you sure? Anyone at all, under *any* circumstances? Think. A confession to a priest..." Right. "A night in a bar... pillow talk with Jeannie or someone else?"

"Nope, absolutely not. I'm a hundred percent sure."

"Ever write about it in a journal or diary someone could have read?" I shake my head. "Or mention it to a shrink in a hospital, or a therapist?"

"No, Miles. I told you: I couldn't even admit it to *myself*. I moved to the far end of the continent just so I wouldn't have to know if there had even *been* an accident."

"So we didn't start the fire. Possibility number two," he says, "there was an eyewitness. Someone saw what happened, maybe got your license plate number, traced it back to you."

Given the conditions that night—dark road, late hour, unpopulated location—we quickly rule out that possibility.

"Which leaves the cop, then," says Miles.

"Right." The cop is the only possible candidate for eyewitness. "Here's the thing, though. I was watching for him like a hawk. I had my eyes glued to the rear-view mirror at the time that I"—I almost say "you"—"threw the bottle. He wasn't behind us then. I'm sure. It wasn't till a short while later he started tailing us. ...Besides, if the cops suspected me of anything, why wouldn't they have followed up?" Miles ponders that obvious question. "Why wait eighteen years to come after me, and why get thugs involved? Doesn't make any sense."

"Right. Which brings us to possibility number three. If neither of us told anyone, and there were no witnesses, including the cop, then someone pieced something together from evidence found at the scene of the accident."

"And the only possible evidence was the bottle itself. If they could somehow trace that."

"Right."

"But wouldn't it have shattered into a skillion pieces?" I ask.

"Maybe, maybe not. It was a pretty thick bottle, as I recall."

An idea light bulb turns on over Miles' head—yes it does; sue me—and he types "Glenmalloch" into the Google search box. He hits the search button, nothing happens. "Shit," he says. The Internet, it seems, has chosen this moment to desert us. "This place has satellite," Miles says by way of explanation. "We'll try again in a few minutes."

Internet on Musqasset is a crapshoot even on a sunny day in June. The concept of broadband is like time travel here. Video streaming is a joke. There are a few DSL lines, but the signal is weak this far offshore. Satellite Internet is popular—that's what Harbor House uses—but its reliability varies wildly from location to location and in bad weather. Some of the B&Bs don't even bother to offer Wi-Fi. They hawk this as a feature: "Unplug, relax, and enjoy a taste of Maine island life off the grid." Quite a few residents still have dial-up Internet, believe it or not, and many people use their cell-phone service for Web access, but cell reception sucks outside the village, where the only cell "tower" (not a tower) is located. Even email is spotty. Texting is probably the most dependable means of communication, but that, too, can be funky. Texts can show up at random times, or not at all.

"Okay," Miles continues, "Let's just stipulate for now that someone has connected you to the accident—they obviously have; we're not sure how yet. So what's the next most obvious question?"

"Why would they want to kill me? 'Motive,' as the cop shows say. And why wait eighteen fricking years?"

"That's two questions, but right. Let's look at motive first. Why would someone want you dead? Not for any apparent gain, it seems. There was no attempt to blackmail you or make demands. Right? Someone just wanted you purged from the census report."

"So that would point to what? Vengeance or 'justice,' I suppose. Someone is pissed off at me and wants me to pay for my... crime."

"Possibly." Miles thinks for a moment. "Or maybe you're perceived as a threat to someone. Are you?"

"Not unless bad computer-game art is a malign force in the universe. Which is a distinct possibility."

"*Do* you have any enemies, though, Finn?"

"I can think of a few people who might want me crossed off their Christmas card lists, but not off the *planet*. And even if they did, why stage my death to look like a suicide?"

"Um, so there wouldn't be a murder investigation." Duh. "Plus, the suicide note comes in handy if someone wants to tell the world you did it. It's a flat-out confession."

"True." I'm still confounded by the fact that the suicide note sounded so much like me, and tapped so uncannily into my feelings of guilt, but I don't want to get into that right now. "Again, though, why wait eighteen years?"

"Who knows? Maybe a new piece of evidence surfaced. Maybe someone just got out of prison after a long stint." *Miles Sutcliffe, Hollywood Screenwriter.* "Without knowing who's responsible, we'll never figure that part out. Let's stay with the who. Someone wanted justice... revenge?... for themselves or a loved one. So who were the parties affected?"

Together we scan the newspaper article and Miles types the names of the victims, as well as the involved motorist who was uninjured, on the laptop:

Paul Abelsen

Laurice Abelsen

Ashley Abelsen

Edgar Goslin

Jeremy Halsey

Seeing the names in stark black font on that plain white screen brings into sharp relief the fact that real human beings died that night in 1999. People who will never have children or grandchildren or taste another spoonful of strawberry ice cream. I feel a burn of shame and grief.

Miles, gleaning my thoughts, says gently, "You didn't know, Finn."

"Because I didn't *want* to know. Because I avoided knowing."

Miles waits a respectful beat, then says, "The Abelsens—we need to talk bluntly about this—all died. But they might have friends or relatives who are seeking payback. Edgar Goslin, he was hospitalized with serious injuries. We don't know if he lived or died. If he lived, he might have a score he wants to settle. Halsey only had car damage; we can probably rule him out."

"So task number one," I say, "is to find out whatever we can about the Abelsens and Edgar Goslin. And that pricey bottle of scotch."

"All without a working Internet," grumbles Miles. No sooner does he say this than a list of results from his "Glenmalloch" search pops up on Google. "Hey, we're back in business, for the moment anyway."

Miles clicks on the URL for the Glenmalloch.com site. The website assembles itself in piecemeal fashion. It's an elegantly designed, hi-res site replete with polished wood grains and vessels of gleaming amber liquid. You can almost smell the barley mash. Miles tools around and finds a page called "Special Release Malts." It shows a pictorial history of all the unique whiskies the company has released over the past few decades. Scrolling through the years, Miles stops abruptly when he sees a product released in 1999 called "Single Barrel 16, Anniversary Edition." The text describes a "premium Islay-style whiskey matured in a single aging cask and offered in a hand-numbered, decanter-style bottle to honor the distillery's 150th anniversary."

The photo hits me like a slap in the face: a squared decanter with a heavy glass cork-stopper and a shockingly familiar black-and-gold embossed label.

"That's it," I say. Unnecessarily. "That's the bottle."

Miles nods, almost hypnotically. "Look how thick that glass is," he says. "If this bottle hit a car windshield, I can see how it would have left pieces big enough to identify."

Wow, a mere twenty minutes into our stupid-ass little "investigation," and we may have already found a key to a pivotal piece of the puzzle. We stare dumbly at the screen.

"So how would someone trace it back to me?" I ask, even as my mind is already supplying possible answers.

"Two ways I can think of," says Miles. "Fingerprints, for one. Either of our prints, or both, could have been on any part of the bottle." He blows out a shaky breath as he weighs the import of that. "Have you ever been fingerprinted?"

"Not that I recall," I say, "though I came close once." I cast him a meaningful glance. There was an incident during our sophomore year of college that we both look back upon with shame—I because I permitted it to happen, Miles because of how he behaved.

Miles and I had been at our friend Doc's apartment, watching Green Bay kick New England's ass on Monday Night Football. We'd had a few beers. Miles was driving me home in his van when we spotted blue lights behind us. He panicked, to put it mildly. "Oh my God, Finn," he shrieked, "what are we going to do?" He started hyperventilating and blubbering like a schoolkid, "I'm screwed, I'm screwed, I'm so fucking screwed."

I was appalled. This was the first time I'd ever seen Miles without the social mask, the first time I realized that behind his polished exterior there lived a terrified child.

"My life will be over if I get charged with DUI," he said. "Over! My father will kill me. I'll never go to law school. My grandparents will freak. ...You've got to switch seats with me." He stopped the van and, without awaiting my answer, dove to the floor and climbed toward the passenger seat, as I, like an idiot, scrambled into the driver's seat. We actually pulled off the switcheroo—thanks to the van's lack of rear windows—but I was taken to the police station, where I had to submit to a blood test. I was finally released, no fingerprints taken, but it was a close call. Not one of our proudest moments.

"You?" I ask. "Ever fingerprinted?"

"I don't think so. No."

"The only other way to connect the bottle to me, then—*if* they could piece enough of it together to identify the brand—would be to trace the purchase data somehow, right?"

"Right. Ordinarily, that would be almost impossible, but this was no Johnny Walker Red. This was sixteen-year Glenmalloch, numbered label. Do you remember where you bought it?"

I think back for a moment but oddly have absolutely no memory of purchasing the bottle. I shake my head no. Maybe it'll come to me later.

"There were only a couple of liquor stores in the Bridgefield area that would have carried a product like this," says Miles. "The Brown Bag sure the hell wouldn't have sold it."

"Right. There was Bridgefield Package Shop"—a snooty place in Bridgefield center that offered a high-end wine and booze inventory—"and maybe that huge place out on route 125."

"Academy Liquors, right. That bottle probably sold for close to a hundred dollars."

"It did, believe me," I say. "I wanted it to be memorable."

Yay, score one for me on that note.

"How many bottles like this do you suppose were sold in our area within a week or two before the incident?"

The answer is plain. It can't have been many. A handful at best.

Maybe only one.

# Chapter 15

We're still staring at the little web photo of the old Glenmalloch bottle when a massive crack of thunder splits the air above us. The lamp in the room loses power, and we go dark. In the absence of electricity, I realize how black the morning sky has grown. We've lost the Internet signal again too. And I can't get online with my phone.

We're instantly back in the 1920s again.

Miles' phone rings. "I'm on my way," he answers. "Beth," he explains to me. "She doesn't know how to use the generator. I'd better head out." There's not much more "detective" work we can do at the moment anyway.

Miles slaps his thighs and rises. He gives me a light goodbye hug, but I catch his eyes probing mine like a doctor evaluating a wide receiver after a helmet-to-helmet collision. He tells me to call him later and vamooses. A minute later, I look out the window and see him driving off in the golf cart he uses to get around the island.

I'm left alone in my newly rented room.

My *tiny, isolated, powerless* rented room.

I wonder how long we'll be without juice. Minutes? Hours? Days? Even though it's late morning, it's surprisingly dark in the old inn without lamplight and under this dense cloud cover.

With no Internet to focus on, my mind hurtles back to the danger I'm in. I have no idea who my stalkers are, where they're staying, what they want, what they know, or how insane they are. I don't know whether they're watching me 'round the clock or not. The idea that I'm going to somehow figure these things out by digging up facts on an ancient scotch bottle suddenly seems like magical thinking of the looniest order.

To complicate matters, my mind, ridiculously and unproductively, keeps gravitating to Jeannie. *Does she really have a kid? Is she still with that asshole who —*

Stop!

I wander downstairs to the lobby to borrow a candle lantern. JJ always keeps plenty of them on hand. The L.L.Bean family is sitting around a low table by the fireplace, playing a board game by firelight. The daughter gives me a little finger-wave and a crooked smile. Damn, she's *more* than cute. Under different circumstances, I might...

Enough. Stick to the task at hand.

Which is what?

• • • • •

Back in my candlelit room, I'm peering out the window at the village below, trying to calculate my next move. I spot a man in a dark raincoat — hard to tell its exact color — standing in the shadowy area to the right of the post office/donut shop. He seems to be staring up at my window. I reflexively draw back. A moment later I look again, and the figure is gone.

A woman bustles by the post office, carrying a big, floppy handbag that reminds me of one my sister Angie owns. Angie. *Call Angie!* Of course! Why didn't I think of that before? Angie works at the city clerk's office in Wentworth, and she can find out anything about anyone. Luckily, my phone is working as a telephone, if not as an Internet portal. I give Angie's work number a try and manage to catch her at her desk.

"Hey Ange, it's me."

"Oh, Finn. Hi. Listen, I'm sorry I haven't been up to see you yet, but I—"

Up to see me? Oh crap. She thinks I'm still in the hospital. "Um, I'm not at Saint D's anymore."

Short pause. "What? What do you mean?"

"I discharged myself."

Another pause. "Do you think that was wise?"

"I'm on Musqasset right now, Ange. It's a long story, and I might lose phone service any second. Listen, I was hoping you could help me with something." I take her silence as encouragement to go on. "I need some information on a couple of people in the Wentworth area. I'll explain it when we both have more time."

"Okay..." she says, not exactly blasting me off my feet with her enthusiasm.

I describe the newspaper account of the accident in some detail and tell her the kind of info I'm looking for—who the Abelsens were, their friends and relatives, who Goslin is/was, what became of him, any follow-up stories on the accident, and so on.

Angie is quiet for several long seconds. "What goaded you into digging for this information, Finn?" What *goaded* me? Sort of an oddly phrased question.

"I'll explain later," I reply. "I'm afraid of losing my signal in this storm, and I've got more calls to make. Can you do me this favor? Ange?"

"I'll... see what I can find out," she finally offers. "If you think that's a good idea. But you *will* need to tell me what you're up to. I'm worried about you, Finn."

I thank her, asking her to email me and Miles whatever results she finds, and hang up.

*Why the worry?* I wonder. *Why the suspicious attitude?*

Because Ange is nuts, that's why.

I'll let her do some digging into Goslin and the Abelsens, though. Meanwhile, I'll try to focus on the scotch bottle—that rare and highly traceable scotch bottle that seems to be the sole thread tying me to the accident—with my phone as my only investigative tool. If only I could remember where I bought the damn bottle, there's a chance the owner of the store, or an employee, might recall someone asking questions about it all those years ago.

But I *can't* remember. And it *was* almost twenty years ago. The store that sold it probably doesn't even exist anymore, and if it does, what are my odds of reaching someone who worked there in 1999? Still, it's *something*, I guess. I have to try. I should have asked Angie for the phone numbers of all the well-established liquor stores in the Wentworth/Bridgefield area. Now *that's* information she would have had at her fingertips. But I don't want to call her back, the skittish way she's acting. Where else might I get that information?

I actually have to think for a moment to remember how phone numbers were disseminated in the pre-smartphone era. Books, oh yeah. Do phone books still exist? Yes, they do, because once or twice a year I dutifully transfer one from my front porch to the recycling bin. I recall that the Musqasset library houses a large collection of them—yellow and white pages—from all around New England.

Island Avenue is half underwater as I trudge the two hundred muddy yards to the library, getting peppered by the wind-blown rain. Every few steps, I check behind me for followers. I have a strong sense of being watched; every window looks like an eye. The instant I step inside the one-room building and stomp the rain off my shoes, Lester Hughes, the octogenarian librarian, chimes, "So the rumor mill was right."

Fabulous—the *town librarian* already knows I'm on the island. Hooray for keeping my presence on the down-low.

Lester shows me, with a wistful shake of his head, the corner of the room once reserved for phone books. It has been converted into The Story Nook, as the hideous fairytale mural attests. "So what do people do if they need a phone number and the Internet is down?" I ask him.

Lester shrugs and offers me a toothless grin. "Call 411 and invest a buck."

I'm back in the rain, my eyes scanning every shadow for movement. I'm trying to probe my brain for memories of that ill-fated booze bottle, but my thoughts insist on flowing to one topic only: Jeannie. Let's face it, I *need* to talk to her at least one more time. Just to learn the facts and be done with it. Is she in a relationship? Married? Happy? A mom, as rumor has it? I never got the chance to ask her last night.

Maybe I should resolve this distraction once and for all, since I can't do any online work at the moment. I'd love to see Jean face to face, but I can't just show up at her door asking questions. I don't have that privilege. Especially if she's living with AssFace von TurdClown.

If I had a legitimate *excuse* to visit her, however...

The Internet.

Wonder if she still has that shitty old dial-up Internet connection. Dial-up is a travesty, of course, but sometimes it's more reliable than anything else on the island. *Can I borrow your Internet?* That would be a pretty lame excuse for showing up at her door.

But it's legit. Sort of. It would let me kill two birds with one stone: grab myself some Internet access *and* see Jeannie again.

Nah, too thin. Too awkward. Too intrusive. Too risky.

• • • • •

Seeing my old home on Fishermen's Court brings up a knot of mixed feelings I can't begin to disentangle. I'm assuming Jeannie still owns the place — a tiny blue-gray cape with a small fenced-in yard and an English garden (i.e., mass of untamed growth with a few tall tiger lilies sticking out). Out back sits an oversized storage shed I insulated and turned into a small painting studio. The location of the house, fittingly enough, is just a jig's cast away from Studio Row, where the "legit" artists live. So near and yet so far. Story of my life.

One glance at the old shed/studio unleashes a torrent of memories — light-filled images of painting at my easel for hours, then catching a fish off the pier in the late afternoon and cooking it for Jeannie over a bottle of wine. Seems like there were hundreds such vintage days, but maybe there were only a handful.

Dare I approach the door? My brain says no, but my feet don't get the memo.

Standing on Jeannie's front stoop in the rain, I feel as if the eyes of the world are upon me. I don't want to bring any danger down on her. And what if ClownAss von TurdFace answers the door? I should have brought a bag of dog shit along to light on fire.

Ignore that last remark.

Okay, if I'm going to do this, I'd better do it fast—before I attract attention. I lightly tap the cat gargoyle knocker I gave Jean for Christmas six years ago (not that I'm counting). Secretly relieved at the non-response, I knock a bit more bravely. Nothing. The house feels unoccupied.

I should just duck and run while the ducking's good, but I can't resist the urge to take a quick peek around. A plastic play castle in the overgrown yard tells me the child rumors are true. I look for signs of a live-in male but don't see anything obvious. No wheeling tool chests, no golf clubs, no recycling-bags bulging with Bud empties.

Oh well, time to make my absence felt. I start down the road to the village and freeze mid-step. Standing in the middle of the road about three houses down, legs splayed, facing straight toward me, is a man in a Davy's grey rain slicker. His face is shadowed by a large hood, but I can see a salt-and-pepper beard climbing high onto his cheekbones.

I'm paralyzed into inaction. I stare at the man. His unseen eyes stare back. Malevolence streams toward me like an electric beam. Or so it feels.

"Finnian Carroll," a man's voice shouts from behind me. Crap, boxed in!

I turn to see Andy Rusch, an old painting buddy, plodding toward me, smiling, in waders and a fireman's jacket. I take an awkward moment to greet him before whipping my body around to face Davy Grey again. He's gone.

"I heard you were on the island," says Andy as he draws up beside me. (Is there a Sherpa on a Himalayan mountaintop somewhere who doesn't know I'm here?)

We shoot the breeze for a minute, but the rain and wind—and my anxiety level—put a damper on real conversation. Andy tells me he thinks Jeannie is working today, and then asks, with almost comical earnestness, "Is everything okay, Finn?"

"Any reason it shouldn't be?"

"'Course not," he says, but I don't love the fact that he waits half a beat before saying it, or that he turns back to me after walking down the road a bit and repeats himself. "'Course not."

The walk to Pete's Lagoon takes around eight minutes, and I find myself looking over my shoulder every few strides. Halfway there, I hear a TV set pop on in a nearby house. The power must be back, at least for now.

As I step through the door of Pete's and shake off the rain, I experience one of the strongest déjà vu moments of my life, one that instantly purges my mind of Davy Grey. Jeannie is behind the bar cutting lemon wedges, her back to the house, and she turns to see who has entered. It's almost an exact replay of the moment I walked into Pete's about nine years ago. On that day of yore, she turned and looked at me from that same spot. I hadn't seen her since college but had thought about her plenty. I'd come to the island for a week with a painter friend who insisted I couldn't call myself a New England artist until I had painted Musqasset Island. Jeannie was about the last person in the galaxy I expected to find tending bar thirteen miles off the coast of Maine, but the instant I saw the twinkle in her eyes, I was hooked like a swordfish. I *knew* in that moment she and I had more history to write together. Maybe lots of it.

Today the twinkle isn't *quite* there, but it isn't *totally* absent either.

Unless I'm misreading. Which I am known to do on rare occasion.

"I was wondering when you'd wash up on the rocks again," she says, in that dry-as-sandpaper tone of hers. "What can I get you?"

"Dazzle me," I say, claiming a stool at the underpopulated bar.

She lifts an eyebrow, then turns and lets her hand flitter along the top shelf of the back bar, feeling out the choices. I feel anything *but* surprise when she reaches for—was there really any other possibility?—the Glenmalloch. It's odd that a bar like this would even stock such an obscure brand of whiskey, odder still that she reaches for it as if it were magnetized to her hand. And yet I'd have fallen off my barstool, literally, if she had chosen anything else.

She pours me a dram of the golden nectar. "Is it hard?" I ask, and she takes my meaning—working in a bar when you don't drink anymore.

"Not really," she replies. "At least once a day some drunken pinhead says or does something that reminds me just how fargin' glad I am to be sober."

We chat about the weather for a bit, for the usual avoidant reasons, but also because, in a storm like this, it's really the only topic.

"I went by the house," I finally say, amending it to "*your* house."

"You probably shouldn't do that, Finn," she says, losing her bantery tone. She looks around, confirming there's no one within earshot. "Listen, I came to see you last night, but I hope I didn't do anything to give you the impression the door was in any way open between... you know..." Us. "Because that ship sailed, sank, ran aground, and washed back out to sea a long time ago." Jesus with the metaphors, Jeannie. "We both agree on that, right?"

Piss. Fuck. Shit.

"Of course," I say. "No, I didn't get any other impression. I just..." I find I can't trot out the I-needed-to-borrow-your-Internet excuse, now that I'm talking to her face to face. "I just wanted to see how you were doing, how your life turned out."

"Turned out? Crikey, I hope it's still a work in progress."

As she goes back to slicing lemons, she gives me the sanitized, Cliff Notes version of her life since I do-si-doed. No, she didn't stay with AssTurd del ClownFace. Hallelujah. Yes, she has a daughter, Bree, who's spending the holiday on the mainland with Jean's sister. Bree will turn three next month. A quick calculation dashes any hope that she might be, well, a blood relative. The numbers don't add up. Jeannie had one other brief relationship after TurdAss de la FaceClown, she says, and that was the one that prompted her come-to-Jesus reckoning with herself. Since then she has lived dude-free and alcohol-free and has been putting all her attention on herself and her daughter. She's finally taking her writing seriously too, and has had two horror stories published. Wow, amazing what a little non-Finn time can do for a person.

And me? Oh, right, forgot this was a quid pro quo. I try to put a charitable spin on my life of the last few years, essaying valiantly not to make it sound like, "After we split up, my life went rocketing down the shitter so fast you'd think it was fired from a bazooka," though I'm pretty sure that's what comes across anyway.

When I'm done my awkward PR spiel, Jeannie leans on the bar, stares me in the face, and says, "So why'd you come back to the island, puffin boy? Real reason."

I draw a deep breath and lift the whiskey glass to my mouth with a hand that's taken on an unwelcome tremor. Some alien form of terror must be lurking in the black of my pupils as I stare back at her, because Jeannie drops her lemon on the floor and says, "Jesus, Finn, what the hell happened to you?"

"Not here... not now."

I order the fisherman's platter, hold the fisherman.

## CHAPTER 16

Miles rings me as I'm finishing lunch and says he's coming to pick me up. He's suddenly getting Internet reception at the house, he tells me, even though the storm seems to be worsening by the minute. The rest of his family is at a holiday charity event at "the club," so we'll have the place to ourselves for a few hours. I'm still worried about the possibility of leading my stalkers to Miles' house, but a live Internet signal seems like an opportunity too good to pass up.

I say goodbye to Jeannie and am about to leave when, to my own surprise, I hear the words, "When do you get off work tonight?" leap from my mouth.

She shoots me a suspicious look. *Why?*

"If I were to show up at your place around seven with a garlic, mushroom, and artichoke pizza from The Barnacle, would you slam the door in my face?"

"Not without grabbing the pizza first." The Barnacle makes seriously good pizza. Not just good-for-an-island-off-the-coast-of-Maine good, but *good* good. "But I don't know if that's a wise idea, Finn."

"Just two friends sharing a pizza," I say. "Unless you've got other plans."

She is silent for a few seconds, then says, "I guess it wouldn't kill me to throw together a salad and stick a dessert in the oven." Jeannie *bakes* now too? Peace in the Middle East. "Just as long as we agree that..."

"Yeah, yeah. See you at seven?"

• • • • •

The rain buffets us in sheets as Miles and I tool down partially flooded Island Avenue in his canvas-topped golf cart. I'm not thinking about ancient bottles of scotch and bad guys in Davy's grey raincoats, as good sense dictates I should be; I'm thinking about dinner tonight. I'm both fired-up and scared to death about spending some time alone with Jean, but I also can't help feeling disheartened by the way she characterized our relationship. I certainly couldn't have expected otherwise, though, could I? The fact is, until an hour ago I didn't even know she was unattached. Until forty hours ago, I had no reason to think I would ever see her again. And until my attempted murder a week ago, I had no clear idea I even wanted to.

So I can hardly expect her to be laying down a trail of rose petals to her bed. But still, "sailed, sank, ran aground, and washed back out to sea"?

The memory of her words triggers a thought. I ask Miles to drive up Lighthouse Road. We park at the top of the hill and I walk to the seaward edge. I tell him to follow me down the steep path that descends to Table Rock. Miles is reluctant to brave the rain and the slickened trail, but he eventually brings up the rear. We stop partway down and take in the scene below. The Shipwreck—*our* Shipwreck, Jeannie's and mine—has shifted its angle again and worked its way two or three yards closer to the edge of the great bed of slate. The whole bow of the *K.C. Mokler* is now jutting out over the water. The waves continue to assault it.

"Holy shit," says Miles Sutcliffe in an awed whisper.

"A few years ago," I say, "if you'd asked me to name the two most iconic sights on Musqasset, I'd have said Fish Pier and The Shipwreck. Looks like they'll *both* be gone soon."

We exchange a look that encapsulates our entire history on the island.

Not long after I came here on that painting excursion nine years ago and ran into Jeannie, I moved here. I loved the island for many reasons, not the least of which was that it was *my* discovery, *my* place. Not Miles'. Miles had barely even heard of Musqasset when I talked him into visiting me here a year or so later, even though Beth was a Maine native and the Sutcliffes had become full-time residents of Vacationland. Miles' decision to buy a summer home on the island was based almost entirely on my relentless hammering.

And boy howdy, did he make me regret it. Where I saw beauty and balance and thriving community on Musqasset, he saw economic opportunity. Where I wanted to preserve the place like a lost Winslow Homer painting, he immediately set about trying to change it.

Miles turns and heads back up the trail. I follow him. We make our way toward his electric cart, wet and winded from the climb. I ask him if I can drive. He knows where I'll be taking him, and he doesn't like it, but he signals *be my guest*.

I might not make it off this island alive, but I refuse to go to my final fishing grounds without saying some things that have needed saying for years. Tonight with Jeannie and right now with Miles. Before he and I do another thing together.

I take the road to old Fish Pier, now marked with a bright new sign pointing to the "Marina and Yacht Club at The Meadows." Miles sighs as I make the turn.

I park the covered cart on a hillock overlooking the landward side of the new marina complex. The white-capped ocean churns beyond it. Gazing out at the rain-soaked cluster of stained-wood buildings that looks as if it belongs in a different locale, I no longer feel the same anger I felt last night but rather a sad sort of resignation. About what? The inevitability of money winning every battle, I guess. My feelings are not even directed at Miles at this point. Today I feel as if we're just two actors in an ancient play mankind has been staging and restaging since the first coin was minted.

I don't feel a need to speak for a while, and neither does Miles.

At last I break the silence. "I said some shitty things to you when I left the island, and I'm sorry. One of my many, many, many—did I mention many?—flaws is that I hold things in, and then when I finally blurt them out, I say more than I intend to. ...But you *do* understand why I felt betrayed by you?"

Miles takes his time replying. "This thing was never about you and me."

"It was *always* about you and me. At least to me it was."

"That's why you'll never be a businessman, Finn. You don't understand that business isn't personal."

"You don't understand that it *is*. Especially in a place like Musqasset. *I* invited you to this island. That's personal. *I* talked you into buying a house here. *I* introduced you to people here who could make things happen for you. That's personal. When you came up with your original development plan, I put *my* ass on the line to help you sell it to the locals. A lot of people hated the idea of a yacht club on Musqasset—hated it—but *I* opened their minds by pointing out how great it could be for Fish Pier. And for the fishermen. And the island."

"It was a good plan, Finn."

"*Was*. What happened?"

"Things change. I had partners. They wanted a surer return on their investment. They saw a better way to leverage the assets at hand."

"Assets at hand? Fish Pier wasn't just a chunk of planks and pilings. It had meaning to people, history. It was the heart of the island's economy."

"The *old* economy. Time marches on."

"It was the soul of the island, Miles. The anchor. The root system. Couldn't you see that? This is a working island, not some trust-fund babies' playground. Generations of islanders docked their fishing boats and lobster boats at that pier. Island kids caught their first fish there. Hundreds of artists painted it, in every light and every season. Fish Pier *was* Musqasset."

"I did fight for the pier, Finn. I know you don't believe that, but I did. But I was outnumbered and out-moneyed. The other partners didn't live here. They had no sentimentality about Fish Pier whatsoever. But I fought my damnedest for it."

"Did you give them the letters?"

He glares darkly at me. "I gave you my word, didn't I? The letters didn't matter. You don't know these people. You didn't see what went on behind closed doors. I had no influence. I didn't have any real skin in the game, I was just the front man. I don't know how much money you imagine I have, Finn—Beth's the one with the real money in our marriage—but the *vast* majority of the financing came from people who gave not one shit about Musqasset tradition."

"Then why'd you throw in with people like that?"

"Not everything in my world is as pure and simple as it is in Finn World."

"Don't do that, Miles. Don't dismiss me as some kind of moral purist who doesn't live in reality. Can you not see the position you put me in? I was a newcomer myself, but there were people here who had grown to like and trust me. I used that trust to help *you*. Can't you see that when you abandoned Fish Pier, you abandoned *me*? How could I stay on the island after that?"

"So it's *my* fault you left the island? Breaking up with Jeannie had nothing to do with it?"

"Maybe we wouldn't have *broken* up if this thing hadn't put so much strain on our relationship."

"Oh wow, Finn. This is classic. You're actually blaming me for your break-up with Jeannie."

"I'm not, Miles. All I'm saying is your actions have consequences. Human consequences. Sometimes I wonder if you've ever really understood that." Again I'm tempted to blurt out some things that must remain unsaid.

"Here's what I think," Miles says. "Much as I miss Fish Pier, I think this new complex is saving Musqasset's ass. It brings in more income, and employs more people, than half the rest of the island combined. Ten, twenty years from now, people will look back on this development as a turning point for Musqasset. A positive one. And Fish Pier will be a quaint bit of history."

"You don't get it."

"*You* don't. The future of Maine's coastal economy is tourism, not fishing. That's a fact. I'm sure when the printing press was invented, the people who ran Scribes R Us thought the world was ending. Change sucks, until the money starts rolling in."

"It's more complicated than that, Miles. And if you don't know that, you don't know Musqasset."

"See that flat rooftop over there?" he says, pointing. "You know what that is? A helipad. We threw it in as a gift to the island. People can now be safely medevacked to the mainland in an emergency. Two lives have been saved this season already."

I don't respond. We stare down at the rain-drenched marina complex, and I'm sure we're each seeing a wholly different sight. If I'd known what sort of atrocity this thing was going to morph into, the fight Miles and I had four years ago might have involved dueling pistols.

"I do recognize you stuck your neck out for me," Miles says at last. "And I am forever grateful for that... So let's get back to the house and get to work."

I could hyper-analyze the subtext of his final remark — he's helping me because of what, a sense of *duty*? — but at this point I don't feel like arguing anymore. I've said all I can say. I need an ally, and I'll take one any way I can get it.

• • • • •

As we're stepping into Miles' house, an email arrives on his phone with a jingle. Random delivery from the weather deities. It's from Angie. Good thing I gave her Miles' email address and asked her to cc him. His phone caught the email, my antique piece of crap didn't.

The email contains a Word attachment. Ange's message is, "Kinda concerned about why you want this information. Promise me we'll talk about it ASAP. Hope it helps you with whatever you're working through." Working through? I guess she thinks I'm still in psychiatric crisis. Take a number in *that* line, sister.

"Can I get you anything to drink?" Miles calls from the kitchen, as I pull up a chair at the desk in his oak-infested study.

"I'll take a beer, thanks."

"How 'bout Diet Coke or O.J.?"

"Just give me a fucking beer, Miles."

He brings two. I move aside Beth's *Power of Words Journal*—which she has been diligently filling with entries, I see—to make some space on the desk. We print up two copies of Angie's Word file. My sister seems to have done quite a bit of research and synthesis in a short time. Getting dirt on people is her mutant superpower. Her write-up:

*As you already know, the Abelsens and Edgar Goslin were involved in a highway accident in the early hours of May 13, 1999. The Wentworth Tribune said the cause of the accident was under investigation.*

*An article in the Trib several days later said the cops had found evidence that an unidentified glass container, possibly tossed from the Carlisle Road overpass, may have contributed to/caused the accident.*

*Paul and Laurice Abelsen were mega-boojie types who lived in Bridgefield. Paul grew up there and had family there. Went to Bridgefield Academy. Owned a startup software company. Father, Gary, is a Mr. Moneybags. Started a scholarship & memorial 5K run in his son's name. Also offered a fat reward for information that would help in the accident investigation.*

*Edgar Goslin suffered head and pelvic injuries. Was hospitalized and unconscious for weeks. After he came to, he told police – S2S – that something had broken his windshield and caused him to lose control of the car. Was wheelchair-bound at first but then had some surgeries and rehab, got his legs back. Arrest record – DWIs, drunk-and-disorderlies...*

*That's the quickie version. I may be able to get more, but first I would need to know what you're up to and where you're headed with this. - Angie*

So Miles and I were right about pieces of the bottle being found. Yay, us. Any sense of self-congratulation is dampened by the ominous implications of same.

There's something in the note that's bugging me too: "S2S." Sorry to say? Is that what she meant? Why put that in there? Ah well, screw it, time to dig into our work. Angie's research gives us a good place to start. We divvy up the workload along unspoken lines: Miles will look into the Abelsens, as they seemed to dwell in his socio-economic stratum. I will look into Edgar Goslin because, well, he's a Wentworth bottom-dweller.

Miles decides to work upstairs, where he says the Wi-Fi is better, so for the next hour or so, we split up and put Google through the wringer. At around three, we reconvene in the study to review our notes together. I turn on my VoxFox app to record our conversation.

Miles says he has learned that Gary Abelsen, Paul's father, was a bit of a crusader, at least in the year or two after the accident. At first he praised the police and asked the public to come forward with information. Later he ranted in op-ed pieces about how his family had been forsaken by the cops. A surprising new detail Miles has uncovered is that Paul and Laurice Abelsen had a second child who was not in the car with them that night—a boy named Theo, three years old at the time, who was later adopted by his maternal grandparents. My heart lightens a bit upon hearing this; I don't know why.

As for my research: Edgar Goslin, yeah, apparent douchebag. Wife/girlfriend had a restraining order on him at the time of the accident. Accusations of battery. Arrests for drunk and disorderly, both before and after the accident. A "friend" set up a charity fund in his name to collect donations to help with his medical expenses, but something fishy happened; the person was hiring hookers with the funds, something like that. Friends in low places.

"Interesting," I say, after we finish sharing notes. "Both of these guys—Abelsen's father and Goslin—might have major axes to grind about the accident, even all these years later."

"True. Abelsen lost his son, granddaughter, and daughter-in-law all at once." Again, a wave of guilt washes over me like hot oil. Miles is right about one thing: when this storm is over, this crime is going to have to be owned. "You never get over something like that."

"Another thing about Abelsen," I add. "He has money. Those guys who came to my house were pros, not local juvies. They were working for somebody, or so they said. It can't be cheap to hire hit men."

"Goslin, for his part, suffered long-term injuries in the accident,"

Miles says. "He seems like the type who might bear a longstanding grudge. Pissed-off dude."

"Right. But a guy like him would want to do the revenge stuff himself, don't you think? My guess is he wouldn't hire professionals, even if he could afford to."

"You're assuming those guys really *were* hired."

"What do you mean?"

"They might have been lying about that. Maybe one of them was Goslin himself."

I hadn't thought of that.

"Possible," I grant. "Whoever it was knew all about me, that's for sure. Including the fact that I was connected to that god-forsaken bottle I wish I'd never laid eyes on."

"Right," says Miles, scratching his cheek stubble abstractedly. "How did Goslin—if it *was* him—link the bottle to you if the cops couldn't? And why wait eighteen years to act?"

"Back to that question again."

Miles leans back in his nine-hundred-dollar Herman Miller office chair, laces his hands behind his head, and stares at the ceiling (no cobwebs in *this* house).

At last he sets his chair back down, stares at his phone and says, "I didn't want to go this route, but..." He scrolls through his contacts list and punches a number. "Hi, Jim. Hey, I want to thank you again for your help, and, listen, I hate to do this, but I need to ask one more favor."

# Chapter 17

Miles wraps up his call and turns to me. "Jim says he prefers the kind of thank-you that comes in a bottle. He and his wife like the Louis Jadot Pinot Noir they carry at the marina."

"My treat," I say. "So...?"

"He says if the accident took place on an interstate highway—which it did—the Mass state police had jurisdiction. He knows some people within that bureau, so he might be able to find out some things. Might take him a while, though."

"That's awesome, Miles. Meanwhile, I guess we keep looking into the scotch bottle ourselves, see what we can learn?" Miles shrugs agreement. "If someone knows it was me who bought that booze, they must have talked to the merchant who sold it to me."

I'm googling liquor stores in the Wentworth/Bridgefield area and jotting down phone numbers when I hear the kitchen door jingle and Beth shout, "Wipe your feet!" at the kids.

"I wasn't expecting them back so soon," Miles says, then calls out, "Finn and I are in here, hon." Warning her I'm in the house. Subtle, bro.

Beth pops her head into the study, greets me with a way big smile, and says to Miles, in a faux-casual tone, "I didn't know you guys were hanging here today." (Read: I thought you'd agreed to keep him safely off the premises, *Honey*.)

Miles explains the Internet situation to her and asks how her party was.

"Pretty small. No one's on the island this weekend. Even the

Gustafsons didn't show. Tons of food, though." She shoots Miles a freighted look and says, "Can I steal you for a sec?"

I can see she's trying to wangle some privacy—a regular Edgar Cayce I am—so I tell Miles I'm going to take a walk and pick up that wine for Jim.

I step out the door and strike off through the storm toward the new marina complex. When I get there, I suppress my gag reflex and enter North Atlantic Charcutiers. It's a pretty nice fucking store, hate to admit. Hell of a lot better wine selection than the Mercantile—and they actually *dust* their bottles. Dandy-looking desserts and pheasant sausages too. I buy half a case of the Louis Jadot pinot for Jim.

I arrive back at the house ten minutes later to find Miles bouncing off the walls. He's cleaning the study as if the Dalai Lama, the Pope, and Oprah are about to drop in for a visit.

"What's up?" I ask him. "You seem a little..."

"Nothing, I just have to deal with some stuff right now."

Right. Message received. We can't continue our work anyway, what with Beth and the kids home, so I leave the wine for Jim, grab my phone, and tell Miles and Beth I'll see them later. They're heartbroken over my departure, I'm sure.

• • • • •

The moment I enter my room at Harbor House, I can tell something's off. The space doesn't feel as empty as it should. I sense the dense proximity of other humans. I freeze in place for a moment and hear the creak of a floorboard. I bend to take a darting glance under the bed. Nope, no one there. But I know I'm not imagining this—someone is nearby or has *just* departed the room, and the floor is resettling in their absence.

I hear another creak. It has a weightiness to it; the sound of a body, a present body, shifting its position. I realize it's originating from the "unoccupied" room next to mine. I grab the drinking glass from its doily on the dresser-top and put it up to the thin wooden wall. Yup, the ol' cup-to-the-wall trick. No technophobe am I.

I hear the muffled tones of a baritone voice. Can't make out the words. A higher voice replies to it, also hushed and muffled. It's the voice of Trooper Dan, I'm sure of it.

Well, *sure* is a strong word. I listen again. Okay no, it's a woman's voice. One thing's for certain, though. There's a clandestine vibe to the chitchat.

I look around my room. For a man who's feeling lethally endangered, I am alarmingly light on weaponry. I notice a two-inch-thick wooden dowel, maybe fifteen inches long, leaning on the inside of the window casing. The sash cord must be broken; the dowel is for propping the window open. Nice touch, JJ. I snag the dowel and, wielding it like a club, step out of my room.

Suddenly the doorknob *two* doors down from mine turns. That room's supposed to be unoccupied too! Out steps Daughter Bean, squinting her eyes like she just woke up from a nap. *Damn*, she is one agreeable-looking individual.

"Oh, hey," she says. "*Thought* I heard something." Her eyes go to the cylindrical piece of wood in my hand. "What are you doing, um, rolling pie crust?"

"Yes," I say without missing a beat, "but I prefer lard to butter. Do you have any?"

"Lard?" she deadpans, slapping her body in a couple of random spots. "Nope, all out. Might have some cream of tartar, though."

I laugh. I like this gal. She's funny and she's got the kind of Emily Blunt vibe that makes my chromosomes do backflips. I'm wishing there was a parallel me who wasn't in fear for his life and wasn't still in love with his ex who could spend this stormy holiday weekend trying to coax young Ms. Bean, of the Beans of Maine, into his private chambers.

"You have neighbors now," she says, referring to herself and her family. "Hope that's okay." She explains that her parents' room had a ceiling leak from the storm, so they asked to be moved. The two rooms next to mine were the only side-by-side ones available.

"Welcome to floor three," I say, "where the elite come to meet. And cheat. And... bleat?"

We chat for a minute, flirting with the edge of flirting, and I learn her name is Leah. I finally pull myself away from her gravity field, saying maybe I'll catch her for a drink later.

Back in my room, I realize, with a slap to the forehead, that the hushed conversation I heard though the wall minutes ago was the sound of a middle-aged couple—Leah's parents—trying to have a little afternoon delight while their adult daughter napped in the next room.

Finn Carroll, ace detective.

Ah well, time to get back to work. I fish out the list of liquor-store phone numbers I jotted down at Miles' house and flop down on the bed to plan a "strategy." Ha.

Both of the booze vendors Miles and I remembered—Bridgefield Package Shop and Academy Liquors—are still in business, according to my earlier Google research. There's also an old standby in Wentworth, the Cordial Shoppe, that's been around forever and claims to have "the region's best selection of single malt scotches." I'd forgotten that one. So, what should I say when I call these places? I doubt any of them have sales records going back to 1999, or that they'd share them with me even if they did, or that their records would tell me anything anyway. I doubt I'll find any employees who were around back then, either.

My best tack might be to try talk to the storeowners themselves, find out if they owned their store back in 1999, and if so, ask them whether they remember anyone, police or otherwise, questioning them about a bottle of Glenmalloch. That might stick out in someone's mind, even twenty years later.

The task would be a lot easier if I could remember where I bought that damn bottle. The memory should be a clear one, but it isn't. True, it was eighteen years ago, but still, it's not every day you drop a C-note on a bottle of booze. I'm still drawing a blank, though.

I go to grab my phone, and that's when the odor hits me. That low-tide smell of rotting sea life. It's a common perfume on the island, one you become nose-blind to after a while. That's probably why I didn't notice it sooner. I sniff around the room. The windows are closed; maybe it's drifting up from the kitchen on the first floor. (If so, remind me not to order the Catch of the Day.) No, it definitely seems to have a nearer, and rawer, source.

I tear open the dresser drawers. Empty. I grab my backpack and unbuckle its flap.

"Yaagh!" I cry, dropping the bag to the floor.

There's a dead fish in my pack. Two-pound cod, I estimate. About twenty-four unrefrigerated hours old. Damn. Someone *has* been in my room. I wheel about, my pulse racing, fully expecting to be jumped. But no one is here.

A quirky thing about Harbor House: the room locks are the original, nineteenth century, skeleton-key type. Room keys are essentially ornamental, interchangeable with one another. Musqasset is an honor-system place, through and through.

I bend down and pull the fish out of my pack by its tail. A nail has been pushed through its head, eye to eye. There's a note wrapped around the fish, written in Sharpie on brown paper. My heart does a drum solo as I read it: "Your next asshole."

I assume the piscine gift is not meant to be a replacement anus for me, so I'm guessing what the author *intended* to write was, "*You're* next—comma—Asshole with a capital A." The clumsy punctuation irks me. Trooper Dan seemed to be, if nothing else, a verbally sophisticated fellow. This doesn't feel right coming from him and his troop. Also, there seems to be no practical value in sending me threats like this; they just serve to make me more pissed off, more vigilant, more likely to seek help. Clearly the sender is more invested in making me squirm than in playing his cards skillfully. Which, again, points to a vengeance motive. Something personal.

Trooper Dan and company, on the other hand, were clinical and detached in their approach. But maybe *that* was all an act. And what's the alternative theory? That *two separate* groups of psychos have followed me from Wentworth, Mass, to Musqasset Island, Maine, in the middle of a nor'easter? Right.

I'm feeling confused and off-balance. Which is probably my stalkers' intention.

I wander down the hall and knock on my new friend Leah's door. She opens it and laughs when she sees the fish I'm carrying by the tail.

"So we've established it's *seafood* pie you're making," she says, then notes the lack of jocularity in my aura. "Hey, what's up?"

"Don't mean to be nosy, but have you guys been in these rooms long?"

"Hour and a half, two hours, I guess. Why?"

"Did you hear anyone go into my room before you talked to me?"

"Just one person, like, ten minutes ago, but that was probably you."

It was. Shit. I go downstairs, still carrying the cod by the tail, and ask JJ, the manager, if he's seen anyone unfamiliar in the building. He replies, "No. Why? Something fishy going on?" Everyone's got an HBO special.

I deposit the fish in the compost bin behind Harbor House, then come back around to the front porch and plant myself on a rocking chair. Sitting out there in open view, I feel as if I have a sniper's laser dot on my forehead. What's my play here? It seems like every move I make is being watched.

Again, the message my stalkers seem to be sending me is: we can take you whenever we want, Sunny Jim, but we will do so at the time and place of our choosing. In other words, Finnian Carroll, you are powerless in this thing.

I refuse to accept that. Though the dead cod has me duly alarmed, I am still feeling more energized than I have in years, and nowhere near ready to roll over. I conclude, once again, that if I possess even the tiniest seed of an advantage in this game, it resides in my ability to figure out who wants me dead and why. That knowledge *might* turn the tables in my favor.

It remains a fish-scale-thin hope, but it's the only one I have. Fuck these guys.

I return to my room with fresh resolve—I know I'm not safe here, but at least I'll hear an attacker approaching, thanks to the inn's astonishingly loud wood floors. As I grab my phone to start calling those liquor stores, I notice my battery level is oddly low. Then I realize why: that damn VoxFox app is still running from when I was at Miles' house. I forgot to shut it off.

Hello. That means I left the recorder running when I went to buy the wine for Jim. Intrigued, I stop the recording and press Play. My earlier conversation with Miles plays back through the tiny speaker. I move the slider bar ahead until I locate the spot where Beth entered the scene and I excused myself to go buy the wine.

I let the sound file play.

No sooner do I hear the recorded sound of the kitchen door jingling from my own exit than the recorded voice of Beth says to Miles, *"So what have you two been up to here?"*

# Chapter 18

There's an audio version of a voyeur, did you know that? It's called an ecouterist. That's someone who likes to *listen* to other people's intimate encounters. I feel every inch the ecouterist as I eavesdrop electronically on Miles' and Beth's private conversation. But the face-burning shame I feel is not quite enough to make me tap Stop.

What must have happened when I left to buy the wine was that Beth joined Miles in the study and sat down right at the desk where I left my phone. It's obvious neither of them was aware my phone was capturing their words in crisp digital clarity.

*"I thought we had agreed it would be best to keep him away from the house,"* says the digitized voice of Beth, *"now that we know what state he's in."*

*"We invited him out to the island, Beth,"* says Miles' voice. *"To our home. It was your idea. We can't just abandon him. We have some responsibility here."*

Beth's idea? Didn't see that one coming.

*"I only suggested it,"* says Beth, *"because I thought it was an olive branch you could offer. You didn't tell me he had just broken out of a psych hospital. I had to learn that from Jim."*

*"He didn't 'break out.' He discharged himself. If the staff had thought he was a danger, they would have kept him under lock and key."*

*"But you do agree he's out of his freaking mind? Right? Jim certainly thinks so. Wandering around the island with a knife in the middle of the night."*

"I agree he's having some mental issues."

"So why are you encouraging him?"

"I'm not. I was just trying to help him figure out if there might be some... external triggers for his fears. Some real-world stuff that's been playing into his delusions."

"He's crazy. You can't fix crazy."

"But that doesn't mean there's no basis whatsoever for his – "

"Crazy, Miles."

"As a screen door on a submarine. No argument from me."

"And you think it's safe for him to be around the kids?"

"No. I don't. That's why I waited till you and the kids were gone. I thought you'd be at the club all afternoon. Finn understands the situation here. Notice how he made himself scarce the minute you guys showed up. He needs a friend right now, Beth."

"He needs a syringe. Loaded with Haldol."

This from a woman who just yesterday at dinner was explaining to me, with a perfectly straight face, how the words we say and think "with focused intention" can alter the nature of physical reality itself, thanks to *The Power of Words*. And yet *I'm* the crazy one. Okay.

"So what exactly have you been doing for him 'as a friend'?" Beth inquires.

"Just talking, you know, processing, helping him sort out a few things."

The recorded voices pause as I hear papers being shuffled around. The printout of Angie's write-up. Our research notes. Shit. There's a long pause as Beth, presumably, reads some of the notes. "Jesus, Miles, what *is* this stuff? What the hell have you guys been doing?" I'm surprised by the heat of her concern. "What the hell is *this* stuff?!"

"Just, like I said, some online research I was helping him with. He can't get any Internet over at Harbor House, so I – "

"But what's all this junk about some old car accident?"

"I don't know. He thinks he might have played some role in it. He thinks some people might be after him because of that."

"And you're *helping* him *with* this idea? Seriously, Miles? Is that wise? The man is having paranoid delusions. And you're feeding into them? Helping him cook up some ancient... what? Conspiracy theory? Revenge plot?"

"For the record, I don't believe he's *actually being followed*. I think it's his own guilt that's chasing him. Guilt he's been carrying around for years. Over something he thinks he did. And now some... circumstance has reawakened it. And he's feeling extremely vulnerable. Anyway, I thought if we could put to rest whatever was triggering his fears – "

"Oh really, Dr. Jung? And you've had this treatment plan approved by the American Psychiatric Association?"

"He's not my patient, Beth, he's my friend."

"Well, sometimes I wish you would choose better friends."

"Meaning what?"

Three-second pause.

"I talked to Mom today."

"And...?"

"They're coming to the island."

"Who? Your parents? When?"

"Sunday or Monday. As soon as weather permits, she said."

"Jesus. Why?"

"Why do you think? They want to see the kids. And us. For the holiday. Daddy has some work stuff he wants to go over with you too. As usual."

"Jesus. I come out to the island to get away from all that."

"Well, I couldn't just say no. So they're coming. Deal with it. I think it's important right now – don't you? – that we make a good impression on them. The *right* impression."

Both Beth and Miles, going back to their college days, have always been anxious about the image they cultivate for their parents. I remember when Miles' parents would be coming to campus, he'd spend two days cleaning, as if preparing for a papal visit. He and Beth are the same way as a married couple. They worry a lot about what their parents think, especially Beth's.

My parents, conversely, were happy with me if I didn't torture dogs.

"Which means you can't be doing any *of* this *stuff,*" continues Beth. I hear the papers being rustled. "No Finn and his freakish delusions, for God's sake. No Finn sitting around here talking banana salad. No... Finn."

"Your folks have met Finn before. At our graduation, at Dylan's – "

*"Yes! Which is exactly why he can't be around! At all. They don't get the Finn thing, Miles. They never have. Especially Daddy. Why don't we invite the Shapiros over on Labor Day? They're on the island now. And maybe the Pillsburys. They'll create the right...* ambience."

*"Whatever, Beth. Whatever you decide. But... despite what you've always insisted on believing, Finn is not the devil. Daft as fuck, maybe, but not the devil."*

"Ditch him. Okay?"

With that, she leaves the room. I fast-forward through the rest of the recording. There's nothing more.

Wow. Daft as fuck. Ditch him. Super.

At least I know where I stand with the Sutcliffes. I also know why Miles was so agitated when I came back from wine-shopping. Beth's dad is coming. Simon Fischer. Miles doesn't like to talk to me about the guy because I always razz him for being Fischer's lapdog.

A blanket of sadness settles over me. I had thought perhaps Miles had changed his mind about me and believed I was on to something real. Turns out he's only been humoring me; he still thinks I'm nuts. I'd better be mighty careful about what I say to him from now on and how I interact with him and Beth.

I try to dig into my liquor store inquiry, but my heart and mind are no longer in it. My progress is further hampered by the fact that it's the Friday afternoon before Labor Day. People are just getting out of work for the long weekend, and the liquor stores are hopping. Employees have no time for nosy phone conversations about ancient history.

• • • • •

I stand on Fishermen's Court in the whipping wind and rain, steeling myself to knock on Jeannie's door. I'm holding a bottle of wine and a pizza box wrapped in a plastic bag, and feeling dreadfully self-conscious. I don't want her to think I see this as a date.

Even though I kinda do, a little bit.

I'm also a tad embarrassed by the wine. She texted me to go ahead and bring some, insisting she hates it when people think they have to abstain around her. So I cheerfully obliged, but now I'm feeling selfish about that choice.

I suck it up and knock.

Jeannie answers the door, wearing an apron. I notice it's covering a burgundy-red top that permits a glimpse of cleavage. I must be mindful to do no more than glimpse. Which is going to be a monumental challenge. Did I mention Jeannie is the most beautiful woman on Earth? At least to my eyes. Her beauty comes perilously close to proving the existence of God.

Like garlic.

Allow me to explain. Just as it's impossible for me to conceive of the existence of the garlic plant without the simultaneous existence of human taste buds, so perfectly designed to exalt its flavor, it is impossible for me to conceive of the existence of Jeannie's face without my eyes, so perfectly designed to exalt her beauty. Chaos theory withers with one look into her face, and cosmic purpose reigns.

So, yeah, what could possibly go wrong tonight?

Jeannie takes a sweeping look up and down the street and backs away from the door.

"That pizza better not be soggy," she says, her eyes sparkling like a distant galaxy.

Oy.

• • • • •

We already covered the life basics at Pete's, so we have to dig a little more deeply to come up with our evening's warm-up banter. We talk about our mutual friends on the island—who's still here, who moved, who's boinking whom. The conversation flow isn't exactly effortless, as it once was, but it carries us through dinner. I, of course, want to know more about her daughter, and, of course, that's an easy subject for her. She asks me about my work as a computer artist, a good way to get me bloviating. She also asks me about my sister Angie; the two of them became friends through me but haven't talked much since Jeannie and I split up.

Jeannie has made a nice salad to go with the pizza and baked something deliciously gooey-looking for dessert. I'm impressed. She could not boil eggs when I lived with her. There's something off about her mood, though. She seems stressed, distracted. And I don't believe it's because she's uncomfortable with me. A couple of times I think I catch her glancing out the window watchfully. I *am* daft as fuck, though, as you will recall.

After dinner, she says, "Why don't you get a fire going while I clean up in here a bit?"

Tasks completed, we settle in with our drinks, I with my wine on the loveseat, she with her tea on the sofa. We face each other in front of the fire. No place left to hide.

"I was a coward to leave the way I did," I say, when the timing feels ripe. "I was hurt, but that's no excuse. We had a lot to talk about. I owed you that."

"You didn't owe me much, Finn. I sucked. I was a shitty mate and a shitty friend. I'm ashamed of how I acted. But yeah, I do wish we could have talked about it."

"Why him?" I say, not accusingly but out of genuine curiosity. She knows exactly what I'm asking. Jeannie, as I mentioned, carried on a handful of discreet dalliances with some rather exotic seafaring men during our time together. She kept these encounters infrequent and segregated from our home life, and she always stayed away from island men. Until Cliff.

Cliff was a native Musqasset fisherman whom I discovered she'd been seeing steadily — and *not* very discreetly — for months. Screwing in our house, to put it bluntly. Cliff was rugged, muscular, macho. Good-looking, yes, but about as bright and contemplative as a bucket of chum. So why pick *him* to change her pattern with men and steer our relationship into the rocks?

"He was the next logical step, I guess," she says. I know what *she* means too, without her needing to explain: I allowed her other indiscretions to go on unchecked until they had poisoned our union, so it was time to up the stakes. Force us to confront the issue, win or lose.

"I get that. A strange choice in men, though."

"Not really, when you think about what was going on at the time. All that Fish Pier business. The infighting, the anger, the suspicion. And quite a bit of it was aimed at me."

"At you? I don't remember it that way."

"People questioned my loyalty. I brought you to the island, after all, and you brought Miles to the island. Miles, the great destroyer of Fish Pier. That's how some people saw it."

"How could anyone lay the Fish Pier thing on *you*?"

"Come on, Finn, you know the rules here. If you weren't born on this island, you'll always be an outsider in some people's minds. I came here fourteen years ago. That's *yesterday* in island time. On the surface, most people here have adopted me, but underneath it all it's not so simple. People weren't sure where I stood — with the fishermen or with the moneymen."

"And so when you slept with Cliff, you were…"

"Declaring my loyalties, I guess."

"Choosing the island. Over me. Over us."

"If it makes you feel any better, it didn't last. Cliff was a drunken asshole. A week after you left, I was already wondering what I ever saw in him."

"But your thing with him got the job done."

Jeannie shrugs and tosses her hands up.

"Is Cliff…?"

"Bree's father? God no."

"You mentioned there was someone else after him."

"Let's not talk about that right now, okay?"

"Sure, sorry."

Jeannie gives me a long, appraising look. "Why didn't you ever say anything, Finn?"

Again, I know what she means without her explaining. Why didn't I confront her about her sexual "detours"?

"I didn't think it was my right. You made it clear, from the start, that you had some 'arrangements' in your life that were your private business, and I wasn't to think I owned you in that way. I thought that was a condition of our relationship."

"At the beginning, maybe. When we were still in 'trial run' mode. At that point, I was keeping my options open, playing it by ear. I had a few good things going for myself and, yeah, I didn't want to give them up for... 'light and transient causes.' But for the most part I was just, you know, testing you."

"Testing me? No, I didn't know. I always assumed if I forced the issue into the open and made you choose, you would have chosen your... 'independence' over me."

"Oh, Finn, you frigging idiot." She gets up and tops off her teacup, flicks her eyes warily out the window again, then returns to her seat. "*I* always assumed that because *you* didn't say anything, you were basically okay with the situation. I figured you *wanted* a relationship that was more 'roommates with benefits' than couple. I thought it gave you an easy out."

"God no. Fuck no. I didn't want that."

"Then why didn't you fight for what you did want? Why didn't you fight for *me*?"

The trillion-dollar question.

## Chapter 19

"Do you remember the day we first talked?" Jeannie says.

"Back in college?"

"We were in that Historical Perspectives on Abnormal Psych course. You were staring out the window and the professor, that McCluskey byotch, tried to trap you with a question. You not only had a hilarious answer but you ripped her a new *brain stem*. I remember thinking, 'Who *is* this guy?' I went up to you after class and invited you to a party that weekend."

"At some dot-com clown's house in Ipswich."

"Right. You showed up, and I was flirting with you. Everything was going great, and do you remember what happened next?"

"I'm sure you're going to exhume those blissfully buried memories."

"*Miles* came along and started flirting with me, and then I turned around and you were gone. You'd left. Without saying a word. Sound familiar?"

"I already knew, when it came to women, never to compete with Miles. Miles always got the girl. Always."

"But I wasn't 'the girl,' I was me. And I wasn't interested in Miles, I was interested in you, thicko. *I* had to pursue *you* for the next three weeks, which was not something I was used to, believe me. Then, when we graduated, you just let me go. To Quebec. I would have changed my plans if you'd asked me to, but you didn't ask."

Her words, if true, are breaking news to me. "I never for a moment thought I had a serious chance with you, Jeannie. I mean, you were this wild, brilliant, tough, gorgeous rebel-goddess who every guy at Godwin wanted to go to bed with, and I figured I was just a case of..."

"What? Romantic slumming?"

"Well, yeah." To me, this is a fact as obvious as barn-red acrylic paint.

"I ought to slap you in the face for that."

"Jeannie. Reality is reality. You've always been out of my league. You are literally *the* most beautiful woman I have ever laid eyes on. You know that, right? Not to mention the smartest, the funniest, the bravest, the most talented..."

Jeannie's eyes suddenly well with tears. "Oh, Finn," she says. "That's your whole problem right there. You don't believe you deserve good things, so you don't *claim* what's yours. ...And I don't think you ever will."

She gets up and starts moving dishes that don't need moving.

I take the cue. I stand and prepare to say my goodnights and goodbyes. But she surprises me by grabbing the bottle of wine and marching into the living room with it. She pours me another glass, looks me in the eye, places her hand on my chest, and pushes me back down onto the loveseat. It is a gesture she used to employ when she was fixing to have her sexual way with me, and it thrilled me to no end, but this time I know her intent is not amorous.

Instead, she flops down beside me on the loveseat and takes my hand. Again, this is not a romantic gesture but rather one that says *I require nothing less of you than consummate honesty.*

"You're going to tell me why you're here on Musqasset," she says.

• • • • •

I spill the beans. I tell her everything that went down in my house the night the bad men showed up. I tell her about my stay in the hospital and the "suicide" note. I realize that in order for her to appreciate the significance of these things, I must place them in their proper context. So I also explain my previous *real* suicide attempt (halfhearted though it might have been), my years of hiding out at my mother's house, my precarious mental state prior to the incident, and the fly-below-the-radar lifestyle I have adopted for the last four years. I do this even though I know it will destroy whatever vestiges of respect, if any, she still harbors for me.

Worst of all, I tell her about that doomed night after our college graduation party.

She takes it all in, betraying no judgment, seemingly accepting every detail. Except one. When I'm done telling the whole story, she gathers her brow and bites her lip.

"So *Miles* threw the bottle?" she says.

"Yeah."

She faces forward on the loveseat, arms folded in contemplation.

"Why?" I ask. She doesn't respond. "Jeannie? Why do you ask?"

"Can we stop there for tonight, Finn? That's a lot for one evening. I think I need to sleep. On all of this. Is that okay?"

"Sure," I reply. Her reaction to that one detail of my story puzzles me, but I'm keen to make my getaway. Now that I've stripped myself naked before her, I don't want to be in her presence any longer. I don't want to see the diminished regard in her eyes.

I am eager to find a horizontal surface and go unconscious for as long as my brain will stay on power-down. It's nearly eleven anyway. The electricity will be shutting off on the island any minute. The unwritten code of lovers on the island is that if you don't leave by lights-out, you're staying the night. The minutes before eleven can be an awkward time.

I stand and say goodbye. Jeannie takes my face in her hands and shakes her head, then collapses against me in a tired hug. I bury my face in her hair, inhaling its exotic mix of fragrances—even though I don't feel entitled to—then silently pluck my rain jacket from a chair and schlep to the door.

At the precise moment I step outside, the island plunges into blackness. I hear Jeannie follow me out.

"Are you going to be safe tonight?" she whispers.

"Probably not." Why start lying at this point in the proceedings?

"Then stay here," she says. "Sleep on the couch."

I grunt my refusal. The last place on Musqasset I would sleep tonight is Jeannie's house. Not because I don't want to but because I've put her in far too much danger already.

"You be careful, then," she says. "You be very fucking careful, Finn Carroll."

I realize I forgot to bring a flashlight along, a major blunder on Musqasset. I meant to buy one today. Shit. Jeannie doesn't offer one, and I don't ask. I start off down the road in the enveloping darkness. I hear Jeannie patter a few steps after me.

She aims her voice at the night sky, and I'm honestly not sure whether she's addressing God or me. "I'd have done anything you wanted. I was just waiting for you to ask."

I want to say, "Is it too late now?" but the words stick in my throat.

I hear her door close quietly. Musqasset darkness swallows both of us.

• • • • •

The walk from Jeannie's to Harbor House takes maybe eight minutes in broad daylight, but the going will be a tad slower in the black island night. Luckily, the route is by open dirt road—no winding forest trails this time—and the rain has let up.

I've gone no farther than two kicks of a can when I hear the sound of heels crunching in the muddy gravel behind me. Three or four pairs of feet. Moving as a coordinated unit. About ten or twelve yards behind me. This time there's no attempt to be stealthy. My followers *want* me to hear them. Clearly they've been waiting for me outside Jeannie's.

Shit. I should have been expecting this.

I stop. The footsteps stop.

I walk forward again. The footsteps walk forward.

I stop. The footsteps stop.

So that's the game we're playing? It's such a primitive scare tactic, it would almost be laughable... if it weren't so damned effective. Few fears are more deeply embedded in human DNA than that of being followed in the dark by an unseen enemy.

"Fuck off, gentlemen," I say, trying to sound nonchalant. No response.

I can't imagine they would really try to assault me, or worse, right here on this open road, in one of the most populated parts of the island. Even in the pitch dark. If I screamed for help, a dozen people would come running with flashlights. But still.

I walk again. The footsteps follow again.

I stop. *They* stop.

I take a stutter step just to catch the men off guard. One of them stumbles as he tries to stop on a dime. Ha. If they're going to screw with me, I'm going to screw with them. I peel off at a sprint. Their flashlights turn on and light my back as the men take up pursuit. The instant I turn my head to look behind me, their lights go off again.

I slide to a stop in the dirt. My pursuers stop. They wait patiently in the dark, thirty feet behind me.

I stand there silently for a full minute. Two minutes.

I crouch in the roadway, wait some more.

I've got all night, lads.

If I just camp here indefinitely, I wonder how long they'll remain at a distance. At some point, will they get bored and make their move? What if I remain here till sunrise?

I'm feeling an urge to taunt them, to draw them into action and get this over with—whatever *this* is going to be—but my unarmed state makes that a foolish option. Why have I stepped out without a weapon?

I try to put on my gamer hat again. If I were a game character, how would I gain some advantage in this situation? I almost laugh out loud as I remember an actual puzzle from a game I worked on a couple of years ago. I pat the dirt road around me and lay my hand on a nice, egg-sized stone the rain has laid bare. I stand, take my shoes off, and remove my socks. I insert one sock into the other to form a double layer, then drop the rock inside, creating a homemade blackjack. I slide my bare, gritty feet back into my shoes and swing my new weapon around.

Damn—this thing could do some serious damage. It's got a nice reach too.

I suddenly don't feel quite so vulnerable. I'm guessing my pursuers have weapons of their own, but even so, if they try to come near me, they're going to have regrets.

"Do you have your lopper with you tonight?" I call out to them. "Why don't you bring it over here? I've got something for you too."

No response. No movement.

"Or do you only attack people who are drugged and strapped into chairs?"

Again, nothing.

I turn to start walking, and my foot slips on some more wet rocks. I've stumbled upon a cache of excellent throwing stones, loosened by the erosion of the rain. I gather six or eight of them and stuff them into my pockets, then collect a couple more to hold in my hands. If these guys continue to follow me, I'm going to start pelting them with rocks. I can sense their general location well enough that, even in the dark, I'm confident I can score some hits.

I start walking. *They* start walking.

I stop and turn. They stop too. I'm about to hurl a rock in their direction when I freeze my arm. I realize they haven't technically threatened or assaulted me yet. If I injure one of them, *I* might be guilty of criminal assault. I probably owe them a warning at least.

"Listen to me," I announce. "If you follow me one more step, I will consider that a threat. And I will defend myself. With rocks. I have a good throwing arm and you *will* get hurt. If you try to come near me, I've got a weapon I will use with force. Consider yourself warned."

I turn back toward the road ahead and start walking again. I am gratified to note the men don't immediately follow. I've at least put a hiccup in their confidence. They seem to be conferring amongst themselves back there. Fine, confer away. Assholes.

I hear them start walking again, but farther back now. They're keeping a greater distance. Good. Still, I warned them not to follow at all. I stop, turn toward them, draw my arm back like a fastball pitcher's, and throw a rock as hard as I can. I hear it go skittering and clacking down the dirt road. I'd better be careful not to bust someone's window.

No reaction from my pals.

I load another rock into my right hand, an angular one, and go into my windup. This time I hear the rock whistle through the air and strike one of their rain-jacketed bodies with a solid *thwhack*.

"Ahh! Fuck!" cries a voice. Good.

All at once, three flashlights turn on and the men start chasing me at a gallop. I run. They're keeping their lamps trained fully on me now. This lights the road for them, enabling them to run full-throttle. But it also lights the road for me, allowing me to keep pace ahead of them. I can't stop and throw another rock, though; that would allow them to close the gap between us. I keep running.

The men chase me till we're about twenty-five yards from the village, and then, as if on cue, they shut off their lights and melt silently into the night. Like they never existed.

• • • • •

The upstairs rear hallway of Harbor House is dimly lit by a rechargeable night-light. As I pass the room where Mr. and Mrs. Bean — I probably should learn their real names at some point — are staying, I see a faint glow highlighting the crack under the door. A laptop or a Kindle in use. For some reason, I take comfort in this. I don't want to be alone tonight.

I grip my homemade blackjack tightly as I unlock my door with my pointless skeleton key. The room is black. Reflexively, I flip the wall switch, even though I know there won't be electricity till morning. I have never felt more fear of a dark room. I know I left my stalkers behind outdoors, but still I feel an absolute certainty that someone is hiding under the bed or behind the door.

My phone is on the dresser, where I left it charging. That is, it *should* be there.

I cross the room in two quick bounds, grope for the phone on the dresser, and find it. I quickly locate the flashlight app. It lights the small room like a crypt in a ghost-hunting show.

No one behind the door. No one under the bed. No one under the work table.

No dead fish anywhere, at least that I can see — or smell.

I jam a wooden chair under the doorknob and allow myself to relax a bit. I take off my jacket and shoes and flop on the bed with my phone. There's a text message from Jeannie: *Be safe.* A well-intentioned, if utterly non-actionable, sentiment. There's an earlier text from Miles too: *Talked to Jim. We were right. Call me!* Right about what? Intriguing, but too late to call.

I see there's also a voicemail from Angie. It arrived just a few minutes ago. This one fills me with unaccountable dread. I touch the "play" arrow.

"Finn? It's me," says recorded Angie. She's drunk. Kind of like saying Yao Ming is tall. "You have to talk to me. I don't understand what's going on. Why is everybody calling me? Why is everybody suddenly so interested in ancient history? I'm confused. I'm scared. What's going on? Call me." She mumbles something I can't decipher, then says, "You're a good person, Finn. Don't let anyone tell you different. You're a good person. Call me."

Ange, over and out.

Hmm, strange. Who does she mean by "everybody"? Has she talked to someone besides me? About the accident? About something else from the past? I wonder who and what. And why would she say she's *scared*? Maybe about my mental health — is she still flogging that mule?

I punch Angie's number. Might as well get this over with; I know she's still up. Sodden as a mezcal worm but up. The call rings through and she picks up, but then the line goes dead. A moment later, I see a return call come through from her. I push Answer, but again the line goes dead. I try calling her again. Same thing.

The Musqasset phone gods are not going to cooperate tonight. Oh well, I tried. I'm about to fall asleep right there with my clothes on when I hear the phone *bloop* the arrival of a text-message.

I look at the screen.

A single character. An emoji. Of a dead fish.

Before I can identify who the sender is, the message disappears from the screen. Poof.

My brain can't handle any more. I shut down.

# Chapter 20

*I dream I'm on the ferry to Musqasset. I've just sold my parents' house, and the new owners are scheduled to move in later today. I suddenly remember that, gosh darn it all, I have left several dead bodies in the basement. I buried them years ago and forgot all about them. I need to get back to the house NOW and move the corpses before the new owners show up. I jump into the water and follow a slimy, miles-long rope that leads back to the dock.*

*From there I embark on an epic journey to the sold house. I encounter endless obstacles and detours on the way and make numerous attempts to call the new owners to dissuade them from showing up as planned. But I can never get a call through.*

*At some point in my frantic journey, it dawns on me the bodies aren't even buried; I've left them lying right out in the open. If the new owners take one look in the basement, they will see them. I recall I've left some wrecked cars down there too. The license plates will clearly identify who the dead people are.*

Dreams are so mysterious. Dagnabbit, if only I could unravel the arcane symbolism behind this one.

*As I finally near my house, I see the neighborhood has been cordoned off with police tape. Dozens of police cruisers, with blue lights flashing, are parked on my street...*

I wake up, fully alert, heart jackhammering.

I realize it isn't the dream itself that has awoken me, or even an external stimulus, but rather my own pressured thoughts. Yes, I have awoken myself from an anxiety dream with an *even more* anxious waking thought. My brain is telling me there's something critically important I need to remember from earlier in the evening.

I strip off my jeans and shirt as I try to think. What could it be?

It has something to do with an encounter that occurred in the village.

The encounter itself was seemingly insignificant. I stopped at the Mercantile on my way to Jeannie's—before grabbing the pizza at The Barnacle—to buy the bottle of wine. As I approached the store, I noticed a trio of young men sitting on the covered porch of the closed gift shop next door, trying to stay dry.

"Excuse me, sir, can I ask you something?" spoke the tallest of the three from under a hooded rain visor. "My friend T-Bone here is twenty-one," he said, pointing to one of his buddies, who flashed me an insincere grin, all teeth. "Honest to God, but he left his ID on the ferry. Right, T? We wondered if you could possibly grab him a twelve-pack of Coor's Light." He held out a twenty and said, "Keep the change?"

Tempted as I was to risk prosecution for a cool $4.71, I politely declined their business offer and wished them well. And that was that. Finis.

So why is this scene playing insistently in my head, driving me from sleep?

Finally, "Light dawns on Marblehead," as my mother used to say.

Twenty-one!

The reason I can't remember buying that bottle of scotch for Miles all those years ago is that *I didn't buy it. I wasn't twenty-one yet.* I was a year younger than my classmates all through college, thanks to an accelerated academic program I was shoved into in high school. I didn't like to advertise my age difference, but when I graduated college I was still only twenty. Anytime I'd gone into a liquor store during my college years, I'd been with Miles or some other older friend.

I couldn't legally buy booze yet, and I couldn't ask Miles to buy that particular bottle for me, because it was a gift for him. So I asked someone else to buy it for me.

With a shudder, I remember who that someone was.

• • • • •

A knock on the door awakens me from deep sleep. My phone shows five past eight. I must have crashed heavily when I finally fell asleep again.

"Who is it?" I ask, groping for my makeshift blackjack.

"Me." Miles.

I throw on last night's clothes, remove the security chair from beneath the doorknob, and open the door. Miles enters, holding two large coffees from Mary's Lunch and a bakery bag. He sets them on our worktable and sits down as if ready to dig into another day at the office.

"I can't stay long," he explains. "Beth's on the warpath. Her folks are coming for an unplanned visit, as soon as they can get over, and she's freaking out." Right, *she's* freaking out. "I promised I'd help her with the shopping and cooking and housecleaning."

"You and Beth do your own housecleaning?" I gasp, pulling back in silent-film horror.

"Our help's not on the island this weekend," he replies, straight as a nail. Alack, the human tragedy of it all. "So listen," he says, slapping the table, "I talked to Jim."

"And?"

"He talked to the Mass police. He confirmed that the cops did find bottle fragments at the scene. Mostly in Goslin's car; the bottle punched through the windshield as it shattered. There were some fingerprints on a couple of the pieces too, but no matches popped up in the database. But listen: the investigators *were* able to figure out the make of the whiskey by fitting together a few of the label pieces."

"Holy shit," I say. It was exactly what we deduced must have happened, but still it's a shock to hear we were right.

"According to Jim, they tracked down three of those 'special anniversary' decanter bottles of sixteen-year Glenmalloch that had been sold locally. All three bottles, evidently, were bought with credit or debit cards. So they were able to identify all of the buyers."

My blood runs chilly when I hear this.

"Here's what's weird, though," he says. "You weren't one of them."

"Are you sure?" I ask (even though *I'm* sure).

"Yes, because they talked to all three of the buyers. Two of them still had the bottle on their shelves. The third guy said he had finished the booze and put the bottle out in the recycling bin the previous week. It was a few weeks after the accident by that point. The police had no reason not to believe him."

"Who was this person, this third buyer?"

"Jim didn't say. Anyway, after that the bottle angle dried up for the cops. But obviously they didn't know what we know."

"Which is...?"

"That there was at least one other bottle sold. Somewhere. The one *you* bought. I wonder why that one didn't get reported by any store owners."

I know one very good reason: because *I didn't buy it*. But I am not ready to tell Miles that just yet, or to remind him I wasn't twenty-one. My mind is laser-focused on the almost certain identity of that third buyer and why he told the police what he did.

"You still don't remember buying that bottle?" Miles asks.

"No," I say, which is the truth, but not the whole truth. "Was Jim able to find out anything else?"

"He got some dirt on this Goslin character too. The guy's not just a bad actor; he's an ex-con. Did time at Walpole. Runs with some seriously shady people. And apparently he had alcohol in his system the night of the accident, but it was just below the legal limit. He'd also had a run-in with his wife, or live-in girlfriend or whatever, twenty minutes before the accident. So he may have been 'emotionally impaired' if not drunk enough to blow a point-oh-eight.

"They think he was speeding too. And listen to this: the bottle didn't actually hit *him*; it hit the passenger side of the windshield and blew a hole. If he'd been fully alert and in control, he should have been able to pull the car into the breakdown lane. But instead he freaked and started swerving all over the place. And that's when he smashed into the Abelsens."

I see what Miles is doing: trying to paint Goslin as at least partially, if not mostly, responsible for the accident himself. It's a touching gesture, meant to lessen my guilt. Little does he know, I'm not the one who most needs the moral strokes.

"Oh, and something else I hate to tell you," Miles says, "but it seems Goslin's... *junk* was crushed in the accident. When the steering column got pushed in. That wasn't in the papers. I don't know how much repair work the surgeons were able to do, but..."

I feel a wave of queasiness move from my stomach to my groin.

Miles looks at his watch and says, "Shit, I've got to get going." He stands, grabs his coffee, and says, "Text me, call me, keep me in the loop. I'll be in touch later." And with that, Miles blows out as fast as he blew in.

• • • • •

All-righty, then. Thanks, Miles. I'm surprised, considering what I heard in his recorded chat with Beth, that he is still continuing to help me at all. He thinks I'm delusional, so why is he still invested in this thing, or even pretending to be? Maybe Jim's new info has swayed him?

Whatever his motivation, I wish he could have stuck around this morning. Two heads are better than one. When I work with Miles, all this stuff feels real to me. I feel like we're getting somewhere. When I work alone, I feel like a crazy person.

And I've just been given a fresh load of crazy-making information to digest here.

I open my coffee lid and turn on the laptop Miles has lent me. As I wait for it to boot up, I think about Edgar Goslin. Considering what he lost in the accident, and the kind of guy he seems to be, it's hard to imagine he wouldn't have a major axe to grind, even after all these years.

One thing's for sure, Goslin is the best "lead" we've turned up. I need to find out more about him, but I don't know how much more I can learn from the Web, even if the Wi-Fi decides to cooperate.

*Talk to him directly. Yes. Good idea. Call Goslin under some phony pretext. Try to push his buttons in some way, see what he spills.*

To do that, though, I'll need his contact information.

Okay, so that's a place to start. Maybe I'll try one of those "people finder" websites and see what I can turn up. *If* I can get on the Internet. Major if.

I give Safari a whirl on the laptop. Still no Wi-Fi. I try my phone's 3G network. Nothing but a spinning circle.

I lean my chair back, pecking at a donut and staring at the ceiling.

Sitting in my room at Harbor House — alone — is making me feel like a lobster in a trap, just waiting to get pulled up onto someone's boat. The feeling is more than metaphorical. I'm suddenly getting a strong sense of actually being watched.

I stand and pace around the room, trying to shake it off. No luck. Most people think it's bullshit, this idea that you can tell when you're being spied on, but ask anyone in the surveillance trades: the sensation of eyes on you is real and palpable. Science is starting to back this up.

I walk over to the window. I feel framed and exposed, but there's not a soul to be seen in the storm-whipped village below, except an orange-ponchoed Dorna Caskie collecting recycling bags from the shops in her electric cart. So why this under-a-lens feeling?

I return to my chair. That's when I notice it: a brand new white plastic smoke detector on the ceiling.

## Chapter 21

Was the smoke detector there when I checked in? I didn't notice it, but why would I have? Across the ceiling is another detector made of yellowed plastic. Why would there be two detectors in one room? One for heat and one for smoke? Nah.

Smoke detector: easiest place in the world to hide a web cam.

I glance again at the new detector and then casually look away. If there's a camera inside it, I don't want to betray my suspiciousness.

No question about it, I can feel eyes burning my skin, and I am absolutely sure there's a live camera on me. I need to get the hell out of here. Not just for an hour or two. For good. I need to relocate. But I don't want whoever's watching me to know what I'm thinking.

I stretch and yawn, then stand up and look offhandedly at my phone's clock. I react to the time in fake surprise. Pretending I'm late for something, I stuff Miles' laptop into my backpack. Luckily, most of my clothes and other belongings are already in there, so I don't have to look like I'm packing for an overnight. I deliberately leave some of my clothes strewn on the bed and chairs, as if I intend to return here, then throw on my raincoat, feeling in the pocket for my homemade blackjack. Taking pains not to look up at the smoke detector, I exit the room.

Rain is blasting the upstairs hall window in micro-pellets. As of last evening's weather report, that hurricane-like system is still parked out in the Atlantic, and the forecast is for more intermittent wind and rain and continued high seas. A craptastic Saturday-before-Labor-Day, in other words. Oh well, I'm not hosting a Kiwanis club cookout.

I'm tempted to go ask JJ if he recently installed new smoke detectors, but I decide to just get the hell out of Dodge. I exit by the fire escape on the third floor, to avoid the lobby, and slip down an alley behind the island's mini-laundromat (two washers, one dryer, don't ask). The storm is whistling through clapboards; it's worse than it looked from the upstairs window.

I'd already planned on dropping in on a few old friends. That mission has now taken on urgency. I need a place to stay. Not someone's house—I can't ask anyone to take that kind of risk—but maybe a toolshed or a guest cabin that's not being used this washed-out weekend.

Dennis and Billy's place is pretty close by, so I head there first. I still haven't returned Billy's rain suit, but now I need to ask him for a bigger favor—the use of his storage locker as a hideout. I make my way to his door, on the bay side of the building. I have to time my way past the waves, some of which are crashing into the base of the sandwich counter. No crab rolls today.

Dennis answers the door. He's holding a mop and looking frazzled. Water must be getting into the building. "Billy's in the shower right now," he declaims, unsmiling. The cold shoulder he showed me earlier has metastasized into a serious case of frostbite.

I see no light on in the bathroom, so I say, "Looks like he may be finished."

"He hasn't started yet."

"Okay, well, can you tell him I came by and I'll probably drop by again later?"

"He'll probably be in the shower later too."

Dennis doesn't quite *slam* the door, but he shuts it with feeling.

Hoo-ah—my friendship mission is off to a rollicking start. So whom else can I hit up for shelter on this fine late-summer morn? Most of my other island friends live either in the Greyhook neighborhood or out on Studio Row—at least they did last I saw them.

I haven't been to Greyhook yet, so maybe I'll head over there first. As I start off in that direction, the wind is whipping so hard I feel it's going to lift me off my feet. Salt from storm-blown spindrift is mixing with the rain, stinging my eyes.

Greyhook occupies the eastern side of the bay all the way out to Seal Point. As I may have mentioned, Greyhook is where the working folk live—fishermen, dockhands, bartenders, shop clerks, and a number of "village artists."

FYI, there are three basic types of professional artist on the island. First you have the "rock star" artists, who own the large ocean-facing properties at the far end of Studio Row and whose work is represented by top galleries in New York, London, and Paris. Then you have the almost-famous Studio Rowers, who own the studio/galleries on—wait for it—Studio Row. Finally, you have the "village" artists. Like I was. These are painters who sell their work for three figures, occasionally four, in the village shops and coastal tourist galleries. Village artists are tradespeople, nothing more, nothing less. Like lobstermen and boat builders. Most of them do other jobs too, like tending bar and working the boats.

Many of my friends on the island are—or were—village artists. When I lived here, we had a loose club of sorts. We often hung out together, doing *plein air* sessions around the island, then hoisting a few at The Rusty Anchor or Pete's Lagoon at the end of the day. We kept each other sane and motivated.

Enzo was a diehard member of the gang. I decide to head for his place first. I keep my head down so as to cut through the wind and keep the salt out of my eyes.

Enzo is a crusty old socialist and conspiracy theorist who lives in a rundown Greyhook cottage near the point. He taught political science at a New Hampshire college for decades, then retired here to let his freak-flag fly. Enzo is a throwback to the days when liberals were the ones worried about government conspiracies. His paintings are sad, muddy-hued things layered with political symbolism. They don't sell, but Enzo doesn't seem to care. Enzo was one of the earliest adopters of personal computer technology back in the eighties. When he's not painting, you can usually find him at his high-end computer, blogging about secret government agencies and warning people they're being spied on.

Not today, though. When I knock on his peeling, lockless door, only his dog Herbert (Marcuse) comes to check me out.

I poke my head inside, just in case Enzo's on the crapper, and shout, "Come on, Enzo, I'm dying out here." His place boggles the mind. If you looked only at his computer system, which occupies a whole wall, you'd swear you were in the office of a top IT guy for Prudential or the CIA. The rest of the house looks as if it's inhabited by a caveman.

If anyone on the island has Internet access during a storm, though, it's Enzo. But I can't use his equipment if he's not home. Can't ask him about a place to stay either.

Maybe later.

The tiny house next door is the polar opposite of Enzo's. Meticulously painted in three tones and rimmed with lush window boxes, it is home to another village artist, Miranda. She's only fortyish, but she dresses like an old hippie and listens to Incredible String Band music from the sixties. She's a good soul, though.

"Finny!" she shrieks, standing in her doorway and opening her arms for a hug. She invites me in for tea, which I gratefully accept. Miranda tells me that in the years since I left, the island has taken on bad juju. There is infighting, ill will, negative energy, she says. Something about the *way* she's saying it, though, with her hand clamped on my wrist, feels more like a warning than an idle observation. "All I can do is paint about it and hope my paintings heal," she says. Ah Miranda, God bless her. I decide not to gum up her chakras with my housing woes.

Maybe the Bourbon triplets can help me: Matt, Zack, and Mike. They own a party fishing boat they take turns captaining and one of the island's few apartment buildings, a four-unit affair. They're all painters too. They learned to paint because art is a sellable commodity on Musqasset. If they'd been born in Brooklyn they'd have learned to make pickles. But oddly (or maybe not), they're among the best artists on the island.

I knock on Matt's door, and he answers. His expression is more puzzlement than hostility. He looks around to see if anyone is watching. "Hey, Finn, kind of surprised to see you here."

"Kind of surprised to *be* here," I half-shout over the wind.

He lobs me a couple of polite catch-up questions from behind his screen door, but there's no "Come on in and dry off" or "Let me show you my latest work." Pulling teeth to keep the conversation going, I learn that his brother Zack got married last year and moved to the mainland, and that Mike had a gallery showing in Boston. Matt's not expending one syllable more than required. Okay, fine. I was planning to ask him if any of his apartments were unoccupied, but clearly that would be unwise.

I next make my way through the eye-stinging rain to Pop's, the world's most inconvenient convenience store (opens at 8:30, closes at 5:30). Pop's sells dairy products with adventurous expiration dates and a random assortment of overpriced canned and dried goods. But I have no need for cocktail wieners or Indian pudding this fine morning; it's the house *behind* Pop's I'm interested in—a small saltbox where the Harpers, Gerry and Ginny, live. They're a lobstering couple who also paint in oils and make sea-crafts from found objects. When Jeannie and I lived together, Gerry and Ginny were our best "couple" friends. Gerry is one of the funniest humans on the planet, and Ginny is the sweetest genius you'll ever meet. And man, can they cook. I probably should have tried them first—they'll know a place I can stay, for sure.

As I'm tromping toward their house, the phone rings inside. Through the wavy old window glass, I hear the muted sound of Ginny answering, and I know, without question, the call is about me.

I knock on the door, but no one answers. I knock again, harder. Nope. They've been warned off. Tears rush to my eyes, ambushing me. I flick them away and watch them mingle with the salty rain. Onward I march.

As I head down rain-swept Camden Avenue, past the half-dozen weathered homes and rooming houses that line the street, I feel as if I'm being watched from windows. At one point I actually see a curtain close at my approach. Maybe I'm just being paranoid.

I decide to swing by The Rusty Anchor to dry off and see if anyone

I know is hanging out there. Bad idea. The way Big Al eyes me from behind the bar makes me feel like a guy on a Wanted poster stepping into a saloon in an old Western. He ambles toward me, cranks out an effortful smile, and says, "Finn Carroll, in the flesh."

I ask him how he's been, and he replies, "Can't complain..."

"...since they closed the complaints department." It's an island moldy oldie.

I order a coffee—it's a bit early for a beer—and Big Al says, more out of compassion than animosity, "I'll get you the one, Finn, but then maybe it's best if you get rolling." Wow, am I actually being kicked out of The Rusty Anchor? Customarily you have to rip a urinal from the men's room wall to accomplish that feat. I reach for my wallet. Big Al waves off payment.

I look around. The place is pretty empty. Back in the day, there'd be a fair crowd of morning drinkers at the Anchor on a Saturday, but it seems the weather is forcing folks to do their sorrow-drowning at home. The only patrons in the joint are a threesome of silent drinkers in raincoats, two of whom are facing away and the third of whom I don't recognize, and, over in the corner, Enzo, the raving socialist painter, huddled over a breakfast tumbler of house red.

"Grizzled" doesn't begin to describe old Enzo; he looks as if the last tool he shaved with was made by Husqvarna. He gives me a surprised nod, which I take as an invitation to join him. One great thing about Enzo: he gives not crap one what anyone thinks of him. If he feels like talking to you, he'll do so, even if the rest of humanity is treating you like an Ebola carrier.

Still, I notice he does keep his voice down. "So I take it you've been getting a heaping helping of island hospitality?" he says, as I sit at his table, pulling back my dripping rain hood.

"You might say that," I reply, matching his turned-down volume. After we ply our pleasantries for a minute, I pursue the topic further, since he brought it up. "I don't get it, Enzo. I mean, I know some people are pissed at me, but why am I being singled out for an Amish shunning?"

"*Homo sapiens* is a pack-hunting beast motivated by fear and self-interest and unmoved by reason..."

"And how do you *really* feel about it?"

"...But to be fair to the beasts in question," he continues, "you brought a lot of it on yourself, wouldn't you say?'

"Why? Because I spoke up for that development plan—in its early days, when it still had merit? So did a bunch of other people."

"You did more a tad more than 'speak up' for it, *amico mio*."

"What? What did I do that was so terrible?"

He peers at me over the rim of his glass tumbler. "Are you asking that rhetorically or...?"

"It's a real question, Enz."

"Come on, Finnian. Don't be coy. We're both too smart for that."

"What?" I really don't know what he means. "I introduced Miles Sutcliffe to a few people. Big whoop. I talked some of the fishermen and selectmen into listening to his plan, but that's all I did—grease the wheels of conversation."

"You vouched for him, among other things."

"Because he was my friend. And because I thought his plan was exactly what the island needed—a way to rehab Fish Pier and also bring in some new tax and retail money. I didn't tell anyone how to think or vote, I just brought people together across tables; that was all."

"On this island, vouching for someone means something."

"Of course it does."

"And when the vouch*ee* lies and deceives, there are consequences for the vouch*er*."

"I get that, Enzo. But here's what I don't get. Miles struts around the island like he owns the place. No one seems to be shutting doors in *his* face. But he was the one—him and his partners—who *actually* screwed Fish Pier, not me."

"And the Romans were the ones who *actually* nailed a certain influential carpenter to a stick of lumber."

"What do you mean?"

"Whom does history blame for Calvary, Finnian? Not the people who did the literal stabbing and flogging and hammering."

I see where he's headed with this, but I allow him to make his point.

"There have always been, and always will be, Romans," he says. "People with power and money who seek to enforce their will at everyone else's expense. Romans are a given. A force of nature. Like weather. We don't take what they do personally. Miles Sutcliffe is a Roman. No one expected any better of him. You, on the other hand..."

"I may be many things, Enzo, but I'm no Judas. I didn't betray anybody."

"You might want to take an opinion poll on that, Buckaroo Banzai."

"I didn't know Miles' plan was going to change! I didn't know Fish Pier was going to be shit-canned! Once that started happening, I washed my hands of the whole thing!"

"Interesting choice of words." He smiles slyly.

"I was as pissed as anyone when those plans started changing, Enz. More so. I was the one who came up with the whole letter-writing idea and got all those letters to the developers."

Enzo leans back and appraises me with a hoised brow.

"What?" I ask. "Are you saying you don't believe me?"

"What I believe is unimportant. I'm not a member of—" He cuts himself off, looks around the barroom, and softly growls, "of a certain 'fraternity' that need not be named."

"What are you talking about, Enz?"

"I think you know exactly what I'm talking about."

Maybe I do, but I want to hear him say it. "Can I buy a vowel here?"

Suddenly the silent drinkers at the other table rise in tandem, sliding their chairs back. Enzo flicks his eyes toward them and knocks on the table in a wrapping-up gesture. "The wine's done too much yapping already. ...Besides, you probably want to get on with your day." He says the latter in the tone of a strong suggestion.

The raincoat posse heads toward the door en masse. Enzo stares at the floor, waiting for them to exit. After they do, he pauses for a few seconds, then stands and zips his raincoat up to his chin. He tosses a scratch ticket on the table as a tip and walks to the door himself. Before leaving, he peers out at the street, then shoots a glance back at me that I interpret as a warning.

I stand and amble toward the rear of the bar as if I'm going to use the men's room.

I duck out the back door.

# Chapter 22

I make my way out of Greyhook, sticking to the back alleys and right-of-ways. I haven't found a roost yet, but right now the village seems like a more welcoming place than Greyhook. I'm passing the row of old fishmonger shacks that serves as the unofficial borderline between the two "districts" when I spot Jeannie, in a blue poncho, talking to someone in a side alley. I can't see the other person; they're blocked by a stack of beat-up lobster traps.

Jeannie notices me, and I think I see a "caught" look flash across her face before she covers it with a smile. She says something to the other person, who turns briskly in the opposite direction. I catch a glimpse of motion behind the stacked traps as the figure stalks away.

Jeannie marches toward me. Before I can ask her any questions, she says, "Walk with me. I'm on my way to work. Let's take the long route."

We're only a pebble's toss from Pete's Lagoon, but we take a detour loop around the small residential neighborhood north of Island Ave. Jean pulls down the visor of her rain poncho as if she doesn't want to be seen with me. "I hear you've been snooping around Greyhook, looking for trouble," she says, aiming her voice at the ground.

"Can't a person take a crap on this island without CNN doing a Special Report?"

"It was on TMZ, actually. ...Hey listen, I'm sorry about the way I slammed the brakes on last night."

"It was late. I'd been blathering. It was time for me to go."

"No. There was something I *wanted* to tell you. Something that might be important to you, but I couldn't. Not till I checked with someone first."

"And?"

"Well, I did that."

"And?"

"It's not something I can just blurt out in thirty seconds. It needs… context."

"Okay. So what time do you get off work tonight?"

She trudges ahead for several yards before saying, "Ten."

Fine. I'll take that as a "date." We walk in silence for a bit. I want to know who she was just talking to—my gut is flashing warning signals—but she doesn't volunteer the information, and I don't feel it's my place to pry.

Instead I say, "Hey Jeannie, can I ask you a big favor? Promise you'll say no if it makes you uncomfortable." I ask her if she still has dial-up Internet at her house, and how she'd feel about my using her place while she's at work.

I expect some reluctance, but she quickly replies, "Sure." I don't know if she's agreeing so fast because she wants to help me or because she wants to distract me from asking about her back-alley conversation.

"I promise to respect your privacy. I'll just plug my computer in and work. I won't poke around or look in anything."

"You didn't have to say that, Finn. I trust you. That's why I said yes."

She hands me her key chain with the tiny stuffed Cthulhu doll on it (another old gift from me) and tells me where to find the logon instructions for the Internet. "Use the landline too, if you want, and help yourself to anything you need."

"Thanks. I *will* masturbate into your underwear drawer; I hope that's understood."

"Well, duh. It'd almost be creepy if you *didn't*."

We're approaching Pete's again but from the opposite direction. I say I'll meet her at ten. She doesn't argue. She's about to step inside when she says, "I'm worried about you, Finn."

"Why?" Like there aren't 457 good reasons to be.

"Just a vibe I'm picking up."

"Do you know something I don't? Have you heard something?"

She pauses pregnantly. "It's more what I'm *not* hearing. Something *not* being said to me. I don't know. But also—" She cuts herself off.

"Also *what*, Jeannie?"

She shakes her head dismissively.

"Come on, Jeannie. Spit it out."

She sighs. "It's probably nothing, but… Danny called me. Asked if I knew if you were okay. Said he had a bad feeling."

Uh-oh. When Danny gets an intuition, it's time to sit up and pay attention.

"How did he know I was on the island?"

"He didn't. Not till I told him. He was just calling out of the blue."

Yipes.

• • • • •

Danny Mawukura. One of my most beloved friends on Musqasset. I was already hoping to see him this morning—to say hello and maybe hit him up for a place to crash. Now I have an even more pressing reason to pay him a visit.

If I've ever met an enlightened human being, it is Danny Mawukura.

He has a bungalow that sits all by itself on the hilly northern side of the island. To get there, I follow a winding trail off Studio Row marked by a brightly colored sign, "Dreamsong Studio." His place is tucked away on a grassy terrace partway down North Hill where it slopes toward the water. The homes of the rock-star artists perch elegantly atop the hill; Danny's place peeks out from the middle like a kittiwake's nest.

His yard and house are an explosion of hand-painted color.

Everything Danny touches becomes a work of art—his guitar, his refrigerator, a hammer from Ace Hardware. He paints all his possessions in a trademark palette of bright earthy colors, creating forms out of clusters of dots. Danny has no formal art training, but his animal-themed paintings, influenced by his indigenous Australian heritage, tap into some primal dimension of the psyche completely inaccessible to crude brush monkeys like me.

I'm not a formally religious person, but you can't hang around with Danny very long without coming face to face with the mysteries of the cosmos. The guy's a freaking shaman. He visits other dimensions with the ease most people visit 7-Eleven.

Case in point, as I approach his house on its walkway of hand-painted stones, not only does the rain stop but the sun makes its first appearance since I arrived on the island. It shines down *only* on Danny's color-crazed quarter-acre—I swear—as he emerges from his studio and says with a grin, "I asked for a sign to mark your arrival, mate, but this is a bit showy, no?"

We give each other a hard hug. As to how he knew I was coming, I learned long ago not to trifle with such questions. Danny just knows stuff. Not because he's tapped into the island's gossip network but because he's tapped into a network of an entirely different frequency.

As we sit down for tea in his glowing-artwork kitchen, I am heartened to see his eyes light up with pure affection for me. At least there's one person on the island who doesn't think I'm lower than barnacle turd on a bilge pump.

Danny was never a hang-around-with-every-day type of friend, but he was my spiritual touchstone when I lived on the island. I'm about to ask him why he called Jeannie about me when he lays a hand on my arm, closes his eyes, and says to me in his hybrid Aussie accent, "Spirit has been knocking on my door about you, mate. Hard. Shall I find out why?"

He looks the question into my eyes and I nod. If Danny has any insight about what's been happening to me, I need to know what it is.

Danny goes into a small room off the kitchen and draws the curtains closed, darkening the room. He lights a sage smudge-stick and wafts the smoke in the air as he faces in the four compass directions, bows, and mutters some words I can't make out. He sits on a cushion, picks up a hand drum, and taps it rhythmically. The drumming goes on for about ten minutes. Then he stops, stands, bows in the four directions, and returns to the kitchen.

"Something came through," he says. Uh-oh. Careful what you wish for.

He lays his hand on my arm again, looks down at the floor, and says, "Spirit tells you've been carrying a burden for a long, long time, Finn. This burden has been sapping your power and now it is threatening to literally kill you. It's not your burden, but you don't know how to lay it down. That's because you've *always* carried other people's burdens. Kept other people's secrets. Preserved other people's falsehoods. You thought that was your way to have value in the world. But in doing so, you've leaked your own power away. And now you must reclaim it. You must *fight* for your truth, *fight* for your worth, *fight* for your power. Or… else."

Jeez. Well, what did I expect? When Danny gives you advice, you don't get "cheer up and look on the bright side" stuff, you get a sucker punch to the soul. Twelve years of therapy condensed into forty-five seconds.

He lets me marinate in the message for a minute or two, then moves on to lighter fare. He asks me about my work, and we talk about painting for a while. When I get up the nerve to ask him if he knows a place where I can lie low for a day or two, he offers to make up his back room for me. Of course he does; that's Danny. But I refuse to stay in his house, so he leads me outside. The sky is busy with barreling clouds again, but the rain is still on pause. I follow Danny to his storage shed, which is down the hill a bit, a safe distance from the house. He thrusts the door open with a ta-da gesture. "Be it ever so abominable," he says.

The shed is actually decent sized and fairly clean and uncluttered, with a window and a wooden floor. It'll do just fine. I'm happy to have a "home" at last.

"I'll bring a sleeping bag and a lantern down for you in a bit," Danny tells me, "and a bite to eat." He points to an inflatable boat with an outboard motor. It is currently deflated and packed onto a hand-pulled, two-wheel trailer. "If things really come a gutser for you," he says, "take the raft down to my little dock and get the hell off the island."

"Thanks, Danny, but I'd never make it across in this weather. Not in *that*."

"I ain't sayin' it's your 'A' option, mate, but if you find yourself facing a choice between the worst possibility and the second worst, take the ruddy thing and go."

I nod and thank him. He clasps my shoulders and looks me up and down. "And if you're thinkin' of goin' walkabout again, switch into this."

He grabs a bright yellow rain suit from a hook and hands it to me, then hangs a pair of binoculars around my neck. Lastly, he reaches into his pocket, pulls out a small black stone and places it in my hand. "Obsidian," he says, "the stone of truth. It'll awaken the warrior within and help you speak your truth."

Those words might sound ridiculous coming from another mouth—such as mine—but not from Danny's. I accept the stone with gratitude.

Danny gives me a hug of pure love and starts back toward his studio.

After a few steps, he turns and our eyes meet again. We both burst out laughing for no apparent reason. Then he taps his heart, points to the sky, and slips away in the wind.

• • • • •

It's only a five-minute walk from Danny's to Jeannie's, but I'm making it stretch. Trying to digest Danny's words to me. Actually, Danny would be the first to tell you they're not "his" words at all—but wherever they came from, they're right on target.

It's true that I've always derived my sense of worth and power in a secondhand way. From other people. For some reason, I decided early in life that my value as a human being lay in enabling others to have the happiness and peace of mind I inexplicably denied myself. And now life has painted me into a corner, and I must find my own power. Or… else.

As if to challenge me on this very point, a figure appears in my vision, about seventy yards ahead on the road. Wearing a hooded rain slicker — yes, Davy's grey in color — and sporting a high black-and-gray beard, the man is pacing around in an overgrown driveway two lots down from Jeannie's. He's talking to a shorter guy, lightly bearded. They seem to be watching the road for someone — someone whose name rhymes with Bin Barrel, I'll gamble. I'm glad I'm disguised in Danny's yellow rain gear.

Faking an old man's penguin walk, I turn into the driveway of a vacant home and stroll behind the house, shielding myself from the men's view. I creep into a patch of scrub pine behind the house from where I can watch the men, unseen. I remember that, miraculously, I have just acquired a pair of binoculars from Danny. I put them to my eyes and adjust the focus.

Davy Grey has his back turned, but the shorter man's face gels into clear view.

Oh.

It's the first time I've laid eyes on him since the inn trucks left the dock.

E-cigarette guy, from the ferry.

# Chapter 23

This could be the break I've been hoping for. A chance to pivot from mouse to snake. These guys don't know I've spotted them. That means I can now watch *them*, maybe find out where they're operating from and what they're up to. Make a move on them before they make their next move on me. I feel electrified.

My new bright yellow rain outfit suddenly seems a liability. It glows like a road-hazard sign. I take it off and stash it in the bushes.

I watch the men as they confab on the side of the road. Once or twice, the shorter one points to the road itself, as if examining the very path I trod last night. They must have been part of the posse that followed me. Which means they are almost certainly Trooper Dan and Chokehold. Clearly they're waiting for me to show up at Jeannie's. How would they know I'm heading there? Only Jeannie and I know of my plans. Same as last night.

An image in my mind tries to flag my attention: the person who was talking to Jeannie in the alley. No. I foul it off like a bad pitch. *Watch the men instead.*

The two guys finally turn and walk off in the direction of the village. Guess they're sick of waiting for me. Good. Now I can follow them. Here's where my knowledge of the island will pay dividends. I know how all the properties interconnect and where all the shortcuts are. I feel confident I can tail these guys anywhere on the island without their knowing it.

I watch them from a distance as they proceed toward the village. At one point, the smaller one crouches and studies a rain-eroded section of the road. It's the exact spot where I picked up my throwing stones, I believe. What are they looking for? They continue to walk, and take a right on Island Avenue. I cut through a series of back yards and overgrown lots, then jog lightly down Thistle Path to pick up their trail as they reach the west end of Island Avenue.

There they are, still walking west. I track their progress down Island Ave as I move light-footedly behind a row of shops. I temporarily lose sight of them.

Suddenly I hear the men take a brisk right turn into a narrow alley that runs alongside the very shop I'm crouched behind! I barely have time to duck around the opposite corner. Miraculously, they don't spot me. I watch as they head down an overgrown path to Town Road 1, the dirt lane that leads to the town barn.

The town barn, where Musqasset keeps its maintenance equipment, sits all by itself in the wooded center of the island. So *that's* where these guys have been hiding out the last couple of days? Makes sense, actually. They probably figured no town employees would be working over the long holiday weekend, so the barn would be a safe, out-of-the-way place to stay dry and use as a temporary headquarters. Avoid checking into any B&Bs or hotels.

• • • • •

I watch from a behind a row of dripping beach-plum bushes as the men approach the rusty old Quonset-hut-style building with the peeling, painted sign, "Musqasset Public Works." There's a walk-in door to the right of a large garage door. Trooper Dan—if it really is him—looks around, then jiggles his hand on the knob for several seconds, using either a badly cut key or a lock pick. The two men go inside.

There seems to be only one window on the building—to the left of the garage door. I want to sneak up and peek in, but, of course, that would be imprudent. I decide to creep around to the rear of the barn and see if there's any way to look in from the back.

Untrimmed foliage presses in on both sides of the barn. (The maintenance building, as always, is the one place in town that never gets maintained.) I need to be careful, as I pick my way through the wet bramble, not to jostle any branches that might scrape or brush against the sheet-metal wall, giving me away.

I'm halfway to the rear of the building when a shockingly loud buzzer alarm goes off, making me literally jump off the ground. I spin about in panic, expecting to be gang-tackled, but then I realize the sound is not a burglar alarm but the building's ancient motorized garage door. The sheet metal walls are further amplifying the crazily loud, oil-thirsty, metallic grinding sound.

I dash back through the brush till I'm near the front of the building again. The unbelievably loud garage door is still on its glacial upward journey. I wait for it to finish. Finally, blessed silence reigns. The door is open wide. I listen for sounds of the men inside. Nothing.

I wait a minute longer. Still no sounds. The men *must* be in there—where else could they have gone? From deep within the structure I can hear the slow, steady drip of water from a leaky roof onto a plastic tarp. But all else seems still.

Maybe the place has an inner room the men have entered. I slink up to the building and crane my neck around the garage-door frame, taking in a small section of the interior. I gradually increase my angle till I'm able to look fully into the open space. No signs of life.

I do see a pickup truck, parked beside a huge pile of road sand in the middle of a dirt floor. Arrayed around the perimeter of the room is the typical assortment of landscaping tools and snow removal equipment you'd expect to find in any small-town New England maintenance garage. I spot an area in the far left corner of the room that's set up like an office, with a desk, an old computer, and some file cabinets. Deserted.

Where could the men have gone? I saw them enter—and they just opened the garage door.

Dare I risk stepping inside? If the men are staying this quiet, they probably know I followed them and are hiding in the shadows, waiting for me.

I still have the blackjack in my pocket. I take it out and swing it around a few times. Emboldened, I enter the large, open space, keeping my weapon in constant motion.

Still no sign of humans.

I'm about to shout, "Come out and show yourselves"—that one works about as well as "Come back, thief"—but some vestigial trace of intelligence keeps my lips sealed.

I slink around the pickup truck and sand pile. No one's lurking on the other side. Plenty of hiding spots around the room's perimeter, though, in amongst the plow attachments and road signs. I notice a lopper hanging on the wall, along with some other pruning tools. Instantly my throat goes dry and my feet gain weight.

I take a few steps closer to the "office" area. That's when my eyes catch sight of a back door—a small one sheathed in galvanized tin. Leading to where? It's all wild woods out behind the barn, I think. Is that where the men went? Out back?

As I tiptoe closer to the door, I see its lever-style handle turn clockwise. Fuck!

I dive for cover behind the desk. The back door opens and then closes again, and I hear the sound of feet striding purposefully through the garage.

A few muffled words are exchanged, then that monstrously loud grinding sound hammers down again, making me jump halfway out of my skin. The garage door is closing!

As the big door slowly comes down, daylight is eclipsed and the room is plunged into blackness. Beautiful. Now I'm locked *in* here with Davy Grey and company. I walked right into their trap. Somehow I've pivoted back to being prey again.

A minute passes in the dark. Two. Three.

Not a peep from anywhere.

Is it possible they didn't see me follow them inside and they've simply gone away, closing the garage door behind them on their way out? Is the pickup truck still there? I'm debating whether to chance a peek with my flashlight app when my phone rings, shattering the silence.

Shit! I bolt toward where I *think* the back door is, about fifteen feet away. My hand fumbles sightlessly for the door handle and snags it first try. I thrust the door open and dive through it into the daylight, slamming the door behind me with bone-crushing force.

I hit the ground rolling, in a patch of grassy gravel, and then spring to my feet, already in a full run. I see I'm in a little penned-in area with a propane tank, some gasoline cans, and some rusted engine parts. I think I hear running feet behind me. I hurdle the four-foot-high chain-link fence cleanly and plunge into the wet growth beyond it.

I plummet through the brush, snapping branches and scratching my hands and face on thorny blackberry bushes as I go. My phone's still ringing, but I ignore it.

I run, run, run through the wild woods.

It takes me several long, hushed stops to conclude no one is pursuing me.

• • • • •

After recovering Danny's slicker from where I stashed it, I creep up on Jeannie's house from the rear. I've taken the woodland route to her place so as to avoid attention.

I shouldn't have come here, I know; it's far too risky. For me, for Jeannie. But I *need* a dry shelter to get my bearings and use the Internet, and I don't know where else to go.

It feels invasive to enter Jean's house without her here. Of course, it used to be *my* house too, but it no longer carries my energy.

After peering out the windows in all directions and closing the shades, the first thing I do is strip off my sopping-wet clothes and toss them into the dryer, then wrap a towel around my waist. Getting semi-naked in Jean's house feels like a creepy thing to do, but I have no choice.

I need to get my business done as quickly as possible and get out of here.

For a minute I can't remember where the dialup modem is, and then I find it on the desk in the living room. I peek out a couple of windows again—no signs of company yet—then plug the modem's cable into my borrowed laptop.

I'm about to try to get online when my phone rings again, flooding my nerves with adrenaline. Angie. I see it was her who called while I was in the town barn, too. It's after eleven a.m.; I guess she's up and semi-conscious by now. I tap the Answer icon, and the call seems to come through, then disconnects. Here we go again. Cell service is still frigged.

I do need to talk to Angie, though, I realize. For reasons of my own. May as well do it now. Luckily, I have Jeannie's landline at my disposal. I dial Angie's number on it.

I need to handle this call carefully. My sister is acting bristly about my questioning, and now I have an even more bristle-inducing question to ask her.

"Jeannie?" croaks Angie; her first vocalization of the day. Her caller ID must be showing Jeannie's number. "What's up?"

"No, it's Finn."

"Finn? What are you—I've been trying your cell." Yeah, thanks for that, sis. "Hey listen, did I call you last night? If so, forget it. It was nothing." Ah, the Angie Saturday Morning Soft-Shoe: who did I drunk-dial last night and what did I say?

"Ange, I need to ask you a question, and it might seem weird."

A beat passes. "Does this have to do with all that skeevy crap you've been poking into? I told you, no more help with that until you tell me why you're so interested."

"Why do *you* care what my interest is?" I ask, flipping the question on her. "Why are you acting so touchy about this?"

Silence. I can feel dark energy massing at the other end of the line.

"Angie? Why?"

She finally blurts out, "Because you and I both know this is not a random, innocent line of questioning!"

Ah, there it is. On the table at last.

"Well, clearly it's not random to you," I say. "You seem to have something on your mind. Why don't you tell me what it is?"

"No, no, no. I asked you first. Why are you poking into ancient history?"

"Why do you care?"

"Why the poking, Finn?"

"Why the concern?"

Mexican standoff. She emits a protracted sigh. "Just ask your damn question."

"When I left for California after my graduation..." Angie is three years younger than me. She was still living at home when I blew town for the West Coast. "Did the police ever come by and question Dad about anything?"

She doesn't answer right away. Her silence is a yes.

"Like what?" she asks at last.

"Like anything? Like a bottle of booze he might have bought with a credit card?"

More silence.

It was *my father*, you see, who bought that bottle of Glenmalloch for me before my graduation. I was a few months shy of twenty-one, and he knew the bottle was a gift for Miles, who *was* twenty-one at the time, so it was hardly a shocker that he would consent to buy for me.

What *is* surprising is that the police questioned him about it. And that he never told me.

"What did they ask him? What did he say?"

Again I wait for an answer.

"I really would like to know what this is about," she says.

"Angie, come on."

"Fine! They asked him if he bought some high-priced scotch, some Glen-whatever-the-bonnie-fuck. He said he did. They asked him where the bottle was. 'It's off being recycled into a dozen aspirin bottles,' he said, 'which was exactly what I needed by the time I finished the scotch.'"

"Why would he say that?" I ask her.

"Um, because he was being Dad?"

"I mean, when did you ever know Dad to drink hundred-dollar-a-bottle scotch?"

"How do you know it was hund—?"

"Because he bought that scotch for *me*, Ange."

She says nothing for a long count, then blows out a breath. "I know."

"Then why were you pretending you didn't? And why did Dad lie to the police?"

"For the obvious reason, I assume. You weren't twenty-one yet. Buying for you was illegal."

"Uh-huh. Does that sound like Dad to you? Lying to the cops to protect himself from a minor misdemeanor charge no judge in the world would convict him on?"

More silence from Angie.

"Angie, does it? Does that sound like Dad?"

"You weren't here, Finn! That's what happened and I don't want to talk about it!"

Angie hangs up. A moment later my intuition whispers another question—seemingly out of left field—that I want to ask her. But I know if I call her back now, she won't pick up.

Angie often responds better to texts than calls. I know my cell isn't working for voice calls, but it might be working for texts. I type into the message box: *One more question, then I'll leave you alone: Did Edgar Goslin ever approach Dad?* I hit Send. It seems to go through.

While awaiting a reply, I make another circuit of Jeannie's house, peeking out the shades. Coast still clear outside, as far as I can tell.

A reply text from Ange comes through in screaming caps: *YOU OBVIOUSLY KNOW THE FUCKING ANSWER SO WHY ARE YOU ASKING ME?!!!*

The truth is, I *didn't* know, but now I do. Edgar Goslin did talk to my dad. Holy crap. So Goslin *does* know something that connects me to the accident. But how? And what did he say to my father?

My cell phone pings another text message.

Two emojis. Two dead fish. And an exclamation point.

In the "from" space at the top of the screen I see a mishmash of numbers that don't even look like a phone number. And then, once again, the message disappears from the screen as if it had never arrived.

# Chapter 24

I'm wearing dry clothes again and pacing Jeannie's floor like a tin shark in a shooting gallery. My brain is overheating, trying to synthesize all the information I've been bombarded with—about my father, Goslin, Angie, and the twisted tale of the scotch bottle—and make sense of it. It's all interconnected. But I can't see the invisible thread stitching it together.

I need to keep moving, keep pushing forward. Like a real shark, not a tin one. That's all I *can* do. That means trying to talk to Goslin, as I was planning to do earlier. In fact, my exchange with Angie has doubled my incentive to find out what he knows.

Turning my attention to my borrowed laptop, I attempt to go online, using Jeannie's pre-Cambrian dialup service. It's like traveling back in time to hear the phone modem kick to life and do that scratchy-sounding "handshake" that was the soundtrack of the nineties.

I grow a full beard waiting for the linkup to happen. And then... hallelujah, connected at last. The web browser creaks open. I navigate to Sure Search, a top-rated people-finding and background search site. It lets me do a trial search for Edgar Goslin of Wentworth, Massachusetts. The site tells me it has located some information on Goslin, but, of course, it won't part with that info till I cough up sixteen magical digits and an expiration date. I choose the Premium Passkey membership, pay the fee, and wait to see what pops up.

And wait. And wait.

A webpage appears, piecemeal—"Search Results for Edgar Goslin."

In the "Contact Info" section, I spot what I'm looking for: Goslin's phone number. I hope it's current. Under "Known Associates," I see a couple of other Goslins. I also see a Sam Kubiak, a John Woodcock, a Frank Torrissi, a Gary Abelsen, a Theo Abelsen, and a Priscilla Begley. The Gary Abelsen connection snares my attention. Does this mean Goslin and Moneybags Abelsen associated with one another after the accident, or is the software linking their names simply because they've appeared in the same news articles?

As a duly authorized Premium Passkey holder — yes sir, that's me — I'm entitled to search as many people as I want (for thirty days). I decide to look up Abelsen. I find his current address listed as a place called Neighbors Village, which turns out to be a high-end assisted living program. I call the place on Jean's landline and ask to speak to him. I expect to be given the runaround due to HIPAA regulations, but I easily find out he's living in the Memory Care unit. Gary Abelsen is an Alzheimer's patient. Another dead end.

Time to try calling Goslin. Of course, if he is involved in all this, he's not going to just blurt out the truth to me. I need an angle. Wish I had Miles to bounce ideas off.

So what do I know about Goslin anyway? Precious freaking little. From what Miles and I have been able to gather, though, he seems like a real charmer. My instinct says he'll react aggressively to any approach that even hints of prying or pressuring. Maybe, though, if I massage his ego and offer *him* something of value...

I quickly compose a talking script and pick up the phone. Not wanting Jeannie's landline to be identified, I key in the "block caller ID" code, then dial the number Sure Search provided.

Goslin's voicemail picks up. His "greeting" is a gruff "Goslin, leave a message," with no attempt to sound even remotely civil.

I've prepped myself in case of voicemail: "Hello, Mr. Goslin, sir, I'm calling on behalf of a group of... 'investors' who would be grateful for the opportunity to speak with you confidentially." I'm giving it the John Malkovitch treatment; genteel but quietly deadly. "We understand you may have certain information regarding an incident that took place in 1999, information that has eluded the police. We have reason to believe this information might be valuable to us, and we may be willing to compensate you generously for it. Please call us back at your earliest convenience, sir. Ask for a Mr. Slade."

I don't want to leave Jeannie's number as the callback. I need to keep her out of this. I can't leave my cell number, either. My cell isn't working correctly—but also, if Goslin is involved in this, he might recognize my cell number. I have a work number that forwards to my cell, so I leave that as the callback. Then I quickly take the steps to have all calls to the work number forwarded to Jeannie's landline instead.

Barely a minute passes before Jeannie's phone rings.

"Hello?" I answer neutrally. It might be for Jeannie, after all.

A woman's voice—seasoned by ten thousand packs of Winstons—replies in a "Nawthshaw" Massachusetts accent, "Lemme talk to this Mr. 'Slade.'" She pronounces it "Swade" and says it in quotes as if she knows it's fake.

"Speaking, Madam."

"Yeah, so what do you need to talk to Edgar about?"

"We'd prefer to speak to Mr. Goslin directly."

"Yeah, well I'd prefer to be married to George Clooney"—says it *Jawdge Cwooney*—"but that ain't workin' out so good. I speak for Edgar when it comes to money matters."

"Well, Mrs. Goslin... *Is* it Mrs. Goslin?"

"It's Begley, and there's no 'Missus' involved." I think I hear her mutter, "thank Christ." According to Sure Search, Goslin co-owns his house with a Priscilla Begley. She must be the live-in girlfriend who's been mentioned.

"Well, Ms. Begley, we're not sure if we're talking about a monetary situation or not. We would have to speak to Mr. Goslin to make that determination. If he does have the information we think he has, then we could be talking about a substantial sum."

"You sure as shit better be."

"Why is that, ma'am?"

"How should I put this? There may be a, ah, existing *marketplace* for this, ah, *commodity*, which you might not be, ah, *cognizant* of." She chuckles, proud of the verbal triple-Axel she has just stuck.

"Has he talked to someone else?"

"You'll have to ask him that."

"May I do that, please?"

"He ain't here."

"Can you tell me when he'll be back?"

"No, I can't. He's off on one of his, what do you call, 'unscheduled junkets.' Why don't you tell me what kind of money we're talking about, so I can know how many five-star hotels I should try ringing him at?"

"I'm not authorized to talk with anyone but—"

"Good luck with that."

She hangs up.

I can tell she's interested in the (fictitious) money, but she's wary, too. Wants me to show more of my cards. Hanging up on me is Negotiations 101 for Priscilla Begley.

Fine. I can play Negotiations 101 too.

I take a quick look out a couple of Jeannie's windows again, scanning for unwanted company, then call the number back. Begley answers with a sigh, affecting boredom. "Yeah?"

"Perhaps I wasn't clear, Ms. Begley. Our offer is time-sensitive. We're prepared to wire Mr. Goslin the money, but we need to know within the next twelve hours if he has the information we're looking for." I'm sounding more and more like a B-movie extortionist, but I can't seem to dial it back. "After that, our offer may no longer be on the table."

"Offer? What offer?" she replies. "I ain't heard no *offer*."

"We'll talk numbers with Mr. Goslin as soon as we—"

"Edgar ain't here. Are you deaf? I ain't seen him for days. But I know everything he knows, so you can—" She stops herself and says, "Hey, wait a second. I see your number, pal."

Shit. I forgot to block caller-ID when I called her back!

"Listen, asshole, you probably know where Edgar is better than I do. Who is this, really?"

"My name's David Slade and I—"

"Yeah, and my name's Katy Perry, and my tits are insured for twelve million bucks. Listen, whoever you are, you're going to tell me your real name and why you want to talk to Edgar, or this conversation's over."

"Mr. Goslin has twelve hours to—"

"Go fuck yourself."

The line goes dead again.

• • • • •

I'm pacing like a shooting-gallery target again. I should be galvanized by what I've learned about Goslin and Begley—they *definitely* know something the police don't—but my mind wants to focus on only one thing right now: the way the conversation ended. Begley reacted to Jeannie's phone number as if she recognized it! How could that be? The Begley-Goslins and Jeannie in communication with one another? I don't even want to consider the implications of such a thing. But the implications are inescapable.

Peering out the windows again, I think about the two times I was followed in the dark. In both cases, I had just left Jeannie's presence. I also recall Jeannie's secretive conversation with the person in the alley behind the lobster traps. A visual detail from that scene—one my mind has been diligently trying to Photoshop away—now insists upon revealing itself in blazing hi-def. When that person strode away from Jeannie, I saw a flash of color through the traps.

It was a tone we painters call Davy's grey.

Shit. No, Jeannie, no.

I feel as if the bottom is dropping out of my world yet again, and I'm tumbling through space. I'm starting to think Miles might be my only friend in this after all. I want to call him and tell him everything I've just learned, but the Miles/Beth situation is delicate.

I don't know what to do. But if I don't get out of Jeannie's house right this minute, I'm going to pop a blood vessel.

As I'm locking the door behind me, an idea strikes me.

# Chapter 25

"Mr. Carroll, oh wow! How's it going?"

I'm at the front door of Preston Davis, the young deckhand I spoke to on the ferry.

Preston's mom invites me in, and we exchange the requisite whatcha-been-uptas. I'm something of a hero in the Davis household because I took young Preston under my wing when he was ten or eleven and gave him free art lessons. And now, I've just learned, he has a full scholarship to study art in college. Wow — occasionally I fail to fuck people's lives up despite my most valiant efforts.

The moment Mrs. Davis departs the room, Preston looks me hard in the eye. He can tell by my energy this is not a social call. "What's up, Mr. Carroll?"

Preston is a young man now, so I decide not to sugarcoat my answer. "Someone followed me to the island on the ferry, Preston; someone who wants to seriously hurt me, maybe kill me."

"Jesus, Mr. Carroll."

"Does Trombly Boat Tours keep records of passenger data?" I ask him point-blank. I hate to put him on the spot, but, fear not, I'll get over it.

"We collect a lot of information on passengers, actually," he says. "Contact stuff, especially. That's 'cause sometimes, like when we cancel a trip for bad weather, we have to get in touch with passengers at the last minute."

"What happens to all that data?"

"It's stored on a hard drive at the mainland office, but we also export some of it to an online database our webmaster uses to send out ads, newsletters, other stuff."

"Who's your webmaster?"

"You're looking at his ridiculously handsome face."

"You're kidding, right?"

"Well, they don't give me that title, 'cause then they'd have to pay me webmaster bucks, but yeah, I designed the site and do most of the—"

"You have access to that database?"

"'Course."

"Is there any way you could take a peek at it for me, without getting in trouble?"

"It's not the Pentagon Papers, Mr. Carroll. Even if it was, I'd do it for you."

"Do you keep records of who was on every trip?"

"The company does. But all the trip-ticketing stuff is done on this antique Dell system in the office. *That* data's only stored locally, not on the Cloud. Every few weeks, I export any new names and contact information it collects into the database I use."

"So there's no way for you to find out if a particular person was on a particular trip? Like on the same trip I came over on."

"I *could*, but I'd have to call someone at the mainland office, and come up with a good excuse why I want that info. If you need it, though, I'll get it for you, Mr. Carroll."

"First things first. Can we check out *your* database?"

We go to the computer in his bedroom. He he quickly navigates to the Excel file he wants and pulls it up.

"What's the person's name?"

"Edgar Goslin. G-o-s-l-i-n."

"You sunk my battleship. We got a hit. He's been a passenger."

He points to the screen. My heart does a little jig-step. Not only is there an Edgar Goslin on the spreadsheet, but there's a home phone number, a cell number, and an email address too. The home number I recognize from Sure Search, confirming it's *my* Edgar Goslin. The cell number and email address are new information. I hungrily jot them down.

"There's no way we can find out when he used the ferry?" I ask.

"I can't pin it down to an exact date from here, but there is something I *can* do." He clicks through his folders with a techno-speed unattainable by anyone over twenty-two. "Every time I update the database, I create a new file. But I save the old versions. I can step back through them, one at a time, and see when his name shows up. Here's an old one I saved on August eighth."

Less than four weeks ago.

Preston opens the file and says, "Dude."

He tilts the screen toward me. There's a "Goski" and a "Gosselin," but, as of 8/8, no "Goslin" in between them. Aha, so Edgar Goslin was added to the database *only on its latest update*. That means his ferry trip has been *very* recent. That information, coupled with Begley's news that he is currently away on a multi-day trip, is all the proof I need that Goslin is indeed on Musqasset Island right now.

He *is* one of the guys who followed me here from Wentworth.

He *is* Trooper Dan or Chokehold. Probably the latter.

Not only that, but I now have his cell phone number and email address.

Holy shit.

Holy Sanctified, Consecrated, Beatified Shit on Toast.

I stand up and take a deep breath, feeling something approaching exhilaration. For the first time since that fateful evening in my parents' house, I have my hands on something real and actionable. Something I can base a strategy on.

Even better, I feel an emotional anvil lifting off my heart. Maybe Priscilla Begley didn't recognize Jeannie's *actual phone number*! Maybe she just recognized the *prefix* — the three numbers after Maine's 207 area code — as that of Musqasset. If she knows Edgar took that ferry here, then she would definitely react suspiciously to receiving a mystery call from the same obscure island thirteen miles off Maine's coast.

I give Preston a bear hug of thanks and head out. I have things to do.

Yes, I am a living, breathing man with *things to do*.

• • • • •

The moment I step back into Jeannie's house, the smell hits me like a tire iron. Rotten seafood. My nose leads me to her bedroom first. Someone has tucked a half-dozen spoiled mackerel into her bed, pulling the covers up to their nonexistent chinny-chin-chins. A decaying jellyfish-looking creature has been mashed into the keyboard of Miles' laptop with a rubber spatula, and the kitchen and living room are festooned with dead crabs, fish, and smashed shellfish that smell as if they've been sitting in a boat's hold for days.

I make a dash through the whole place to ensure the perpetrators are no longer on site. I don't see anyone—but I'm not convinced I'm alone; I sense human presence nearby.

I throw open the cabinets and closet doors in every room, exactly as I swore I wouldn't do, and open some windows to air the place out.

If this stunt is supposed to piss me off, it's working. On the bright side, this is proof that Jeannie has no involvement in this. No way she would allow her home to be desecrated in this way. Another voice in my head immediately retorts, *On the other hand, what a perfect way to throw suspicion off herself.*

No. I can't allow myself to be eaten up by this cancer of doubt. I have to trust Jeannie. Period. She let me into her home because she trusted *me*.

The cartoon demon on my left shoulder fires back, *But why were those guys waiting outside her house like they knew you'd be heading here?*

*Maybe they saw her hand me her house keys,* the cartoon angel on my right shoulder rebuts. Yes, of course! That would explain it. She handed me the keys right in front of Pete's!

I realize there's one easy way to find out who Jeannie's been chatting with lately—by checking the call history on her landline. I know how to do that; I bought the damn phone system when I lived here.

No. Again, no. Not only would that be breaking my word to her, but it would be breaking my fundamental trust in her. And once that dam breaks, it might never be rebuilt. Screw that.

I grab a small garbage bag from under the sink and begin collecting the animal corpses from around the house, using a doubled-up plastic grocery bag as a glove.

When that task is done, I throw on Danny's rain slicker, unzipped, and step out the back door, checking for attackers as I exit. No one in view. I look toward the green trash bin across the yard, beyond Bree's play castle. That's when I notice more "gifts" strewn about the tiny, overgrown yard: eight or ten piles of rotting fish entrails, oozing their juices into the muddy ground. The stink is ferocious, even though the wind is blowing the other way.

I march toward the trash bin, ready to blow a gasket. My shin catches on something unseen, and I go sprawling on the ground, my chest landing smack in a pile of fish guts.

My head whips about to see what I tripped on. I spot a length of clear nylon fishing line strung bow-taut across the yard, about eight inches above the ground, hidden by the tall grass. Hilarious. You guys are a serious laff riot.

The bio-muck I have landed in is quite possibly the most abhorrent physical substance I have ever come in contact with. As I try to push myself out of it, something hard strikes my skull with brutal force, rocking my head back. Stunned by the blow, it takes me a moment to realize I've been hit by a rock. I'm dazed and disoriented.

Next thing I know, I'm being *bombarded* with rocks from more than one direction. I dive for the ground again, using my arms to cover the sides of my face. Several lemon-sized rocks strike my back and side like hammer blows. This must be payback for *my* rock-throwing.

Another rock connects with my head and I hear a sickening crack. For a moment I think my skull has been split, but then I take a quick look and notice the "rocks" are actually clams. Hard-shelled clams of cherrystone or quahog size, still in their closed shells.

After a couple more direct hits to my thighs and ass, the air assault stops, and I hear two sets of footsteps running away. By the time I get to my feet, my attackers are gone.

Once I determine I haven't suffered any serious injuries—perhaps a mild concussion, though—the first thought that crosses my mind is, "I am going to *get* Goslin. Fuck him."

My second thought is that I have a lot of work to do now. I can't go anywhere covered in this vile-smelling filth, and I can't leave Jeannie's home and bed befouled.

Before I start my cleanup, though, I need to send a couple of text messages.

The first is for Miles, to let him know what's been happening to me. I go back inside the house, strip off my shirt and pants (again), toss them into the washer, scrub my hands, and grab my phone. For a moment, I forget why I grabbed it — maybe I *am* concussed. I shake my head clear and type the message: *Lots to talk about. Goslin is the man. He's here on the island right now. He just attacked me, but I'm okay. Can we meet somewhere?*

The second message is for Goslin. I find a dead fish icon on an emoji app and select it as a text message for him. I would love to see his face when he receives this message from me to his personal cell number, which there's no way in the world I should know.

It's time for *me* to start messing with *his* head.

# Chapter 26

I'm about to hit Send when an alien impulse—I think it's called wisdom—intercedes. If I text Goslin that emoji, I may gain a moment of satisfaction, but I'll also be playing his game. And tipping my hand in a way that doesn't serve me. I need to maximize my advantages.

What *are* my advantages, as things stand? I shake my head again to reboot the synapses. One: I know who Goslin is, and he doesn't know I've figured that out. Two: I know he's on the island—*and* I have ways to contact him here; he doesn't know that either. Three, and this might be the biggie: I know he has anger management issues. That might be his Achilles heel; I can't afford to let it be mine.

Whatever my plan of attack is going to be, I need exploit his weaknesses and leverage my advantages to the fullest. Yes.

First things first. I toss Jeannie's sheets into the washer with my clothes. Dressed in Danny's slicker and some men's sweat pants (not mine, alas) I found in a closet, I grab a couple of trash bags and a snow shovel, and go to work cleaning up the fish guts in the yard.

After triple-bagging everything I can pick up, I thoroughly hose away the residue from the grass. Wasting water is a capital offense on Musqasset, but I can't count on the rain to do this job. Next I set to scrubbing the indoors clean.

The whole time I'm doing these tasks, I'm thinking about how to deal with Goslin (who may be watching me every moment). Casting this as a game scenario, I realize my range of options hinges on one key variable: *if* I can find out where Goslin is staying on the island, *then* I can employ a "first strike" strategy of some kind and surprise him. If I *can't* find out where he is, then I must lure him into some sort of trap, which involves an entirely different type of strategy.

So, first and foremost, I must try to determine Goslin's whereabouts.

When I was in the maintenance barn, I saw no evidence he was camping there, but I still can't rule out that possibility. Nor can I rule out the idea that he's rented a room. I do know his cell number, though. That's huge. I don't want to call it directly; not yet—not until I know what my play is. But I wonder: is there a way I can locate him based only on his cell number, via GPS? Or is that something only the police can do?

I don't know the answer to that, but I know someone who might.

The wash is finished drying, so I make Jeannie's bed and strike off into the storm again.

• • • • •

"Private property is an illusion," shouts a voice in response to my knock. I *think* that's Enzo's way of saying, "Come in, please."

I shake off the rain and step into his rattletrap house. He's working at his computer wall. After our last exchange, I'm not sure what Enzo's attitude toward me is, but I elect to believe our old friendship means something.

I sit on the edge of a low bookcase, and he surveys my bruised and nicked-up face. He doesn't ask how it got that way, and I don't explain. "Hey Enzo, you're a pretty paranoid guy, right?"

"It's not paranoia..."

"If they're really out to get you. Tell me about it. What do you know about tracking someone's location by using their cell-phone number?"

"What do you *need* to know?"

"Well, like... can it be done?"

He grunts as if to say, *It's not a simple answer.* "Is this a hypothetical situation or...?"

"Let's call it quasi-hypothetical."

He laughs a bone-dry *heh-heh*. "Well, question number one is: do you have the person's permission to track them? If so, you just download an app. Your friends and family sign onto your list, like good little sheep, and then you can all find out who's sneakin' off to the no-tell motel when they're supposed to be in church praying to the Flying Spaghetti Monster."

"And if you don't have the other person's permission?"

"Then you have to get more creative. It all comes down to whether you can get your mitts on the person's phone. I mean physically. If so, there are GPS trackers you can plant that act like human LoJack systems. The software sits there completely invisible; the person has no idea it's on their phone. In fact..." He leans back in his chair and wiggles his brow. "If you can get hold of someone's phone, you can do a whole lot more than track their location."

"What do you mean?"

"There are programs you can install—not strictly legal, mind you—that'll let you turn that phone into a spying device J. Edgar Hoover would have creamed his tighty-whities for. You essentially gain complete control of the person's phone, remotely."

"Holy shit." That would be handy as ass.

"Holy shit indeed."

Unfortunately, there's no way I can get my hands on Goslin's physical phone, so that route is moot. "What if you only have their number, not the phone itself?"

"Then you're shit-out-of-luck. If it's an emergency situation—a missing person or someone threatening to rape your cat—the cops can get a warrant and work with Lord Verizon to triangulate the person's location. But that option is generally unavailable to the merely curious private citizen."

He turns back to his computer screen and cracks his knuckles. I take the hint and stand up to say goodbye. But then a thought occurs to me. "Hey Enzo, can I ask you something else?"

He hears a note in my voice that makes him turn and give me his full attention.

I decide to skip the hypotheticals this time. "Some pretty scary people planted a document—a letter—on my home computer. The letter claims I wrote it, but I didn't. But here's the crazy part: anyone who read it would swear I did. It has my humor, my writing style, personal stuff about me. Even *I'm* half convinced I wrote it in some kind of fugue state. I can't freakin' figure it out."

"What type of scary people are we talking about? Criminal? Corporate scum? Government scum? High-level? Low-level?"

"I think it's just a personal revenge thing, but I'm not a hundred percent sure."

"The reason I ask is... Well, let me back up a bit." He leans his chair back and thinks for a moment. "Do you know the main reason most second-rate scams and hoaxes fail? Shitty writing. I kid you not. Most people can't write and have no clue what it takes to create fake letters and documents that are convincing. That's why you can usually spot an email scam; something's a little *off* about the wording and punctuation.

"But there *are* people out there who are good at this stuff," he continues. "Literary forgers. They're like art forgers but with words."

"Wasn't there a book out a few years ago by someone who did that?"

"There was, but this is bigger than just writing fake Dorothy Parker letters for fun and profit. Government agencies and criminal enterprises—as if there's a difference—employ these folks too. They're talented writers, but they're also cunning linguists. Ha! I knew if I lived long enough I'd find an excuse to say that! They can recognize any linguistic style and emulate it. And now they have technology on their side too. If they can access your computer, directly or remotely, they can run everything you've written—emails, docs, online posts—through a software program that scans for all sorts of writing tendencies: commonly used words, sentence structure, literacy level, punctuation and formatting habits, common errors, even personality markers. With that kind of help, these forgers can write a letter even your wife or mother would believe you wrote. Fool the experts too."

Well, well, well, I am certainly getting an education from Enzo today. I feel the coil of anxiety that has been tightening in my chest for the past week start to loosen a little. Why? Well, now there is at least one plausible explanation for how that suicide note got written that doesn't involve my being bat-shit insane. It also would explain why Troop and company spent so much time dicking around on my computer that day.

It's hard to believe a guy like Goslin would go to the trouble and expense of hiring a "literary forger," though. But then again, if he runs in criminal circles that might have access to that kind of specialist, it's not so farfetched, is it?

I thank Enzo for his help and get up to leave. As I'm heading out the door, he shouts in a movie-Amish accent, "You be careful out among them English."

# Chapter 27

As soon as I leave Enzo's, I notice a reply from Miles to my earlier text. It reads, *Beth and I want to buy you dinner tonight. How about the Mermaid at 6:30?*

I recognize the purpose of the invite. Treating me to dinner at a restaurant will allow Miles and Beth to buy off some guilt about shunning me, while still keeping me away from their home, their family, and their prying friends. Still, I suppose I'll have to eat something one way or another. So I text him: *Sounds good. Thx.* Miles texts back: *Why don't I pick you up at 5? That'll give us time to talk about Goslin first. We'll meet Beth at the Merm.*

Good. Miles has managed to wangle some Beth-free time with me so we can strategize about how to handle the latest developments.

I have a couple of errands to run—buy a flashlight and some trail mix and also, now, some first-aid supplies to treat my wounds. Once I've completed those tasks, it's time to start getting ready to meet Miles. I'm still officially a guest at Harbor House, so I decide to shower there. Anyway, Miles still thinks that's where I'm staying.

There are no private bathrooms at HH, as I've mentioned, only a suite of shower and toilet stalls in the middle of the second floor. As I take my clothes off in front of one of the large mirrors, I see I've got three quahog-sized bruises blossoming on my sides, and a couple of nice ones on my back. The right side of my forehead is cut and bruised from where a cherrystone struck it, and my lip is puffed up—don't know how that happened. I have another cut on top of my head, with a visible lump under it. This new "fighting hobo" look is not going to play well with Beth.

The worst thing I see in the mirror is not the cuts and bruises, though; it's the hollow look in my eyes and the tremor in my muscles. Each encounter with Goslin and his goons has been more extreme than the last, and I have a pretty good idea what it's all leading up to. The torment they're putting me through now is just foreplay. Payback for all the years of suffering Goslin believes I caused him. But the real payoff is yet to come.

I need to come up with a plan *tonight* to deal with Goslin and, if possible, execute the plan tonight as well. Tomorrow morning at the latest. I don't want to wait around to find out what his next move is going to be. *I* have to make the next move. Somehow.

• • • • •

I sneak out of Harbor House by the fire escape to find Miles already waiting for me in his golf cart. He looks... tense. I slide into the cart beside him, and off we go.

It appears the rain may finally have stopped for good.

Miles waits till we're out of the village and then starts peppering me with questions. "Are you sure Goslin is one of the guys who attacked you?" "How do you know?" "Are you sure he's on the island?" "How do you *know* Goslin and Begley have inside information about the accident?"

The more I provide credible answers, the more agitated he becomes. Again I find this odd. If he really thought I was nuts, he wouldn't be grilling me this way. And he wouldn't be getting so worked up about my answers.

I would love to believe his concern is solely for my safety, real or psychological, but I know Miles well enough to suspect there is more to it than that. He only gets *this* concerned about things that affect him personally.

As if to confirm my suspicions, Miles pulls the cart over, jumps out, and starts pacing in circles. "Fuck," he says. "Why does this have to be happening *right now*? Could the timing be any worse? Jesus Christ! Jesus Christ!"

"What is it, Miles?" He doesn't answer. "Does this have anything to do with the career moves you were telling me about?"

"Yes, damn it to shit!" He continues to pace a groove in the road.

"What's going on with all that?" I ask.

"I'm not supposed to talk about it."

I can tell he *wants* to talk about it, though, so I don't say a word. I just fold my arms and wait. It'll come.

It does.

"Remember I told you there might be an opportunity coming up for me in Washington?"

"No, I forgot. Of course I remember."

"It's in the Senate, Finn."

"Holy crap."

"Yeah. I don't know if you keep up with political news, but there have been rumors in the press about Pat Aldridge being in poor health, possibly resigning before his term is up." Aldridge is one of Maine's two U.S. Senators. "All pretty vague stuff, but my name has been tossed around in a couple of newspapers—very purposefully, by the way—as a possible replacement. Anyway, within the next week or so, Aldridge is going to announce he's stepping down. Turns out, he has terminal cancer and wants to spend his final months with his family. This isn't public information yet."

"And?"

"In the state of Maine, it's the governor who appoints an interim senator in a situation like this. And... it turns out I might have an 'in' there. Some kind of 'favor-owed' situation. Anyway, things have been heating up behind the scenes and now, well, it's..."

"Time to buy a Keurig machine for your new office on Capitol Hill?"

Deflecting my lightness, he says, "This could become more than just a Senate seat too, Finn. A *lot* more, if a certain group of people have their way."

Is he saying what I think he's saying? "Wow, Miles. That's pretty freaking exciting."

"Try *terrifying*. If there was ever a time in my life when I had to be absolutely, positively, boiled-in-a-sterilizer clean, it's right now. I can't afford to have even the *whiff* of a scandal floating *anywhere near me*. Why does this stuff have to be surfacing *now*? Why?"

"Whoever is pursuing me, Miles—Goslin and his gang—has no knowledge of you being in that car."

At this, Miles' face flashes red and he stares hard at me for several seconds. He holds up his phone like an accusation, showing me a text message on the screen: *Carlisle Road, Bridgefield, MA. 1:20 am, May 13, 1999.* Jesus. What? In the Sender box is a garble of numbers, like the one I saw on my phone when the dead fish messages came in.

"Who... Who sent this? When did you get it?"

Miles says nothing. His eyes dig into mine with almost physical force.

"This is impossible," I say. "There were no witnesses, and the bottle connects *me* to the scene, not you. The only person on Earth who can possibly put you in that car that night is..." I leave the unspoken "me" hanging heavily in the air.

A storm cloud passes over Miles' expression.

"Jesus, Miles. You don't think *I* sent this text... do you? You don't think *I'm* the one who's been—"

"No. Well, not... deliberately."

"Meaning what?"

"Meaning if you were... in ideal mental shape—the Finn I've always known—of course you would never..."

"Do you still think I'm delusional? Do you still think I made up that story about being attacked at my parents' house? That *I'm* the one stirring all this old stuff up? Even after what I've told you about Goslin? He's *on the island*, Miles; that's a fact." I lift my shirt and rotate my torso to show him the bruises on my sides and back. He gasps. "Do you think I did that to myself? Real events are happening here."

"I know. I know real events—*some* real events—are happening. But I also can't forget the fact that you *did* just get out of a psychiatric hospital. I'm sorry, Finn, but I can't help but wonder how much of what's happening to you is—okay, I'll say it—your guilt *orchestrating* events so you somehow get punished for your misdeeds."

"God, Miles."

"People do that, Finn. I've seen it. They bring down upon themselves the punishment they think they have coming to them. And if that's what's happening here, then maybe part of you wants to make sure *I get punished too!*"

Ah, the nub of it. We face each other on the road like unarmed gunslingers. "You've been watching too many old Hitchcock movies," I say. "Tell Beth thanks for the dinner invite, but I have a date with Chef Boyardee this evening." I start off down the road.

After a few seconds, I hear the *bloop* of a text message coming through on Miles' phone. Miles pulls up next to me in his cart and stops. His face is the color of a cadaver's. He shows me the text he just received. It's identical to the last one: *Carlisle Road, Bridgefield, MA. 1:20 am, May 13, 1999.*

And I sure as hell didn't send it.

• • • • •

We drive around the island in silence for many minutes. Miles is chewing his lower lip like it's calamari. Finally, he releases a few tight syllables. "All right, assuming Edgar Goslin is on Musqasset right now—and that's still a big assumption in my mind..."

"He took the ferry here, Miles. He did. Ask Preston Davis."

"...Then where does that leave us?"

I tell him about acquiring Goslin's cell-phone number from Preston. I also tell him about the money-for-information ploy I used on Priscilla Begley.

"That wasn't a terrible idea," he concedes, stopping the cart to think. "Actually, I don't see any reason it can't still work."

"Begley hung up on me. She knew I was conning her."

"No, I mean we approach Goslin directly. Leave Begley out of it."

"But he may have talked to her by now. If so, I'm sure she told him about my call."

"So? What's to say we can't still reach out to him? We call his cell, tell him we know he's on the island, tell him that we're an interested party, that we're on the island too, and that we have cash for him *if* he can provide us certain information. Act like we're the ones with all the leverage. Play it coy, don't give him any details, just say we want to meet him. If I'm Goslin, I'm going to be curious enough, or suspicious enough, to show up."

"Maybe. But I'd be super-cautious too, if I were him. I'd definitely bring my goons along. And let's assume it works: we get him to show up—either alone or with goons—at a meeting place. Then what? I mean, we're not really going to hand him a wad of cash, so...?"

Miles pauses and thinks. "Right, we need to be crystal clear about our objective, and our move. Also—shit!—we'll have to find a stand-in to do the actual meeting for us; Goslin knows who you are, and he might know who I am too." He looks at his watch, blows air out of his cheeks. It's obvious this thing is going to require more strategizing than we have time to do in the ten minutes remaining before we meet Beth.

"Let's plan on doing something in the morning," he says. "Meanwhile, let's enjoy a..."

"Last supper?"

"Nice meal." He starts driving again. "Needless to say," he adds, needlessly, "don't tell Beth what we talked about."

• • • • •

Beth is a better actor than I remembered her to be. She orders a nice bottle of wine to get dinner rolling, makes lively conversation throughout the meal, and, in general, plays the perfect hostess. She even accepts, unchallenged, my obvious lie about slipping on some wet rocks at Mussel Cove as the explanation for my cuts and bruises. A neutral observer would never imagine: (1) she thinks I'm criminally insane, (2) she loathes my relationship with her husband with every mitochondrion of every cell of her being.

The only time I see tension cross her face is when I bring up her parents' upcoming visit. She covers immediately, though, saying how nice it will be for her kids to see their grandparents for the holiday. At one point, I catch her flashing Miles an eye signal. Half a minute later, she excuses herself to go to the bathroom. "I'll walk with you," says Miles, who gets up and heads in the same direction. In the mirror over the bar, I see Beth walk past the rest rooms and around a corner. Miles follows her. They've gone into the back hallway to discuss something; probably how to ditch me now that the food-ingesting portion of the festivities is over.

I notice Miles has left his phone on the table. Dare I peek? Better not. It's probably locked anyway. But then I remember him checking his email only moments ago; maybe it's still unlocked from that. Keeping my eyes on the bar mirror, I slide his phone across the table onto my lap. His email is still open; the phone is unlocked! I tap my way to his text-message log and find half a dozen texts from random-looking sets of numbers — going back to yesterday. They're all the same message: *Carlisle Road, Bridgefield, MA. 1:20 am, May 13, 1999.* I note the first one came in yesterday at 10:22 a.m. That would have been right after I showed him the old newspaper article in the chapel. Damn.

So *that* explains Miles' sudden change of attitude — when he showed up at Harbor House with his laptop, ready to work. And why he's been "helping" me with this whole thing. And hiding it from Beth. Someone has placed *him* at the scene of that accident. His concern is not for me. Never has been. His concern is for Miles. Why didn't I see that before?

Underneath his calm, "empathetic" exterior, Miles has been shitting cinder blocks since he got that first text. Because, to him, it meant one of two things: either *I* was sending the texts because I'm a nut-job hellbent on seeing both of us get our karmic comeuppance, or else a third party, perhaps a political rival, really *has* figured out a way to tie him to that fatal accident, a job the police couldn't do. And even though Miles didn't actually throw the bottle — in *his* mind, anyway — just the fact that he was in the car with me, drunk, when people were killed, makes for the kind of story a state senator would hardly want anyone tweeting about.

Especially a state senator with tall ambitions.

I spot Miles returning from the back hallway with Beth. I slip his phone back onto the table, screen-side down.

• • • • •

On my way back to Danny's shed in the deepening darkness, I catch the scent of herb in the air and pass within ten feet of a trio of young men in raincoats standing under the eaves of a large woodshed. It's my three beer-buying buddies with the $4.71 business offer. The alleged eldest of the trio flashes me his toothy grin again, but it comes off as creepy now.

I feel a ping in my gut and realize something is still bugging me about my earlier encounter with these guys and their whole "twenty-one" story. I can't put my finger on what it is, though.

I try to shake off the feeling as I walk on. I wonder if the lads are going to follow me.

My cell-phone rings, startling me. Is my phone service working again, or will this be another dropped call?

I duck behind a rack of kayaks-for-rent, seemingly unfollowed by the lads. The number I see on Caller ID does not warm my heart. It's Angie's. The sun is long past the yardarm, so *that* can't be good news. I tap the Answer button.

"Okay," says the gin-thickened voice at the other end. "You want to dig into this shit, have it your way. Grab a bloody shovel."

# Chapter 28

What comes tumbling out of Angie's mouth over the next few minutes causes tectonic plates to shift in the psychological foundation of my life.

"He didn't think you were a bad person, Finn," she blurts out, as if she's been holding her breath for two minutes. "He knew it was an accident. He was worried about it ruining *your* life."

"Who, Angie?"

I know damn well who.

"You know damn well who."

Dad, of course.

"What are we talking about here?" I ask her.

"He knew, Finn."

I'm pretty sure I know what she's saying, but I need to hear the words aloud. In a voice that sounds hollow and distant to my own ears, I say, "Knew what?"

"Don't make me say it, Finn."

"Knew what, Ange?"

"That you caused that crash! The one that killed those people. That's why he lied to the police. Not to protect himself. To protect *you*. But you're not a bad person. You're not a bad—"

"Angie!" I snap. I can feel her slipping into maudlin incoherence, a stage in her drunkenness progression from which there is no return. "I need you to stay focused."

"I can't promise anything," she slurs.

"How did he know? What made him come to that conclusion?"

"I told you. It was in the papers. That the cops suspected"—she mangles that word—"a bottle was thrown from that bridge. One day they showed up at our door with a credit card receipt. Asked Dad if he bought a bottle of that Glen-fuck-me-sideways crap. Dad remembered the way you were acting the day after your graduation. Dropping grad school, heading off to California with some losers you hardly knew. He knew *something* had happened to you, but he didn't know what. When the cops started asking questions about the bottle, he put two and two together. Told 'em the bottle went out with the recycling."

Jesus. My whole "No one else could possibly have known about that night" theory has just flitted away like a flock of startled gulls. Dad knew. Which means Mom knew. Angie knew. And any of them could have told anyone, at any time. This changes everything.

"How long have you known what happened?" I ask my sister.

"Since back then. There was no hiding from it." Angie seems to sober up all at once. "Things got super-weird after you left, Finn. Dad started staying up late at night, drinking at the kitchen table. In the morning we'd find notes he'd scribbled about the Abelsens and Goslin. The whole thing was killing him, but there was no way he was going to turn his own son in."

Unreal. All of this was going on while I was learning how to make burritos in Mission Beach, blissfully unaware anyone had even died that night.

"So *that's* when Dad started changing?" I say, as much to myself as to her. I remember when I came back from California, my dad was a different man. He looked twenty years older, and his eyes had a dark, pleading look. I'd always thought it was his mounting health problems that caused the depression of his later years, but now I see it was probably the other way around.

"Him and Mom had started having problems too," says Ange. "The house was not a fun place to be, believe me. I started 'going out' every night just to get away from there."

Suddenly the whole Carroll Family Holiday Tragicomedy Special sharpens into focus. To protect Miles' secret, I blew town and began steering my life into the breakdown lane. To protect *my* secret, Dad allowed guilt to consume him. Which, in turn, put the final nail in the coffin of his marriage to Mom. Which, in turn, caused Angie to start avoiding home like a communicable disease. Which, in turn, caused her to "fall in with the wrong crowd" and pick up her lifelong love of liquor, among other unhelpful tendencies.

My God, it's an O. Henry tale on acid! An entire family brought down by a single thoughtless act *none of us even committed*! I don't know whether to laugh or break down crying. But I do know this: if I start laughing I will literally never stop. They will haul me off the island on a gurney, singing "Camptown Races" in a Daffy Duck voice.

It's my turn to deliver a blow to Angie. "I need to tell you something," I say to her, "and I need you to be sitting down." I hope what I'm going to say will help her in the long run, but it might do the opposite. "Dad was mistaken. The night of that accident, it was Mi—"

Suddenly the phone connection cuts out as if I've hit End Call. I redial. The call goes through but then cuts out again. I try several more times; same result—connect, disconnect. Angie calls *me* back, but when I try to answer, the line goes dead again. Thank you, oh Mighty Phone Gods of Musqasset, for your ever-impeccable timing.

I couldn't have left Angie dangling at a worse moment. By the time I reach her again later—*if* I manage to do so—she'll be too drunk to communicate with.

*Bloop.* A text message comes through. A knife emoji, a gun emoji, and a coffin emoji.

Come to think of it, maybe I'm the one who needs a drink here. I make a beeline for Pete's Lagoon and plant myself at the corner of the bar. Jeannie looks at me as if I'm a suicide bomber with my finger on the detonator. She doesn't even ask how I'm doing; she simply fetches the bottle of Glenmalloch from the top shelf and pours me a finger.

Six seconds later, she pours me a refill. "Are we still on for ten o'clock?" she hazards.

I probe her eyes to see if there's some dark secret hiding in there I should be worried about. If there is, she's covering it well. I remind myself of my commitment to trust her.

I nod; yeah, we're still on.

· · · · ·

I lie on my bed at Harbor House, warm from the good scotch but cold in my gut. My decision to return to my rented room instead of Danny's shed was unplanned and automatic. For the first time in days, my mind is devoid of thoughts about men with loppers trying to kill me. Or about friends who think I'm psychotic. I am oblivious to text-message threats and to the fishy smoke detector hovering right over my face. I am even indifferent to the astonishing note I found under my door when I returned to my room just now: "Hey, want to meet for a drink later and share seafood pie recipes? – Leah." It's been ages since a pretty woman courted my attention, but even lust can't set its hook in my mind.

All my thoughts are on my fucked-up family.

I think about my father crawling into an early grave, at the age of fifty-seven, believing himself partially responsible for the Abelsens' tragedy and believing his son to be an unredeemed killer. Lying to everyone *about a lie.* A falsehood. If only he had talked to me about it, just once, I could have lifted that burden from his shoulders. But of course, that would have broken the Carroll family code. The code of secrecy. In Dad's mind, keeping mum about my "crime" was the greatest gift of love a father could bestow on a son. That's how the Carrolls showed love, after all; by protecting one another's stories.

I clearly see, for the first time in my life, exactly how septic we were as a family. A meal at the Carroll home was not an open-hearted gathering of family members. It was a weighty affair, filled with innuendo, in which each of us related to the others through a filter of secrets each alone was privy to. The layers of who-knew-what-about-whom and what-it-was-okay-to-talk-about were insanely complex, and power dynamics were always in play because each of us was hoarding private knowledge we could use to blow the others' lives apart.

My older sister Grace knew I had been caught shoplifting and also knew where I hid my porn stash. I knew she was using contraception and sneaking around with an older guy who liked to get rough. Angie knew I sometimes stole beer from Dad's private fridge. I knew she liked to cut her skin when she was alone. And so on and so on. Layer upon layer. But ultimately we *kept* all our secrets, at least the big ones, because that was how one behaved with honor — yes, honor — in the Carroll household.

Suddenly a memory swoops, full-blown, into my mind, flooring me with its vivid detail.

*I'm seven years old and I bound off the school bus, excited because my class has been dismissed early for a teachers' meeting. I run into the house to tell my mother I'm home, but I don't see her anywhere — maybe she forgot I had a short day. I figure she must be napping, which she often does in the middle of the day, so I dash upstairs. Before I get to my parents' bedroom, a man slips out of the room, closing the door behind him.*

*"I just needed to find your mother," he explains to me, flashing a smile that doesn't spread to his eyes, "so I could give her a special package." Yes, that's the phrasing he uses; talk about Freudian slips. That's when I notice he's wearing a brown UPS uniform. With lots of undershirt showing. The thing that strikes me the most, though, is that he is a black man. This is the first time I can recall seeing a black man in our house. This random moment of racial awareness distracts me from the more obvious questions I should be asking.*

*The man hustles off downstairs, and my mother emerges from the bedroom, tying her bathrobe sash. She gives me her biggest smile, a rarity, and says in a hushed voice, "Come downstairs with me, Finnian; I need to tell you a great big secret."*

*As she scoops me a heaping bowl of ice cream from the freezer, she explains to me, "That delivery man was bringing a birthday present for Daddy. Birthday presents have to be kept secret, right? So you can never tell Daddy about the man who came today."* **Man who came** — *again with the Freudian stuff. "Can you keep that a secret, Finnian? Mommy likes to give ice cream to little boys who are good at keeping secrets."*

*True to her word, she randomly gives me ice cream, with a wink and a smile, not once but several times in the ensuing weeks.*

*I have pretty much forgotten the whole thing when we are at a neighborhood cookout the following summer. I'm looking for my mom, to show her a salamander I've caught. I find her sitting at a picnic table next to the same UPS man who had been in our house that day, only this time he's wearing a tank top and shorts. I notice their bare thighs are touching. Silly. My mother makes the "shh" gesture and winks at me. And the random ice cream treats start up again.*

Until this moment, I had no conscious memory of that whole episode. "Conscious" is the operant word here. Because it doesn't take a Manhattan psychoanalyst to see the subliminal thread that has woven through my entire life. I suddenly realize, as insane as it sounds, that I was actually seeking Jeannie's *approval*, on some level, when I looked the other way regarding her infidelities. I thought somehow she would *credit* me for my discretion. Yep, I did.

God, what a rancid stew we Carrolls were steeped in.

And I'm still steeping in it. Look at Angie. She is a raging alcoholic and I have never confronted her on it; have, in fact, covered for her on countless occasions. Look at my friendship with Miles. Ever since college, my value to him has derived from how well I could help him maintain his lie of being the perfect guy. The list goes on.

Danny's message for me was absolutely on target. My whole life, I have sought to gain my power from lies. And — surprise! — there *is* no power in lies. Lying has sucked the life out of the Carrolls for decades. But maybe Danny was right about something else too. Maybe the crisis I'm in is offering me a chance. A chance to explode this old pattern once and for all.

Yes! That power *is* in my hands. These truths I've been learning about Dad, these memories I've been unlocking, are not necessarily here to condemn or shame me but to offer me clarity. I don't have to live the Carroll Way. I *can* reinvent myself.

I roll off the bed, fired up with fresh energy and resolve. It *is* possible to change; I have to believe that. Life has been holding that door open for me ever since I stumbled out of my parents' kitchen, clinging to a pulse, eight days ago. I will not piss that chance away.

I look at my cell-phone clock. Nine fifty. Jeannie will be out of work in ten minutes.

Before I leave my room, I take the sweet note Leah left for me and write on the back, "Would love to exchange seafood pie recipes with you, but, alas, I am a man in love. Next lifetime for sure. – Finn." I slip the note under her door as I walk past.

It's a small act of truthfulness, but it feels good.

## Chapter 29

The Shipwreck teeters on the edge of Table Rock like a truck trailer dangling off a bridge in an action movie. I'm surprised by how much integrity the hull still possesses. I'd have thought the punishment this storm has been meting out would have broken it apart by now, but the old mail boat hangs stubbornly together; determined, it seems, to make its final voyage as the *K.C. Mokler*, not as a pile of anonymous sea shrapnel.

I was expecting Jeannie and me to go someplace quiet to talk, but the first thing she said when I met her at Pete's was, "It's going. Tonight, I can feel it." I knew what she meant—The Shipwreck. And I knew we had to be there to witness it. We borrowed Pete's ancient pickup truck and drove to Lighthouse Hill as fast as we could.

Now here we sit, looking down with flashlights at the wreck once again, waiting for one final monster wave to sweep it away. The rain has ended and the winds have finally calmed, but the sea is still pounding ferociously.

I've always been of the persuasion that places and objects hold onto "memories"—energetic traces—of emotionally charged events that take place in and around them. I think maybe that's what ghosts are. And so, when The Shipwreck lifts anchor tonight, I think it will be taking the ghosts of Jeannie and Finn's old love with it. Not just metaphorically but in some energetically real way. I believe that. I do.

The idea lashes me in the heart like a stingray's barb. But then I think of all the lies, all the hurt silences, all the drunkenness-in-place-of-intimacy that took place in and around that old husk. The ghosts of *those* things will be going out to sea too. And maybe that's not so terrible.

We remain wordless for several minutes, and then at last I cast her a line. "So you had something you wanted to tell me last night?"

Silence resumes as we watch the old wreck rock and groan on its great slate bed. I don't want Jeannie to speak until she's ready. Maybe I don't want her to speak at all.

She finally says what's on her mind. "When you told me last night about Miles throwing that bottle, I was... surprised."

"What do you mean?"

"Angie told me about the accident, Finn."

"Jesus. When?"

"Years ago. When you and I were living together, here. She told me *you* had thrown that bottle—because, well, I guess that's what she believed. But she told it to me in confidence and made me swear I would never tell you."

"How the hell did it come up?"

"You and I were having... issues. I used to talk to Angie about them sometimes. She knew you better than anyone else did. I just wanted to understand you." We watch another wave assault the wreck. Not the big one yet. "I always felt there were things... kinda major things... holding you back from really being in a relationship with me."

"Those things were named Stavros, Captain Jim, and Peter," I point out. I have never named her secret lovers aloud in this way. It feels pretty good, actually.

She allows my remark to pass unchallenged and says, "I was on the phone with Angie one night and we were talking about it. She was drinking..."

"Do tell."

"...And she let it slip that you had this... burden you were carrying around that had been weighing on you for years. I asked what it was. I probably had no right to ask, and she probably had no right to tell me. But she did. On the condition I would *never* tell you."

"But you just did."

"I called her last night. After you left. Told her I might need to rescind my promise. I couldn't talk to *you* till I told her that."

So Jeannie was the "everybody" Angie was ranting about in her drunken voicemail.

"This certainly puts a new face on things," I say. "Half the time we were living together, you were going around thinking I was a killer?"

"Not the 'malice aforethought' kind."

"But still... You've known about these deaths for years. And I've only known about them for — what? — three days. Things might have been different for us if you'd told me."

"I made a promise to Angie, Finn. What good is a promise if you don't keep it? To my credit, I did try to pry it out of you several times."

Thinking back, it's true; she did. She used to harp, to the point of genuine annoyance, on this theory that I was carrying some old secret that was dragging my life down like an anchor.

"I was actually a lot more surprised to learn you *didn't* throw that bottle," she says.

"Why's that?"

"Well, because I remember the bizarre way you were acting the day you said goodbye to me in '99 and left for California. And because it explained so much. I thought guilt was the whole reason you were so... What was the term I used to use?"

"'Insufficiently entitled.'"

"Right. I figured you were a textbook case of Catholic guilt. You believed you should have been caught and punished for your crime, but you weren't. Therefore, you didn't think you deserved to have good things happen to you. Therefore, you would never ask for anything you really wanted. Even if it walked into the room naked and gave you a lap dance."

"I don't think you were wrong about that part."

"I don't either. It's the *degree* of guilt I don't understand," says Jeannie. "Don't you think you're exaggerating your role in this thing? Miles threw that bottle. You didn't do anything."

"Exactly. I didn't *do* anything. I was the one — the only one — who had the power to act, but I didn't. Miles passed out. He had no idea he caused any harm."

"Neither did you."

"Because I *chose* not to know. I heard sounds that night, Jeannie. Sounds of glass and metal. After he threw that bottle. But I never followed up to find out what they were. In fact, I fled the freaking *state* so I'd never have to know for sure."

"And if you *had* known, that would have changed the outcome how? You said yourself the cops sped off, blue lights flashing. They must have been going to the accident scene. Everything was handled. The only thing that would have changed if you had come forward is that blame would have been placed on Miles. And you didn't want to see your friend's life ruined. I don't see how that makes you the devil. But I do see how it makes you an insanely loyal friend. You took on the moral burden that should have been his."

"Neither of us took on the moral burden. That's the point, Jeannie."

She emits the most rueful laugh in the history of rueful laughs. "Riiiight."

Thinking back on my life over the last eighteen years, I have to laugh too.

Part of me desperately wants to accept the shot at exoneration Jeannie is trying to offer me, but my conscience — that infallible inner calculator — tells me a debt is still owed. It seems Jeannie's inner ledger is coming up red too. I can see in her downcast eyes that she has not said all she needs to say to me tonight.

"What is it, Jeannie?"

She stares at the wreck as if she was personally responsible for its ruin. "I kept my promise never to tell *you* what Angie said... but she never asked me not to tell *anyone*."

As I wait for her to complete this revelation, we both turn our heads at the exact same moment. The horizon is rising eerily to meet the cloud-covered moon, and we know what we are seeing. A mammoth wave is rolling in. Instinctively, we scramble up the cliff-side several yards and watch it advance, mesmerized.

I brace myself for the drama that will be unleashed when the killer wave breaks — the violent clap of water, the bomb-blast of exploding spray, the shriek of hull-metal on rock...

But the wave doesn't break. It arrives instead as a gigantic swell; black water rising quietly up the cliff-side by fifteen feet or more. The Shipwreck silently lifts off its stone berth, straddles the water's surface for a few seconds, and then sinks out of sight with a sigh of bubbles. The massive swell retreats to sea.

When Table Rock becomes visible again, it is a literal blank slate. The wreck is gone.

A tear runs down Jeannie's cheek. But I don't think it is for the *K.C. Mokler*, off on its final mail run. Jeannie squeezes my fingers as if she wants to break the bones.

• • • • •

For reasons I can't quite fathom, it now seems a foregone conclusion that Jeannie and I will sleep together tonight. This tacit understanding fills the cab of the truck like secret perfume as Jeannie drives to her house. It gels into a certainty when, halfway there, the lights go out on Musqasset — eleven o'clock; lovers' hour — and Jeannie lays a finger on my hand, ever so lightly.

Why, oh why, is it that life only gives us the things we crave the most when we no longer crave them? Not that I don't want to sleep with Jeannie. I do. Oh fuck yes, yes I do. But now I care about the reasons. I don't want it to be a one-and-done thing, an impulsive act committed for reckless or poetic causes. I don't want a farewell fuck. I don't want a closure fuck. I don't want a "two lost ships in a storm" fuck. I don't want Jeannie sleeping with me out of abandon, pity, grief, desperation, existential loneliness, or even good ol' glorious randiness. Two days ago, I wouldn't have given two shits about the why. Now I do.

So I must navigate these waters mindfully. The conditions, the *understandings*, will need to be right, or I won't be able to go through with it.

Jeannie steers Pete's truck down a meandering, unmaintained dirt road and parks in the woods behind Fishermen's Court. It's a token stab at privacy that will fool no one, least of all Goslin's gang if they're watching for us, but I tip my hat at the effort.

We approach her house, treading softly, without flashlights, and slip into its cinnamon-scented darkness. I still know by touch where the rechargeable battery-operated lamp is located, but before I can turn it on, Jeannie presses me against the wall and kisses me. Her lips have a wet, silky warmth that dissolves all reason. I kiss her back without a *nanosecond's* hesitation. The idea that I was going to dictate the rules of this engagement—via a mutually agreed-upon set of emotional parameters, stamped in triplicate and duly signed by both parties, grumble, ahem—now seems as absurd as the idea that I could dictate the course of the ocean storm that has stranded me here on Musqasset.

Before a coherent thought can even begin to form in my head, we are pulling at each other's clothes and lurching toward the nearest horizontal surface, which, in this case, happens to be the living room sofa/rug combo.

I've always been a "lights on" kind of guy when it comes to lovemaking, especially with Jeannie. I never wanted to be robbed of the visual feast of her nakedness or the flush that comes over her face and neck when she is in the throes of lust. But tonight, darkness is the perfect milieu. It makes the tactile exploration of each other's bodies all the more pressing, the moments of touch-meeting-touch all the more mysteriously synchronized.

Every cliché ever written about lovemaking applies here. Jeannie and I proceed to consume one another sexually with a hunger and ferocity I've never imagined even in my most debauched fantasies—and yet each urgent, darting movement is feathered by an exquisite gentleness of touch that turns it into art. Time disappears. Individuality disappears. There is only the act of love, performing itself, with Jeannie and me as the stunned and grateful witnesses. God enrapturing Godself and inviting us along for the party.

And stuff like that.

Somehow we end up in her bed. And that may be the best part of all. Jeannie, naked, soft, and warm, wrapped around me like a blanket as sleep comes prowling for us in the dark. Still not a word spoken since we stepped out of the truck.

A thought intrudes. I wonder if the men are standing outside the house right now, watching, waiting. I don't even care. As long as they leave Jeannie and me alone right now, they can do whatever they want. Fuck them.

But of course, my mind can't rest, now that I've thought about the danger. I slink out to the kitchen and fumble around in a drawer until I find a sharp knife. When I come back to bed, Jeannie is curled away from me on her side.

Fuck them. Fuck them and the ferry they rode in on.

• • • • •

It's been years since anyone served me a hot breakfast without expecting a tip. I awaken to the smells of coffee brewing and eggs cooking in the rain-washed island air. For a moment I am able to pretend life is just good. Here I am, with Jeannie, on a Sunday morning, in the home we once shared, my concept of lovemaking recalibrated to new heights—and now coffee and eggs await. A man can dream, can't he?

When I enter the kitchen, the dream evaporates like water on a hot griddle. Jeannie is sitting at the table, staring out the window, her back to me. She doesn't turn to greet me. I know she has rowed away to her own private island, the one with no visitors' dock.

I grab a cup of coffee and sit behind the plate of toast and eggs she has made for me. If I detect even a whiff of regret from her over what happened between us, I'm going to jam a fork into my neck.

"I'm not going to say last night was a mistake," she offers at last, still turned, "because clearly it wasn't *that*."

"Clearly," I say. At least we agree on one thing. "But..."

"But..." Here it comes. "I hope it hasn't raised any unrealistic expectations on your... on *either* of our parts."

"And by 'unrealistic expectations,' you mean..."

"Once the ferry is running, you need to be on it and we both need to just... resume life as normal."

I have to chew on that before responding. First of all, there is no "life as normal" for me. Hasn't been for years. But especially not since a trio of strangers showed up in my parents' house and tried to boot me permanently from the good ship Lollipop. But that's beside the point. Do I have a right to ask Jeannie to change her life for me, based on one night of intimacy? Do I even want that myself? We have not remade enough ground with each other to be entertaining such thoughts. I haven't even met her daughter, for God's sake. So I certainly cannot argue with Jeannie's logic. And yet, why close doors?

"I'm not going to make any awkward suggestions," I say. "Don't worry. But at the same time, I'm not going to pretend, for the sake of convenience, that last night was only a casual hookup. It wasn't. And I'm not going to lie and say it was. I'm done with lying."

"Finn, please, can we...?"

"That's all I'm going to say about it, Jeannie. The end. Let's just enjoy each other's company this morning. No demands. No promises. No heavy silences. You and I pissed away enough of our time together that way."

That seems to mollify her, and she lightens up. We eat our breakfast and chat for a while, mostly about Bree, who's due back on the Tuesday morning ferry. I steer Jeannie onto the topic of writing and convince her to read me a short story she wrote. It's good. I mean *holy shit* good. Wow. Jeannie has become a bona fide writer, with her own voice.

I ask what happened to the paintings I left behind. She leads me out to the storage shed I converted into a mini-studio, and I'm surprised to find it largely as I left it. A manual lawnmower and some boxes have been moved in, but my paintings are still here, and the place still looks like a studio. Just laziness on Jeannie's part or something else? I'm afraid to ask.

Looking at my paintings — both the finished ones and the eternally frozen works-in-progress — is like reading a forgotten diary. When you're a painter, stumbling upon your old paintings can release more stored memories than an electrode to the brain.

I point at a canvas of a dry-docked boat with a hole in its hull. "That was the week you had your breast cancer scare." No symbolism there, doc. Flipping through a leaning stack of canvases, I find a good one of a Musqasset meadow blowing in the wind.

The day I did that one, I recall, I was wandering around the island with my French easel, looking for something to paint. I spotted a guy in a straw hat working on a canvas near Tucker's Field and asked to join him. We had a memorable day together. He asked my advice on a few things and gave me a tip or two. We laughed a lot.

Weeks later, I was thumbing through an art magazine and I learned the man was Jamie Kent, quite possibly the world's most famous living representational artist. And he had been asking *my* advice. I'd almost forgotten about that. Maybe I wasn't crazy to believe I had some genuine talent; maybe I was crazy to believe otherwise. Delusions of mediocrity, is that a thing?

Looking around my old studio, I realize I didn't leave just *one* lover behind when I walked away from my life on Musqasset. I feel a physical, almost sexual urge to hold a paintbrush in my hand again and spar with a canvas.

I notice Jeannie studying one of my pieces, trying to decide whether to share it with me or not. I signal *give it up,* and she reluctantly angles it toward me. It is a nude. Of her. The one and only attempt I ever made to paint her, to bring my two lovers together. That was an arrangement that didn't work out—for one embarrassingly simple reason: when she posed nude for me, I couldn't keep my mind on my work. I'd painted other nude models before and had never had any trouble maintaining artistic detachment. But not with Jeannie. I couldn't look at her naked without getting all riled up. We had a lot of fun in the studio that week, but we more or less agreed it was not a workable long-term solution.

Jeannie must be having the same memories I am, because she drops the canvas and stares at me baldly. Time elongates. She unbuttons the top button of her denim shirt, eyes never leaving mine. I stare back at her, transfixed as always, powerless before her beauty. But as I step toward her, she breaks eye contact and scuttles out the door.

# Chapter 30

I find Jeannie outside, sitting on a sawhorse in the wet grass. Whatever "moment" was about to happen—as the Viagra lady in the TV commercial might say—is now a fleeting memory. I try to sit beside her, but she waves me away.

"I didn't realize I still had a thing for you," she says. "Obviously my self-awareness needs some work in *that* department. But I have to act like a sober person now. For my daughter... and for myself. The bottom line is this: you and I are not going to 'be together.' Na ga happen. There are some... barriers to that, which we don't need to get into. But if I make love to you again, I'm going to start talking myself into believing it actually *could* happen. And I'm going to make myself miserable. For months or years to come. So we need to pull the plug right now. Cauterize the wound instead of making it deeper."

Somehow I knew she was going to say something like this.

"Maybe *I* can have a say in what's a 'barrier' and what isn't," I tender, insisting myself onto the sawhorse.

"No, you can't, because you don't know all the facts. If you did, you would turn your back and walk away without saying a word... again." A dig about the way I left last time.

"Facts about *what*, Jeannie? What could be so—"

"I did some unforgivable things, Finn. After you left."

"What kinds of things?" I honestly can't imagine what would be worse than screwing Cliff the fisherman on the same sofa I watched *Breaking Bad* on.

"Things that... well, they're the reason I stopped drinking."

"Those things can remain your business, Jeannie. Forever."

"I thought I'd never see you again," she says, as if I haven't spoken. "And I was pissed at you and thinking *good riddance to bad ass-clowns*. I never in a million years thought we would have another... opportunity with each other. Or that I'd want one. That doesn't make what I did right; it just explains my frame of mind."

"You don't need to explain anything."

"Yes, I do. I did things in order to hurt you and get back at you. I let my guard down and got involved with the wrong people."

"We both had reasons to try to hurt each other back then," I say. "But whatever you did after I left, it was only emotional acting-out. It didn't *actually* hurt me, because I was gone. I don't ever need to know about it, whatever it was. It has no power to affect me now."

"Yes, it does, Finn. There are... circumstances I have created that are... *ongoing*. And you *will* be hurt. Unless you leave the island on the first ferry run and stay away for good."

"What if I decide not to do that?"

"You need to."

"What if I decide I want to move back to Musqasset, start painting again, build a new life here, meet your daughter...?"

"Christ, Finn!" She jumps up off the sawhorse. "What is wrong with you? You need to go. Now. I have to get ready for work, and if you stay any longer I am going to say things that will..." — her voice loses its edge — "ruin a memory I want to hold onto. Please, Finn, go. ...Please."

She looks wrung out, flattened by a bus. I have no words for her. And yet I don't seem capable of locomotion.

My phone rings, breaking my paralysis. It's Miles. I text him, *Call u in a few*.

Jeannie leans over me, places her hands on my face, and gives me a lingering and delicious kiss. It is deeply infused with "goodbye," though. When she stands up, I can feel the connection between us sever like a snapped cord. She walks off into the house and into her private future.

• • • • •

"Are you ready?" says Miles on the phone as I step out onto the road.

"For what?"

"What we talked about yesterday! To flush out Mr. Edgar Goslin."

"Are we really going to do that?" My brain—not to mention other select portions of my anatomy—is locked into a Jeannie groove right now. I have trouble switching tracks to Goslin. I force my feet to commence the painful trek away from Jeannie's house.

"We'd better be," replies phone-Miles. "I've recruited some helpers." He explains that a pair of young men who work at the new marina have agreed to serve as our "muscle" in the utterly insane event Goslin does agree to meet us in person.

"But we don't even have a plan," I point out.

"I've been working on that," he responds. "Here's the deal. If—and I know that's a giant if—we can get Goslin to agree to meet, we'll insist the meeting take place at the gazebo on the west side of the village. It's private enough to hold a discreet conversation, public enough that no funny business can go down there. My two guys have already staked a claim to it, and I planted a webcam and a recorder there. I've also thrown together some cash, which we can flash at Goslin to, you know, lubricate the gears of conversation."

"And then what?"

"Then we just... see what we can get him to say."

That's our plan? I'm glad my health insurance is paid up.

Miles proposes that *he* make the initial call and conduct the actual powwow with Goslin. He's decided the situation is too sensitive to use a stand-in—he's probably right—and so he will do the meeting himself, wearing oversized sunglasses and Billy Staves' hooded rain suit with the the super-high collar. Our two beefy young conscripts will conspicuously stand guard nearby. In theory, there should be no real danger of violence. But in theory, bumblebees can't fly. We don't know how Goslin will play this, or whether he will bring his own goon squad along. We're messing with things we are eminently unqualified to deal with. As usual.

"I'll meet you at Harbor House in fifteen," says Miles, "and we can phone Goslin from your room."

I hit End Call and step up my pace. The weird clash of emotions I'm feeling — post-coital bliss, raw heartache, and mortal terror — is one I've never quite experienced before. I still feel oddly *vital*, though, in a way I haven't in years. And I'll still take this jacked-up emotional goulash over the low-grade depression that was devouring my soul in Wentworth.

I'm feeling so enlivened, in fact, I barely break stride when I spot a dead crab lying on its back in the middle of the road. Someone's dropped catch? Nope, it's been cut cleanly in half. I see another demi-crustacean about twenty-five feet ahead. And another one after that. Intended for my eyes, no doubt. So my buddies *did* stake me out at Jeannie's after all, and they knew I'd be heading back toward the village on this road. Can't say I'm exactly shocked.

I march on, less fearful than I probably have any right to be.

As I'm about to pass a trailhead on my right, I see a dead mackerel nailed to the wooden trail sign, festering merrily in the morning air. This routine is starting to feel a little childish, guys. I stop and take a look down the bush-lined trail. I see three or four more rotting fish nailed to trees, ten feet or so apart. Do my stalkers actually think they're going to lure me into the woods by planting a trail of dead fish like breadcrumbs? How stupid do I look?

Wait, don't answer that.

I have no intention of walking into a trap, but I do jog down the trail a few yards to see how far ahead they've marked the path. Through the foliage, I spot another fish-nailed-to-a-tree just beyond a fork in the trail, and another after that. I guess they want me to follow their trail toward the abandoned orchard in the middle of the island. Right, guys. That'll happen.

I turn around to head back to the main road when I hear the rustle of branches and the scuffle of shoes on dead leaves. Two men grab my arms from behind. A third one yanks a band of stretchy material over my head, forming an instant blindfold.

A fist slams into my side. I collapse to my knees.

One of the attackers ties a rag around my mouth to gag me as another one tries to pull my hands together behind my back. I thrash and kick in resistance.

A paralyzing kick from a shoe-heel is delivered to the side of my head, and I instantly see stars (yes, I've just discovered, that really happens). I give up the fight. They tie my hands.

The men carry me along, face down, my shoes dragging in the dirt. They trot me across the road and into the brush on the other side. They're moving in a half-run as if they want to get this thing handled quickly, whatever this thing is going to be.

The blindfold is working; I can't see a thing. The men drag me for fifty yards or more over rocky, brambly terrain. Then they lift me and toss me, not at all gently, into what feels and sounds like the bed of a pickup truck. I yelp in pain as my face meets the molded metal, but my cry goes nowhere, thanks to the gag.

A motor starts and the truck drives off.

The truck bounces along a rough road and makes a series of sharp turns that have me slipping and sliding in every direction. I can feel the grit of loose sand in the truck bed.

After a couple of minutes, the truck stops.

The men yank me from the bed and drop me roughly on the ground. The surface I land on feels and smells like a dirty carpet. The guys position me on my back, my tied-up hands behind me, and pull my legs out straight. They bind my legs together with a series of bungee cords—thighs, knees, ankles.

Next, they roll me up inside the dusty, filthy-smelling carpet and wrap some more bungees around the roll. I feel myself being lifted and carried along by the men. These guys must have planned this out like Ocean's Eleven; not a word has been spoken by any of them.

They toss me, rolled up in the rug, onto another hard surface. It is instantly evident, from the rocking of the "floor" and the sound of surf, that I'm in a small metal boat. I hear an outboard motor kick over. That's when I realize how screwed I am. How many benign reasons can there be for hauling a person out to sea in a rolled-up carpet?

Try as I might, I can't conjure up a list.

The boat starts off. The waves feel fence-high as we maneuver over them. We must be in the bay, though, because the water would be even rougher if we were in the open Atlantic.

It's hard to keep track of time, I've noticed, when you're rolled up in a carpet on your way to your own execution, but I estimate eight or ten minutes pass as the boat chugs and dips over the rolling waves, which grow steadily steeper as we go.

Finally, one of the men can no longer keep his mouth shut. He says to one of his cronies, in a voice meant for me to hear, "Should we toss him out here?"

Another voice—slightly familiar?—snarls a "No," then adds a moment later, "Let's lower him into the water *gently*."

They both start laughing as if this is the grandest joke e'er told. The engine winds down.

I am edging toward panic. For the second time in just over a week, I am facing the near certainty that I'm about to die. And I still do not want to die.

Still do not, still do not, still do not.

The motor cuts out and I hear a hollow thump that makes my heart leap with hope—the small boat has bumped up against what sounds like a larger boat. So maybe they're not going to dump me into the Gulf of Maine with weights attached. Maybe I've been granted a stay of execution. Probably not for pizza and DVDs, though.

The men stumble and bump about as they attempt to tie the smaller boat to the bigger one in the high-rolling surf. I hear footsteps climb a step or two up a metal boat ladder, then voices from the higher deck engaged in a debate. From what I can pick up through the muffling of the carpet, they're trying to figure out how to maneuver me up into the larger boat. The rough water is making their job difficult. Good. Fuck them—in case I haven't said that for a while. I hear the word "winch" being bandied about. Two of the men clamber back into the smaller boat and secure a couple of ropes around my carpet roll.

I feel myself being slowly lifted out of the boat via electric motor, my body sagging between the two rope-holds.

The men release me from the winch boom, dropping me onto the deck of the bigger vessel. They undo the ropes and the outer bungee cords, and unroll the rug I'm in, leaving me still blindfolded with my hands tied behind my back, my mouth gagged, and my legs bound together. The deck is pitching from the waves, but these guys seem to have seasoned sea legs.

The men haul me roughly across the deck. One of them digs my cell phone and wallet out of my pockets. Another one throws open a heavy-sounding hatch in the floor.

A horrific—nay, *apocalyptically* bad—stench is unleashed from below. Rotting fish, several days old. A muscular guy (Chokehold?) grabs me around the torso, hoists me in his arms, and carries me down a steep, short set of stairs, grunting and panting. He releases me with a shove and I splash-land in a shallow pool of liquid, amongst a clutch of slippery objects I immediately identify as dead fish.

The man clangs back up the metal steps, escaping from the smell as fast as he can. I hear the clink of a string-operated light switch, and he shuts the hatch behind him.

It's me and the dead fish. Together in the dark.

## Chapter 31

The boat dips with the storm-driven waves, and the rotten-fish soup goes sloshing across the floor. It collects against the other side of the chamber, pooling in the canted angle between the wall and floor. My body topples and rolls with the fish, and I go plunging under the putrid liquid, face down.

My mind races toward panic. I'm going to drown in this stuff! My lungs itch to inhale.

*No*, I tell myself. *Hold your breath; the boat will shift back in a few seconds.* Those seconds stretch out into a thousand distinct microseconds, and then I feel the liquid shifting back the other way and spreading out thin again. My face finds the air. I haul in a breath as I try to gain control of my tumbling body. Oh my God! That smell! I don't have time to dwell on it, though, because the awful broth splashes up against the other side and repeats its puddling effect. Again, I go underwater. Again, panic tries to rise.

The boat shifts back again, the inner tide flows the other way, and I manage to gulp in another breath. As I slide across the floor again, in pitch blackness, my mind grabbles to define the physical space I'm in. The chamber is maybe seven or eight feet wide. The surface feels slick. Plastic-coated?

I mustn't allow myself to be submerged again. *Keep your ass down and your face up*, I command myself. That's my new life-purpose: ass down, face up.

The next time the hellish soup hits the wall, I'm ready for impact. I pull in a breath and allow the liquid to *buoy* me this time, instead of going under. Okay, I get how to do this now. The secret is to *ride* the liquid, rather than fight it. I'm sure there's a spiritual lesson in there somewhere, but I'm not exactly in the headspace to receive it.

Staying afloat is the key. I'm finding it devilishly hard to control my body position, what with my limbs bound and the floor tipping from side to side like the tilty room in a York Beach funhouse, but I must keep my face aimed skyward and remember to float.

The rancid air envelops me like a second layer of liquid. It feels thick and overpowering and almost viscous. It makes breathing seem like a last-resort option.

My mind wants to run away from this situation and never come back, but I must stay grounded. I'm not dead yet. I'm alive. In this minute. And if I play my cards right, I can be alive in the next one.

A minute. I can shoot for that. One minute. Then maybe another one after that.

I need to be fully present and mindful.

I journey back to my old Zen practice. Clear the mind of judgments, I tell myself. Accept what *is*. Suffering is not caused by the conditions we find ourselves in but by the way we *judge and label* those conditions; by our resistance to reality. Suffering is resistance. Yes.

So stop resisting.

Nonjudgmentally speaking, then, my conditions are as follows: My hands are tied and my legs are bound. I cannot see. I am engulfed in an extremely powerful—not "bad," necessarily—odor of putrefaction. I am sliding back and forth amongst a pile of rotting fish in several inches of liquid. The fish are wet and slimy. My gag reflex is firing and my stomach is lurching.

Those are the facts that comprise my present reality. My reality is neither good nor bad. It just *is*. Om Aranam Arada. Accept what is, do not resist it.

I slosh across the floor again, my head slamming hard against the wall. Damn!

Breathe! Breathe! Breathe! Breath is the key.

My lungs are telling me they *can't* breathe because the odor in here is so pressing, but in fact they can. The chamber is not airtight. I am not going to suffocate. I force myself to take a full mouth inhale, through the wet bandana-gag, and allow my body to move like driftwood in the shifting liquid. *Don't fight it, go with the flow.*

I feel my heart rate slowly come under control, even as my body tosses back and forth in the dark. The danger of losing my mind begins to subside.

Acceptance, not resistance, Grasshopper.

Okay, okay. I accept.

I accept. What is, *is*.

Good. Fine. Better.

*Now* what? What variable can I control here?

The constant shifting of the floor and slopping of the fishy liquid is out of my hands. But maybe I can find some way to anchor my body. Yes. That would be a good start.

Anchor. Body.

If I can make my way to the metal steps, I should be able to brace myself against them somehow. Or at least grab onto them. My wrists are tied together behind my back, but my hands can still grasp.

Get to the metal steps, then. Right. Okay, so how? As the liquid flows across the middle of the chamber, thinning out, I flip onto my side and try to inchworm my way toward where I think the steps are. No traction on the slick floor. And the flow of the liquid is too strong to overcome. Is it my imagination or is this soup getting deeper? I hold my breath and let the liquid lift me again as it pools in the wall/floor angle. I think of another idea.

I ride the liquid — I swear it's deeper than it was when I landed in here — till it pools again on the other side. This time I hold my breath and deliberately go underwater. My legs are tied together, but I find I can flip them as a unit, like a dolphin's tail. I paddle furiously toward where I think the stairs are. When the water shifts the other way, my body slams full-force into the stair unit, cracking my elbow on the metal. Damn, that hurts, but I manage to grab the side of the metal structure with my bound hands. I cling to it with an iron grip. Pumping my feet against the floor to create friction, I push myself to a sitting position, still gripping the stair unit behind me.

Hallelujah! I'm stable and anchored against the flow. For the moment. The fishy water goes sloshing past me. Yes! I'm a dock-post now, not driftwood.

I can hold on like this indefinitely, I think, if the stench doesn't kill me. Or can I? It suddenly becomes glaringly obvious to me: the water *is* getting deeper. Listening carefully, I pick up a sound I didn't notice before. The whooshing of water through a hose or pipe. Not a garden hose, either, but a big fat inch-and-a-halfer, by its sound.

The chamber is being pumped full of water. Those twisted fucks.

The thought sends me into physical panic. I start thrashing my legs and making terrible sounds with my throat.

*Stop! Calm down.* I need to get up the stairs, that's all. Up. That's doable. Up the stairs.

Of course, even if I manage to do that, and then somehow, miraculously, open the hatch — with no hands, mind you; ha — my buddies are still waiting for me topside.

But if I stay down here I'm going to drown. So up the steps it is.

*One minute at a time, Finn. Just get through the next minute.*

Shinnying my hands sideways along the bottom bar of the step structure behind me, I am able to inch my way around to the front of the stairs. My ass is now up against the bottom step. After much contortion and pistoning of feet, I somehow push my butt up onto that first step. I rest and breathe through the wet gag, listening to the water rush in through the hose/pipe.

Through sheer willpower, I push my ass up two more steps. My head bumps up against the hatch with a loud thud.

Damn! I freeze, waiting to see if the sound has aroused any attention from above.

No footsteps approach.

The water is now covering my feet at all times, I notice — whichever way the boat is leaning. This chamber is filling up fast. *Come on, come on, Finn, do something.*

I push my head up against the hatch and am surprised to find it opens. Is gravity the only force holding it closed? I quietly lower the heavy hatch back down into its frame and wait to see if my topside buddies have noticed the sound or motion. No reaction.

I push the hatch open with my head again, this time by a foot or so. I hungrily pull in a lungful of cooler air through my ick-soaked gag. I wait for my captors' feet to come running. They don't.

I push my ass up onto the next highest step, holding the hatch open, awkwardly, with my head. One more stair and I should be able to roll over onto the deck and be free of the hold completely. It's going to hurt like the bejaysus because the heavy hatch cover is leaning all its weight on me.

And my kidnappers are probably standing around the hatch in a circle, grinning at each other, waiting for me to make my move. But I've got to do it. No choice.

In a fast tumbling maneuver — which hurts as anticipated — I roll free of the hatch and onto the deck. The hatch slams loudly shut.

Again I hold my breath in dread. Again, no feet come running.

I realize that somehow, in rolling out of the hatch, my blindfold came free. It ripped right off my head. Yes, there it is, stuck to a splinter on the side of the hatch. I can see!

I look around. The deck is unoccupied. I pull in a few grateful breaths as I lie on my side, relishing the partial escape I've just pulled off. The relative dryness of the deck prevents me from sliding as the boat rocks in the waves.

From what I can see from here, the boat appears to be a mid-sized fishing vessel.

Next task: figure out a way to get my wrists and legs untied.

I wriggle my way to a tie-down cleat and use it to pry off the bungee cord that's around my ankles. I then writhe and twist my legs until my calves can move a bit more freely. Over the next several minutes, I'm able to squirm out of all the leg bungees, using the cleat as an aid.

Next, I back up against the rusty corner edge of an old motor casing and use it to saw through the rope binding my wrists. It takes a while, but at last my hands are free.

I stand and stretch my arms. I rip the wet gag off my mouth and fill my lungs with pure, unfiltered ocean air. It tastes more delicious than

French champagne.

Now I'm able to take a walk around the deck, using handholds to steady myself against the pitching of the boat. I see it's a trawler I'm on. The smaller boat that brought me here has departed, and I seem to be alone on this vessel—which, I note, is anchored at the outer reach of the bay, well beyond the harbor.

I spot a slop sink with a faucet and rinse my face and hands with the running seawater, then make my way to the wheelhouse. It's a trashy little room containing the steering wheel, the boat controls, a two-way radio, and the fish-finding radar gadgetry, in addition to a dozen scattered Mary's Lunch coffee cups, a plastic fryer-oil bucket full of men's magazines, some coffee cans containing rusty fishing hardware, and several wall plaques bearing gems like, "It's almost beer-thirty," "S.S. Boobie Bouncer," and "I'm a drinker with a fishing problem."

The engine and electrical system are key-operated, like a car, but the key isn't in the ignition; why would it be? I discover I can't operate the radio without the key.

Looking around, I spot a small metal basket attached to the wall. A catchall for to-do items, looks like. Moving closer to it, I see a familiar object inside: my confiscated wallet. Underneath it sits a plain white envelope, unsealed. With a sick sense of foreboding, I open the envelope. When I realize what I'm looking at, my feet turn into deep-sea sinkers. I'm weighted to the deck.

The envelope contains printouts of three newspaper articles about the 1999 accident on Carlisle Road and the follow-up investigation.

Delusional my ass, Miles.

Keen to learn whose boat I'm on, I snoop further. I find a compartment in the piloting console that contains the boat's paperwork. When I see the name of the owner, I tug in a breath. I should not be surprised, but I am. Clifford Treadwell.

Cliff. Jeannie's Cliff.

I drop my ass into the captain's seat to steady myself against the rocking of the boat—and the rocking of my universe. Hold on, hold on. Does this mean Cliff Treadwell and Edgar Goslin *know* each other?

Those two worlds should not be connected in any way, except in my own mind and experience. And yet here they are, brashly intersecting with one another in reality—the world of Musqasset, a remote island off the coast of Maine, and the world of Edgar Goslin, a low-life creep from Wentworth who was involved in a freak accident eighteen years ago in which I played a role.

What is the hidden root system connecting them?

A theory begins to assemble itself in the dark folds of my cerebrum. It is a theory that makes my gut feel poisoned. And yet it would explain not only the link between Cliff and Goslin but also Jeannie's guilt and discomfort with me.

The theory soon gels from wild hypothesis into near certainty.

Here are the facts whose logical connection I cannot ignore: Jeannie believed, for years, that I caused the accident in 1999. Jeannie was having an affair with Cliff when I left the island. Cliff hated me. Jeannie was livid with me at the time. She admits to having done something hurtful to me after I left. She even implies that she blabbed off to someone about the accident.

Conclusion—and really, you'd have to be a concussed sea cucumber living in a dark cave not to see it: *Jeannie* told Cliff about me and the accident. Cliff, thrilled to have found a way to make my life miserable, did a little research, just as I did, and learned about Edgar Goslin. The two men, being birds of a dysfunctional feather, hit it off, and Bob's-your-uncle, a partnership was born. Why they waited so long to take action against me remains unexplained, but one fact seems inescapable: Cliff and Goslin are working together, and their connection occurred through Jeannie.

The tectonic plates shift again as another fundamental assumption crumbles. From jump street, I have assumed my troubles began in my kitchen in Wentworth and followed me out to Musqasset. But what if that assumption was ass backwards? What if, instead of *escaping from* my problems by coming to Musqasset, I was *running toward* them? What if, all along, Musqasset has been reaching out its tentacles and pulling me into its tooth-lined maw?

If so, then, weirdly enough, my father was the one who set it all in motion. After all, it was he who concluded, years ago, that I was guilty of manslaughter. Angie got her ideas about my guilt from him. Angie told Jeannie, then Jeannie told Cliff...

As I think about the cascading implications, I suddenly feel—bizarre as it sounds—acutely drowsy. Maybe it's emotional fatigue, maybe it's reluctance to face my fate, maybe it's fish-rot fever, or maybe it's the ceaseless rocking of the boat like a damn cradle, but I drop off to sleep right there in Cliff's "captain's" chair.

• • • • •

I awaken some time later to an urgent realization. My captors didn't leave me in the fish hold to die. If that was their intention, they would have done the job more decisively. No, they left me there to torment me, to break me. Which means they will be coming back to finish their business.

I must prepare for that eventuality. How? Well, for starters I need to do something about the alarming odor clinging to my skin and clothes. I don't see any spare clothes around, so I grab a canister of Boraxo from the sink, climb down the hull ladder, and jump into the ocean. Holding onto the ladder railing at all times, I peel off my clothes—now dyed a nasty reddish brown—and scrub them with the soap powder. Not an eco-friendly thing to do, but...

Now that I'm in the water, I weigh the idea of swimming for shore. But the boat is anchored pretty far out, and the seas are still rough. I *might* be able to make it, but is that my best move? Right now I've gained a strategic advantage by escaping from the hold. My captors won't be expecting that. I'll have the element of surprise in my favor when they return.

I climb back on deck, wring out my newly laundered clothes as best I can, and put the wet items back on my body. They're freezing cold, but I hardly notice. Embarking on a weapons search, I find several fish-skinning and filleting knives. I select one with a six-inch blade that's all business. I lash it to my shin, near the ankle, with a Velcro strap I find.

I make mental note of a brutal-looking gaff hook with a long handle hanging on the outer wall of the cabin. Might come in handy at some point. God, I hope not.

Before I'm able to construct a real plan, I look toward shore and see a small metal boat with an outboard motor laboring over the rolling waves.

It's them, coming back.

# CHAPTER 32

If there was room in my psyche for fear, I'd be terrified, but there is room only for strategizing. The seeds of a plan start to gestate. It's one that's going to require a lot of luck, but I don't have the time—or, oh yeah, the mental resources—to concoct MacGuyver-level crap.

Taking a page from my tormentors' book, I find a spool of heavy-gauge fishing line, cut a length of it with the knife, and shove it into my pocket. Then I return the envelope with the news stories in it to the "to-do" basket, under my wallet, wipe the captain's seat clean, and straighten up the wheelhouse a bit, so it looks exactly as it did when I entered; i.e., like drunken dogshit.

Next, I creep across the deck, trying to keep a low profile. I gather up all the bungees I removed from my legs and search for more. Luckily, Cliff is a bungee-and-duct-tape kind of guy, and I find a huge stash of the cords in one of his low cabinets. I gather fifteen or twenty of them and place them all in a bucket on deck for handy access, keeping a couple in my pocket. I quickly wipe up the bloody footprints and puddles I've created.

I gulp in a lungful of fresh air and descend into the foul-smelling hold, leaving the hatch open to allow daylight in. The stench hits me like the flat of a shovel as I get my first clear look at my former prison. As I surmised, it's a small chamber, maybe seven by ten feet or so, lined with molded plastic. It's almost half full of murky, brownish water, with dozens of dead pollock floating in it. The flow of water through the hose seems to have stopped. The pump must have been on a timer, or else there's some kind of float-device shut-off valve.

Fortunately for my plan, the steps have a metal handrail on either side. I tie the length of fishing line tightly across two support posts for the handrails, at shin height.

I climb back upstairs, shut the hatch after me, and duck under a tarp covering a piece of deck equipment. I slip the knife out of its Velcro leg-strap and wait.

• • • • •

I hear the engine of the small craft shut off and the men clamber up the hull ladder and onto the trawler's deck. From my low vantage point, I can see their feet moving about but not their full bodies. They're all wearing rubber boots.

There are three guys, as I more-or-less expected. Three is my lucky number. One of them says, "I'll check on Fuckface," and throws open the hatch to the hold. I mentally cross my fingers as he starts down the steps. Just as I hoped, I hear a muffled "Aaaagh!" as he trips over the fishing line I tied there and plunges into the bloody fish-water with a splash.

"What happened?" shouts one of the guys on deck.

"I fuckin' fell, that's what!" a muted voice from below shouts back. "Aww, Jesus! FUCK! Hey, where the hell is he?"

"Huh?" yells one of the deck guys, and then, in act of stupidity worthy of Yosemite Sam's dumber brother, he scampers down the steps to check out what happened to his buddy and me. Then, blammo, just as the first guy is yelling, "Hey, watch out for the—," guy number two falls. With a splash. Amazing. A twofer. Now there's only one bozo left on deck. As I peer out from under the tarp, I see he's a tallish dude. He is hovering near the hatch, looking down.

I note he's wearing a slicker. The color? Davy's grey.

This is my chance. I've always wondered: if I needed to attack someone in cold violence to save my own skin or someone else's, would I be able to do it? I'm about to find out.

I spring from beneath the tarp and charge across the deck, keeping my footfalls silent. Just as Davy Grey becomes aware of movement behind him, I jam on the brakes and grab him by the neck using the same chokehold that was used on me not long ago.

"Don't fuckin' move," I growl, placing the point of the knife against his bearded cheek. "And don't make a sound." I take a couple of sideways steps, dragging him with me, until I can reach the open hatch with my foot. In a swift move, I flip the hatch closed, then drag the guy on top of the hatch cover with me, trapping the other two guys below. Luckily I've got my sea legs by now, because the boat is still rocking and rolling to a lively backbeat.

Okay. As of this moment, I have control over all three of these assholes. Aren't I awesome? Right. Well, I won't be able to maintain status quo for long. Second law of thermodynamics and all. I need a plan.

"Stand right there or I will stab you," I instruct the bearded guy. He nods and I release him just long enough for me to dash over to a coiled chain I scoped out earlier. Holding the knife in my teeth, I quickly drag the heavy coil onto the hatch. That should hold the men below, temporarily.

Wielding the knife in my hand again, I whip my attention back to Davy Grey. It's only now I get a look at his face; his recently grown beard was throwing me off from behind. It has more white in it than I'd have expected, but still the man is irritatingly handsome.

"Hello there, Cliff," I say, "Long time no see."

"Not long enough," he replies, flashing me a grin that somehow comes off as both shit-eating and menacing.

"You and I are going to chill for a while and shoot the breeze," I tell him. "So I want you to walk over to the deck rail"—I point to my intended spot—"and sit with your back against that post."

"What if I'm not in the fuckin' mood?" he asks.

"I WILL CUT YOUR GOD-DAMN FACE OFF!" I shout, lunging at him with the knife, my eyes wide and my teeth bared.

He drains of color and shoots his hands up in surrender. Sometimes good ol' crazy is the only way to get a person's attention. He turns and marches docilely to the rail. I can hear his buddies yelling from the hold and thumping against the hatch. The weight of the chain coil is holding them below for the moment, but...

Cliff sits on the deck, facing me, as instructed. I dash over to the bucket where I placed the bungees and grab a handful of them. I order Cliff to join his hands behind the post; he complies. I put the knife in my teeth again, and he permits me to reach through the rail and bind his hands together. Next, I bungee his feet and legs together, then wrap a couple of the bigger cords around his torso and the rail post, securing them snugly.

Now: what to do about his buddies? I *could* pile more weight on the hatch cover and keep them trapped below deck, but I feel an urge to confront them all together, to get to the bottom of this thing once and for all. I crab-scuttle over to the hatch, drag the chain coil off it, then scuttle back to Cliff. Holding the knife against his neck, I wait till one of his buddies throws the hatch open and starts to emerge. He's a wiry guy with zero body fat who looks as if he's spent a lifetime running around on fishing boats. He's painted head-to-toe with bloody water.

"I'm going to kill your friend," I say calmly but loudly while Wiry Guy is still on the steps. "Unless you do exactly what I tell you. ...Step out of the hatch."

He looks at us both, wide-eyed and frozen, but Cliff snaps, "Do what he says," and Wiry Guy complies.

I order the third guy out of the hold using the same technique. He's a gym-jacked dude who is probably Chokehold — and might very well be Goslin himself. Holding the knife-point against Cliff's neck, I order Wiry Guy to grab some bungees and tie Gym Bob to the railing post beside Cliff's. Spurred on by Cliff's enthusiastic encouragement, both men cooperate. Next I tie Wiry Guy, the same way I did Cliff, to the post after that.

Done.

Three little pirates all in a row, two of them wet and foul-smelling.

I can't believe I've managed to pull this off. *Now what the hell do I do?*

Seizing the gaff hook on the wall to give myself some added authority, I march back and forth in front of my three tormenters, all tied helplessly to the deck rail.

"So, who wants to start?" I say cheerily. "Okay, I'll go. You guys have been having some yucks at my expense, haven't you? Well, I'm not a huge fan of assault and attempted murder, FYI. So now it's my turn." Deliberately echoing the words Trooper Dan used in my kitchen, I say, "The way we work is this: I ask questions, you answer them without a moment's hesitation. Thus you avoid the gaff. Are we clear on that?"

Moving the huge, needle-sharp gaff-hook back and forth between Gym Bob's and Wiry Guy's eyes, I say, "Which one of you is Edgar Goslin?"

In their eyes I see only blank confusion.

I march over to Cliff and press the tip of the hook sideways against his neck skin. "Which of these guys is Goslin?"

"What the hell are you talking about?" Cliff replies. Cocky dick.

"I know Edgar Goslin is here on Musqasset," I tell him evenly. "And I know you're working together. If he's not one of these two clowns, he must be the one I saw you with yesterday at the maintenance garage."

"Ronnie Milloy? The road guy? He works for the town. I was just borrowing his truck. I think you know why."

"Then which one of these two is Edgar Fucking Goslin?"

Cliff rolls his eyes. "I *heard* you went off the deep end," he says. "Guess the rumors were true." Boy, do I want an excuse to rip this guy a blowhole.

"Don't even bother denying it, Cliff," I say. I march into the wheelhouse and grab the envelope I found in his to-do basket (and my wallet along with it). I march back to Cliff and, with the flair of a movie lawyer doing his big reveal, I whip out the news articles about the highway accident and dangle them in front of his face.

He does not break down and blurt out a courtroom confession. Instead, he laughs. "That? You think all this is about *that*?"

"You're going to try to claim it isn't?"

Cliff shakes his head as if in pity. "Jeannie told me you were the smartest guy she ever knew. Guess she didn't get around much." He pauses and reconsiders his words. "Although you and me both know *that* ain't true."

I almost punch his clown-sphincter face. "I'm running out of patience here, Cliff. I know Jeannie told you about me and this car accident."

"So what if she did? You think *these* guys give a shit about that?" He tosses his head contemptuously toward his compadres.

"Well, given that they tried to kill me in my own home," I say, my voice tightening, "and went to great lengths to write a convincing suicide note in which I confessed to the crime, then yeah, I'd say they give A LITTLE BIT OF A SHIT."

Wide-eyed, he backs into the steel post he's tied to. "Jesus," he says. It's not the "Jesus" of a man who's thinking, *Dang, I've been caught redhanded*, it's the "Jesus" of a man who realizes he's dealing with a truly unbalanced individual.

"Are you seriously going to tell me you don't know about what happened in my house in Wentworth?" I ask him.

He looks me fully in the eye and says, "I. Have. No. Idea. What-you-are-talking-about!" Either he's a better actor than he has the brains to be or he's telling the truth.

"Goslin didn't tell you?"

"WHO THE FUCK IS GOSLIN?"

"Don't act like you don't know! I'm holding the evidence right in front of your face." I read aloud a sentence from one of the news articles in which Goslin's name is mentioned.

Cliff sighs and lets his head slump. After a moment, he says softly, "I didn't remember that was the guy's name. Honest. I barely even read those stories."

"Then why are you carting them around on your boat?"

"They were just supposed to be between you and me. The other guys don't even know about them."

"So why do *you* have them?"

"A little added insurance, that's all. To make sure you got the message."

"Message?"

"The reason you're here on this boat, dickwad."

"Which is...?"

"I think maybe I should let your friends explain that. They'll be here any minute."

"Oh, right. The cavalry is on its way."

"Believe me, don't believe me, I don't give a shit. But they'll be here. High noon. The appointed time of your sentencing."

"My sentencing?" I say, barely able to stifle a laugh. This guy has a flair for cheesy drama. "My *sentencing?*"

He looks at the deck for a long count, then raises his head with a sneer. "Fishermen's Court, asshole."

# Chapter 33

*Fishermen's Court is more than the name of the street I once lived on.*

*If you've dwelt for a time on Musqasset — or certain other islands off the coast of Maine where there is no resident police force — you may have heard whispers of an entity that goes by the same name. Fishermen's Court. What is it? One learns not to ask.*

*A trawler captain finds his net cut to ribbons one morning.*

*A lobsterman discovers sugar in his gas tank has ruined his boat's engine.*

*A heedless clammer gets his teeth knocked in after leaving the Anchor one night.*

*In coffee joints and bars 'round the island, heads nod darkly and someone inevitably mutters, "Fishermen's Court." Conversation over.*

*It is well known that there's a code of honor in the Maine seafood procurement trades. You don't encroach on another guy's fishing grounds. You don't pull up another guy's trap. You don't mess with another fisherman's livelihood. If you do so on Musqasset, you will soon find your luck running thin. The punishments doled out to offenders are not usually lethal — though there was a killing on Matinicus Island a few years back that made all the papers — but neither are they slaps on the wrist.*

*Fishermen's Court aims to send unambiguous messages.*

*But the first rule of Fishermen's Court is the first rule of Fight Club. Best not to chit-chat too much about it. In truth, most people believe it's just an island myth, a poetic way of saying fishermen watch out for one another; an eye for an eye, a tooth for a tooth.*

*But the old-timers and insiders know a different tale.*

• • • • •

"I don't see anyone else here but you and your nasty-smelling friends," I say to Cliff. "So why don't you explain what the hell you're talking about."

"Not my place to say."

I kneel before him and aim the knife blade at his eye—weird how accustomed I've become to playing the demented heavy. "*Make* it your place to say. What did you mean about Fishermen's Court?"

He mulls his conversational options, concludes they are limited. "All you had to do was stay off the island," he spews. "That's all you fuckin' had to do. There wouldn't have *been* any more punishment."

"Punishment? For what?"

"The Court heard your case four years ago, asshole. And found you guilty."

"And what was my crime, exactly?"

"Treason," he says, without a hint of irony. "We were ready to give you your sentence at the time, but you skipped town. We figured you musta got wind of what was coming your way and took off. We said fine, let him go. That was what we all wanted anyway." He thrusts his reddened face at me. "But you had to come back, didn't you? *Didn't* you?"

I hear the distant snarl of a boat engine. Looking out toward shore, I see two small craft chugging in our direction. I get the gut sense that Cliff is telling the truth and that the approaching boats contain the other members of my tribunal.

"So now what?" I ask, feeling the walls closing in. "Now I'm supposed to receive my sentencing and punishment? Let me take a wild guess: death by execution at sea."

Cliff says nothing. Which makes me believe my guess is correct. "Is that it, Cliff? Execution?" No answer. I lay the knife blade against his bearded cheek, unintentionally drawing blood. "Are you guys planning to kill me? Answer!"

"Jesus, no!" he blurts. "What the fuck do you think we are? You *got* most of your punishment already, for Chrissake. All we wanted to do was follow you around for a few days, throw a scare in you, rough you up a little. Then, at the end, toss you in the hold for a while, break you down for good, and give you the fishermen's farewell."

"What the hell does that mean?"

"You know damn well what it means. Shit, maybe you don't. Each member of the court gets a minute alone with you, to do whatever we want, short of killin' you—punch you in the gut, spit in your face, speak our piece. Then, when we've all had our turn, we haul your ass back to the mainland and toss you out near Pemaquid Point. The end."

"And these?" I say, waving the paper printouts I still hold in my hand. "How do you explain these?"

"Those?" He laughs again. Annoying prick. "Those were just a send-off from me to you. A little reminder, so in case you were ever tempted to drag your sorry ass back to Musqasset, or talk to anyone about what happened on this boat today, you would know *I* had something *I* could talk about too. And yeah, that something came to me courtesy of Jean Eileen Gallagher."

I don't think Cliff is capable of making up stuff like this. Thus I am inclined to believe him. The two small boats are drawing near now, and they don't look like a Coast Guard rescue team, that's for sure.

"Can I ask you one last question, Cliff?" The macho has drained out of me.

He shrugs in a slap-worthy way.

"What were you talking to Jeannie about yesterday morning?"

He laughs wearily and shakes his head. "You and me, bro, we're members of the same sad club. The Jeannie Left-Behinds. Miss Jeannie G., she's got a... situation goin' on, but it ain't with me, and it ain't what you think. One thing I can tell you, though—you got a world of hurt comin' your way."

Yeah, I'm starting to get that impression.

· · · · ·

When the small boats draw up alongside Cliff's trawler on the port side, my heart deflates—more with sadness than fear. There are seven guys aboard the two vessels, and I know all of them: Billy Staves, my old Scrabble buddy; Matt and Mike, two of the three Bourbon triplets; Gerry Harper, husband of Ginny and frequent dinner guest of Jeannie's and mine; and three other lobstermen/fishermen I sometimes shared a table with at the Anchor.

As I stand at the rail looking down at them, I can feel a lump forming in my throat. I don't want my voice to crack when I address them.

I wait till I'm sure I can talk steadily and say to the small crowd, "I'm afraid Captain Kangaroo's Court has been canceled for the day, folks. You're going to have to take your lanterns and pitchforks somewhere else." I signal for Cliff to swivel his head so they can see his face, then I point the knife at him. "If anyone tries to board this boat, I'm going to shove this knife into your friend's neck."

Several seconds pass in silence.

"Like the one you shoved in us?" says Billy Staves, staring at me with stony eyes.

"What are you talking about, Billy?"

I look out at the septet of men glaring at me from the boats. Their faces vary in age, race, and ethnicity, but I see only one countenance: cold Yankee rectitude.

"Can someone please tell me what's going on?" I ask. "Because I don't get it. What did I do that was so unforgivable? Yes, I brought Miles Sutcliffe to the island. *Mea* fricking *culpa*. Yes, I vetted him as a friend and asked you to break bread with him. That was a huge mistake. I know that now, but that's all it was: a *mistake*. I didn't mean harm to any of you. Can't you see that? I have apologized to you in every way I know how."

My words are met with arctic silence. "I had no idea he was going to kill Fish Pier," I continue. "I tried to stop him. In fact, I tried to *help you fight him.*"

"Oh, right. That's rich, Finn," says Matt Bourbon.

"What? You know I did, Matt. Once Fish Pier was put on the

chopping block, I started fighting the whole project. That letter-writing campaign was my god-damn idea. Or have you conveniently forgotten that? *I* was the one who proposed it. *I* was the one who organized it and convinced you all to try it. *I* was the one who put my friendship on the line for it."

A few of the boat riders look at one another bemused. "I wouldn't brag about it if I were you," says Billy.

"I can't help it if it didn't work. I never guaranteed it would. I just thought it was worth a try."

"So did we," says a lobsterman named Jean-Claude. "That's why we humbled ourselves to a bunch of rich-bitch assholes. Because you told us to. Because we trusted you."

"And I did everything I promised you I would!"

"Like hell you did!" thunders Billy. "You blew town, that's what you did. You slunk off like a weasel when the henhouse light comes on. And we all know what happened next."

"No, we don't, Billy. *I* don't, that's for sure."

As I stare into the simmering eyes of those men across the short breach of water that separates us, I realize I am staring across a vast gulf of understanding. We are seeing things from divergent perspectives. Operating from different sets of facts. Where does the disconnect lie?

• • • • •

*In the final days of my Musqasset tenancy, as I've mentioned, Miles' marina/yacht club project was morphing into something no one had seen coming. Miles had overcome many of the islanders' resistance to the project by showing them what a boon it would be for Fish Pier and for all of Musqasset. Once the town had fallen in love with the idea of having its own resident police and fire department, a new schoolhouse, a tax surplus, and, oh yeah, a huge increase in the flow of retail money, the bait-and-switch started. Miles, speaking for his partners, began to present amendments to the plan. The most radical of these involved the scrapping of Fish Pier for a more "revenue positive" idea.*

At the town meeting when that amendment was presented, there was, needless to say, a hue and cry — mainly from the fishermen, lobstermen, and artists. But you could feel the tide had already turned. The number of residents in favor of the new commercial development — no matter what changes it entailed — now far outweighed those who opposed it. There was still a vote to be taken, a few weeks hence, but we all knew how the vote was going to go.

After the meeting where the Fish Pier amendment was proposed, the fishermen and their friends gathered at The Rusty Anchor to commiserate and voice their anger. Bo Baines, the guy who ran the Seafood Exchange, stood up on a chair, drunk, and shouted, "Fish Pier's dead! Long live the Mall of Musqasset!"

Saul Guptill chimed in, "Aye, there's nothin' can be done about it now."

Or was there? I was sitting alone in a corner of the bar, thinking. Stewing. About Miles, to be specific. I realized I wasn't completely sure I trusted him. During the whole proposal period, he alone had served as representative for his mainland partners. All information going back and forth between the island and the development group had traveled through him. When I would talk to him privately, he would assure me he was fighting tooth and nail against his partners to preserve Fish Pier. But...

But what if that weren't true? I now began to wonder. Maybe it was the Tullamore Dew talking, but I started to think maybe Miles wasn't fighting quite as hard for Fish Pier as he claimed to be. Maybe he wasn't presenting the full picture to his partners, or to us.

I didn't want to voice my doubts to the fishermen; they were already pissed off enough at me for bringing Miles to the island. But I did stand up and say, "Listen to me for a minute, folks." The place went quiet. "These people — Miles Sutcliffe's partners — are human beings. Right?"

"That's being pretty fucking generous," slurred Billy Staves.

"Maybe we need to put a human face on the pier," I said. "Maybe if the developers knew a bit more about what Fish Pier meant to each of you — not just money-wise but in your lives, in your blood..." Okay, the Dew was definitely having its say. "Maybe if they knew what it stood for, to you and your families, living and dead... Maybe if they heard your personal stories, they might decide to stick with the plan that preserves the pier instead of scrapping it. So why don't we tell them? Why don't we write to them? All of us. Tell 'em our stories."

No one spoke for several seconds. "What you're talking about sounds like begging to me," said Emmet DuPry, one of the old-timers.

"Aye," echoed Saul Guptill.

Drinking recommenced.

But over the next few weeks I hammered away at the fishermen. I went to each of them individually and worked with them to get their memories down on paper. Some of these guys hadn't written a paragraph since high school, yet here they were, pouring out their life stories. Billy Staves, Matt Bourbon, and others rounded up old photos of their parents and grandparents on Fish Pier, and wrote down the old folks' stories as well. Dorna Caskie dug up a children's book she had written about Fish Pier. I even saw a tear on the face of old Gawk Larson, the hardest and proudest of the lobstermen, when he shared his tale of seeing his father on the end of the pier one night, singing "The Bells of Aberdovy" to the mermaids.

In a strange way, the letter-writing project took on a life of its own and became bigger than just a tactic. It became an almost museum-worthy testimonial not only to a beloved physical landmark but also to a fading way of life and set of values.

I didn't claim any official role in the letter "campaign," and I didn't want any credit for it. I didn't even tell Jeannie I was doing it (by that time our communication had gone down the crapper anyway). But I did promise that when the collection of letters was ready to be delivered, I would deliver it. And the way I planned to do that was through Miles.

One fog-shrouded evening, a group of the fishermen asked me to meet them on Fish Pier. They stood in a circle around me, and, like a mother handing over her infant for adoption, Billy Staves presented the bulging folder of letters to me. "You asked us to do this," he said. "It was hard for some of the fellas. But we did it. So we're counting on you to do right by us."

"I'm not promising results, Billy," I said. "But I promise to get this to the people who need to see it."

"Still sounds like begging to me," offered Emmet DuPry.

As I walked away from the pier that night, I knew I had been given stewardship of something fragile and intimate. There was a lot of hope — maybe too much *hope* — bound up in those handwritten pages, but I meant to *fulfill my promise, even if my friendship with Miles took a hit.*

And it did. Later that evening I asked Miles to join me for drinks at Pete's.

"There's no easy way to say this," I told him, "so I'll just spit it out. Some of us — myself mainly, but others too — are starting to have some questions about the way you're presenting this development deal. On both sides of the Gulf. We feel there are... aspects of the situation that maybe your partners aren't taking into consideration. The fishermen have written some personal letters about the pier, and we'd like to get them to your partners. We need you to deliver them."

Miles stared sharply at me, as if I'd slapped him.

"If this is the last thing I ever ask of you, Miles, so be it. But I am asking this."

His face turned lobster red. "How DARE you question my word and try to do an end run around me," he said. "What gives you the RIGHT?"

"What gives you the right to deceive these fishermen, Miles? These people are my neighbors and friends."

"Is that so, Mr. Local Hero, savior of the ancient ways no one else gives a fuck about?"

"You don't give a fuck, that's for sure. You never intended to preserve Fish Pier, did you? You've been posturing about it since the get-go. Your plan since day one has been to — "

"Oh, and what suddenly qualifies Finnian Carroll to analyze high-level real estate deals? Who promoted you from part-time bartender to grownup?"

"Gee, skip the soap and plunge it right in, Miles."

"You'd like that, wouldn't you? You love playing the poor martyr who gets fucked by The Man."

"And you love being the big dick who does the fucking. You're so arrogant it doesn't even cross your mind that the 'common people' can see right through your lies."

"Oh yeah? Well, here's one for you, Finn: I really respect your opinion on this matter."

I rose out of my seat and almost punched him. Things went downhill from there, each of us trying to wound the other with words — and very nearly with more than words.

Finally, after we both calmed down a bit, he said, "If you absolutely insist *on my doing this, Finnian, I will do it, I will deliver the letters. But know one thing: if you ask this of me, you are putting our friendship on the waiver wire."*

"You already put our friendship on the waiver wire," I replied. "Not just this time but **many** times. Many, many fucking times." *I stood up from the table, handed him the fat file folder, and said,* "Deliver the package, Miles," *then walked out. It was the last time Miles and I spoke before I left the island a few days later.*

• • • • •

And now as I face my accusers from the deck of Cliff's fishing boat, I start to get an inkling as to the source of their anger. "So tell me what happened," I say. "Give me the benefit of the doubt and pretend I don't know. Because I don't. I really don't."

"The next town meeting," says Jean-Claude, "when the vote was due, a bunch of your buddy-pal's golf-shirt-wearin' partners and lawyers showed up. Guess they figured everything was gonna go their way, and they wanted to be there when the whole shootin' match was made official. They started barreling ahead with the vote like nothing had changed, and Billy here stood up and asked the head one, the president guy, if he'd gave our letters any thought. Guy was like, 'What letters?'"

## Chapter 34

"The worst part," says Jean-Claude, "was the guy turned out to be a pretty decent fella. Said he wished he'd-a seen the letters, that he woulda took 'em into consideration."

"Bottom line," says Billy, "it was too late to make changes to the development plan by that time. The vote was held and it passed. And now there's a fuckin' cheese boutique where my boat used to dock. Bo Baines went out of business, and the hub fell out of our operation. Now we're all fending for ourselves, those that are still left. Anchoring out in the harbor, selling our catch on the mainland, working till dark every night, scraping by."

"Fuck, Billy," I say. "I never meant for this to happen." And now my voice does crack, and there's nothing I can do about it. "I cared about you. All of you guys. That's the only reason I got involved in the whole thing in the first place. I had nothing to gain from it."

"So say you," says Billy.

"Don't!" I snap at him, feeling my face go red. "Don't you dare suggest I got some kind of payback out of this. If anyone wants to accuse me of that, you step up here on this deck and you say it right to my face."

None of the men move, except with the rolling of the waves. For the first time, I see uncertainty register on some of their faces.

"Here's the truth about Fish Pier that no one wants to remember," I say. "I loved the thing—I painted it a dozen times—but it was a fucking disaster. It was falling apart and sinking into the seabed. And all you guys used to do was bitch about it. Bitch, bitch, bitch. Walk into Pete's or Mary's any time of the day and that's all you'd hear. Everyone bitching about the pier, everyone blaming someone else for it—fighting over it, taking sides—but no one doing a god-damn thing. Yes, I put the bug in Miles Sutcliffe's ear about it. And when he came out with his first plan, the one that included money to rehab Fish Pier, I was all in. It wasn't a perfect plan, but it was going to help you guys, and that's all I wanted. And that's the honest truth."

It *is* the honest truth, so I'm pretty sure it rings that way to the men. But still they stare at me as if they've brought a noose along.

"I'm not a born islander," I continue. "I know that will always make me suspect in some of your eyes. But I actually *chose* this place. I fell in love with Musqasset on my own, and you know why? Because it's a working island, not some tourist trap from the cover of *Yankee* magazine. People just try to make a living here, and everyone mucks in together and helps each other out. I loved that, and I wanted to be part of it.

"Who was it that helped you put up your traps every winter, Billy? Who was it that sanded down your boat with you, Gerry, and helped you get an agent to sell your paintings, Mike? Every time there was a trail that needed clearing or a dock that needed new pilings or a fundraiser for the school, who was in there working elbow to elbow with you guys?"

"He did muck in a lot, give him that," says Billy matter-of-factly to his peers.

"And I was okay in all of your eyes as long as I was doing that. No one questioned my loyalty then. But the first time something goes a little wonky, you're all ready to walk me from the nearest plank." Shame flashes in a couple of pairs of eyes. "*Someone* lied to you about those letters, that's for sure. Maybe it was the president of the development group, maybe it was Miles Sutcliffe—or yeah, maybe it *was* me, but why would you assume that? Why wouldn't you give me the benefit of the doubt over Miles and his mainland cronies?"

"We got our reasons," says tied-up Cliff.

"I busted my nuts to get you guys off your apathetic asses and write those letters. Why would I do that just to sell you out?"

"Payola," says Jean-Claude, but he says it at half-volume.

"Oh, right. Who believes that? Who really believes that? Come on, raise your hands." No hands go up. "The bunch of you make me sick to my stomach."

Suddenly it's as if *I've* become Fishermen's Court, and the fishermen have become the accused. The shift is palpable. It's Mike Bourbon who finally speaks to the others. "He's got a point. We should have talked to him first. Heard him out. We owed him that. We shouldn't have jumped to... *this*. I'm out. I'm done."

No one says a word. Guilty silence reigns.

I untie Cliff and his two buddies, no longer fearing they will harm me — at least not here and now. "Which one of you has my cell phone?" I ask. Gym Bob hands it to me.

I climb over the deck rail and down the ladder into the metal boat that brought me here. Facing my accusers one last time, I say, "I find *you* all guilty of treason."

I start the engine. "I'm taking this boat," I announce. "I'll leave it at the Greyhook launch."

I motor off toward the island.

The waves seem to have calmed just a bit. The storm to the east of us is finally moving away.

• • • • •

I haven't had a chance to look at my phone since before my carnival-o'-laughs in the boat hold. Miles must be wondering what the hell happened to me. I'm so anxious to see my messages, the phone literally feels warm in my pocket, but right now I've got my hands full operating this vessel. I'll check my phone as soon as I'm on terra firma.

I'm able to do some thinking as I putter along, though. It's only now that I start to untangle the Cliff-Goslin situation. I still find it mind-boggling that Cliff and Goslin aren't connected to each other at all. The idea that there have indeed been two separate parties trailing me, an absurd notion I rejected early on, is almost inconceivable. And yet Cliff seems to have been telling the truth. He had nothing to do with the forced suicide attempt at my parents' house. And he didn't follow me out to Musqasset. Those things were all Goslin.

The dead fish and the nighttime stalkings, those were Cliff and his buddies from Fishermen's Court. They had their own reason for pursuing me, which had nothing to do with some ancient highway accident. Cliff didn't care about that accident, either, except to use it as ammo to keep me away from Musqasset. And from Jeannie.

Then what has Goslin been up to since he came to the island? Why hasn't he made any moves? Why has he been so god-damn quiet?

I wonder if Miles has taken any action on the Goslin front in my absence.

• • • • •

As soon as I've hauled the boat aground at the Greyhook landing, I dig out my warm phone. I see voicemails and missed calls from Miles, and texts from Preston Davis and Jeannie. I go to Jeannie's message first. Considering what Cliff told me about her — and the warning she herself tried to give me — I open it with a hefty dose of wariness.

Her text: *There's something I should have told you, but I chickened out. About Cliff. He fell for me pretty heavy back when he and I were... you know.* "Fucking," I mentally fill in. *It wasn't a casual thing for him,* the text goes on. *He was in love with me. Big-time. Still is. Won't let it go. Anyway, he's a pretty scary and super-insecure guy. (He must have asked me ten times how big your dick was.)*

I have the urge to immediately text her back, *How big was his?*

Just kidding.

Sort of.

*After you left the island,* her text goes on, *I got into badmouthing you with him. One night he filled me full of my favorite truth serum. Patron Silver. And - I am so sorry about this, Finn - I told him the whole story. About you, the bottle, the accident. Anyway, I think you ought to watch out for Cliff. He knows you're here and he might be trouble for you. Again, I'm sorry.*

Thanks, Jeannie. This information might actually have come in handy about three hours — or three days — ago. Our timing has always sucked. I am heartened to know, though, that she felt compelled to be honest with me and to *try* to warn me.

Or maybe just she's covering her ass because she knows Cliff and I have already had our little *tete a tete*. Hmm.

There's one final chunk of text from her. It causes a hot flutter in my abdomen, which might be pleasure or pain. *Last night was amazing, you jerk. Wish I could stop thinking about it.*

What Jeannie and I had last night was real. Right? As real as it gets. Right? I have to believe that, or I can't believe anything — truth no longer has an access point.

The voicemails from Miles are of the worried type I was expecting: Where are you? Are you okay? What happened? What are we going to do about Goslin? Call me, call me, call me.

I'll call him in a minute.

The text from Preston Davis is the one that sends my mind careering into crazyland for about the ninetieth time this weekend: *Called the mainland office, asked about those passenger records. Edgar Goslin took one ferry trip to Musqasset, a little over two weeks ago. Stayed one night, then went back the next day. He's not on the island now. Hope that helps!*

Goslin, not on the island. What? So Goslin is *not* Trooper Dan or Chokehold — those guys definitely followed me out here; I recorded their voices. But Goslin's tied up in this thing for sure. My conversation with Priscilla Begley proves it. His trip to Musqasset proves it.

So where is Goslin now? Why has he gone below radar?

I'm about to share Preston's news with Miles when my phone-finger freezes. I'm suddenly uncertain about talking to Miles. Maybe it's because I've been revisiting all that Fish Pier drama — all the doubts I had about Miles back then, our confrontation — or maybe it's because I've learned those fishermen's letters never reached their intended recipients, but my trust in Miles is definitely not at a high-water mark.

I'm wondering, in fact, if it's time to acknowledge the great blue whale that's been doing pushups in the middle of the room since this whole thing started: maybe Miles knows more about *everything* than he's been letting on.

I barely have time to give this idea room to roam when my phone rings. Miles. I hesitate to pick up, but some primal neural override makes me tap Answer.

"Finn, Jesus, where the hell have you been? Are you okay? What happened?"

"There's a lot to tell."

"I want to hear all about it. But listen: Jim dropped by. He learned something new about Edgar Goslin. You need to get over here."

"What about Beth? Won't she—"

"She's out. Having lunch with friends and doing some last-minute shopping. Her folks are coming in today."

"Today? But the ferry isn't running yet."

"They don't use the ferry," says Miles, scoffing at my blue-collar naïveté. "Just get over here. Hurry."

• • • • •

"Goslin's dead," says Miles, meeting me at the door.

He turns and walks back inside.

Dazed, I follow him to his study, where he has two online newspaper articles open on his computer: "Missing Local Man Found Dead in Car" and "Police Find Week-Old Body in Car." Both articles were written yesterday.

The two articles report essentially the same facts. A car was found just off Route 495 near the Wentworth-Bridgefield border in a heavily wooded area. The driver, dead, was Edgar Goslin. His live-in girlfriend, Priscilla Begley, confirmed he went missing on August 22, nine days earlier, and had not been seen since. The vehicle evidently veered off the highway near an exit ramp and remained hidden by foliage in a gully for over a week. Goslin, who was on blood-thinning medication, seems to have died of blood loss from a traumatic wound, the result of an apparent accident in his home workshop. Police believe he may have been trying to drive himself to the hospital when he became unconscious due to bleeding.

Miles stares at me wordlessly. I look at the date again. My stomach sours.

Goslin died on August 22. The home invaders came to my house on August 23.

Goslin was dead before any of my troubles began.

## Chapter 35

All my previous conceptions about how and why I was targeted for extinction by a group of unknown killers are out the window. I have to rethink everything from the ground up.

"Did Jim have any inside information?" I ask Miles. "On Goslin's death?"

"As a matter of fact, he did. There were some details the cops didn't release because they're still investigating. They're assuming accidental death, but they're following up on a few things before they make a final ruling."

"And...?"

"Well, like the papers said, the cops think Goslin injured himself in the workshop behind his house. Priscilla Begley never looked in there, but when the cops checked it out, they found blood all over a work table and an electric hedge cutter he was apparently trying to fix. They think the machine turned on unexpectedly."

"Jesus."

"Yeah. They found two of his fingers on the floor."

My skin flushes hot as a couple of mental gears clink together almost audibly.

"They think he tried to call 911, but his phone was dead," Miles continues. "So he panicked, jumped in his car to drive to the ER, then passed out behind the wheel."

I'm not listening anymore. I've planted myself in front of Miles' computer and am frantically googling Goslin's name. I find another article about his body being discovered, but, like the first two, it does not contain a photograph. I need to see a picture.

A picture, a picture, a picture...

I google "obituary Edgar Goslin," and a link pops up to the Sullivan Funeral Home in Wentworth. I click it and a memorial page for Goslin — freshly posted — opens. In the center of the screen is a photo of the man himself. It's probably fifteen years out of date, but the face is unmistakable.

It's the face of the man in Trooper Dan's video, the man whose fingers Troop removed with the lopper.

"Goslin didn't die by accident," I say to Miles.

"What?"

"He was murdered. By the same guys who tried to murder me. They cut his fingers off, bled him out." Recalling from the video the plastic bag that was wrapped around Goslin's hand to catch his blood, I add, "They staged it to look like an accident. Guess they didn't want him found right away, so they moved his car to a hard-to-spot location, planted the body in it, spread his blood around the workshop and the car."

I have trouble interpreting the stunned look on Miles' face. Is he stunned by the information I've given him or by how deeply delusional I am?

I need to be alone for a minute. To think. To process. I don't want to make a fuss about it, though, so I just excuse myself to that timeless temple of self-reflection, the bathroom.

I'm shaking as if I'm in a walk-in freezer as I sit there on the throne with the lid down. If Goslin was not the agent behind my attempted murder, then who could have been? Gary Abelsen? He's an Alzheimer's patient in an assisted-living community. Who else could possibly have the motivation to take such extreme measures? And why the damn eighteen-year delay?

Suddenly the great blue whale that was doing pushups in the middle of the room stands up on its tailfin and starts Riverdancing. The fundamental assumption on which all my reasoning has been based since day one is that I am the one and only person who has direct knowledge of the lethal events that took place in my car on my graduation night in 1999.

What if that weren't true?

What if *two* of us actually remember what happened?

Since the moment I heard—or *thought* I heard—crashing sounds on Carlisle Road on that blighted drive, I have unquestioningly believed that Miles passed out cold after tossing the bottle. And that he had no idea he threw it off the wrong bridge. After all, I had to take him to the the damn ER. And no one could fake unconsciousness well enough to fool an ER staff. Right?

But then I realize—with a hollow laugh—that I myself, only nine days ago, played possum convincingly enough to fool a team of professional killers.

What if—my mind doesn't even want to go there—Miles *was* just faking? What if he heard the crashing sounds too? What if he knew full well what he did and just didn't want to deal with it? What if he left me to make the moral call and to hold the moral bag, knowing, quite correctly, that I would latch onto it with a death grip?

Miles was an ambitious guy, even back in college, and highly protective of his blue-blood, Teflon-man image. Even back then, he figured someday he'd be living a big life in the public eye. In fact, I believe the reason he decided to marry Beth was that he saw her as his ticket to the show. Her family had money, his family had a name and social connections and a Yankee pedigree. Together they could go places. The night of the bottle-throwing incident, he was agonizing over that very decision, grappling with the choice between following his heart and following the path his career ambition and family DNA had already laid out for him at the tender age of 21. And it was ripping him apart.

Clearly, he ended up choosing the road more traveled.

But what if Miles has always known people died at his hands that night? What if some part of him has always been dreading the day the truth comes crawling out of the ground like a body buried alive in a horror movie? And what if exigent circumstances in his life—such as, oh, I don't know, winning a fast-track ticket to the U.S. Senate and beyond — were suddenly demanding he rid his closets of old skeletons, pronto?

And *if*, let's just say *if*, Miles wanted to clean up this *particular* closet, who would need to be permanently silenced? Who but the one person on Earth who knows exactly what happened in that car? Finnian T. Carroll at your service. And death by apparent suicide, with a signed confession to boot, would be the ideal way to dispense with said Mr. Carroll.

I think about the careful wording of the suicide note. Why did it alter the fact that the bottle was a gift from me? Answer: because if my unnamed "friend" had been the recipient of the gift (which he was), then *he* would have logically ended up with the bottle (which he did), not I. No good. Then why mention the friend at all, and why say we passed the bottle back and forth? Answer: in case Miles' fingerprints ever do get matched to the shards. That is still a possibility; the cops took prints from the glass, and those prints are still in the system. And if Miles' fingerprints were suddenly to appear in a database — say, because he just joined the U.S. Senate and had to be fingerprinted for the federal job — a belated match might pop up. The mention in the note that we both handled the bottle offers a tidy explanation as to how his prints got on the glass, while still leaving me as the guilty party.

Hmm, in this scenario, who else would need to die? Answer: the only other person who seems to know something about what really happened that night — Edgar Goslin. Maybe Goslin figured out somehow that Miles was in the car with me that night. Maybe — oh, shit — maybe he learned it from my own father! I know the two of them talked, Edgar and my dad. That's right! And my dad knew Miles was with me that night: *he bought me the scotch as a gift for Miles*. Maybe that's why Goslin came to Musqasset a few days before his death. To talk to Miles.

To blackmail him.

And maybe that's why Goslin is dead.

Damn. Once I get past my resistance to that single, elemental idea — that Miles has always known he killed those people that night — the dominoes just start toppling.

Whoa there, though, Jumpy Jumpface. Slow down. I'm getting carried away. There's one major kink in this line of reasoning. That is, it turns on a premise I simply cannot bring myself to believe—that Miles would be willing to kill me. That does not ring a true chord in my gut. Flawed as Miles is, I know he loves me. Unequivocally. In fact, I believe he loves me more than he loves any other person alive, except maybe his children. He loves me more than he loves Beth, that's for sure. More than anyone in his family of origin. More than any other friend.

He knows I love him, too, as no one else does. And he *needs* that love. In fact, he gets something from me that goes even beyond love. I think, on some level, I give Miles his center. A big chunk of it anyway. Deep down, I don't think Miles knows who he is without me to reflect and affirm him. To kill me would be a terrifying act of self-annihilation, and that is something I *truly* don't think Miles is capable of.

And yet, the facts are pointing to Miles in a way you'd have to be insane to ignore.

An idea occurs to me. A possible way to put Miles to the test.

In light of the fact that Goslin was the man in Troop's video, I realize there's one other person who might be involved in all of this. It is a name that will be forever branded on my brain cells but that I have never spoken aloud. If I say the name to Miles and his eyes betray recognition, that would go a long way to telling me Miles is indeed hip-deep in this thing.

I exit the bathroom and return to the study.

Miles is waiting for me anxiously, the photo of Goslin still staring belligerently from the computer screen. Miles gives me the perfect opening by asking, "What did you mean about Goslin being killed by the same people who tried to kill you?"

I describe to him the video Trooper Dan showed me when I was strapped into the chair. "It was Goslin in that video," I say. "They asked him who else knew what he knew. He didn't answer, so they cut off two of his fingers. He started screaming a name over and over, and I'll never forget it." I watch Miles' eyes carefully as I say the name. "Clarence Woodcock."

Damned if I don't see a flicker of panic in his eyes. He tries to cover it, but it's too late. He knows the name. And he's thrown by it.

• • • • •

Miles is pacing back and forth in the study. He wants me to believe he's thinking about the Goslin situation, but what he's really thinking about — I know Miles — is that name. Clarence Woodcock. It's eating at him. He looks at his watch in a fake sort of way.

"Listen, I've got to make a couple of phone calls," he says. "It might take me ten or fifteen minutes. Help yourself to a beer or a sandwich. Don't go anywhere, though, okay? We've got to talk about this some more. I won't be long." With that, he trots upstairs.

What is he up to? Who is he calling? Should I be worried about my safety? Probably. But fear of imminent grievous harm is a state I have become oddly accustomed to.

I turn back to the computer and, just for the hell of it, type "Clarence Woodcock, Wentworth" into the search engine.

The top item that comes up is a *Wentworth Tribune* piece, "Former Wentworth Police Officer Found Dead in Home." It's dated August 23. My heart takes a swan dive into my belly.

The article:

*John Clarence Woodcock Jr., a private investigator and former detective in the Wentworth Police Department, was found dead in his Wentworth home this morning by a family member. Cause of death is under investigation but may have been an accidental fall on a staircase. Police believe death occurred sometime between 12 a.m. and 10 a.m. on Thursday, August 22.*

*Woodcock, 62, known to friends and associates by his middle name Clarence, served on the Wentworth police force from 1982 until 1996, when he resigned and started a private investigation business. A widower, Woodcock had lived alone in his home at 4 Boxford Terrace for the past twelve years. His body was discovered by his daughter, Melissa Rodak, 39, who went to the home to check on him when he failed to answer his phone several times.*

*No further information has been released at this time.*

Maybe I'll take that beer after all. I go to the kitchen, pour a third of a Sam Adams down my throat, and bite into an apple. I wonder if my sister Angie knows anything about this Woodcock guy. On the spur of the moment, I thumb her name on my phone. Again, the call seems to go through but then disconnects. I try again, same result.

If I had half a brain, I would run out of the house this minute, try to call the Maine state police, tell them everything I know, and hole up in the woods until the cops arrive. If Miles is involved in all of this, as I am coming to believe he must be, then I don't have to worry about protecting him anymore. I can come clean about the entire mess.

But evidently I am *not* the proud owner of half a brain, because I sit back down at the computer. I retrieve the results of the Sure Search inquiry I did earlier on Goslin. There I see it, the name John Woodcock, among Goslin's known associates. I can't believe I didn't notice it earlier; must have been the "John" that threw me off. (I see another name I also overlooked before — Theo Abelsen — but I don't have time to think about it now.)

I do some more digging online and learn that Woodcock was a well-liked cop in his day and a community advocate for the disabled. However, he "resigned" from the police force under a cloud of suspicion. Seems he was under internal investigation for taking payoffs from known criminals. He agreed to walk away without pension benefits in exchange for avoiding indictment.

The timing of his death leaves no doubt that he was part of the purge that included Goslin and was meant to include me as well. A huge development, obviously. I don't know whether to share it with Miles or keep it to myself. Good sense tells me to play this card close to the vest.

What is Miles up to right now? I take my shoes off and tiptoe toward the staircase leading to the second floor. Listening, I hear nothing but the soft hum of a printer. I quietly ascend the carpeted stairs. Judging by the open bedroom doors and the stillness in the air, Miles' kids aren't home. I approach the room next to the master bedroom, the one Beth uses as her office and exercise room. I see Miles seated at Beth's desk, moving a mouse around and staring at her computer screen, his jaw hanging open and his skin clammy-looking.

The printer near the door is churning out pages.

I step into the room, expecting Miles to react in surprise or guilt, but he doesn't. I reach into the printer tray and glance at one of the pages. Appears to be a printout of a bank statement.

"What is this?" I ask Miles, not really expecting an answer.

"Beth's trust fund," he says numbly.

Ah, the one to which she gained access when she turned twenty-one (and which, of course, played no role in Miles' decision to marry her).

I look more closely at the printout in my hand, then pick up a couple more sheets of paper from the tray. Printed on the pages is a long series of check images, going back to the year 2000. All the checks are made out to the same party: John Clarence Woodcock Agency, LLC.

# Chapter 36

"I don't usually look at her private banking stuff," says Miles defensively, as if Beth's privacy were my main concern at this point. "But once in a while, when we're doing our taxes or something, I... I remembered seeing that name."

He looks into my eyes and I into his. I can tell he is feeling deeply bewildered, deeply betrayed. I feel sad for my friend. His life may be changing irrevocably in this very moment.

Questions, enormous questions, must be asked of Beth, and right soon, but neither of us seems ready to think about how to proceed with that.

The decision is taken out of our hands. We hear the jingling of the bell on the back door downstairs. We look at each other in mute paralysis. Beth's voice calls out, "They're here! Their boat came in! No more laughing, no more fun!" A beat passes. "Miles...?"

Miles seems powerless to use his voice, and it's certainly not my place to answer for him. I expect him to hastily shut off Beth's computer and dash out of her room, but he doesn't.

We hear Beth start up the stairs. "Did you hear me? They're here. My parents. They're anchored outside the harbor because of the storm, but they want to have dinner with... Miles?" She is in the upstairs hall now. Her voice drops in pitch as she realizes where Miles is. "Miles?" She pokes her head around the doorframe. "What are you doing in my room?" She steps fully into the doorway. "Finn! What are *you* doing here?"

When neither of us replies, she marches to the computer. "Miles, what the *fuck*? Why are you looking at my personal bank accounts, and why is *he* here?"

Miles says in a surprisingly neutral voice, "Who is Clarence Woodcock?"

A shock tremor jitters Beth's face before she resets it into a mask of righteous anger. "My private bank accounts are none of your goddamn business!"

"Why have you been writing him checks since the year after we graduated from college?" Miles asks, pointing to the printer tray. He's either forgotten I'm in the room or doesn't care.

Beth fixes Miles with one of the iciest glares I have ever seen issue from human eyes. "You and I will discuss this in private," she says. "In private."

"Actually, Beth, I think—"

She cuts him off. "IN. PRIVATE." She snaps off the final "t" sound as if cracking a bone over her knee.

Miles caves. He says to me, "You better scoot along, Finn, I'll talk to you later."

"I don't think I'll be doing any scooting right now, Miles. I think we need to—"

"Go! Now!" He suddenly looks ready to blow steam out his ears. "Beth and I will deal with this privately, and I will call you later!"

"No," I say, raising *my* voice a bit now. "You don't get to exclude me from this. Not when I'm the person whose neck is on the chopping block, and you two seem to know—"

"Finnian! *I* will handle Beth! That's final!"

"You don't get to make that call, Miles!" I snap. "Beth is a grownup, and she and I have business to clean up."

"Are we finally going to do that, Finn?" she says. Her tone is stark and devoid of clemency.

For a moment, I don't know what she means, but then a light comes on in some dark backroom of my mind. Beth transforms, right before my eyes, into her twenty-one-year-old self, complete with U2 tee-shirt and ill-advised Winona Ryder pixie cut. The doorway framing her dissolves into a hospital entrance. I am seeing her on graduation night, 1999.

"That night, when I took Miles to the ER..." I say, pausing to allow the old memory fragments to fit themselves together. *After Miles was brought in on a gurney and admitted, I went to use the bathroom. When I came out, Beth was already arriving on the scene. I couldn't figure out how she had shown up so quickly, but I was happy to be off the hook. I slipped out the exit and went home, leaving Beth to handle Miles and all the details.* "How did you get to the hospital so fast?"

"BECAUSE I WAS IN THE FUCKING CAR THAT NIGHT!"

She regards our dumbstruck faces for a second, then says, "Graduation night! I was there! Lying under a blanket in the back seat. You two didn't even notice me—but that's nothing new. I heard everything that happened."

She waits for the aftershocks to bounce around the room a few times, then says, "I need a drink."

She stomps heavily out of the room and down the stairs. Miles and I look at each other in open terror and follow her down into the study. She plants herself behind the mini-bar and pulls out a bottle. Will it surprise anyone to learn it is the Glenmalloch? It will not.

She pours herself a hearty two fingers, takes a sailor's swig, and says, in a somewhat calmer but shaky voice, "I had a lot to drink that night. Who didn't, right?" Leaning on the bar to steady herself, she seems resigned to an unburdening. Relieved, almost. She swirls the scotch around in the glass, gazing into the little vortex as if it were an eyehole into the past.

"By eleven o'clock I was wiped and ready to go home. I couldn't find either of you, so I figured you were off doing... whatever it is you two do when you're together. Finn, you had promised to drive us home, so I went to your car and lay down in the back seat. I figured that was the only way to be sure I didn't miss you guys. I fell asleep, passed out, whatever." She takes another swallow. "When I woke up, the car was moving. We were on the road. You two were talking about something private. I didn't want you to think I was listening in, so I didn't say anything. And then the longer it went on, the longer I just pretended..." No need to finish.

My brain has been harpooned here. Is it really possible a third person was with us during the entire drive home that night? It's hard to believe we wouldn't have noticed. But then again, Miles wouldn't have noticed *anything*, the shape he was in. And I was so focused on dealing with *him*... And she *was* under a blanket, lying down, in the dark... Actually, it's not hard to believe at all.

"When that business with the bottle happened," Beth says, "I heard everything. I had this terrible feeling in my stomach all night, and the first thing I did when I woke up the next morning was turn on the news. There it was, a story about a highway accident in Bridgefield. I threw up for forty-five minutes straight.

"When you finally woke up, Miles — *came to*, I should say — I asked you some questions about the night before, and you obviously didn't remember a thing. I had a decision to make: destroy the life we were building together before it even got started — destroy *all* our lives, really; our careers, our dreams — or just keep my mouth shut and pretend I wasn't even there." She stares at the bar-top. "The decision made itself... as they often do."

"So all these years you've known those people died that night?" says her husband.

"Don't you get self-righteous with me, Miles. Don't you fucking dare!"

Miles backs down. "How does Clarence Woodcock factor into this?"

"Just let me talk!" She takes another swig of the ol' country, refills her glass, and says, "I felt horrible about not coming forward. Horrible. What sucked the most was that I had to deal with the guilt alone. Miles, you knew nothing. Finn, you had vanished from the planet. I tried to..." She stops and inhales slowly through her nose. "We got married that summer, Miles, and I tried to be happy. And I was. Sort of. But I couldn't forget what happened. I watched the newspapers obsessively for any follow-up stories — about the accident, about Edgar Goslin and his rehabilitation.

"One of Goslin's friends started a website to collect donations for his rehab and to help him get back on his feet. It was kind of a new idea back then—a charity website. Supposedly you could donate anonymously if you wanted. And that was where I made the stupidest mistake of my life. I started making some donations—pretty big ones, actually—from my trust fund. I had just gotten signing authority on it, and I was feeling my oats. The account wasn't titled in my name, and I didn't think my donations could be traced to me personally. Or *would* be, I should say. Young and stupid, right?"

She drinks again. "Well, no good deed, blah, blah. One day when you weren't home, Miles—this was a year or so after graduation—there was a knock on our door, and two not-very-country-club-looking guys were standing there. One of them was using a walker. They introduced themselves as Clarence Woodcock and Edgar Goslin. I almost peed my pants; how the shit did Edgar Goslin find me?

"Well, he told me how. He started to get suspicious about those donations, he said. He figured—not stupidly, I must say—that when someone gives that much money to a stranger on multiple occasions, they might have more than a casual interest in his case. Maybe they're trying to buy off some guilt. So he hired a private investigator to look into it. Woodcock."

She moves to the window and looks out at the ocean, swirling her booze again as she tries to assemble the story pieces. Miles and I wait.

"This Woodcock creepo—red-faced asshole—tells me he traced the donation funds to my trust account and to me. And then he started looking into *us*. You and me, Miles. He found out where we lived, where we *used* to live, who our friends and family were. 'How's your cousin Helena?' he says. 'Did she ever get that cyst removed?' He had my attention.

"Anyway, he goes on to tell me he has friends on the police department, and they told him they found pieces of the bottle that caused the accident. I knew that from reading the papers, but then he tells me something I didn't know. It was a rare scotch, he says, and the cops were able to track down three local people who'd bought that bottle. 'And that was kinda curious,' he says, getting all TV-detective on me, 'because one of the buyers was a guy named Carroll. Whaddya know, same last name as your husband's best pal.' He taps his temple like he's some kind of special genius. 'Well, Edgar and me paid a visit to this Mr. Carroll,' he says, 'and, knowing what we knew, we were able to... *encourage* him to part with some information he'd lied to the cops about: that the scotch was bought as a gift for one Miles Sutcliffe.'"

So my dad *did* supply the link to Miles. Jesus, what did they do to him to pry that information out of him? No wonder he was so stressed about the whole thing.

Beth proceeds, "I'm on the edge of panic at this point, and Woodcock knows it. He says, 'So I was starting to get the picture on why you made the donations. If only I had proof.' And next he tells me something I'm not sure if it was true or if he was just making it up. At the time, I believed him, but later..." She tosses her arm in a stagy shrug. "He said, 'The cops had already turned Edgar's car inside-out for evidence, but just for hell of it, I asked Ed what clothes he was wearing the night of the accident. Well, turns out the hospital returned those clothes to him when he was discharged a few weeks after the accident. The clothes were ruined, but Edgar kept them for some reason, and damned if they weren't still in their Patient's Belongings bag.' Woodcock tells me that when he opened the bag, lo and behold, a piece of glass dropped out, a nice-sized one. Embossed, not windshield glass. Must have been lodged in a shoe or a pocket of his shirt or pants. Woodcock knew what he had.

"When he examined the glass, he said, he found a clean fingerprint on it. And it didn't belong to Finn Carroll. He didn't have to tell me what that meant.

"'I've looked into you and your husband,' he says. 'I know you got a big life planned for yourselves — country clubs and museum boards — and I know who your daddy is, Sweetheart. So here's what we're going to do.' It wasn't a discussion. 'You're going to... engage my services as a security consultant,' he says. 'I'm not going to do any work for you, but you're going to pay me a monthly retainer, commensurate with the value of my silence. In perpetuity.' Goslin started to grumble about the payment arrangement, I remember. Woodcock explained to him that the payments had to be in his name — Woodcock's — to make them appear as a legitimate business expense but that he would give Goslin his cut every month.

"In case you're ever tempted to change your mind about our… agreement,' Woodcock says to me, 'I'll just be holding onto this.' And he pulls out a little plastic bag with a piece of bottle glass in it. And he laughs this smug little heh-heh-heh, and then—the arrogant fuck—he leers at me and wiggles his eyebrows like he's actually coming on to me."

Beth dumps the rest of the drink down her throat and looks at Miles and me defiantly. "That's who Clarence Fucking Woodcock is."

Miles is seething, I can tell, though he's trying to contain his rage. Oddly enough, his anger seems to be aimed in my direction more than Beth's.

"Let me get this straight," he says to Beth at last. "All these years, you've been making extortion payments to some thug, living in fear, and putting our family at risk because of something *Finn Carroll* did on a drunken night twenty years ago."

"Finn?" says Beth, looking at him strangely. Then she turns to me and says, "You seriously haven't told him? Jesus, you really *must* be in love with him."

"What are you talking about?" Miles demands.

She spins toward Miles again. "Finn didn't throw the bottle that night, Roger Clemens. *You* did."

# Chapter 37

Miles loses his shit, to put it mildly. This is the Miles who, when backed into an existential corner, dissolves into a blubbering, whimpering child. I have seen him like this on only a couple of other occasions, and never to this extreme.

"*I* threw the bottle?" he says, his eyes darting around as if someone else might be watching us. "What are you saying? You're saying *I* threw the bottle? *I* threw the bottle?" His voice is moving rapidly up the pitch scale. "What the fuck, Beth? Finn? What the fuck? No! This can't be happening to me!" To *him*. Ah, Milesy. "This can't be happening! Not now!" He paces back and forth like a leopard in a cage, holding his head with both hands. "Oh my God. No, no, no, no, NOOOO!"

He wheels on me and Beth with wild eyes and says, in a voice a full octave above normal, "You've known this all along. Both of you. Why didn't you tell me? Why the hell didn't you tell me?"

"Because I knew you'd get like *this*!" snaps Beth. "I knew the worry would burrow into your brain like a parasite and eat away at you, day after day, year after year. And somewhere along the line you'd blow it; you'd blurt something out, just to relieve your anxiety."

"Nice to know how highly you regard me."

"People are what they are, Miles. It's not a judgment. I did you a huge favor. I took the decision out of your hands. Like I always do when we face a really hard choice."

"You had no right to take anything out of my hands! Either of you. How dare you withhold this from me? I had a right to know about my own actions. I had a right to know!"

"So you could *what*, Miles?" I say, keeping my voice low and steady to lend ballast to his tottering ship. "Stand up and do the right thing? Step forward and claim responsibility? You and I both know that never would have happened. We saved you from twenty years of mental anguish and bad decision-making."

"It wasn't your place to save me from anything!"

He has a point, but...

"When it comes to the tough calls, Miles," says Beth, "the really tough calls... Well, that's not really your area of strength, is it? That's why Daddy's always been... slow to move forward with you. That's why he hasn't given you more opportunities over the years. That's why he hasn't put you on a faster track."

"Oh Jesus, your dad," Miles says. His face pales. He moves into a weird internal space and resumes his caged-leopard pacing. "Why is this happening to me *now*? Why *now*? Why *now*?" He stares wide-eyed at the hand-woven Persian carpet, but he's not really seeing it. "I'm screwed, I'm screwed, I'm so fucking screwed. I'm screwed, I'm screwed, I'm so fucking screwed." He looks up at us and smiles a pressured, off-kilter smile, then repeats the words in a sing-song way. "I'm screwed, I'm screwed, I'm so fucking screwed." He actually starts dancing to the rhythm of the words—a Vaudeville box step, yep he does. It is a truly unsettling thing to behold. I am watching my friend's mind come unhinged.

"Miles!" I shout, but he seems not to hear me at all. "Miles!"

"I'm screwed, I'm screwed, I'm so fucking screwed. I'm screwed, I'm screwed, I'm so fucking screwed."

"Miles!" I bark sharply, as if trying to call off a dog. "Stop!"

"Get a fucking grip!" shrieks Beth.

"I'm screwed, I'm screwed, I'm so fucking screwed." He's saying the words through an awful amalgam of laughter and tears, and I realize I am witnessing, perhaps for the first time in my life, a person truly "in hysterics." I call his name a few more times.

No response. He keeps laugh-sobbing the words, "I'm screwed, I'm screwed, I'm so fucking screwed."

I don't know how to get through to him. My eyes land on the bottle of Glenmalloch.

"Miles!" I holler one last time, to no effect.

I seize the bottle and, in an act the fates have been trying to place in my hands for eighteen years, I throw the Glenmalloch. It strikes the fireplace, smashing into flying splinters.

There must be hidden power embedded in that Scottish glass, because the sound gets through to Miles where words could not. He goes deathly silent. He looks at me with a *Where am I?* expression.

"Get hold of yourself," I order in a harsh whisper. He nods vacantly. He takes a silent minute to put himself together mentally.

Beth waits till he appears to be back in business, then wails, "What is *wrong* with you?" as if he has been coming unglued just to irritate her.

"What's wrong?" Miles says, his tone now incongruously light. "Your father is here, that's what's wrong. And I'm fucking dead." Miles goes to the bar and takes out a new bottle of scotch, the plebeian blended stuff, and pours a glass. He takes a drink, sits, tries to relax. No dice. Too much nervous energy. He bounces up out of his chair and starts pacing the floor of the study again. Something unsaid is still on his mind.

"Beth's dad is the one who has the 'in' with the governor," he spills at last. "He's the one who's been touting me for this Senate opening."

Ah. Now I see why he's been so guarded with me about the big career move. As I've said, he doesn't like me to know how much power Simon Fischer wields over him.

"But it's grown even bigger than that," he adds. "Last time I saw him... he, he explained to me that there were these... people, these very... *elite* people he was making inroads with. These people were interested in backing someone for a run for... well, Pennsylvania fucking Avenue. Ha!" Beth knows all this, presumably, so he's laying it out for my benefit. "He recommended *me* as their man and—surprise!—they agreed I might have just the qualities they're looking for. If your dad could do his part and get me that Senate seat, they would start working on my behalf the day I took office. I would never meet these people directly, and I would never see their machinery at work. But they would remain extremely active in 'clearing the road' to the White House for me. They were only interested in backing a solid winner, though; someone they could count on to go all the way and to never, ever let them down."

Miles turns and faces Beth. This is a part of the story she doesn't seem to know yet. "So then he looked at me, your dad did, and said, 'Son, before I put your ass in that Senate seat, I'm going to ask you a question. It may be the most important question you will ever answer. I don't care if your answer is yes or no. I only care if it's the truth." Miles pauses for effect. "'Do you have any bodies in shallow graves I need to know about?'

"I said, 'No, sir.'

"He patted me on the knee and said, 'That's good, son.' Then he gave me the patented Simon Fischer death-stare and said, 'Because if I find out otherwise, hell will rain down.'

"And now—*now*—all this old stuff decides to surface," Miles blubbers. "Goslin turns up dead..."

"Dead?" interjects Beth. "What? When?"

Miles ignores her. "*That's* going to get some people asking questions. And this Woodcock sleazebag, you can bet *he's* going to come crawling out of the woodwork..."

"You don't have to worry about him," I say.

Miles and Beth look at me in surprise. "What do you mean?" asks Miles. "Why not?"

"Why don't you ask your wife?"

Beth draws her head back in a theatrical display of affrontedness. "What the hell are you talking about, Finn?"

"You're seriously going to act like you don't know?"

"Don't know what?"

"Come on, Beth. Okay, I'll play along," Watching her face for a reaction, I say, "Woodcock's dead too."

Beth's eyes go blank and her jaw drops. If she's acting, she's pretty good at it. "How? When? How do you know?"

"Google," I reply. I count off the names on two fingers:

"Woodcock... Goslin... The two men who have been blackmailing you for years, Beth. Both dead from 'accidents' within the same twenty-four-hour period. Kind of a mammoth-ass coincidence, wouldn't you say?"

"I certainly would," Beth allows. "But this is as big a shock to me as—"

"Now throw in the fact that someone tried to off *me* at the same time, and I'd say that shifts it from coincidence to monkey-randomly-typing-*Lord of the Rings*."

"Why are you looking at me like that?" Beth says to me. "Finn, get serious. You and I have had our differences over the years—I've *wanted* to kill you a few times, God knows—but there's no way in hell you seriously think I'm capable of...?"

"I wouldn't have thought so two hours ago, Beth. But now...? The three people who have the dirt on your husband get killed—or almost killed—the same day? And, just to tie the whole package up with a neat ribbon, one of them conveniently pens a suicide note in which he confesses to causing the old accident himself."

"Okay, that's enough," says Miles, as if coming out of a fog. "I don't like where you're going with this."

"I didn't ask you, Miles." I continue to press Beth. "And all of this comes at a time when your husband is about to be thrust into the public eye in a very big way. Just like you've always wanted."

Beth stammers, "That's just so.... That's just so..." Her eyes roll from side to side like an overwound cat clock's as she searches for a rational explanation that doesn't include her.

"*Someone* is responsible for these killings and attempted killings, Beth, and who else on the face of the planet—"

"*Alleged* attempted killings," she says. "Alleged. Alleged. By you."

"Oh, that's right, Beth. No one really tried to kill me; that's just a paranoid delusion. I'm clinically insane. A locked-ward psychotic. Right?"

"I never said that!"

"Isn't what you've been trying to convince Miles of since I got here? Since *before* I got here? 'Finn is out of his mind, you can't believe anything he says. He's talking banana salad, he's dangerous, he shouldn't be around the kids...'"

"Where the hell are you *getting* this crap?" she says.

"From here," I say, holding up my phone. "I have you on tape. Both of you." That gets her attention. And Miles'. "The other day, when I went to buy that wine for Jim, I left my phone recorder running on the desk by mistake. I heard everything you said."

Beth's face blanches again. She can't argue with what the recorder captured. "You did just get out of a psychiatric hospital," she attempts, weakly.

"Right, Beth. It's also a mighty handy way for you to discredit everything I have to say. So nothing can land on you."

"It was my idea to invite you to the island! If I felt personally threatened by what you had to say, why would I do that?"

"Maybe to finish the job that didn't get done in Wentworth."

Her head literally jolts from the blow of what I'm suggesting.

"I won't say what I really want to say to you right now, Finn. You know why? Because *words have power*. But I am done with you. After twenty years, I am so fucking done with you." She slams her glass down and storms out of the room.

"When's the last time you saw Edgar Goslin?" I shout after her. She keeps walking. I follow her out to the kitchen where she punches her arms through the sleeves of her windbreaker. "When was the last time?"

"Last time?" she snaps. "I only saw that asshole once. The day he came to our door, back in 2000." She zips up the jacket and steps into her rain shoes.

"That's a lie, Beth. You expect me to believe you're totally clean here," I say, "but you keep lying to me, so why should I?"

"I don't care what you believe, you crazy fuck. You and Miles can stay here all day, working on your conspiracy theories. I'm going to go round up the children so they can see their grandparents. Here in the real world."

Beth exits, slamming the door.

I open the door and shout after her, "I know Edgar Goslin came to

Musqasset a couple of weeks ago."

"And Bigfoot was on the grassy knoll with the second shooter!"

"Are you going to try to tell me Goslin didn't contact you at all?"

She doesn't try to tell me anything.

• • • • •

By the time Miles and I find our shoes and make it out the door to follow her, she is already out of sight. Miles runs up the walkway. I'm right at his heels. He looks both ways on the road, doesn't see her. Neither of us says a word; it's as if we are under a spell of silence that can't be broken until we find Beth and wring the final truth out of her.

Miles runs to the back yard and starts down the trail Jeannie led me down a few nights ago. He veers onto a side path leading to a couple of neighboring properties. I hang back as he bounds up to a neighbor's house. A woman answers the door and I see Kelsey, Miles' daughter, in the background. The woman shakes her head no.

Miles runs back to his house and jumps into his golf cart. I follow him and jump in too. Thinking Beth may have taken the trail to the marina, Miles drives around to the spot where he and I parked the other day, the knoll from where you can view the whole marina property. Beth isn't anywhere to be seen. Miles drives off, crackling with nervous energy.

He heads through The Meadows on its winding main road, checking out all the properties. We spot Dylan shooting hoops in a driveway with another kid, but no Beth. Miles turns onto the road to Lighthouse Hill, drives to the top. I jump out of the cart before it's fully stopped and run to the path leading down to Table Rock. Miles is right behind me.

There she is. Standing on the edge of Table Rock, in the slippery moss and seaweed. No waves are washing over the bare slab of slate right now; either because the tide is out or the storm has weakened, but still... One slip of the foot or errant wave will wash her out to sea.

We scramble down the steep, rocky path toward her.

"Beth!" shouts Miles. "Move back!"

She takes a step *forward*. For a moment I am sure she is going to toss herself into the ocean, but then she turns and regards us, almost like strangers. She looks back at the sea one last time, then slumps her shoulders and shuffles, in resigned fashion, toward higher ground.

By the time we reach her, she is sitting on a dry rock safely above sea level.

In a voice barely above a whisper, she says, "Edgar Goslin and Clarence Woodcock came to our house two weeks ago."

Miles and I wait for more.

"I let them in. What choice did I have? I didn't ask for this responsibility."

"Tell us what happened, Beth," I say in the tone of a friend. "Please."

She looks out into the middle distance and lets the scene form in her mind. "They sat at our kitchen table. Woodcock said to me, 'It might surprise you to know, we read the papers.' He threw down a newspaper with one of those op-ed pieces—the ones Daddy paid to have written—suggesting that you"—Miles—"might be a great choice for that Senate seat if Aldridge stepped down. Then he said, 'Now that your husband's career is about to get a shot of Viagra, this might be a good time to renegotiate our terms.' And he slipped me a piece of paper with his new and improved 'fee' on it."

More puzzle pieces are linking up, one by one.

"He was expecting me to be cowering and meek. I guess he just picked the wrong day to mess with me. Something came over me. Maybe it was the fact that I've had seventeen years to build up hatred for these guys. Paying their hush money every month, knowing they had the power to sink our future anytime they chose. God! I've been seeing that smug red face of his in my sleep my entire adult life!"

She stares, unseeing, into the harsh Atlantic.

"Long story short, I told Woodcock to go fuck himself. ...He didn't see *that* coming, let me tell you. He says, 'You're forgetting what I have sitting in a plastic bag in my office, lady.'

"'I'm not forgetting,' I said. 'A stupid piece of glass.'

"'With your husband's fingerprint on it.'

"'So you claim,' I said.

"'Oh, lady,' Goslin pipes up, 'You do not want to test us on that.'

"For some reason — impulse, really — I decided to call his bluff. 'Yes, that's exactly what I want to do,' I said. 'I don't believe that glass is from the accident, and I don't believe you have my husband's real fingerprint. And I don't want to deal with you anymore until I have proof.'

"Woodcock gets all sputtery and says, 'Even if it wasn't real, which it is, I've got records of you making payoffs to me going back seventeen years. Deal with *that*.'

"'Records cut both ways,' I said. 'Extortion is a crime. Now get the hell out of my house and don't ever, ever come to my door again.'

"He stands up, gets in my face, and says, 'I better see that new fee show up on the fifteenth. Or there will be dire consequences. Dire.'

"'You'll be lucky to see the old fee,' I told him. And then..." She lowers her face into her hands — a bit melodramatically, if you ask me. "I wasn't planning to say it; it just came out. I said, 'If you ever do one thing to threaten me or my family again, I will send people to *your* home who will fucking kill you.'"

Miles and I wait, in frozen suspense, for the final shoe to drop.

"Those were literally the last words I said to them before they left."

She hangs her head as if finished. Miles grants her a moment, then says, "So... what did you do next?"

"Do?" she replies foggily. "I didn't *do* anything. I was bluffing. I don't know any 'people'; you know that. But those were the last words I said to two human beings before they turned up dead in *just the way I spoke*. Don't you think that means something?"

Means something? Yes, I thought it meant she was about to confess to the killings.

"Wait, wait, wait," I say, trying to wrap my head around what's going on here. "Are you actually saying — and I just need your honest answer here, Beth, for once in our god-forsaken lives — you had nothing to do with the deaths of those men or with what happened to me?"

"Not directly. I didn't make a phone call or hire some hit men. But clearly, *words have power*. Look what happened to those men! They're both dead!"

Jesus, you've got to be kidding me. She actually thinks she's *cosmically guilty* of killing these guys because she *wished it on them with her words*. And she says *I'm* the crazy one?

Given the facts at hand, it is almost impossible to believe she had nothing to do with Goslin's and Woodcock's deaths, but, looking at her drained face and sunken eyes, it is equally impossible to believe she is lying. I had no idea this woman was such a nutjob.

Beth stands up, and we all regard one another mutely.

My phone rings, nearly jolting me off the rock I'm standing on. The caller ID shows, oddly enough, JJ, the manager at Harbor House. I step up to a higher rock to answer the call.

"Hey, Finn, sorry to bother you," says JJ, "but Pete called from over at the bar. He's trying to get hold of you, says it's kind of an emergency."

I call the number JJ gives me, and Pete picks up. "Finn," he says, "Have you seen Jeannie?"

"Not since this morning. Why?"

"She's gone. Disappeared. In the middle of her shift. Went out back to get a keg and no one's seen her since."

# CHAPTER 38

Miles flips me his golf-cart keys. I run up the steep trail and jump behind the wheel, pulling for breaths. I'm at Pete's Lagoon within minutes, praying by the time I step inside, Jeannie will have turned up.

Prayer denied. Pete is standing behind the bar in her place, ineptly drawing a pint of Guinness. "She's never done anything like this," he says, a note of accusation in his voice. "All these years, never." *Until you showed up* is the obvious subtext.

"Did she take her stuff with her?" I ask him. He points to a little cubby area in the back room behind the bar, and I see her rain jacket folded up with her shoulder bag on top of it. It's a sight that scares the ever-loving shit out of me.

"Has anyone checked the grounds, the bathrooms?" I ask. "She might have fallen and hurt herself."

"Franca took a look around. Barb too."

I charge off to do my own search of the place. Pete doesn't stop me. I check the bathrooms, the dark corners of the storeroom. I check Pete's office. A coat rack has been tipped over and the rug is rumpled. From someone else's previous search?

I run outside and check the pilings under the building, the bushes and undergrowth on all sides of the restaurant. I've got a terrible feeling.

I scan the water of the bay. No floating bodies visible from shore.

Panic rises in me, and I have the impulse to start running around the island screaming Jeannie's name. Before I can execute on that innovative plan, it occurs to me it might be time to try the police again, now that the storm has abated and the sea is finally starting to settle. Maybe our roving part-time officer can make it over from Monhegan now. Even if he can't, I still need to talk to someone in authority, tell them Jeannie's gone missing, get some advice, go on record with my story.

I find the police number in my contacts list. The call goes through, or seems to. But then, just as with my calls to Angie, it disconnects just as someone picks up. I try twice more and get the same result. I try the state police too. No luck.

Bloody Musqasset cell-phone service — it has a mind of its own.

I've got to do something. I "speed" over to Jeannie's house in Miles' cart. I know I won't find her there, but I need to check anyway.

Predictably, she does not answer the door. I look under the raven sculpture in the garden, where she used to hide a spare key. Still there. I tear through the house, calling her name and looking for her in absurd places, like the fridge, even though I'm sure she's not in the building.

I jump back into the cart, drive around the corner to Studio Row, and run up and down the footpaths, knocking on doors, shouting in windows, asking folks if they've seen Jeannie. No joy.

I floor it back to the village, wringing every watt of anemic horsepower from the cart.

I need to talk to anyone and everyone who knows Jeannie. That includes my fisherman "friends." I start toward Billy Staves' place when I see Billy himself, standing near the rear of his building where Dennis's sandwich counter is. He's talking to Gerry Harper. I hate these two assholes right now, but finding Jeannie is my sole concern.

I stop the cart and jump out. The men go silent.

"Jeannie's missing."

"Missing? How do you mean?" says Gerry.

I give them the seven-second version, and the men seem genuinely upset. Gerry starts off, breaking into a jog. "I'll get some people together, we'll turn the place inside out," he calls out as he goes. Then he stops for a moment, turns back to me, and says, "Don't worry, man, if she's on this island, we'll find her." I nod, and he rushes off.

"Dennis and I will take the boat," says Billy. "Circle the island. See what we can see from there."

"Thanks, Billy," I say. Words I never expected to hear escape my mouth again.

I run back toward Miles' cart. "Finn," shouts Billy, stopping me in my tracks. "I need to say something to you. Real quick."

"Another time, Billy," I reply. "After we find Jeannie."

"This'll only take a sec."

I stand and listen, but my mind is racing ahead to next steps.

"Mike Bourbon was right, out there today. We rushed to judgment. I'm sorry for that. You deserve your say. We owe you that. And I, for one, am ready to hear your side whenever you're ready to talk."

I don't have time for this conversation. "That's mighty white of you, Billy," I say, "but if my friendship meant so little to you, I'm not sure I really *want* to win it back."

"Fair enough. Friends ought to be loyal. In that case, you might want to talk to your own buddy."

"What do you mean?"

"I mean Miles Sutcliffe was the one who flipped us all against you."

I'm itching to move on, but instinct tells me I need to hear this. I lock eyes with my old Scrabble partner. What dazzling word combo is he about to play?

"We did trust you, Finn," he says. "We all figured it was Sutcliffe who deep-sixed those letters of ours. So one night, after the vote, Fishermen's Court paid him a visit. We took him out on the pier to have a little 'heart to heart.' But when we questioned him, he swore blue-faced that he'd passed the letters on to his partners. One of our more skeptical brethren suggested that, just to ensure his veracity, we might perform a 'buccaneer's baptism.' He and another fella grabbed Sutcliffe by the ankles, like they were going to dunk him in the bay, and he started bawling like a five-year-old. 'Okay, it was Finn!' he said. 'I'm sorry! I was just trying to protect him. He's my friend! Don't hurt him!'

"We practically had to beat it out of him," says Billy, "but he finally told us you never gave *him* the letters. The story he heard, says him, was that one of his development partners, the one who was in for the biggest wedge of the pie, got wind of the letters. He was afraid some of the other partners might be swayed by a bunch of sob stories, so he paid you off to lose the letters, leave the island, and never come back."

"*Miles told you this?*" I say, ready to blow a brain-valve.

"We had to drag it out of him, but yeah." He adds with a sheepish note, "You did disappear from the island, Finn, and you didn't come back."

"I left the island because I broke up with Jeannie and because my mother was dying and needed care. I told people that. Why did you believe him over me?"

"Guess it was the *way* he told it, the way we had to wring it out of him, the way he begged us to spare *you*, not him. I mean, you'd have to be an absolute world-class liar to play that the way he did."

"Yes, Billy," I say. "Yes, you would."

I run off.

• • • • •

The story Billy just told me is gnawing at my belly like an ulcer, but I have to focus on Jeannie's safety. I'm trying to decide where to search for her next when a text comes in on my phone. It's from her!

The text has obviously been typed in a hurry or under duress. It reads, *They haven.* Fucking auto-correct. A few seconds later her fix comes through: *Have me.*

They have me?

Blood starts pounding in my ears. I type, *Who has you? Where?*

The reply comes flying back: *Can't.*

I assume that means she can't answer right now, but I try anyway: *Jeannie, who has you? Where did they take you?* No reply.

I type, *Jeannie?* and hit Send again.

I pace back and forth in the middle of Island Avenue, *willing* a reply to come in.

Nothing.

Something feels wrong to me about Jeannie's texts, but I can't put my finger on it. I close my eyes and try to let it come to me. An image pops into my memory. Shit!

I run the stone's-throw distance back to Pete's, fling the door open, and race up to the bar. I look into the back room where I saw Jeannie's belongings earlier. There it is, sitting in the outside pocket of her bag: her phone in its kelly-green case. She doesn't have it with her! So how did those texts...?

I gesture for permission to go behind the bar, and Pete waves me around. I grab the phone out of Jean's purse. The Messages screen is open. I see our most recent text exchange on it. *What?*

"Pete, who's been back here?" I ask.

"No one but the ghost of Captain Bradish." An old bar yarn.

"You sure?"

"Oh wait, the Patriots were doing team sprints in there a while ago; I forgot. Hell yeah, I'm sure. I've been standing right here. No sign of her yet?"

"No, I'll let you know when I find anything."

I consider taking Jeannie's phone with me but slip it back into her purse. I barrel full-speed out of the bar, caroming off L.L.Bean dad as he's entering, almost knocking him off his feet. He looks at me as if I'm a crazy person. He might be on to something.

As I'm about to jump into Miles' cart, I freeze. I realize Pete, and Pete alone, has had access to Jeannie's phone the whole time the text exchange has been going on. I recall the disheveled state of his office — signs of a struggle? I turn around and march back into the bar.

My phone pings another text. One word. From "Jeannie": *Help.*

Pete hasn't budged from his place at the register. Jeannie's phone hasn't moved either.

*WTF? How could text messages be issuing from her phone all by themselves?*

Have I mentioned that I'm a giant freaking idiot?

The answer slams me in the head like a falling air conditioner. I recall the way my own phone has been behaving. Dropping calls in an odd way, feeling warm to the touch when I'm not actively using it, going in and out of service at key moments. I've been chalking it all up to the Musqasset cell-phone gods. But now, Jeannie's phone sending phantom texts?

How could I have been stupid enough not to think of this?

I run to Miles' cart and drive off toward Enzo's.

Before approaching his door, I ditch my phone outside in an empty flower pot. If I'm right about what I'm thinking, such precautions have become essential.

Enzo spots me before I can knock and lets me in. I quickly fill him in on Jeannie's disappearance and then say, "Remember those spy programs you were telling me about? Is there any way to tell if someone has planted one on your phone?"

"Has your phone been acting funny?"

I reply that it has and tell him the myriad ways. "I thought it was just Musqasset cell service in a storm."

"You have an Apple, right?" he asks. I nod. "Like I told you earlier, someone would need to have access to your physical phone, and they would need to jailbreak it."

I don't know what jailbreaking a phone means, but I nod as if I have an embryonic clue.

"Has your phone been out of your physical possession?" he asks.

"It has." It was sitting in my parents' house the whole time I was in the hospital. Someone could have planted the entire digitized Library of Congress on it. I've left it in my room a few times on Musqasset too.

"The only way to know for sure if you're infected is to dig directly into the phone's root file system. That's tricky to do with an iPhone; it doesn't have the right tools built in. But you don't want to do that anyway—if you're really being spied on, you'd tip off your spies that you're on to them. Remember, they can see everything you do on your phone."

"There's no way to look into the files remotely?"

Enzo's eyes twinkle. "Well, look at you, getting all tech savvy. Actually, that's sort of the *only* way to do it." He leads me to his computer wall. "All the files on your phone are probably backed up remotely on the Cloud."

Okay, sure. We figure out how to log into my Cloud account from his iMac, and, sure enough, we find the backup of my phone's files. Using the basic file-search tools available on the computer but not on the phone, Enzo is able to dig into the phone's file system. He pulls in a breath when he spots a well-hidden file with the seemingly harmless name ASAN20.

"Holy crap, I've read about this one," he says, duly gobsmacked. "High-level, pro-grade stuff. Illegal as hell. It's not just spyware, it's a full phone hijacker. There's a tiny chip that goes into the phone when you install it. With the hardware/software combo, you can remotely turn the person's phone on and off, track their location even when the phone's off, listen in on phone conversations, read their texts and emails, *send* texts and emails, delete files, track their online activity, even turn the mike and camera on."

Translation: someone's been tracking my every move, my every word — probably since I left the hospital. Manipulating my calls and files too. Like that recording from the ferry that suddenly vanished. I tell Enzo about the "ghost" texts I'm getting from Jeannie's phone, and he concludes her phone may be infected too.

"You're being seriously watched, my friend, by some serious people."

Not good news but good to know.

At this point, my spies don't know I've discovered their spyware, so I may be able to turn that to my advantage. But from now on I will have to monitor everything I say and do. Obviously, I should have been doing that all along.

"You'll need a burner," says Enzo, "in case you have to talk confidentially." He digs in a drawer where he has several old phones. He finds a wiped smartphone, a couple of years out of date, with a new phone number assigned to it. Thank you, Enzo's paranoia.

He quickly figures out how to import my Contacts list from the Cloud onto the burner phone so I'll have all my important numbers, including his, then hands me the burner. "Let me look for a charger for that."

"No time." I'm already out the door.

"Go find her, man," Enzo shouts after me. "I'll do what I can from my end."

I retrieve my regular phone from the flower pot outside—no new texts from "Jeannie" yet—and then I'm off in Miles' speedmobile.

# CHAPTER 39

I drive a frantic circuit around Greyhook, asking everyone I know, friend and frenemy alike, if they've seen Jeannie. Along the way, I send several texts to fake Jeannie, such as: "Where R U?" "Are U safe? I'm worried!" "Jeannie?" I know she's not really seeing my texts and that if I do get a response it won't be from her; it will be from her captors. But still, I have to play dumb. Not a stretch for me.

I run into The Rusty Anchor. The fishermen stop talking at once and turn to stare at me, but when I shout, "Jeannie's gone missing!" they jump out of their seats, buzzing with questions, their drinks forgotten. As I'm heading back out, a sign on the wall nails my attention. Printed in huge black lettering, it reads, "Be 21 or Be Gone."

My unconscious mind starts sending up flares again. I suddenly realize why my first encounter with the three young beer-buyers has continued to needle me. The eldest of the trio claimed to be twenty-one: the age one would be now if one had been three years old in 1999. From the get-go, Miles and I have been asking, *Why would someone wait eighteen years to seek payback?* Could the answer be as simple as *because he needed to grow up first?*

As I jog toward Miles' cart, I replay the meeting with the wannabe beer-buyers. The name of the oldest one—the one with the toothy smile—was spoken aloud by his wheeler-dealer friend. What was it? I'm trying to drag the name from memory when a new text comes in from "Jeannie."

Instantly I forget about the beer boys. I read the fake Jean text with a critical eye. The first text bubble reads, *In cave at robs head*; the second, *No come 2 dangerous*. Then nothing.

Rob's Head. I know where that is. Okay, so by telling me, as Jeannie, *No come 2 dangerous*, her captors are obviously baiting me *to* come. They know I won't be able to resist. And, of course, they're right. They probably have loads of fun surprises in store for me when I arrive. And it's doubtful Jeannie is even in this "cave"; they just want to lure me there.

• • • • •

Rob's Head is a roundish, protruding cliff face on the north side of the island. I have done my share of exploring there. I know of several small caves where gulls nest but not a cave large enough to hold adult humans. It's possible such a cave exists, though, and I just never found it.

Now... if I were possessed of intelligence, which clearly I am not, what I would do at this juncture is throw together a posse of Jeannie's friends and march en masse to Rob's Head.

What I *do* do is run off half-cocked into the woods, alone, armed only with the fish-skinning knife that's still strapped to my shin. The trail to Rob's Head is not accessible by vehicle, so I have to travel by foot. I know I can't storm the enemy's lair single-handed — I'm not quite *that* stupid — but I'm hoping maybe I can get close enough to the cave in question to survey the situation, then call in reinforcements, if necessary, on the burner phone. Wish I still had Danny's binoculars with me, but I'm not about to go fetch them now.

I make good time running along the network of trails that leads from Greyhook across the island's central wilds. By the time I reach the trailhead to Rob's Head Trail, though, my lungs are stinging. I need to slow down and metabolize some oxygen.

"Old dudes, so pathetic," comes a voice to my right. I turn to see Leah stepping out of the woods with a lopsided grin. And lo, what is she holding but a pair of binoculars? The Beans of Maine, it seems, are birdwatchers. Reading my anxiety level, she drops the levity and looks sharply into my eyes. "What's going on, Finn?"

For some crazy reason, I trust Leah, though she's practically a stranger. "Someone I care about very much is in trouble with some very scary people," I tell her.

"Would this be the love interest you passed up a roll in the hay with a gorgeous twenty-three-year-old for?"

"It would."

"How can I help?"

It's an earnest offer, and I'm in no position to refuse it. "I'm looking for a cave at Rob's Head, one big enough for people to hide out in."

"I think I might know of one," she replies, and dashes off down Rob's Head Trail. My breath restored, I run after her.

Within a few minutes, we're drawing near the head. Leah stops and points down a twisty, muddy trail that leads around to the cliff-face and the water's edge.

"The cave I'm thinking of is down that way. Hope you brought climbing shoes, 'cause it's about twenty feet up the—"

"The people we're talking about are dangerous, Leah. We can't just stroll into their hideout holding a three-bean salad."

"Oh, right, duh. Hey, I know a place where we might able to scope things out from a distance first, without being seen. It's out on Crane Neck."

Crane Neck is an outcropping of high, rocky land northwest of Rob's Head that hooks out into the Atlantic like, well, a crane's neck. Because of the way it curls back on the island, there might indeed be some locations from where we can spy on the face of Rob's Head.

"This way." Leah is off and running again. The old dude keeps up pretty well.

Five lung-shredding minutes later, we're at the base of Crane Neck—far enough from Rob's Head that we shouldn't be noticeable by Jeannie's captors. Leah hands me her binoculars.

To test the lenses, I focus on a boat anchored a few hundred yards offshore. A beast of a luxury yacht. If the yachting set is braving the open ocean again, I muse, the ferry should be running tomorrow. Will

I be on it?

"Come on, Finn." Leah leads me down a jagged trail that runs along the landward-facing side of Crane Neck. Seeking a good vantage point, she steps up onto a rounded rock and points out a flat area a few yards ahead, a bit lower on the trail, surrounded by bushes. "Try looking from there," she says.

As I start to climb down to the lookout spot, a thought slams into my mind, freezing my limbs in place: both Cliff and Jeannie herself have tried to warn me that Jeannie is involved in something that will hurt me. Till now I've taken that to mean *emotional* hurt, but maybe the meaning was more literal. What if there are no "captors" in this scenario? What if Jeannie has not actually been taken at all? What if I'm being played in a more insidious way?

"Something wrong?" asks Leah.

"Just thinking about how careful I need to be." I step down to the flat lookout space Leah has shown me. As I plant my feet and lift the binocs, a cloth sack is pulled over my head.

Around my neck I feel the same rock-muscled arm that held me in its pipe-like embrace nine days ago and hear the voice of Chokehold say, "Miss me, Finnian?"

• • • • •

After a short jaunt across choppy waters in what feels like a skiff, and then a blind ascent up a boat ladder, I feel myself standing on the deck of a seemingly large craft. My hands are bound in front of me with nylon cuffs. Chokehold marches me, roughly, along a carpeted corridor, then down a set of stairs into a lower room. He shoves me onto a padded bench where I land awkwardly, my skull smacking into a wooden wall.

*T-Bone!* The name pops into my head unbidden, as if jarred loose by the blow. That was the name of the eldest beer-buying kid, the one with the creepy smile. T-Bone, T for short. T as in Theo? As in heir to the Abelsen estate?

The bag/blindfold is yanked from my head and I see I'm in a

sparsely appointed, sunken room with slatted wood walls and a series of portholes. The only furnishings are a couple of bolted-down table-and-chair units and the wall bench I'm sitting on. Still, it's clear that the vessel I'm on is a luxury yacht, a fairly massive one.

When I see the trio sitting around the table in front of me, my mind seizes up in incomprehension. The entire L.L.Bean family: Mr., Mrs., and daughter Leah.

"Good afternoon, Mr. Carroll," says Mrs. Bean with her mouthful of small, even teeth. The tone and cadence are instantly familiar. Trooper Dan. That voice, which was in the high-talker range for a man, and which I thought sounded a tad prissy, is completely normal for a woman, I realize. Strange how I didn't pick up on that before. The fake beard she must have worn that day at my parent's house—and yes, her blatant violent cruelty—flipped my brain to assuming, without question, she was a man. I think they call it premature cognitive commitment.

"Our instructions are to treat you civilly," she says. "So we will remove the handcuffs... If you can assure us there won't be any idiocy."

I nod. Chokehold, aka *Mister* Bean, cuts the polymer restraints with a razor tool.

"Take a moment to get your bearings," says the missus.

I look left and right, and it's only now I see who's sitting on the bench beside me. Jeannie. Arms folded, wearing an unreadable face.

It's true, then? Jeannie in cahoots with these guys?

My response to this realization, oddly, is a rush of relief; at least her life's not in danger. Relief evaporates when I notice the animal terror in her eyes. No, she's not in with them. She's a captive too, like me. She and I exchange a silent, guarded look. Chit-chat isn't exactly appropriate, given the circumstances, but I try to project calmness toward her.

An urgent thought stabs at me immediately, one that might make the difference between life and death. These guys are most certainly going to body-search me. I'm surprised they haven't done so already. When they do, they will find my knife and my burner phone. I must not allow that to happen. Those items might be Jeannie's and my only hope of getting out of here alive. These wankers are well aware of my regular phone—they've been using it to spy on me for days—but I must think of a way to hang onto the burner. And the knife.

I survey the room and once again call on my gamer mind. *Another puzzle to be solved, Game Boy, so solve it. Fast. Put the brain in overdrive.*

The room is bare, so there are few props for me to employ.

Shifting my ass, I notice the bench padding slides a bit on the wood surface. It is not glued down to the bench but is attached in sections by ties.

A rough idea hatches in my skull, and a plan begins to assemble itself. Well, "plan" is too generous a word for it—call it the early rudiments of a plan-like thing. Three steps must occur in sequence, I realize: One, I must remove my knife and burner phone from my body and hide them. Two, Troop and company must search me. Three, I must return the hidden items to my body *after* I've been searched.

If I can pull those steps off, I will gain a potentially critical edge.

Easier thought than done.

There is only one possible hiding spot for my knife and phone. I'll need Jeannie's help. Working in our favor is the fact that Jeannie and I can communicate complex messages with the subtlest of eye movements. I meet her gaze and, with a nano-shift of my irises, signal her to get up and walk to the nearest porthole. Amazingly, she picks up on my cue. Without hesitation, she stretches, stands up, and strolls toward the window. The three captors' heads turn and goggle at her; clearly, she's not supposed to be wandering around freestyle like this.

I seize the momentary distraction to slip the knife out of its shinstrap and slide it under the seat cushion of the bench, below my rear.

Mrs. Bean clears her throat at Jeannie, who turns with a *Who, me?* look.

"You didn't tie us up," says Jeannie, "so I assumed we were free to move about the cabin."

"You assumed incorrectly." Mrs. B. tosses her head toward the bench.

Jeannie returns to her seat, but her brief exchange with Mrs. B. has bought me enough time to slip the burner phone, too, from my pocket and under the seat cushion. Both items are pretty thin; I hope they won't make a telltale lump in the cushion when and if I have to stand.

Phase One complete. Easy sneezy.

Now for Phase Two. I want them to search me. I want them to find my main phone, find the Velcro strap on my shin, and come to the conclusion that I am carrying nothing of threat or consequence. Once they've searched me, I see no reason why they'll want to do so a second time. That is my hope.

The Beans seem to be in no hurry to do anything at the moment. Mr. B. is checking his phone for messages. Mrs. B. is sitting eerily still and blank-faced. Leah (or whatever her real name is) is working on a laptop. My sense is they're awaiting word from someone.

I need to engage them, get them talking. Try to make something happen.

I address Mrs. Bean first. "So, did you bring your lopper along today or will you be resorting to the fine selection of *nautical* torture devices available to today's enterprising and psychologically disturbed hit-person?"

Does she crack a tiny smile? "I guess that's for us to know and you to find out, Mr. Carroll," she replies in a not-unfriendly tone.

"I hear three-hooked fishing lures can be used in a number of inventive ways."

"Is that right?"

She seems to have let her guard down a bit. Maybe because she is holding all the cards, and I'm holding a giant heap of fuck-all. Good. I'll press on.

"I hate to admit it," I say, "but I bought that you were a dude. The beard worked. Was it super-realistic or was I just too dense to notice it came from Halloween City?"

"The mind believes what it is cued and predisposed to believe. Gender stereotypes tend to work in my favor."

"Yeah, most chicks wouldn't lay into the lopper work the way you do." I'm deliberately being a dick, just to throw some sparks. "Anyway, the beard sure fooled me."

"It wasn't designed to fool *you*, Mr. Carroll. It was a simple precautionary measure necessitated by the risks of my trade."

"Which is what, exactly?"

I receive no answer. "So let me guess the pecking order here," I say to Mrs. Bean. "You're the crew foreman and chief enforcer." I then project my voice toward Mr. Bean. "You're the muscle and mop-up guy, right? Do you get paid for the hours you spend doing power curls? If not, I can speak to the union steward."

I glance at Jeannie and she shoots me a warning look like, *why are you antagonizing these people*?

"Which one of you is the computer hacker-slash-'literary forger'?" I go on. Trotting out the term Enzo used doesn't trigger any noticeable reaction. "That must be you, Leah, or whatever your name is. I'm guessing you were the person working at my computer while I was tragically attempting to end my life in my parents' kitchen. Kudos on that suicide note. That was some top-notch writing work. Natural talent alone or did you have some software help?"

At this, "Leah" does look a bit surprised. "You're not quite as dumb as you let on."

"Close but not quaahhht," I reply in a dumbass hillbilly voice. "But I thaink I done figgered out what all y'all been up to since the day you like-to kilt me." I drop the shtick, disappointing no one. "Once you realized you'd fucked up and I was in the hospital, not the morgue, you came back to my house. You deleted the suicide note from my computer, tidied up the mess. Things were more complicated now, though. You didn't know whether I'd seen the note or talked to anyone about it. So you couldn't just try to kill me again. You needed to find out what I knew, who I might be talking to, what I was planning to do."

Trooper Danielle raises her brow in a show of amused tolerance. I go on. I'm piecing this together as I go, but it feels right. "You went to work on my phone. You planted a file called ASAN20 and a microchip on it." Both women's eyes flash surprise at this. "I know you've been tracking my location since I left my house in Wentworth, listening to my conversations, reading my texts and emails, watching my online activity, deleting files, blocking phone calls. You obviously sent those fake texts from Jeannie."

They're letting me ramble; they must want to know how much I've figured out. For my part, though, there's method to my madness. I hope I'm not getting too cute for my own good when I say, "Here's the thing, though. You don't know how long I've been aware my phone was hijacked. You don't know how long I've just been feeding you what *I want* you to hear, while conducting my real business — like talking to the police — on a burner phone."

Trooper Danielle sighs through her teeth. It's an annoyed sigh that says, *You're bluffing but, fine, you've forced my hand.* She catches Choke's eye and head-nods toward me.

Choke approaches me. "You, up," he orders.

I obey. He starts the pat-down I've been angling for. He finds my regular phone immediately and tosses it to Leah, who starts examining it. "Oh, and here's hers," he says, taking Jeannie's phone from his pocket and lobbing it, too, to Leah. "I went back to the bar and got it."

The accent: Brooklyn definitely, not Boston.

Continuing his body-search of me, Choke finds my wallet and the small black rock Danny gave me. He grunts and for, no explainable reason, plunks the rock into my hand, letting me keep it. Must be Danny's mojo at work. Patting down my leg, Choke finds the Velcro strap around my shin. "What's this?" he demands.

"I had a knife. ...Past tense."

He removes the strap from my leg.

"Or maybe," I tease, "that was where I hid my burner."

"Okay, asshole, you asked for it." He commences another pat-down of my body, only this time it's more of a smack-down. Each rough slap is designed to inflict pain. He takes particular relish in slamming my gonads with the heel of his hand.

"Easy," warns Mrs. B — a reminder that, for some reason, I'm not to be treated too roughly.

He shoves me into my seat and pulls my shoes off, searching them as well.

Good. This is precisely the kind of body search I was hoping for. Minus the gonad-slamming thing. I want them to be satisfied that I'm cleaner than a Mormon sit-com. I don't want them to have any reason to check me again.

Search complete. Phase Two down.

Now, for Phase Three. Can I somehow sneak the items *back into* my clothing?

A text message comes through on Mrs. Bean's phone. "All right, time to move you two joy-birds upstairs," she says.

Fuck.

## Chapter 40

Troop and company rise and gather their things. They look expectantly at Jeannie and me, waiting for us to stand and accompany them out of the room. It appears I have no choice but to leave the knife and burner phone behind.

Jeannie seems to intuit my predicament. She stares at Troop, wide-eyed, and says, "Are you going to kill us now?"

Choke gestures impatiently, *come on, stand up, let's go.*

Jeannie repeats, "Are you going to kill us? ...That's what's happening, isn't it? You're taking us somewhere to kill us! WHY? What have I done? Why am I even here?"

"Enough of the theatrics, Ms. Gallagher," says Madam Troop. "Let's move it along."

"No!" Jeannie shouts, a quaver of panic in her voice. "I don't want to die!" I *think* she's creating a distraction for my benefit, but I'm not absolutely sure she isn't freaking out for real. Maybe it's some of both. "Please, no! I'm not ready to die! I have a daughter. She needs me! Please!"

Choke grabs her by the shirtsleeve, yanks her to her feet. "Come on, lady, let's go."

Jeannie jerks her arm from him with a sharp "NO!" She starts backing toward the far end of the room, away from the stairs. The three captors close in on her as she shrieks, "NO! NO! NO!" over and over in authentic-sounding existential terror.

I take advantage of the distraction. I grab the phone from under the cushion and slip it into my left pants pocket, lightning fast, then grab the knife. Choke has my leg strap, so the knife will have to go into my right pocket. It's hard to angle it into my pants while sitting down, but I don't dare stand up and draw anyone's gaze. I slide it in as best I can, blade first. Shit. It doesn't fit. The handle sticks out of the pocket.

Jeannie is kneeling on the floor now, wailing, "I don't want to die!" like John Turturro in that haunting woodland murder scene in *Miller's Crossing*. It is a terrifying spectacle.

I try to force the point of the knife through the bottom of my pocket, but for some reason it snags. Won't poke through. What are these pants made of, woven titanium?

Jeannie shouts, "NO! NO! NO!"

"SHUT UP!" Choke orders, standing over her. He produces a black oblong object from his pocket. "Do you know what this is, lady?" I do; it's a stun gun. "Do you want me to use it?"

"I don't want to die!" screams Jeannie in reply.

"*Do you want me to use it?*" he repeats, moving the weapon closer to her.

Jeannie "comes to her senses," shouts, "No!" and thrusts her hands up in surrender. She lets Choke jerk her to her feet. He turns her body toward the stairs.

The knife, the knife. Why won't it poke through?

I give it a hard shove and the blade finally pops through the fabric with an audible *fup*. I feel it slice my skin as it shoots down the inside of my pant leg and stops at the handle. Shit. *That* did some damage. Well, at least the knife is hidden, for the moment.

Troop and company surround Jeannie and march her toward a doorway to the right of the steps. Choke gestures for me to follow.

I comply. I don't know how badly I've cut myself. It's not the injury I'm worried about; I'll live. It's the blood. If a red stain starts blossoming on my pants, I'm in deep guano.

I place my palms on my thighs as if I'm doing the docile, hands-down walk, but I'm really trying to hold the wound closed and hide any blood that might appear. The positioning of my hands looks slightly awkward, but Troop and company are giving most of their attention to Jeannie, who resists every step as if she's in mortal terror. Which she probably is.

We are led down a corridor with windows revealing a pair of staterooms that look like five-star hotel rooms. We come to a T-junction. Chokehold ushers me down a short corridor to the left; the two women escort Jeannie to the right. Choke points to a doorway. I step through it.

It's a bathroom, probably the most aggressively elegant one I have ever set foot in. The floor, tub, toilet, bidet, shower chamber ("stall" doesn't do it justice), and sink are dark green marble—you'd swear they were cut from a single piece. The fixtures are polished brass, the cabinetry cherry wood buffed to a gemstone finish.

"Get out of those filthy fucking clothes and take a shower," orders Choke. "Then get dressed." He points to the cherry wardrobe wherein clean clothes presumably reside.

This is not what I foresaw happening next, I must say. I guess it's thoughtful that they want me tidied up for my own execution, but really, they shouldn't have.

Chokehold stands near the door, hands on hips. He's waiting for me to disrobe, maybe even to hand him my clothes. No, no, no. That mustn't happen.

"I have a thing about undressing in front of other dudes," I say, still shielding my wounded thigh from view. "Traumatic gym class experience."

Choke doesn't seem to appreciate my humor. "Boo fuckin' hoo," he replies. But he doesn't fight me on it. He points to a tasseled gold rope dangling from a brass eye in the wall and says, "Ring when you're done," then leaves the room. Yup, you can actually ring for service on the S.S. Ostentatious. With a gold fucking rope, no less.

Hoping there are no hidden cameras in here, I take the knife and phone out of my pockets and hide them in a cabinet. Danny's rock too. I strip off my clothes—there is indeed a bloodstain on the pants—and toss them into the trash. I don't want anyone seeing them.

I examine the knife-cut on my leg. It's two or three inches long; can't tell how deep. Steady stream of blood, though.

After I shower in the outrageously soft water, the cut is still bleeding. I press several layers of toilet paper onto it, hoping that will stanch the blood-flow for now.

I open the cherry-wood wardrobe. It's empty. Very funny, fellas. Guess I'll be promenading al fresco this evening. Eventually I notice some inset drawers, with no hardware on them, on the left side of the wardrobe. Within them I find some new men's underwear, a folded pair of chino-style pants, and a blue Oxford shirt. In a bottom cubby area is a pair of boat moccasins, which I guess I am supposed to wear sans socks, as is custom for the island-hopping set.

I don the clothes. Luckily, the chinos are pretty loose-fitting. Recovering my stashed items from the cabinet, I stab the knife-blade through the bottom of the right pocket, hiding the knife pretty well. Now seems to be the right time to turn the burner phone on. Its battery power is at about sixty percent or so. I don't know how fast this particular model eats up the voltage, but I'll just have to hope its power lasts long enough.

Long enough for what, I have no bloody clue.

I silence all the phone's sounds, then scroll through the contacts list and select a name. I send a text: *Call coming from me. Not a butt dial. Don't speak. Leave phone on. Might be long.* I then push Call and wait for the phone to be answered on the other end.

Before I can confirm that the call has gone through, there's a rap at the door. Darn, I didn't even get to pull the gold rope and ring for Lurch.

I slide the phone into my left pocket, mike facing outward, and hope for the best.

"Come in," I say.

•  •  •  •  •

I didn't think my brain had any room left for surprise, but evidently I was in error. It's not Lurch—i.e., Chokehold—who enters the bathroom. Nope, it's a waiter in a short tuxedo jacket and bow tie. A slim Korean-American man, he says, "The pleasure of your company is requested for dinner. Would you please follow me?"

Sure, why the fuck not?

I follow the waiter down a corridor with a glass wall showing a stunning vista of the rocky northern side of Musqasset, then up a set of stairs. We pass a private dining room with a table made up for dinner and enter a small side room off the dining room. It features a couple of tables and a little bar. A cocktail lounge. Quaint. The waiter seats me there.

"May I start you with a refreshment? Mr. Fischer will be joining you for dinner shortly."

Mr. Fischer. The name comes as a blow, but then again, not really. Simon Fischer. Who else's boat could this be, after all? The Abelsen theory dries up and blows away like dander.

"Water will be fine," I reply to the waiter. I sit in silence on my brocaded chair as he fetches a glass and fills it with ice water.

He scampers off. A few minutes later he returns, ushering Jeannie into the room. She's wearing a simple black tennis-dress-type thing, presumably provided for her by "management." Her eyes bug with terror.

The waiter fetches her some water, then leaves us alone.

And so, here we are, Jeannie and I, together for dinner on a fine yacht at anchor in the Gulf of Maine. If we didn't know we'd both been kidnapped and dragged here against our will, this might be the start of a lovely evening. Alas, we do know.

"Are you okay?" I ask her in a throat-whisper.

"No permanent damage."

"Nice work back there."

"You too. What you were trying to hide? I couldn't quite see."

I shake my head, don't want to say the words aloud.

"You know whose boat this is, right?" she says. A confirmation, not a question.

I nod. "Beth's dad's."

"So do you have any idea what in the Jumping Jiminy Fuck is going on here?"

"I wish I didn't, but... Jeannie, I think Beth's dad had some people killed, and I think he's the one who tried to have me killed too."

She filters this information for a moment. She must have a jillion questions, but she asks only one. "Do you think... don't lie to protect my feelings... they're going to kill *us*? Tonight?"

"Taking all the facts into consideration, honestly, I don't see what other path they have."

"Shit. No! Bree! What am I going to do about Bree? How is she going to—"

"Shh. That may be *their* path, but it doesn't have to be ours."

"What are you saying?"

"I'm saying I have no intention of letting them go through with it."

"What can *you* do about it?"

I don't much care for the way she says that.

"I don't know yet," I reply, wrapping my hand around the piece of obsidian in my pocket, "but I do know one thing: I'm done with accepting whatever cards I'm dealt. I'm playing this thing out all the way. To win. So be ready for anything."

"Don't do anything stupid and heroic. Not on my behalf. I don't want to live in a world that has no Finn Carroll—"

"Shh. Listen, Jeannie, I don't know how much time we have alone here. It might be just a minute, so I need to say something to you." I grasp her hand. "I love you. Remember that, no matter what happens. I love you so much it literally hurts."

She squeezes my hand, hard, but her eyes have retreated to a shadowy place within.

"I wish I hadn't let you go the first time," I continue. "I wish I had made you the center of my universe the second time around. I wish I had told you I never wanted you to touch another man as long as I was alive. I wish I had just said 'I love you' every single waking minute, instead of moping around like a wounded jackass."

She's fighting tears and losing the battle. "Why couldn't you have said this to me years ago, when it would have mattered?"

"Because I was damaged goods, Jeannie. *Am* damaged goods. I spent the first half of my life believing I had no worth and the second half believing I had *negative* worth. Well, fuck that. I'm ready to be whole. I am so, so ready. And that means owning the fact that I love you. I always have."

"Oh God, Finn, our timing; our pathetic, miserable timing..."

"When we get out of this thing, Jeannie—and I'm saying *when*, not *if*—I want to meet your daughter. And if meeting me doesn't make her puke, I want to start spending some time with the two of you. And if that goes well, I want—"

"Stop! Finn! Please. You need to stop. I've told you over and over, that can't happen. I have made choices that cannot be undone. I didn't want to tell you. I wanted to spare your feelings and—yes, okay—to enjoy the brief fantasy that you and I could be together again... But that's all it was. A fantasy. There's something you need to know, and it—"

"Jean! Finnian!" booms a growling baritone from a few yards away. Simon Fischer enters the cocktail room with his arms out in welcome, as if he's greeting two long-lost friends. Barrel-chested and bald as Mr. Clean, he has an Albert Finney/Jonathan Banks kind of vibe and exudes the absolute confidence of a man accustomed to having his way in all things. "Please. Join me. Let's have some wine and a bite d'eat."

## CHAPTER 41

"Mr. Fischer, not to be a shitty guest or anything," I say, glued to my seat, "but I think you have a bit of explaining to do."

"Pleasure before business. Come. Everyone needs food." Fischer tends to speak in short, bark-like bursts. Punctuated by brief silences. Which somehow gives his words. Added weight. Whether they deserve. It. Or not.

"Seriously, Mr. Fischer, what the fuck?"

"Call me Simon." He actually looks mildly peeved that I'm not jumping at his offer of hospitality. What planet does this guy live on? Actually, I know the answer to that: Rich-Guy Earth, a parallel dimension to mine with an entirely different set of rules.

"Look. If there was any unpleasantness," he says. "In the way you were brought here. I'm sorry. I told my crew to go easy on that stuff."

Oh, well, okay. Guess all is forgiven, then. Kumbaya.

"Come, come." He beckons with both hands. "A little wine, a little yip-yap. There's no reason we can't be civilized here."

"With all due respect"—I almost say "sir," but I won't give him that—"being spied on, mugged, blindfolded, and kidnapped could be construed as reasons."

"Don't test a man's generosity, Finnian. Come. Eat."

When I don't move, his shoulders slump in dismay, and he casts an eye toward Chokehold, whom I hadn't noticed in the background. I grasp the meaning Fischer intends: this can get ugly if need be, but must it? Point taken. I don't feel a crying need to be manhandled by Chokehold again. I rise from my seat. Jeannie follows my cue.

The long formal dining table is set for five, with all the place settings grouped at one end. Simon Fischer moves to the head of the table and gestures for Jeannie and me to take the two seats to his right. The waiter appears out of thin air and pulls Jeannie's seat out for her.

"Bring us a bottle of the Margaux, Hoon. The '10 should be fine."

"Yes, sir. Right away."

We're all seated. Fischer rubs his hands together.

"So... Finnian... I think the last time I saw you was on Dylan's seventh. Beth and Miles had that big do. Whatcha been up to since you left Musqasset?"

He's really going to do this? The cozy chit-chat thing?

"Living in a dump, getting drunk, and trying to commit suicide," I reply. He barks a laugh. Doesn't know if I'm kidding or not. "You, Simon?"

"Little this, little that. Trying to keep the books in the black. And the ass in the pink. Jean, you're looking stunning. I see what all the blather's about. How's life treating you?"

"Can you please tell us what's going on here, Mr. Fischer?" she says.

"Relax. You're among friends. No more hostilities." Hoon arrives with the bottle. "Let go of the past. Don't sweat the future. Embrace the present. Isn't that what Eckhart Tolle says? I love that guy. Let's just enjoy some nice wine in a lovely setting."

"I don't drink," Jeannie says.

"Shame. Oh well, the more for us, Finnian, right? Hoon, get the lady a sparkling water, would you?" Hoon scampers off. "Nervous fella. Must be genetic. So, Finnian... Been enjoying your stay on Musqasset?"

"It's been a pip."

"That so?"

"Ayuh."

Before the crackling wit of our dialog can put Aaron Sorkin any further to shame, an even more uncomfortable development occurs. The other two guests arrive. Miles and Beth. They must have just boarded the craft; Miles still has his jacket folded over his arm.

Upon seeing us, the Sutcliffes feign pleasant surprise, a titanically inappropriate response, given the circumstances. Jeannie and I stand to greet them, playing our parts in the absurdist guerilla drama unfolding before our eyes.

"Sit, sit," says Simon Fischer after kissing Beth on the cheek. "Your mother won't be joining us this evening. Migraine. She sends her regrets."

Hoon appears with San Pellegrino for Jeannie and fills the other glasses with thousand-dollar-a-bottle Bordeaux.

I notice that Troop and company have moved silently into the periphery of the room. "No, they don't sit at the table," Fischer explains to me, though I didn't ask. Read: there's only one alpha hound in *this* room, sonny boy.

Once everyone is seated, Fischer cracks his knuckles, stretches his lips in a parody of a smile, and says, "So..." He drums his fingers on the tabletop a few times, clucks his tongue, chuckles to himself at some inner amusement, then takes out his cell phone. He starts reading something on it. He swipes to another screen, chuckles again, makes a little "hmm" sound, swipes some more. This behavior goes on for a solid minute as the rest of us sit there in silence. I look across at Miles and Beth. Neither of them wants to make eye contact with Jeannie or me.

Simon Fischer puts his phone away, looks at the four of us, each in turn for three full seconds, then says, "I had the weirdest damn dream last night." He leaves the statement dangling in the air.

Neither Jeannie nor I is in the mood to take the bait. Miles is looking as if he just wants to shrink into his Sperry Top-Siders, tap-dance out of the room, and fling himself into the ocean. Beth is steaming, her arms folded; I guess she knows this routine.

And so the silence goes on. And on.

At last Beth hisses, through clenched teeth, "What was the dream about, Daddy?"

"I forget," he replies. He looks at us all again for a beat or two, then starts laughing uproariously. He fixes his gaze on Miles until Miles has no choice but to join in. As soon as Miles' laughter gathers momentum, Fischer stops abruptly, leaving Miles laughing alone.

Miles haltingly silences himself.

Fischer continues to stare at him with darkly hooded eyes and says, "What's the matter, son? Feeling uncomfortable?"

"No, sir, not real—"

"Don't lie to me!"

"Yes, sir, I'm feeling uncomfortable."

"Good. I *want* you to feel uncomfortable. Do you know why? Because you have put *me* in an uncomfortable position." Long pause. "The last time I sat down with you... I asked you a very simple question. And demanded a truthful answer. I asked if you had any buried bodies. That I needed to know about. I thought I was being... what's the word? Metaphysical? Meta*phor*ical. Ha."

He takes a slow sip of wine, relishes the taste. It *is* good damn wine, but I can only allow myself a few sips; I need to stay clearheaded.

"I explained to you," Fischer goes on, "that I was in the process of joining a... *fellowship* of sorts. With some extremely influential people. International people. With a keen interest in U.S. politics. The kind of people you absolutely do not fuck with. I told you I had taken a huge risk on your behalf. Recommended *you* as a potential candidate. For their backing and support. Do you think I did that because you're my son-in-law?"

"No, sir."

"Do you think I did that because I *like* you?"

"No, sir."

"Do you think I did that because you're handsome and make the ladies warm in their woolies?

"No, sir."

"You're damn right I didn't! I did it because it was good business. I'm handing you the keys to the fucking universe here. And I expect the world in return."

"Yes, sir."

"Anyway... these potential... 'partners' of mine. They liked what they saw in you. For whatever reason. Liked your 'fight for the cause' image. Liked the way you come across for the mikes and cameras. Your ja-na-say-kwah." He takes another slow sip of wine. "The one thing I told you... was that if they were going to consider 'backing' you... they wanted no baggage. None. Not even a shaving kit. So you can imagine how... disturbed I was. When I learned you had lied to me. Not on just one major count. But two."

Miles' eyes bulge out of his head as he stares at the table.

"Lies of omission, the filthiest kind."

Fischer makes a fist with one hand and rubs it with the other, as if polishing it.

"What upsets me, Miles... is not that you lied. Be clear on that. In the career path you have chosen, you will lie on a daily basis. An hourly basis. Lying will be your rice and beans. And you'd better do it well. No, what upsets me is not that you lied. But that you lied to *me*. I am THE MAN YOU DO NOT LIE TO. Do you understand?"

He glares at Miles with the wattage of an inquisitor's lamp. Miles stares equally intensely at the table.

"Did you really think I wouldn't do my own follow-up? Did you really think I would take you at your word? I can find out anything I want about you. ...Like that." He snaps his fingers. "I can find out what you ate for breakfast on March fifth, 2008. I can find out which tree you pissed on at a graduation party in 1999. When I asked you if you had any secrets, I wasn't looking for *information*. I was looking for fealty. And you let me down."

Miles and Beth look as if they'd rather be facing an ISIS firing squad than sitting at this table. It has become increasingly clear to me that the reason Jeannie and I are here is to bear witness to Miles' humiliation. And once we've served our purpose, we're going to be disposable.

"Let's look at your lies of omission. One by one. Shall we?"

"Sir, can we please do this in private?" pleads Miles.

"No! We cannot. Let's start with Lie Number Two." Simon Fischer turns to the rest of us and, in an almost playful voice, says, "Quick quiz. Who can tell me what *filia nothus* means?" I think Miles, the lawyer, probably knows, because he winces in dread. "No one? Oh well. Don't be embarrassed; I had to look it up myself. It's an antiquated term.

"Hint. It has to do with a situation that exists amongst your little foursome. Two of you know about it. Two of you don't. But you all deserve to be on the same page. Miles, you're among the cognoscenti. Why don't you start?"

Miles doesn't speak, just continues to stare laser beams at the table.

"Courage. That's what you lack, son. That's what frightens me most about you. Come on, tell them what you've done. Say the words."

Miles says nothing.

"Come on, Miles. Okay, let me get you started. Repeat after me: I..." He pauses. "Fucked..." Another pause. "My... best... friend's..."

"Filia nothus!" shouts Jeannie, slamming her fist on the table, jangling the tableware and causing all our heads to turn. "Means bastard daughter." With everyone's attention settled on her, she says, "Miles is my daughter's father."

I feel a knife blade slip into my soul and twist.

"I'm sorry, Finn," Jean says. "This is what I've been trying to tell you."

Silence descends. Seconds pass like big, heavy objects.

Jeannie picks up a butter knife, twirls it slowly in her fingers. She stares at her eyes in the blade's reflection. "After you left, I wanted to punish you in some way," she says softly, to me alone, "and I... That's no excuse. I'm sorry — so, so sorry. That's all I can say."

Something vital slithers out of me. I long for my parents' ragged sofa, a bowl of cold cereal, and an evening of watching Animal Planet alone. Bring back the dead life.

"B-Beth," stammers Miles, "I was going to tell you. I — "

"Enough!" thunders Fischer. "When you lie to my daughter, you lie to me." He turns to Beth and says, "While you were paying hush money... to hide *one* of your husband's indiscretions... He was busy creating a second one. *That's* who you married. *That's* who you've given me to work with. Which brings us to Lie Number One..."

His attention suddenly swings toward the kitchen. "Hold on," he says. "Dinner is served." Hoon wheels in a table containing five covered plates and a basket of steaming focaccia bread. "I took the liberty of ordering for all of you," says Fischer. "The stripers are running right now. There really was no other choice."

Hoon serves and uncovers the plates. In a high, delicate voice, he says, "Pan roasted sea bass with a light drizzle of fennel aioli."

"Whatever the hell aioli is," blares Fischer. "Ha! I don't like to over-season fish. When it's fresh, let it speak for itself. Am I right?"

"The sides are a roasted okra with bacon and tomatoes," continues Hoon, his light voice trembling slightly, "and a popover shell with fig and chestnut stuffing."

"Me, I prefer mashed potatoes," says Fischer. "But whatever. Dig in."

He's going to have us eat dinner under the weight of the steel girder he just dropped on us. And he's going to enjoy watching us squirm. Human discomfort is a recreational sport for this guy, I realize. What a piece of work.

I'm glad to have the plate of food to concentrate on, though. I can't look at Miles; I despise the man. Can't look at Jeannie. Beth's not really an option either, never has been. Judging from the torpid pace of the silverware clinks around me, no one seems to have an appetite but Simon Fischer.

"I've always been aware of your payments to Clarence Woodcock, Elizabeth," says Fischer, picking up his former conversational thread. "I have access to your trust account. Did you imagine I didn't? I'm the one who set it up. I'm the one who funded it. I'm still an accountholder." He chews his food for a moment. "I knew Woodcock was a private eye. I figured you had him on your payroll to keep tabs on Mr. Wandering Dick over here. Your business. And probably a wise idea. Considering.

"But over the past few weeks... With this new 'political opportunity' shaping up... I needed to take a closer look at everything. Do my due diligence. So I had my crew..." He angles his head toward Troop and company. "...turn up their eyes and ears. If this Woodcock *had* anything on hubby dearest—hotel room videos, whatever—I needed to know about it. We learned that Woodcock had booked a ferry trip to Musqasset. Noteworthy, given the timing.

"I know he came to your house, Elizabeth. Along with this Edgar

Goslin character. I know everything that was said."

"You were spying on me, Daddy?" says Beth, petulantly, like a teenager.

"Spying *for* you, Sweetheart. I found out this Woodcock was putting the squeeze on you. But not over some hotel-room photos. No. Over something I didn't understand. So we decided to put the squeeze on *him*. And Goslin. And what did we find out? That your husband did a very bad thing. One night a very long time ago."

"It was an accident, sir, I didn't even know about it," says Miles. "I wasn't hiding anything from you."

"Quiet! So now these people, Goslin and Woodcock, they had to be... made into a non-liability. Which, of course, creates additional exposure. For me. My crew handled it efficiently. I'm sure. Exactly how, I don't know. And I don't *want* to know. And I don't have to. Do you know why, Miles? Because when you attain my position in life... you can pay others to live with that kind of knowledge. So you can sleep at night. But—and here's what you need to understand—YOU HAVE NOT EARNED THAT PRIVILEGE YET!"

"*No one* earns that privilege, Mr. Fischer," I break in. "Not you, not me, not anyone. Your 'crew' murdered Clarence Woodcock by pushing him down his stairs. Your crew murdered Edgar Goslin by bleeding him out and then staging it to look like he died in his car. Your crew *tried* to murder me by forcing me to swallow a bottle of booze and a bunch of pills. But they screwed up. Didn't get the job done. Hence, here I am. Hope that didn't ruin your sleep."

Fischer laughs sourly. "You make a lot of assumptions, you little shit."

"Is that so, Mr. Fischer?"

"For instance, you assume I *wanted* you to die in that kitchen," he says. "You assume I didn't realize you were the best source of information I had. About the 'incident' in 1999. You assume we didn't just give you a..." He looks to Trooper Danielle.

"...non-lethal dose of benzodiazepines along with some sugar pills and enough Rohypnol to lay you out on the floor," she supplies.

"You assume we didn't *want* you to find that suicide note," says

Fischer. "You assume we didn't *want* you to go into a panic after you'd read it. Wondering who could possibly know such facts about you. You assume we didn't just tap your phone, sit back and watch. To see what you'd do. Who you'd call. Who you'd email. What you'd google. What you'd write. Who do you think sent those 'mystery messages' to Miles? And why do you suppose we sent them?"

I don't reply.

"Same god-damn reason," he says. "To stir the pot. See what bubbled up."

# CHAPTER 42

"You're claiming you *faked* my overdose?" I say to Simon Fischer. "And you've been spying on me this whole time, just to find out who knew what about Miles?"

"All I'm 'claiming,'" says Fischer, "is that for such a wise-ass, you make a lot of assumptions. Eat your food. You're skin and bones."

I think he's lying. I think he's just one of those guys who needs to win in every situation — at least in his own mind. He can't stand the fact that I "beat" him by surviving his attack. I forced him to go to Plan B, and now he has to make it seem like Plan B was Plan A all along. Either way, lying or not, this guy is in serious need of a grenade up his ass.

"You're not as clever as you think," I say to Fischer and friends. "I know you planted that fake smoke detector in my room. And those emojis were a dead giveaway that you were tapping my phone." They weren't, of course, because I'm mentally deficient. "You think I didn't notice you blocking my calls to the police and to my sister Angie?"

"Maybe the emojis were a warning," Leah replies. "A courtesy. Maybe if someone blocked a few calls to your sister, they were doing you a kindness."

"A *kindness*?"

"Your sister Angie still thinks it was you who threw that bottle. If you had been permitted to correct her on that point..."

She doesn't need to say the rest. Angie would have had to join the ranks of Goslin and Woodcock. Maybe Leah does have the remnants of a soul.

"That's enough!" bellows Simon Fischer. "All of you. I've heard way more than I want to. The point I'm trying to make, Miles... is that things have gotten messy. Very messy. For me. Because of you. And now there may be serious egg on my face."

Simon Fischer chews both his food and his thoughts, then says, "I'm a powerful man, son. More powerful than you will ever be. Even if you one day hold the highest public office in the land. But there are men more powerful than me. Pass the salt, would you? Even the gods have greater gods, eh? Ad infinitum, so it seems.

"Let me tell you something about these people I've been cozying up to. I'll never tell you everything... but let me tell you *something*. These people aren't the PACs or the Super PACs. They're not the L-L-Cs or the five-o-one-c-four political charities. These are the people *beyond* the Super PACs. These are the people with the resources to make things happen... directly. Need a senior congressman to get caught with a teenage dick in his hand? Need the stock market to get jittery before a vote on the hill? Need a truckload of military weapons to fall into the wrong hands? That's what these people do. They influence things. In the real world.

"This business of ours. Yours and mine. Getting you that Senate seat. That was meant to be... a 'test.' For me as much as for you."

He chews some more.

"The governor of our fine state, you see... we golf, him and me. We schmooze. Visit each other's summer homes. And as you and I have already discussed... in the state of Maine... when a U.S. Senator resigns in the middle of a term... it's the governor who names their replacement. So when I heard about Aldridge getting a visit from ol' Johnny Carcinoma. And with you getting some good press lately. And that state Senate seat. The stars were aligning. I saw an opportunity. I suggested to my pal. The governor. That you'd make a fine member of Congress's upper chamber. When Aldridge threw in the towel. But it turned out Governor Rick had his own guy in mind. Shame.

"I turned to my... document specialist here." He indicates Leah. "She'd already helped me in a couple of business situations. I knew the quality of her work. With my access and her skills, we were able to place some... *things* on Governor Rick's computer. Written, anyone would think, in his own words. Then 'leak' them to me through an 'anonymous source.' I won't tell you what those *things* were, but... Devastating. Take a bow, Leah. Fine work, fine work."

So Leah *is* her real name. She responds with a tiny nod.

The fact that Simon Fischer is letting Jeannie and me hear all this stuff is not an auspicious development for either of us.

"Anyway, the governor is now enthusiastically on board. So..." He wipes his hands and mouth, fires his napkin at the table. "What I'm trying to tell you is... I have been stepping out on a slippery ledge for you, Miles. And what have you been doing in return? DICKING ME IN THE ASS!"

"I didn't lie about that accident, sir," pleads Miles. "I didn't *know* about it. I was drunk that night. I passed out cold. I had to be taken to the ER." He looks to Beth, but she's not going to bail him out—not this time, no siree. "I only found out about it today!"

"Today? Even if I believed such grass-fed horseshit... you lied to me about the *filia nothus*. So I must assume you lied to me about other things. So be it. That's the situation we are in. Accept what is. Right? That's what Eckhart says. But before this day is in the books... we *will* clean up our loose ends, you and me. All of them."

"What are you planning to do, sir?" asks Miles, an audible cringe in his voice.

"What am *I* planning to do?" says Fischer. He stands and gazes out at the sinking sun through the enormous dining room window, stretches his arms, then locks eyes with Miles. "*I'm* going to take a nap. I don't have to redeem *my*self. I don't have to prove *my*self. You, on the other hand..."

"What? What do you want me to do, sir?" says Miles in a little-boy voice that makes me pity him in spite of the circumstances.

"Handle the situation."

"How?"

"By making a decision and acting on it, that's how. Prove to me you are worthy of my absolute trust and confidence."

"I've proven that to you over and over, sir. With the Camden situation, with the golf course at Belgrade Lakes, with Fish Pier..."

"Fish Pier was nothing. You were just following my orders. I told you what I wanted to happen. And you carried out my wishes."

So Simon Fischer was the silent money—the big money—behind the marina development on Musqasset. Should have known. Should have fucking known.

"What I'm talking about here, my boy, is an *executive* decision," he says. "*You* evaluate the situation. *You* decide on a course of action, whatever it might be. *You* ensure that it's carried out to completion. That's what needs to happen. And then we will reassess where we're at."

On that note, Simon Fischer departs the scene.

• • • • •

A minute or two later, no one has spoken yet. Miles is pacing the floor, grabbing at his hair as if he literally wants to tear it out. "What should I do?" he asks Beth at last.

"You're on your own," she says, "and I mean that in every possible way." She pushes her chair away from the table and walks out of the room, slamming the carved mahogany door behind her.

Quiet takes over again as Miles paces back and forth.

At last he stops, apparently having come to some kind of decision. He turns to Chokehold. "You," he says, "stay here and guard them"—meaning Jeannie and me.

"I take orders from Mr. Fischer," says Choke. "Not you."

"Well, I'm giving orders on Mr. Fischer's behalf. If you want to verify that, you can go drag him out of bed and ask him."

Choke waves his hand in concession.

"You two," says Miles, pointing to Leah and Trooper Danielle. "Come with me. You're my consulting team."

Miles exits the room, muttering, "Sorry, Finn," with a lump in his throat. Leah and Danielle follow him out. Jeannie and I are left alone, with Chokehold standing guard.

• • • • •

An eternity seems to pass, Jeannie and me sitting side by side, not looking at each other. I want to say something, but my vocal cords absolutely refuse to make a sound.

Jeannie finally ventures, "Miles had been... 'expressing an interest' in me since college. I never reciprocated. Never. Until..." She chews on her inner cheek, stares abstractedly ahead. "We only hooked up three or four times, and then I came to my senses. ...I said I did it to punish you, but that's not really true. I did it to punish myself. You were the only person in the world whose opinion I cared about."

I feel an urge to point out she had a funny way of showing it, but my tongue clings to muteness.

"I figured you already thought I was... well, maggot slime," she goes on. "Worse. So I asked myself, what can I do to live down to your opinion of me, to really *earn* the feeling that I'm fully worthy of your contempt? Miles started hitting on me almost the moment you left the island. I said to myself, 'That'll do the trick.'"

"All right, that's enough, you two," says Chokehold. "Save it for Maury."

"That was hitting bottom for me," continues Jeannie, undeterred. "That's when I quit drinking. That's when I started examining my life and making some changes." She takes a long, shuddery breath. "After a month of sobriety, I was already seeing things more clearly. I decided I was going to go to the mainland, track you down, tell you I loved you, try to win you back. And that was when I found out I was..." Pregnant. "And that was the end of that."

"Ah, Jeannie," I say, finding my voice. "Jeannie, Jeannie, Jeannie."

"Because I *do*, you know," she says in a papery voice. "Love you. So much. I don't know why I could never convince you of that. You've always been the one. Ever since I laid eyes on you in that Abnormal Psych class. No one else ever had my *heart*. No one."

"I mean it, you two," says Choke. "Shut up. You're giving me a fucking toothache. In fact... *you*" — he points at me — "in there." He nods toward a nearby men's room.

Having seen his stun gun, I comply with his order.

Perhaps it will even play into my hands.

• • • • •

The men's room is tiny, half the size of a jail cell, with only a toilet and a sink.

Chokehold shuts the door on me. Good.

What I just learned about Jeannie and Miles has knocked the wind out of me, for sure, but still I must keep my wits about me. I take the burner phone from my pocket and check it. The call I placed earlier seems to have gone through and is still live. But the battery power is down to about twenty percent. I might be stuck in here a while. I need to conserve what little juice the phone has left. I whisper, "I'll call back," into the mike and shut off the phone.

I'll have to reboot it and place the call again later. That might not be easy, though.

• • • • •

After a good chunk of time has passed—at least an hour—I hear the dining-room door open and footsteps cross the room. Words are exchanged, and the footsteps depart. Listening against my door, I hear Choke's chair creak as he stands up. Sounds like it might be time for him to get the show rolling. Whatever that means.

I slide my ass back toward the middle of the bathroom floor and turn the burner phone back on.

I hear Choke push his chair away from the table.

I stare at the burner phone, willing it to power up faster. It is taking its damn sweet time. I know I turned the volume off, but I'm not familiar with this phone model. I'm praying it doesn't make an electronic jingle of some kind when it reboots. If it does, I'm fucked to the gills.

I hear Choke's heels walking in my direction. He's about fifteen feet away.

The phone shows only *black screen with logo, black screen with logo, black screen with logo.* Come on, turn on, you piece of shit! Come on, come on!

Finally, the phone lights up, in blessed silence, and is running again, with its small reserve of battery power. Choke stops at the door.

I frantically navigate to the Recent Calls list and redial the earlier number—Enzo's—then slip the phone back into my left pocket, mike facing out, just as Choke opens the door.

He enters, wielding his stun gun. My hand is still in my pocket. I ease it out, hoping the glow of the phone screen doesn't show through the fabric of my pants. Choke orders me to stand up and jerks me out into the dining room. Jeannie is still waiting there.

Outside the yacht's big windows, I notice the sun has set and full darkness is rapidly descending. The decks are now tastefully lighted for nighttime.

To Jeannie's surprise and mine, Choke hands us both back our confiscated cell phones. He also returns my wallet to me. Why? He then gives me a knowing grin, reaches over and pulls open the top of my left pants pocket—the one with the burner in it.

My heart sinks.

He stares at me for a long moment, waiting for me to surrender the burner voluntarily.

I start to say, "Take it," but then he reaches into his own shirt and pulls an item out: a folded-up piece of paper in a sealed Ziploc sandwich bag.

He slips it into my pants pocket. As his fingers slide down into my borrowed chinos, I'm sure they're going to make contact with the burner phone, but they miss it by a hair's breadth. He pulls his hand away.

"Leave that there," he says, referring to the ziplocked paper in my pocket, then gives Jeannie and me a shove and tells us to move our asses. To where, we don't know.

As we march along, I hear my regular phone—the one Choke just returned to my hand—ping a text-sent signal. Jeannie's phone pings a text-received tone a second later. I look down at my phone screen and see a Sent text from me to Jeannie. Ah, so Leah has taken control of our phones again. The text from "me" reads, *I just wanted to say I'm sorry... I've been thinking a lot about what you said... And, of course, you're right.*

A few seconds later, another text exchange pings. This time it's Jeannie's hijacked phone replying to mine. *It doesn't mean I don't love you,* texts phantom Jeannie. The real Jeannie hasn't touched her phone's keyboard. Jeannie and I exchange WTF looks.

Choke marches us down a set of stairs to a lower deck, and we head toward the stern of the craft. If there's going to be an opportunity to use the knife in my pocket, it will have to come soon.

My phone texts Jeannie's again: *I know. I get it. I was letting my little head ☺ do my thinking... I know we can't have a life together... And I know that doesn't mean you don't love me.*

Jeannie's phone to mine: *Glad you see it that way. Sorry. ☹*

My phone to hers: *I'll be heading out on the ferry in the morning... It should be running again... But hey, before I go, want to see something amazing?*

Jeannie's phone to mine: *Not if it's an anatomical feature! Haha. What?*

Choke leads us down a final staircase to an exterior deck at the stern, a few feet above water level. I don't know what this type of deck is called. It's an open area on which people can sunbathe and around which small craft can moor.

Tied to the rear of this lower deck is an inflatable boat with an outboard motor. It's Danny Mawukura's—the boat he showed me yesterday; his trademark designs are painted on it. Jeannie and I look at each other in mute puzzlement. Why is Danny involved in this? A motorized skiff with a squared-off bow and stern—probably the same one that carried me to this yacht—is tied up beside it. Both boats are accessible by a single short ladder.

My phone sends another text to Jeannie's: *Turns out our shipwreck didn't go far out to sea...* Clever, Leah is, bringing The Shipwreck into this text exchange, knowing it had special meaning to Jeannie and me. *It's 100 yds off shore, underwater... And it's doing something incredible...*

Jeannie's phone: *Doing? What do u mean?*

My phone: *I can't explain. You have to see it... Can you meet me?*

Jeannie's: *U have a boat?*

Mine: *Danny's letting me borrow his... Meet me at that little dock of his in, like, 15?*

Jeannie's: *K bye.*

Ah, yes. I remind myself that Troop and company have been listening in on me via my phone's mike everywhere I've been in the last few days. They must have heard my conversation with Danny when he offered me his boat to use. They probably sent a couple of Simon Fischer's lackeys to go fetch it just now. Smart. When Danny is questioned by the police, he will affirm that he did indeed offer to let me use the boat.

The police? Yes. See, I'm starting to piece together what's going on here. A chain of evidence is being established whereby I'm inviting Jeannie to Danny's boat and we're going to take a ride on the still-choppy waters. I have a feeling we're going to have an "accident at sea."

Miles cannot seriously be in on this.

No sooner does this thought occur than the man himself appears on the deck above us in the soft night-lighting. He's talking with Trooper Danielle and Leah and looking out at the water.

"Miles, you've got to be kidding me!" I shout up at him. He doesn't look at me, but I can see his face looks ten years older than it did two hours ago. "I know what you're planning to do here. Murder Jeannie and me? You've got to be fucking kidding me!" He flinches as my words hit him, but he refuses to look at me.

"Seriously, Miles? Seriously? Murder?"

Miles nods to Choke: time to get things moving. I've never seen such a miserable, drained expression on my friend's face. The stress of this decision must have stripped something elemental out of his soul.

"All right, you two, into the boat," Chokehold orders Jeannie and me.

"Snap out of it, Miles!" I shout at the upper deck. "If you do this, it can never be undone. You think what happened with that whiskey bottle was bad, try living with murder on your conscience. For the rest of your life!"

Miles is staring at his phone to avoid making eye contact with me. He's trying to appear focused and in-command.

Suddenly a voice rings out from the interior of the upper deck. "What the hell is going on here, will someone please tell me?" It's Beth, in her bathrobe, trotting out to see what the commotion is. Thank God. Beth and I have never been besties, but she *will* provide the voice of reason here. She won't condone *this*.

"Beth!" I shout up at her. "Miles has lost it! He's trying to have us killed!"

"Miles, what are you doing?" she demands, eyes popping with disbelief.

"Beth, go back inside!" shouts Miles.

"Miles, answer me!"

"Go back inside, Beth! I am handling this."

Beth trots down the stairs to the lower rear deck where Jeannie and I and Chokehold are standing. She inserts herself between Choke and me, arms folded, awaiting my explanation.

"They're going to take us out on the water and kill us," I tell her. "They planted fake texts on our phones to make it look like it's going to be an accident."

Beth grabs my phone from my hand and studies the recent text exchange. "Did *you* write this?" she shouts up at Miles, incredulous.

"The three of us did," says Miles defensively, indicating Leah and Trooper D. "It's what has to be done, Beth. Stay out of it!"

"I'm in shock," she responds, staring up at him with her head cocked back. "It's actually pretty good." She wipes her prints off the phone and places it back in my hand.

"Let me know when it's over," she says to her husband and starts back up the stairs.

# Chapter 43

"Beth, no!" I yell after her, my voice going high with panic. "You've got to help us, you're the only sane one here. Come on, Beth, please. As a friend."

"Friend?" She freezes on the stairs and spins her head toward me. "Is that what you said? Friend?" She turns and walks back down a couple of steps, staring at me slack-jawed. "You're not my friend. I fucking *hate* you, Finnian Carroll, don't you know that? Ever since that night in the car, I've wished you were dead."

"Jesus, Beth, I didn't throw that bottle. All I did was—"

"I'm not talking about the bottle, jagoff; that was an accident. I'm talking about before. When Miles had his meltdown. When he was crying and thrashing on the ground and saying he was jealous of you and what you had with *her*." She juts her jaw toward Jeannie. "Do you remember what you said to him? I do. 'You don't love Beth,' you said. 'And if you marry her, you will be profoundly unhappy for the rest of your life.' Well, those words crawled under his skin and laid eggs, you ass-fuck. And those eggs hatched in *our home* and *our bedroom*. And now every night it's like *you're* lying between the sheets with us.

"Who does he call whenever he's having doubts about our marriage? Who does he visit whenever he needs time away from the ol' ball and chain? Who does he *claim* to visit whenever he slips away for a Hilton Weekend Special with the intern of the month? Finn Carroll, his blood brother in Beth hatred. *Help* you? *Help* you? I can't wait till fish are eating your dead eyes."

"If you believe *I* planted those thoughts in his head, Beth," I say, "you are delusional to a degree even I didn't imagine. If Miles really loved you, you wouldn't have to—"

"Stop right there, Finn!" shouts Miles. "Don't say another word. It's time for you to go. Get on the god-damn boat."

"Are we really going to do this, Miles?"

"Get on the *boooooat*." He looks as if he's about to cry.

Choke steps closer to Jeannie and me, nudging us toward Danny's inflatable boat.

A seed of a strategy has germinated in my mind. I eye-signal Jeannie to go first, then, with a very small gesture of my hand, mime the act of starting the boat motor. I hope she reads me. Jeannie knows her way around boats, big and small.

My plan won't help *me*, but it might help Jeannie.

She steps toward the short ladder leading down to the tied-up inflatable. I notice as she descends the ladder and scrambles into Danny's boat that the lower part of her body is shielded from view from above. I'm counting on that small bit of shielding—and the rapidly deepening darkness—to buy me some cover when I follow her.

I stall as a long as I can, giving Jeannie a chance to scope out Danny's boat and its engine. Then I start down the ladder after her. The moment my waist is blocked from view, I slip the knife out of my pocket.

I grab the rope that's mooring Danny's boat and whisper to Jeannie, "Start the engine." I slice the rope with a couple of brisk swipes of the blade. The moment the engine kicks over—it must have been warm; it starts first pull—I give the boat a big kick-shove away from the yacht's stern. I turn and take a step back *up* the ladder.

"Go! Go! Go!" I shout behind me at Jeannie.

The reason I didn't climb into the boat with her? Because I know we can't outrun a skiff in a rubber inflatable. But if I can buy Jeannie enough time to escape alone, she might be able to make it back to shore—it's only a few hundred yards away. I stand on the ladder, prepared to defend it against all comers.

"I'm not leaving you here, Finn!" Jeannie shouts.

"Go! No time to argue!"

"Jump in!" Jeannie pleads, refusing to go without me.

"No! You have a daughter, don't screw around!"

Those words get through to her. She shifts the prop into forward and gives the small engine some gas.

Chokehold steps toward the ladder I'm standing on. I know he's armed only with a stun gun. In order for that weapon to work, it will need to make solid contact with me. I don't plan to let that happen. Before Choke can reach the ladder, I lash out at him with the knife, swiping the blade from side to side.

I don't intend to let him, or anyone, onto this ladder.

I don't intend to let him get close enough to stun me or to climb into the skiff.

"This doesn't mean I'm leaving you!" shouts Jeannie as she aims Danny's boat toward land, maxing the throttle. What she's telling me is she's coming back with help. The truth is, I was hoping help would already have arrived. But I guess my little burner phone ploy didn't work. It was a long shot anyway.

The good news is that the sea has finally calmed a bit. For the first time in days, the waters are reasonably safe for small craft. Jeannie ought to be able to make it to land if I can buy her a head start. I swing the knife back and forth as I watch Jeannie start to make progress toward shore in the rubber boat.

Suddenly I'm blinded by a brilliant light from an upper deck, and I hear a voice shout, "Drop the knife, asshole!" The light-beam shifts its angle for a moment to show me that the holder of the high-intensity flashlight has a pistol in his other hand. Then the light strikes my face again. I see a second beam of white light hit Jeannie, as another voice shouts at her, "Freeze! Stop the boat!"

Jeannie hasn't traveled far enough to be safely out of pistol range. She stops the boat and lifts her hands in surrender. I drop the knife and do the same.

It never occurred to me that Simon Fischer would have armed bodyguards. But of course, why wouldn't he? Troop and company are mission specialists; they're not around him 24/7. A guy like Fischer would naturally have round-the-clock personal protection.

Have I made it abundantly clear yet how giant an idiot I am?

"Bring that boat back, NOW!" Chokehold shouts at Jeannie. She obediently putters back toward the stern of the yacht.

• • • • •

I stand on the rear deck with Chokehold and the two armed bodyguards, my hands held aloft. Jeannie waits in Danny's boat at the bottom of the ladder, a gun trained on her.

Miles descends the stairs from above, carrying himself with an erect, shoulders-back posture meant to look commanding, presidential even. He sells the effect pretty convincingly, if you don't know him too well. As he approaches me, he and I can't avoid making brief eye contact. He casts a glance up at the rail of the second deck for my benefit.

His glance is meant to tell me, *Sorry, but I'm being watched; there's nothing I can do about this.* I look up to see Simon Fischer and Beth, side by side, leaning on the upper rail and looking down on all of us like the Lannisters watching a death match.

So I guess I'm supposed to forgive Miles for what he is about to do. Why? Because he'll be in hot water with his wife and father-in-law if he doesn't. Jesus, Miles, get a grip.

"Into the boat," Miles orders me, his voice cracking slightly.

I have no choice but to obey. I climb down into the inflatable craft, eyeing Miles every step of the way. He evades my glance with care.

"You two," Miles says to one of the bodyguards and Chokehold, "into the skiff." Choke and Bodyguard clamber down into the larger of the two small crafts.

I know Miles so well I can watch his thoughts play out on his face. At this point he's still thinking he's going to be able to delegate this whole operation. But then he looks up at Simon Fischer, and I see awareness blossom. Miles realizes this is a test. Of his mettle. Of his "courage." Of his hands-on leadership and decision-making. Delegating won't do.

He climbs down into the rectangular skiff and takes the wheel, a general with his two lieutenants. He reassesses the personnel arrangement and orders Choke out of the skiff and into the rubber boat with Jeannie and me. Damn, I was hoping he'd leave Jeannie and me alone.

It's tight quarters on the inflatable with Choke aboard. The boat *can* hold three adults, but not in "style, comfort, and class"; Choke's a sizeable dude, in case I haven't mentioned.

Jeannie is left to helm the tiller. Maybe Choke doesn't know how to operate an outboard.

"Go!" Miles orders, pointing eastward. *Why east?* I wonder.

We strike off toward the black horizon. The full dark of night is upon us now, and the moon is only a high sliver in a cloudless and oddly starless sky. The island lies to our starboard side. In a few minutes we'll be clear of it, and out into the depths of the open Atlantic.

Miles follows us in the skiff without any lights. Even though I can hear his motor a few yards behind ours, I can barely see his boat, so dark is the night.

I don't understand why we're going in this direction. The way the fake texts were written, I thought we were supposed to have our "accident" near Table Rock, which is on the northwestern edge of the island, in the opposite direction.

But eastward we go.

The only bits of light we can see are from the scattered homes to our right, on the northern side of the island. Soon the last of the lighted world will be behind us.

I am heading into blackness, never to return, it seems. How strange. A mere nine days ago, I was living a marginal existence in my parents' decaying home, feeling unloved and alone, wallowing in low-level melancholy and despair, failing to savor the life that was mine for the grabbing. Then I was given the gift of attempted murder. Yes, *gift*, because it made me hunger for life again. The past several days have been terrifying, exhausting, and more stressful than anything I've ever endured, but they've been electrifying too. I've tasted true love again and had my heart ripped to the core. I've made love as only the angels can. I've used my mind and body in ways I didn't know I could. And I've discovered I'm not a coward when my back is against the wall. These are life-changing revelations.

Alas, there is little life left for the changing. It's all going to be over soon. My crazy hope was that, even if I couldn't figure out a way to escape this mess, help would arrive. That's why I called Enzo on the burner phone and let the line stay open all through dinner and beyond. I was hoping he would listen in on what was happening and send in the reinforcements. Maybe fetch our policeman from Monhegan or figure something else out.

But no. Maybe my call didn't really go through, maybe Enzo wasn't listening, maybe he couldn't make out anything being said, or maybe he just didn't give a crap.

I still can't believe Miles, my best friend, actually intends for Jeannie and me to die out here, but that seems to be the course he's committed to.

Ahead on the right I see the lamppost at Mussel Cove. That's the last light we'll pass on the eastern end of the island. Then it's nothing but blackness till Ballyconneely Bay in County Galway, my ancestral home.

I look behind me at the western horizon. It's still showing some faint luminescence from the setting of the sun. Enough to create silhouettes. If anyone was following us in the distance, even with their lights off, I think I'd see them. But I see nothing. We're all alone out here.

If I'm going to die on the black ocean, though, I refuse to die in servitude to Miles' lies. I refuse to make this easy for him. I still have a few things to say to him. And I want to make sure that on the off chance Enzo is still listening and my burner phone still has power, there is a record of what is about to go down. But the hitch is, if we go much farther, we'll lose cell-phone reception. The island's lone cell "tower" barely covers the island itself, on a good day. So I need to stop this boat somehow. Force the endgame to happen close to shore. Make it harder for Miles to pull his crime off cleanly.

Time is running out, so I have to try something fast.

"I wonder how much gas this thing has," I say to Jeannie, lading my words with meaning I hope she will unpack. What I'm really saying to her is, "Can you make the engine quit somehow?"

"Shut up," orders Chokehold. Silver-tongued rogue.

We cruise along for a minute or two, followed by the skiff. We steer past the Mussel Cove light and its protruding apron of rocks. Now the last thing we'll pass on the right is Seal Point, which has no lights, and George's Knob on the left. George's Knob is not as obscene as it sounds. It's just a rock formation lying off the northeastern edge of the island; large enough to merit a name, too small to be called an island. Once we get through the channel between George's Knob and Seal Point, it's $H_2O$ as far as the eye can see.

Suddenly the engine starts to cough and sputter. *Yes! Good work, Jeannie. Whatever you did.*

"What's going on?" says Chokehold. "Did you pull the choke out? Push it back in, lady."

The engine dies. Chokehold whips out his phone and hits the flashlight app, illuminating Jeannie. One of her hands is holding the engine tiller, the other is holding a now-empty bottle of spring water. She grins. Bless her pirate soul. The cap of the gas tank is off and Danny's emergency kit is open, revealing the source of the water bottle.

"Did you just dump water in the gas tank?" Choke asks Jeannie, aghast.

"Sure the fuck did, asshole," replies Jeannie.

# Chapter 44

"All right, everyone calm down!" shouts Miles, the least calm person on the high seas tonight. He has drawn the skiff up aside the crippled inflatable. "I need to think."

"Yes, you really should do that," I say, turning on my phone's flashlight and shining it in his face. I need to engage his attention before he settles on a course of action that might be unstoppable. "Think about what you're about to do, Miles. Do you really want to murder—*murder*—your best friend and the mother of your child?"

"I don't *want* to do any of this! Things are out of control! Things have been set in motion. And now what needs to happen needs to happen."

"You're not thinking clearly, Miles. You're in panic mode and your lizard brain has taken over. Step back and take a deep breath. You still have options."

"Like what?"

"Speak the truth. Come clean. About everything. About the accident. About Fish Pier. About Bree. About this sleazy puppet show your father-in-law is trying to orchestrate. Hold your head up high, look people in the eye, take accountability for whatever you've done, and then push the restart button on a new life. A better life, a freer life."

"Ha!"

"You haven't done anything irredeemable yet. You won't go to jail for those highway deaths. It was an accident. There'll be consequences, but you can handle them."

"That's easy for you to say, Finn. You don't know what it's like to have as much to lose as I do."

"Ah, there it is."

"What? There *what* is?"

"The premise of our friendship, in black and white." Part of me is trying to stall, buy some time, but part of me is also saying what needs to be said.

"I have no idea what you're talking about."

"You know exactly what I'm talking about. You just said it yourself."

Now he shines *his* phone-beam on *me*. "Enlighten me, Finn. What premise?"

"That Miles Sutcliffe, scion of the Old Greenwich, Connecticut Sutcliffes, carrier of destiny's torch, has more to lose than crooked-toothed, working-class Finnian Carroll from Wentworth, Massachusetts."

"That's ridiculous. That's your own low self-esteem talking, not me."

"It's been our story since day one, Miles. When you got pulled over for that DUI and begged me to slide behind the wheel of your van, why did we both agree to that? Because I could afford to have an arrest record, you couldn't. Same with the cheating thing on our philosophy final and that bio paper I wrote for you. When you got caught with that high school girl in senior year, I said she was with me. Why? Because you were about to get married and couldn't afford to fuck *that* up." I'm surprised he's letting me carry on like this; maybe *he's* trying to stall the inevitable too. "We never talked about the underlying premise, but we both understood it."

"Maybe *you* did; I sure the hell didn't. I don't even *remember* this stuff. None of it. It's gone. It has no foothold in my mind."

"What about Fish Pier? Does that have a foothold in your mind? I know what happened the night Fishermen's Court paid you a visit. You threw me under the bus again."

"You're full of shit."

"You told them I never gave you their letters!"

"I said no such thing!" he fumes with overblown indignation.

"You promised me you would pass those letters on to your partners. Those letters were important, Miles. They had people's *lives* bound up in them. Their hopes, their pride, their stories."

"Those letters were a joke. They weren't going to do a damn bit of good. Simon Fischer had already made up his mind that the pier had to go. And Simon Fischer always gets his way. Our other partners were going to rubber-stamp it. Period."

"That's not the fucking point, Miles. Those letters mattered *to the fishermen who wrote them*. They mattered a lot. And you told those guys *I* sold them out!"

Miles' eyeballs lose focus and start dancing from side to side. I know the look. "You had left the island and you weren't coming back," he says. "I still had a home here. I had to *live* with these people."

"So that makes it okay? Expediency trumps truth? These people were my friends. And for the past four years they've hated me, all because of a lie you told them."

"Those letters were a stupid idea. *Your* stupid idea. All they did was create false hope. You *deserve* to take the blame for that."

Time has frozen by this point, and no one exists but the two of us. We're going to finish this thing—despite the insane circumstances—and nothing is going to stop us now.

"Fuck you," I say. "From the day I made the mistake of inviting you here, you have taken the one thing of value I ever built for myself—my life on this island—and shat all over it. In every conceivable way. And all because of that one lifelong belief."

"Which is?"

"That Miles Sutcliffe's life is more valuable than Finn Carroll's. That you *matter more than I do*!"

"You're wrong, Finn." Miles laughs glumly and shines his light into my eyes. "That's what *you* believe. That's always been the *real* story of our friendship."

His light feels painfully bright.

"From the first time you met me," he says, "you thought I had a big life, and you wanted in. But you didn't think you were *enough*. On your own merits. You thought you had to *buy* your way in. *Serve* me in some way, make yourself indispensable."

Fuck this guy. Fuck Miles Sutcliffe.

"*You* held yourself lower than me," he continues. "I never asked that of you."

"Come on, Miles, you know you never saw me as equal to your preppy friends and your Sugar Loaf friends and your Greenwich friends." Something raw and primitive is being exposed in me, and I hate it. I feel on the verge of tears, and now I *want* someone to interrupt us, but no one does. "I was a sociology experiment for you: can people from different social castes be friends? But when you were with your real peers, I embarrassed you."

"You did embarrass me. Not because of your cheap shoes or your crooked teeth, but because you tried so fucking hard. *You* felt you didn't belong, so you were always *auditioning* — with your humor, with your intellectual gymnastics, with your willingness to be the fall guy — trying to win a spot on the varsity squad."

He shines his light up and down my body, as if taking stock of the totality of me for the first time.

"I'm going to let you in on a little secret, Finn. The reason the rich get richer and the poor get poorer isn't because the privileged have the key to some special club. It's because life gives all of us what we *expect*. Most of my family's fortune ran out two generations ago, but the Sutcliffes still expect great things of ourselves. That's why I have a house in The Meadows and another in Cape Elizabeth, and you're living in your parents' house in Wentworth. You expect shit and you get shit."

"You have two homes on the ocean because you married money. You were too scared to follow your dreams. Don't give me that 'great expectations' bullshit."

"You've always been cleverer than me, Finn, but you've always eaten my table scraps. Why? Because you don't think you belong at the table. Every bad thing that happens to you, you see it as confirmation of your essential worthlessness, punishment for the sin of being you."

"Go to hell, Miles."

"Whereas I view setbacks as speed bumps, aberrations. That's why I can't even *remember* those stupid incidents you mentioned. I don't cling to the negative stuff, I let it go."

"That's because you're never the one who pays the price!"

"That's because *you* pay the price for things that aren't even yours to pay for! Look at that bottle business. You've been letting it eat at you for eighteen years, and you didn't even throw the stupid thing. Me, I took one look at those news stories, saw there was nothing that could be done about the situation, and purged it from my mind."

"Wait. What?" It takes me second or two to process what I've just heard. "Are you telling me you *knew* you caused that accident? That you've known all along?"

His eyeballs start the dance routine again.

"Those are two different questions," he says. "With two different answers. But all right, yes, I'll admit, the night of the accident, I heard everything. I didn't know what to do, so I just... shut down. Pulled the plug, checked out. The next day, I turned on the news. I saw what had gone down. But I asked myself a simple question: will my taking the blame change anything for the victims? The answer was no. So I pushed 'delete file.'"

"And what, just erased it from your memory? Click, gone?"

"Absolutely. I had a lot to think about—the wedding, law school, finding a new place to live. I literally never gave that night another thought, never fed it another watt of mental energy. Not one. For eighteen years. Even when you came back here and started rehashing the whole thing, I honestly didn't remember throwing the bottle. I'd purged it that thoroughly.

"It was only today, when Beth said it was me, that the actual memory came bubbling up. And it threw me for a loop for a minute, I'll admit. But let me ask you something, Finn—and this is the point I'm making: who's been better off for the last eighteen years, you or me?"

At that, my rational brain shuts down. Animal rage takes over. I launch myself off the inflatable boat, across a couple of feet of black water, and onto Miles' skiff.

I take him down like a linebacker courting a penalty flag.

The second he hits the deck, I am on top of him, hammering his face and torso with my fists. I punch him for my father, for my sister, for Beth. I punch him for Jeannie and Bree and for his betrayal of our friendship. I punch him for Edgar Goslin. Most of all, I punch him for the Abelsens, an innocent family whose lives he wiped out by a careless act he decided he was never going to own. I've never struck Miles in my life before, but it feels so fucking good.

Am I wrong or does Bodyguard take his sweet time before intervening? After fifteen or twenty blows, though, I feel a hollow cylinder press against my temple.

"Enough," orders Bodyguard, with no particular emotion.

"Get him out of here!" Miles shrieks at Bodyguard in a shaky voice. "Get him back on the other boat!"

Bodyguard presses the gun barrel to my ribs, forcing me to maneuver back into the inflatable.

"What are you going to do now?" I ask Miles from Danny's boat. "Murder Jeannie and me? Then what? Click — delete file? On with your blissfully ignorant life?"

"No, *you're* going to do it, fuckin' smartass."

The hairs go up on my neck and arms.

"What do you mean?" I ask, shining my phone-light on him. His eyes are wild with the fury of a wounded child. His nose is oozing blood.

"The News at Nine team will call it a 'tragic murder-suicide,'" he says. "You've explained it all in the note you wrote. The one we stuck in your pocket, in a waterproof bag. Leah outdid herself this time, I must say. The note says how you've been living a tortured life, wracked with depression, ever since you killed that family on route 495. But how things were looking up lately. You hooked up with your old flame again, and life was good. You trusted her so much, you even confessed to her what you'd done all those years ago, hoping it would make the two of you even closer. Whoops, major turn-off. She shut down the love train, and now she's insisting you go to the police and admit what you did.

"She had to be dealt with, the meddlesome bitch," he goes on. "So you lured her to your friend Danny's boat, as your phone texts will show, and now it's time to do the dark deed. Just like in that old folk song you used to sing..."

And then, most bizarrely, he begins to sing. *"Polly, pretty Polly, come go along with me...."* The look I see in his eyes tells me the Miles I've always known has left the building.

*"Polly, pretty Polly, come go along with me."* He reaches under the seat of the skiff and drags out a heavy object. It's an anchor, of navy design, with a curved bottom and two vertical up-posts, plastic-coated. A rope is attached to it. My God, he's really thought this through.

*"Before we get married, some pleasure to see..."*

He lugs the anchor to the edge of the skiff, then heaves it across the gap onto the inflatable, where it lands with a dull thud. It must be a twenty-pounder.

"Tie the anchor rope around her ankles," Miles orders me, no longer singing.

"No, I'm not going to do that, Miles," I say, lighting his face with my beam.

"Tie. The rope. To. Her. FEET."

"No."

Miles, seething, shines his light on Choke and says, "*You* do it." Choke grabs the anchor rope and, from a kneeling position, tries to tie it around Jeannie's ankles.

"Don't touch me!" Jeannie screams, kicking wildly at him with both feet. Choke reaches for the stun gun in his back pocket. I time my own kick perfectly. My shoe connects with the device and sends it flying out of his hand and into the coal-black water. He growls his rage at me, but what's he going to do? It's two against one, on a wobbly boat.

"Lie still, lady," shouts a voice from the skiff—Bodyguard's, "or I'm going to shoot your friend." Bodyguard shines his light on me.

"Fuck you!" shouts Jeannie, still kicking frantically at Choke.

"I have a gun aimed at his head," Bodyguard says, "and I *will* pull the trigger."

I shine my light on Bodyguard. He is indeed aiming a pistol at me. As soon as Jeannie sees this, she goes perfectly still.

"Now, LET HIM TIE YOUR FEET," shouts Miles at Jeannie. And then, as his next words—"YOU MISERABLE FUCKING BITCH"— come spewing out of his mouth, something astonishing and inexplicable happens.

His words boom out across the water at five or ten times their normal volume, crackly and distorted and with a slight, echoey time delay—they seem to be issuing from an electronic speaker of some kind.

"WHAT THE FUCK?" cries Miles. Again his voice is unexplainably amplified.

Suddenly we are all bathed in light, beaming from a dozen or more sources. From both sides of the channel. Searchlights, spotlights, heavy-duty flashlights.

"Put the gun down!" shouts a voice, issuing from the same loudspeaker as Miles' voice did.

We hear the sound of multiple boat engines turning over in unison.

What the hell is happening?

## Chapter 45

As my eyes try to adjust to the spotlight assault, I see boat headlights and red and green sidelights switching on. Two rows of fishing boats begin closing in on us, one from the north, one from the south. They've been sitting there, lining the channel in the dark, their silhouettes subsumed by the larger silhouettes of Seal Point and George's Knob.

As the two rows of boats churn closer to us, the searchlights and flashlights are lowered from our faces, with the exception of one that stays trained on Bodyguard and his gun. The whole area remains awash with light, though, from the headlights and crisscrossing beams. I see familiar faces at the wheels of most of the boats, other familiar faces manning the decks. Even Cliff Treadwell is here with his trawler. Some of the fishermen are holding rifles and harpoons. Some are holding phone cameras, recording everything that's going down.

The two rows of boats stop, about twenty feet from us on either side, hemming us in.

My eyes are drawn to the Bourbons' party fishing boat. It's equipped with a loudspeaker the captain uses to talk to the passengers. I see Matt Bourbon standing at the helm on the upper deck and Enzo beside him, holding his cell phone up to the microphone. My phone call from the burner in my pocket must still be beaming live to his phone. That's how Enzo has been blasting Miles' voice across the water!

Standing on the lower deck of the Bourbons' boat is Jim, the statie, now wearing his badge and holding his gun. This has become official police business.

"Drop your weapon and put your hands where I can see them," Jim commands. "All of you. That's a police order."

Bodyguard drops his weapon.

"Miles, you're under arrest," Jim shouts, "and so are you two, whoever you are." He points his gun at Bodyguard and Chokehold. Then he orders, "All of you, aboard this vessel."

A couple of the fishermen toss out lines to our two small boats. I grab one of the ropes, and Jeanie and I start pulling the inflatable toward the larger boat. Miles tries to lift his hands in surrender, but the instant he moves he is blasted from all directions by searchlights and flashlights. He covers his face with his hands to block the dazzling light.

A man's voice issues from a smaller speaker on another boat; I can't tell which one. "Miles Sutcliffe," it announces in a formal tone that defies challenge, "Fishermen's Court finds you guilty of treason."

A woman's voice—it might be Ginny Harper's—shouts from a megaphone on another boat, "Leave this island and don't come back. If any of us ever see your face again, your sentencing will commence. And it *will* be harsh."

I half expect Jim to make some sort of pronouncement about how there'll be no vigilante justice here, yada-ya. But he says no such thing.

He's a cop, but he's an islander first.

• • • • •

I stand on the high bridge of the Bourbons' party boat with Matt and Enzo, as Matt navigates around Seal Point and steers toward the harbor on the south side. Jim is holding Miles, Bodyguard, and Chokehold—his real name turns out to be Bela Negrescu—below on the first deck. Jeannie sits alone in a passenger seat at the rear of the upper deck.

"How did you find us in the pitch dark?" I ask Enzo.

"GPS. On your burner. We figured you had to come through the channel."

It was a total shot in the dark that he'd get my call and figure out what was happening, but if anyone could do it, it would be Enzo.

"Keeping the line open was smart," he adds. "I'm just glad the mike was decent and the battery held up. I recorded everything."

"You must have worked your ass off to pull all this together," I say to him.

"Nah. Once I put the word out, everyone mucked in." He winks.

"Whoa. What have we here?" says Matt, looking out a fair distance beyond his bow.

A private yacht—Simon Fischer's—is chugging around the island from the opposite side. Two smaller craft fan out from behind it and flank it on its starboard side—they're "herding" it into the harbor. I can't read the lettering on the escort boats, but both of them have blue lights. Police. The smaller of the two, I'm guessing, is Kelvin, our part-time peace officer. The bigger one must be the Maine Marine Patrol or State Police. Kidnapping, murder, and conspiracy to commit murder are evidently frowned upon in these parts. I'd still love to shove a grenade up Simon Fischer's ass, but watching him get hauled away in handcuffs will have to suffice.

I turn to Matt Bourbon and say, "I was surprised to see the whole gang show up tonight. Especially after... today. I thought Fishermen's Court only looked out for its own."

"We do," says Matt. He doesn't look me in the eye, but he reaches out stiffly and touches my arm. "We do."

I want to say something, but nothing comes.

I have no idea how to feel about Fishermen's Court right now, and maybe I never will. But I am happy, so bloody happy, to be alive.

I wander toward the back of the upper deck. Jeannie is standing now, looking out over the deck rail. Not at the parade of fishing boats churning up the brine behind us but across the Gulf, toward the mainland. I stand beside her and look out too.

"Going back on the ferry tomorrow?" she asks. "Back to Wentworth?"

"Ferry, yeah. Wentworth, nah. Just long enough to pack my stuff and settle things up with the house. It's not my home anymore. It should have been Angie's all along."

"Uh-huh. And your long-range plans?"

I make my way over to the opposite rail so that I'm facing the island. Jeannie moves along with me. "I already told you those."

She shoots me a questioning glance.

"I'd like to meet your daughter. And if meeting me doesn't make her puke, I'd like to start spending time with the two of you. And if that goes well..."

"Shh, Finn," says Jeannie. "Stop... Please." But there's no anger or acrimony in her voice.

Fine. I'm good with silence. I gaze across the short stretch of water, locking my vision on Musqasset's town dock. Jeannie studies my face for a long moment, as if to see whether any trace of falseness is showing in my eyes. Then she settles her gaze on the town dock alongside mine.

After a few silent moments, her hand sneaks tentatively toward me and grasps the loose fabric of my shirt with two fingers. This is an old, old move of hers, going back to college. Whenever she wanted to be close to me but wasn't quite sure where we stood at the moment, she would lightly clasp my shirt between her first two fingers and wait to see how I responded. It was a gesture I found irrationally endearing.

I reach my arms around her and pull her to my chest, pressing her head to my heart. And I just hold her there, hard. This is not a move I would typically make, because it smacks of possessiveness, of territoriality, of dominance, but right now I don't much care what it smacks of. And neither, it seems, does Jeannie.

I feel her warm tears soaking my shirt, but they are good tears, cleansing tears, tears we have earned together. She wraps her arms around me and clutches me like a life preserver.

I look back at the line of fishing boats pushing us onward from behind, then at the harbor pulling us forward with ever-widening arms, and I feel peace. Maybe for the first time in my sorry-ass life. I don't know what tomorrow will bring. I don't have a plan. I don't have a goal. As of this moment, I know only three things with certainty.

This is my love.
This is my island.
This is my life.

The End

# Acknowledgements

Many thanks to my wife and soul-partner Karen for tirelessly insisting I was a novelist, despite my many years of well-constructed arguments to the contrary. Thanks to my late parents, Bob and Irene, and to my sisters, Carol, Maureen, and Diane, for their delirious love affair with the English language over the years — and to my daughters, Phelan and Quinn, for continuing that affair. Together, you've been my writer's institute.

I also wish to thank Jill Marsal of Marsal Lyons Literary Agency, who was the first "industry" person to believe in *Fishermen's Court*, and whose generous notes made it stronger. Immense gratitude goes out to friends and family who read various beta versions of the book and gave me much-appreciated feedback — Ken Laverriere, Tom Vittorioso, Ken Mokler, Matt Sughrue, and Chase Fraser. Ken L., you will never know how much your ongoing enthusiasm for *FC*, and your gorgeous photographs, buoyed me. I'd also like to thank my first "professional" reader, Danielle Winston, whose comments grew on me over time and helped me make some needed changes.

Many thanks, too, to the folks at Black Rose Writing for launching *Fishermen's Court* into the world.

Finally, I would be remiss not to thank Mr. Warren Hayes of Central Catholic High School, Lawrence, Massachusetts for teaching me, and thousands of other teenage imbeciles, what the craft of writing was all about. May your retirement be ever free of comma splices, Mr. Hayes.

# About the Author

Photo by Ken Laverriere

Andrew Wolfendon is a ghostwriter of over sixty books for adults and children. His screenplays have been optioned numerous times in Hollywood. He has written/designed over twenty-five computer and video games, many of which have won major industry awards, and has penned the song lyrics for several children's entertainment titles. Andy has done scriptwriting work for Blizzard Entertainment, Disney, Titanium Comics, and other entertainment companies. Fishermen's Court is his first novel.

Thank you so much for reading one of our **Thrillers**.
If you enjoyed our book, please check out our recommended title for your next great read!

*The Tracker* by John Hunt

"A dark thriller that draws the reader in." *–Morning Bulletin*

"I never want to hear mention of bolt-cutters, a live rat and a bucket in the same sentence again. EVER." *–Ginger Nuts of Horror*

View other Black Rose Writing titles at www.blackrosewriting.com/books and use promo code PRINT to receive a 20% discount when purchasing.

BLACK ROSE writing

Made in the USA
San Bernardino, CA
11 September 2019